I0682649

They Called Me

JO

A
White

Slave Girl

By: Jacqi Fromauex

DIGITAL PUBLISHING

2011 Jacqi Fromauex

ISBN: 10 0983305765
Library of Congress: 2012930179
Printed in the U.S.A.

ACKNOWLEDGEMENTS

I wish to express a special thanks to my children who urged me to write this novel: Christine, Jean-Paul and Marcel Fromond. I will be forever grateful to Christine F. Fromond, Betty Drew, Gary Puliam, Ginger Cucolo and Virginia Seideman who gave up many precious hours in helping me with the formatting and editing of this book.

INTRODUCTION

A compelling human-interest story of mystery, suspense and a realistic portrayal of the culture of the era, rounds out this tumultuous life. Child of an autocratic tyrant of a father, this "slave girl," raised in the delta swamps on a plantation in a culture that seemed as though the depression was never over. However, role models befriended her in her early years, who led her to believe that she could do anything, if the mindset was there. She wanted to be exactly like them

With a hard work ethic, a young girl who was haunted by "a murder," clawed her way out of the darkness of naïveté to find and experience a world she had never known. This gave her the incentive of breaking the chain of ignorance where most would have succumbed to the norm of time and place, and perpetuated the cycle. Instead, she chose to rise above an environment that would have stifled most.

She became one to learn, to conquer, to overcome adversity as well as succeed. Her life was determined by time, place, environment and parenting. In later years of adult hood, she faced a life affected by circumstances and relationships, which would intrigue any reader. Its compelling interest and issues transcends anyone's imagination. She had her mind toward a different perspective for her survival.

TABLE OF CONTENTS

INTRODUCTION   4
CHAPTER 1   7
CHAPTER 2   63
CHAPTER 3   76
CHAPTER 4   85
CHAPTER 5   103
CHAPTER 6   110
CHAPTER 7   117
CHAPTER 8   119
CHAPTER 9   122
CHAPTER 10 125
CHAPTER 11 131
CHAPTER 12 135
CHAPTER 13 136
CHAPTER 14 141
CHAPTER 15 146
CHAPTER 16 153
CHAPTER 17 155
CHAPTER 18 161
CHAPTER 19 171
CHAPTER 20 175
CHAPTER 21 177
CHAPTER 22 180
CHAPTER 23 184
CHAPTER 24 189
cHAPTER 25 196
CHAPTER 26 198
ChAPTER 27 205
CHAPTER 28 208
CHAPTER 29 218
CHAPTER 30 223
CHAPTER 31 224
CHAPTER 32 227
CHAPTER 33 231
CHAPTER 34 232
CHAPTER 35 233
CHAPTER 36 234
CHAPTER 37 237
CHAPTER 38 239
CHAPTER 39 241
CHAPTER 40 243
CHAPTER 41 250
CHAPTER 42 254
CHAPTER 43 257

THEY CALLED ME JO: A WHITE SLAVE GIRL

CHAPTER 44 259
CHAPTER 45 261
CHAPTER 46 266
CHAPTER 47 271
CHAPTER 48 276
CHAPTER 49 281
CHAPTER 50 283
CHAPTER 51 284
CHAPTER 52 285
CHAPTER 53 289
CHAPTER 54 294

CHAPTER 1

My Name"s Jo

Gift of the Photo League, New York: ex-collection Lewis Wickes Hines GEH NEG: 30195
77:0183:0033 Image revised: Hines, Lewis W. (1874-1940) Boy picking cotton ca. 1912

It was quite ironic when I was born and was a girl. My Papa was ecstatic when Mama first told him that the pregnancy was just like all the other boys. He would be happy with nine boys, one right after the other. However, when delivered at home by the "help maids" my Papa was somewhat disappointed. He wanted another boy. Therefore, when all the naming began, he had to get in on it. Not many people had four names, but I did. It happened like this. Mama named me Mary, and Isabelle named me Beth, and Papa named me "Jo." This was part of his name, Joseph.

I didn't get to be Mama's girl for long because I liked playing with my older brothers, all eight of them. My brothers had me outside as much as possible and I loved it. Outside activities began with them watching over me as they worked. I was in "hog-heaven!"" This made my Papa happy, because he had plans for me, that my Mama knew nothing about.

It was not long until I was old enough to do some of the outside chores almost without help. Papa was glad because he could see another free hand to learn how to work in the fields. I was the "ninth boy," so-to speak and the name "Jo" was just the way he planned to keep it.

I know that I can remember when I was less than three and a half years old. Oftentimes my Mama would work in the fields during cotton-picking times and I would lie on her cotton sack as she picked cotton. This was done especially if there had been a "hell raising" during the early morning chores with the boys.

As Mama picked cotton along with the others, I would jump up, pick a little cotton and put it in Mama's cotton sack as well as my brothers. It depended on who played with me the most. That was fun to me and they enjoyed me playing with them as well. This play didn't last long in the field because Mama had meals to prepare at home with one of the hired hands (Lili), who was just like a mama to me. She was just a baby of one of the rescued slaves who worked hard in the kitchen, enjoyed me as well, since I was the youngest and was a girl. (The story of the slaves will be told in the Chapter 2.)

Soon Mama was not going to the fields as she did every day. I am sure that I whined about it sometime, especially if I felt as if I was not getting enough attention. I didn't notice that Mama was getting fat like Lili, "her side-kick" in the kitchen, but I didn't care.

Mama was just getting so big that she couldn't pick me up like she use to do. She and Lili cooked for about 50 hired hands at that time. It was not long until there were eighty or ninety. Later, Mama couldn't do much of any playing with me and going to the field at all. That took some of my fun with my brothers away. Eventually, it stopped altogether for a while. All the help went for Lili, because she knew that all of the crew had to be fed.

I didn't know that she noticed me moping some about not getting to go to the field, so she fixed me up for picking cotton with an old flour sack, and made a shoulder strap to go around me, so that I could be just like the others. I know that I felt just as important as the rest of the crew. I only picked with one and then with another. The blacks loved me and called me sweet names; therefore, they got the most help on their row.

I sure was a little "tot" out working in the field and acted as tired as the rest of them when dinner time came along. My Papa was proud to see me happy like that. I was so short, that no one could see me from a distance but I was "squirreling" around from one to another.

Mama and Lili kept getting fatter. All I knew was that Lili was Mama's "right and left hand" in the kitchen. I was not old enough to understand all this, but in two months, my younger sister "Evette" was born. Mama was seven months pregnant working in the fields just as hard as the hired hands. She had no business in fields at all, especially with the amount of the work she had to do.

She was such a blessing to all, because she went to keep peace with the boys and help settle any arguments they might have been brewing. She put herself out to let everyone know that she could be a part of the team. Her love for us permeated each with joy, love and peace. If there was a fuss before any of the boys went out to work, you can bet she went along with them to make sure Papa didn't hear about a ruckus. The whip would've been popping all around. He was out at the same time every day with his horse, a whip, rifle, pistol and rope, to take care of every type of problem or situation that might pop up.

Time went by too fast for me. I enjoyed every bit of the work. Some of it was messy, but if the boys could do the work, then I made sure that I learned how or helped them with the tasks. I was right in there each year, picking a little, chopping with someone, riding with the team on a slide or on the mules every year. I couldn't do much in the wintertime, but you can bet I tried. I was proud to be as "good" as they were.

The Burn

One winter was a very hard one when I was only five and a half years old. It snowed 12 inches and no one could go anywhere. It was a blistering cold winter with rain, sleet and snow. Not much outside work was done except the milking of all the cows in the pen and feeding the rest of the animals. There was plenty of hay and corn for them so there was no use to make them go out into the pasture, but the gates were left opened for them to go, as they wanted.

All the fireplaces were roaring with big oak fires. Boulean had the flu and Mama used "smoothing irons" heated by the fireplace, which she placed in the bed with Boulean. Mama wrapped them in old sheets and feed sacks, and then she put them on top of the "salve" she had rubbed on his chest as well as his feet. This was supposed to keep the fever down as well as keeping him warm. He would have chills with very high fever, which required all the extra quilts to stay warm. These "smoothing irons" were rotated often because they lost too much of their heat. This method kept him warmer as he began to get well.

While still sick Boulean would call on me to get something for him. He was bored and just wanted the company, but I was not allowed to be there except to give him water and usually a biscuit with syrup, or some other sweet. I was the one who stayed cold from running to him back and forth to get warm.

Evette, stayed in the kitchen with Mama and Papa. She helped keep the firewood for the stoves, while Papa kept the large fireplace going with an even heat. He surely didn't want to burn the big pot of stew meat and potatoes, as well as the pot of beans, which hung from the fireplace. These long rods were on a hinge, so that they could be pulled away from the heat as they began to get too hot or when a log had to be added for more heat. These were only used when the weather permitted.

It was for me to get warm in the living room with the boys. I had to squeeze my way through with all the boys hovered around the living room fireplace eating roasted peanuts. I would just stand in front of them until my legs were blistering through my overalls from the running around.

Once, after a trip to satisfy Boulean, I ran in to warm up shortly after the boys had just put fresh logs on the fire. While I was getting warm, flames were lapping under and around one of the fresh logs. As soon as I knew that I was too close, I was already on fire. The overalls were burning as I jumped and screamed for the boys, YEEAKS, HELP ME, Y'ALL!" WOW, Y'ALL IT HURTS ALL OVER!"

They tried to hold me down and put out the fire. The right leg of my overalls had burned up to the back pocket with my flesh burning.

"IT'S STILL BURNING, ISN'T IT?" I asked as I was still yelling.

It had a dreadful smell. Each of the boys helped put out the fire of the burning clothes as well as one leg with their bare hands. It got the ligaments behind the right knee. The boy's hands were burned rather badly from using them to put the fire out.

When Mama heard those screams, she knew something bad had to have happened, and she beat Papa getting to me. Immediately, Papa sent Ted off on the fastest horse to the store, three miles up the road to get some sulfur. That took some time with the deep snow, but all the attention was to keep my leg as straight as possible until Ted returned. This caused concern from all. While Mama waited for the sulfur, she mixed the ashes and molasses.

When Ted returned with the sulfur, Mama blended the ashes and molasses with the sulfur. After blending, she spread it on a clean strip of flour sack and wrapped it around and around beginning with my heel and on up to just below the rump. The back of the knee, mid-calf and heel had an extra mix put on it.

There was plenty of help to hold me down, though. Mama then took extra strips of the torn flour sacks to wrap the leg to hold all this "bandage stuff" to my leg, as well as to help prevent infection.

As soon as everyone turned me loose, the leg bent backward. If they had known to make a wooden brace for my knee, I would not have been of capable bending it. The ligaments were burned too badly to keep the leg straight. According to the old country doctor who was told to check on me, this was a third degree burn. Whiskey mixed with honey was the medication for pain, which would soon put me to sleep. The sleep was what I needed,

When they needed to stop me from crying, the whiskey and honey mix was given immediately. Ted's slapping the horse to make her run faster to the store caught the attention of all who lived along the three-mile trip. They were wondering what had happened at our house. This commotion brought people along the way out to ask. Ted hollered back to tell them without stopping.

Three days passed and the snow began to melt. People who heard Ted cry out about what had happened spread the news quickly. They were very concerned and came out in their wagons to see how bad the burn was. Mama would carefully unwrap the wound as I screamed.

I would scream, "Mama, it hurts too much to show, and they know what a burn looks like. Just tell them that you can't do it."

Each time it was unwrapped, the bandage would pull more skin and off. Nonetheless, mama felt it needed to be unwrapped for some more of her "curing" medicine to help the healing process. The crying didn't stop the unwrapping, though.

I believed that my Papa and Mama had some kind of concoction to keep anyone from suffering very much from any illness, sprains, cuts and burns. Who in their right mind would've thought that these concoctions would've healed such a burn, or anything?

I became pretty good at hopping to be capable of moving from place to place. This bothered everyone because I never wanted to be still for very long. I began to use a dining chair to scoot around the wooden floor.

When Ted saw this, he and Papa braved the snow and went to the "sapling area." They cut two small ones down and carefully split them with a wedge from the top down. They left about one-half foot for the end of the crutch. With the "cut off" small pieces, they spread each half piece open so that they could place them for "underarm" supports as well as supports for the hands, and screwed them in tightly. Then Cedric and Joe cleaned the bark and pine-tar off with Kerosene.

Before long, I had a pair of crutches. Mama padded them with strips of an old cotton sack under the armpits and for my hands for comfort. The crutches were used from January through May when the healing took place. Who in their right mind would've thought that this concoction would've healed such a burn?

The doctor came out to check on me and told them to take the crutches away and not to allow the use of them anymore. He told them that I would never be capable of stretching the tendons if I continued the use of the crutches. I had to try to walk. So, away they went. I hobbled around from side to side. This hobbling was actually stretching the ligaments and tendons very well as I got older and began to grow taller. Soon I could put my toes to the floor.

I would try to run a little every day and this helped a great deal. When the weather turned warmer for me to be outside, I would ride one of the mules as the plowing was done because this would force me to stretch my leg even more to keep from falling off. The mules back was wide, and that was why they would want me to ride. This was fun for me for a few hours, especially if there was someone to talk to me. Then, I would want to ride even more. I would ride with one worker and then another as they turned the soil for planting.

Later in September, when I started school, I was older than most in my grade. The younger ones had their sixth birthday before the first of the year, but I was born in April. Therefore, since I was cripple She wanted me to be a "pretty cripple" starting her first day of school. I didn't have very long hair, but Mama made sure I looked pretty. She "French braided" my hair tightly so that my hair would not come down while I was playing around at school. Mama would dampen each tress as she pulled to plait. I was so tender headed that tears would just roll down my cheeks. I never wanted to hurt Mama's feelings by letting her know that it hurt. She wanted me to be a "pretty cripple." I would frown so wide that I couldn't "undo" the frown, when Mama finished pulling my hair back. I just had to deal with it until I could loosen it later. Each of the two braids hung straight back and always had a piece of "flour sack" ribbon tied at the end.

Mama asked often for me to help her in the kitchen, but the Slave Driver would not give in. He needed another slave to work in the field and he got one. If my Mama had won that, or if I had insisted and listened to Mama, I probably could've had Papa change his mind. However, I was not aware of how important I was for him, until it was too late. I was just good; I liked it and was fast. I would've learned a lot from Mama, and perhaps she and I would've had a better life.

How could he be so cruel though to a young girl, even though I liked being outside? I enjoyed being with the animals as well as singing the spirituals with the black men and women. This kind of fieldwork never left me and the sacks got longer and longer as I got older. Soon, I learned how to plow, work heavy equipment, and how to do other "slave labor" just like the others and Papa was glad that I did, but Mama didn't feel the same way. She couldn't believe all he was having me do.

His own Papa objected. I was working rather hard to be so young. This work was done all without praise to me or anyone else in the family. I should've rebelled, even if I was going to get a whipping, because I got'em anyway. However, I thought that one day; I would make him proud of me. That didn't happen until 23 years later.

After the cotton was chopped and cleaned of weeds, the cultivator dragged the old chopped dead grass out past the end of the row, and then the "sweep" was used to get moist soil up and onto the small cotton plants. Joe (the grandchild of one of the slaves) liked to use the sweep.

He was in the south field plowing with the sweep with a mule that he preferred using. This work had to be done. The "sweep" work was slow work. He also had the oldest mule, which knew when to go slow, with the slightest of "grunt", as well as to "woe." Joe would do something like this while the rest of the laborers were in another field.

Joe was my buddy and he liked me. He was older than Papa, but in great shape, tall and strong as an ox. He was older than Cedric, and Lili was the youngest. He and Cedric probably learned more from Grandpa Thibodeaux's teaching than any of the others. They were smart at working on the milling machines as well as running it to cut lumber for building.

One day Papa sent me down to the field with a bucket of treats and a cool jug of water for Joe. He was plowing and it was time for his biscuit with syrup and a slice of bacon. Just before he finished, he grabbed at my overalls and started pulling up on the buckle. This caused my overalls to cut me in the stride. I began hollering for him to stop. I had no idea what was happening, but I wanted the bucket back and for him to leave me alone.

I yelled, "What's the matter with you, Joe? Leave me alone. Leave me alone, you hear?"

"STOP IT JOE, YOU ARE HURTING ME, OKAY." I screamed as loud as I could.

He had to be losing his mind. I started to run but couldn't jerk away from this giant of a man. I knew that somehow I had to get away and get the bucket back for Mama, 'cause she said not to leave it. Before I knew it, Papa slipped up behind me. He cracked that whip loud around Joe and got me a little on the arm. Neither Joe nor I heard him coming. It was as if Joe was in another world. The whip didn't faze him. He just acted as if the whip had not touched him at all. I kept pulling my clothes to where they belonged and not stuck up in my rear where Joe had yanked on them and bent the buckle. When that whip came at him again, he reached out and this time he grabbed the whip.

"RUN TO THE HOUSE JO." Papa was yelling.

"HURRY, JO. GET TO THE HOUSE!"" Papa yelled.

Joe had that whip; and was pulling on it so much, that he was getting too close to Papa.

"RUN TO THE HOUSE, JO!" Papa kept yelling.

"WHY AREN'T YOU HURRYING, JO? GET TO THE HOUSE!" Papa screamed!

I tried to run, but I was still a "Crip" and my buckle to the overalls was bent up. I couldn't hurry, so I hid in the plum orchard to finish trying to straighten that buckle, and peeped at what was happening. Oh, I was horrified at what was going on. The horse was frightened raising up on his hind legs as Papa was trying to get the whip away from Joe. The horse kept backing up. Joe kept coming toward Papa as he pulled on the whip.

"JOE, DO YOU KNOW WHO I AM?" Papa asked.

"ARE YOU SICK, JOE?" Again, Papa asked him something, and there was only a glaze in his eyes.

"JOE, STOP IT RIGHT NOW, YOU HEAR ME?" Papa was screaming.

Joe just kept pulling on the whip, trying to get to Papa, who was frightened by then, and Papa knew that "bad things were about to happen right away. He hated it that Joe was acting like this. He was very fond of him and he had been one of the most reliable slaves. He was smart at working on anything and loved each one of us.

Then Papa saw that he had to kill Joe, or be killed. He had no choice but to shoot Joe. He shot him in the leg first, to get his attention, but it seemed as if the first shot didn't faze him. He kept pulling on the whip to get to Papa, so Papa shot him again as Joe was getting closer to him. I couldn't believe that It took two bullets to put him down.

Then Papa got off the horse, wrapped the rope around Joe's shoulders. and under his arms, tied the knots and started dragging him down the row toward the bayou. The old mule just stood there as if nothing had happened. He would've stayed until someone yelled at him to "gee" or "haw." He was an old, easy-going mule and that was why Joe liked to use him for plowing.

I began hobbling back to the house when Papa turned toward the bayou, but I kept hiding to see what he was going to do next. That was when I saw the rest. I was shaking like a leaf. I didn't want Papa to see me watching, but curiosity got the best of me as I hid behind one plum bush to the next one. He was not paying any attention to me. He told me to hurry to the house and thought that I had gone. He was too busy with Joe to watch to see if I had indeed left the field. I wished that none of it had happened and I also wished that I had not seen any of it. However, I kept watching and hiding.

As soon as Papa disposed of the body, he rode the horse to where the mule and plow were. He finished that row to the end, hooked the plow into the chain on the slide. He hopped on the slide with the mule pulling him, holding the plow and rode it to the barn with his horse following close behind.

He was fortunate that Cedric, as well as all the other hired hands were in the field at least a mile from where Papa shot Joe. They would not have heard any shots at that distance. I think that was the first time Papa had done anything with a plow since he ran away from home when he was about twelve years old.

When I got home, I was just about out of breath. Mama and Lili were just doing their stuff in the kitchen. I gave Mama's bucket to her and I didn't mention anything about what happened in the field. I went to my bedroom right away to settle my nerves and peeped out the window watching for Papa. I was glad to see him get back quickly, so that no one could see him with Joe's mule. Soon Papa came in.

He got Mama into the living room (next to the bedroom) and whispered what had happened, so that Lili couldn't hear the conservation. I could hear the mumbled whispering, but Mama never said a word that I could hear. He told Lili later, that Joe said he was leaving, as well as what he told Joe. She was shocked that he had never said anything about being unhappy and certainly nothing about leaving. However, I knew for sure; I would always wonder if Joe survived the gunshots.

The gun didn't go off again. I didn't know how far Papa took him, but if he was dead or just put in a coma.

I was glad when everything returned to normal. Papa told everyone at "pay time" that evening that Joe had told him that he was leaving. Papa said he told him to do whatever he wanted to do. He said he told him that he was a free man and could go where he wanted. I suppose all believed him, even Cedric and the other great grandchildren of the slaves.

Papa told all the workers and especially as he looked at Cedric, "You know how Joe kids around a lot? Maybe he will show up soon." This ended the farming for me, I thought.

Back at school, as most of the summer had just vanished, it seemed, I was still the "Crip." The high school softball coach and math teacher heard about all the cruel remarks made at me by other class-mates, and became very concerned. Coach came up to me on the school ground, chatted with me and had me stretch my leg as often as I could. I showed her that I could run well also. I didn't think that I was as cute as my classmates were, and certainly didn't have the store bought clothes and neat school supplies. However, those who made fun of me thought they had it all. I didn't care, because I enjoyed school more than they did. They didn't know what farm work was ei-ther. I worked like a slave and had fun at it. They didn't have more than "maybe" a little tiny garden.

After moving up in grade levels, I was a happy student. Occasional-ly, I had five pennies (that Jay had hidden from all but me) and I ran to the store for a piece of "store-bought" candy. This was fun, but to me I was growing up and working harder than I thought I would have to. I was beginning to work longer hours, with a longer cotton sack. I thought that one day I might be called to work in the kitchen for Mama, but that never happened even as I was got older. I needed to know how to cook and help Mama and Lili. However, Papa never mentioned it.

One evening after I was coming in from one of the sweet potato digs Papa said, "You are going to take piano lessons."

I thought he had gone mad. Had he lost it and gone mad like Joe? I knew Joe had gone mad, and I thought that I could see the same "dull" look in Papa's eyes. I was frightened at first, but Papa told me to go to the old man at school who taught piano lessons three times a week (Monday, Wednesday and Friday). The old man was the owner of the sugar cane mill which we used.

I had to tell the coach about the piano lessons that Papa had me take. She was comforting to me when I told her that I didn't know why he was giving them to me because I didn't have a piano at home. I was going into the fourth grade that year. She would keep up in how I was doing in my classes as well as the piano. I needed this encouragement, and she evidently could realize this lack of self-confidence. They knew that I had a lot of farm work to do, cripple or not.

We had a long harvest table with an oil-cloth covering which was red with white checks about three fourths inch wide, and two inches long. They were about the size of a piano key, but I wondered if these lessons were my pay for hard work. I thought this is not going to work. He remembered enough music from school to know if I was using the correct finger as well as the hand. It was a pain for me with him watching my entire lesson, which I had that evening. I had it to do the next evening, and the next from then on. I could see that I was going nowhere, and fast, at that.

At the end of nine months, he had me to quit, because he said that my ring fingers and little fingers went down on the keys at the same time. How he could tell, I never knew. Years later, Ted told me that the old man owed Papa some money and this was the only way he could pay him back.

I think if Papa had told me that, I would have taken all this more seriously and learned to play the "table-cloth" well, and the teacher would have bragged on me enough that he would have bought an old piano for me.

As time passed, the coaches kept their eyes on me, seeing to it that I ran for each of them from one grade to the next, and I got better each year. Of course, she knew how hard I had to work back on the farm, even as a Crip, but both were a "safety net" for me.

Keeping my leg in motion was what I had to do, so I never stayed still very long. I tried to be the best at any play or creative stunt attempted, I would try to "out-do" Boulean. This was cruel, but I didn't know any better, and Boulean never fussed at me for it. He should've given me his fist a time or two. Even though I was the little Crip, I would still try to do stuff faster than him, or I would try something he couldn't do at all. He probably was afraid HE would get into trouble for doing it. And, he probably would have if I hollered for him to stop it. Then, I would have gotten one and I deserved it.

He didn't like farming or school. I competed with him in spelling and always beat him. He just didn't try, and never had the fun that I had. I would make up fun things to do. Boulean was just an unhappy boy and not interested in anything except building a playhouse across the road. It was done well and had a small "thatched red clay fireplace." He let me see in it two times. I told Mama how cute it was.

If he could've had a chance to have books at home, he could've done anything. He built his own home after he married and then built Papa's house. He was smart, but never had a chance to prove it. Teacher's just didn't give a darn. They were afraid to tap his abilities, I think, or were not that interested. He just worked his butt off and was still beaten for doing something wrong, or not fast enough. Papa could come up for many reasons, for Boulean to get a whipping. I felt bad for intimidating Boulean, especially as I got older.

Isabelle, my oldest sister, was good to me. She was one of my role models. She went to college without paying anything right after I was born. This was during the depression era. I always wondered what she did to deserve this. I was enslaved to get to go to college, and I left without a dime given to me for an education. Maybe she was enslaved also, working with Mama and all the babies and miscarriages that Mama had. I had always thought that she got off too easy. That was certainly unfair for me to think that, because she did a lot for me. Don't for a second; think that Isabelle did favors for us for nothing. There were always ulterior motives.

Isabelle was the slave driver in that family. She knew that she would get a lot of work out of us as well as her oldest child, Paulette. This work was usually in the garden as well as cleaning up in the house. Paulette would clean up and fix "leftover's" at a young age. I didn't know how to do what that child was capable of doing. She would do this while Isabelle took a nap after teaching all day.

One Christmas, Paulette got a tricycle and since there was only six and a half years difference in our age, I enjoyed playing with her. Evette was no fun. She would always cause an argument and I was the one who got the whipping. However, Paulette was thrilled to have someone to play a few grown-up games with her.

We didn't mind helping Isabelle, though because we were away from Papa's whip. Sometime the "payback" was a perm for me. I don't know if Papa bought the perm or not. I was so tender-headed that I didn't like them until it was all over. She rolled my hair so tight that I couldn't even grin or cry. It reminded me of the "French braids," which Mama would do. I didn't know which was worse, the perm pulling on my hair or Mama plaiting my hair into French braids. When I got either "hair-do," my hair would be pulled back so tight that my jaws pulled back also. If I tried to relax my jaws, the hair would still pull and hurt. I was so tender headed. What a life with French braids or perms!"

After my paternal Grandpa died, Papa bought out the heirs to add to his plantation. All the other slaves were older than Grandpa and had died before he did. They were buried in the pasture close to where their "rescuer" lived. Only one grandchild was left after Joe was killed and later on, several great grandchildren of the younger sets went to live with other families near town. Soon they married some of the hired hands who worked for us, but wanted to live in town, but still worked on the farm, but not as often. Cedric, who was about five years older than my Papa was, wanted to stay with us so he would not be alone. All were happy that he wanted to stay near us since his brother, Joe, was gone. Therefore, Papa hauled the first old school bus to the back under the pin-oak tree and set it up like a camper. The camper now had everything Cedric needed except for food, and Mama kept him supplied with plenty of that. He would be on the back porch ready to work before we were up. Cedric was a hard worker and just like a member of the family.

His camper had a wood heater in it to heat leftovers, make coffee or for warmth in the winter time. He never got over his brother not telling him and Lili about leaving. He was bothered by him not leaving a note to either of them. He had left without telling Cedric anything about it and they missed him a lot. They never knew that he had gone crazy and Papa had to put two shots in him. I am glad that Cedric didn't know this. I guess that both shots went into him. Nothing was ever mentioned about Joe after that day,

However, I kept being afraid of him slipping up on me. Nevertheless, I didn't say a word about the ruckus. I always had the thought that the bullets just put him in a coma for a while. No one else ever knew about what happened to Joe. I doubt that Papa knew that I saw all but, where he pulled the body. I felt sure that he took him down as far along the bayou as he could get without anyone finding him. I am so glad that I kept it a secret also. I am glad Evette didn't know about Joe. She would've told everyone about it at one time or another. If she had known and told it, Papa would've been killed for sure or be put in jail.

Soon after this episode, and between crops and storms, Papa had the time to supervise some building. He had my brothers, Cedric and some other hired hands build two small houses for the "tenant farmers." Before the tornado hit Grandpa's place, Papa rented it out to a family who would work on the farm, which paid for part of their rent. These other two homes were for share-croppers for families with a couple of acres for them to have their own garden. The men of these families worked for Papa for their rent plus some income. The other renter had the gift of leather-craft. He could make most anything after the tanning was done. It reminded me of the same skills, which Grandpa Thibodaux had. He had all the hides he needed because Papa kept him supplied with those. Papa bartered for work by the leatherman's which went for of us to have a saddle and a whip.

He also did a lot of work for others in and around the community for extra income. Their wives would work in the gardens or helped Mama, if she needed them. However, their children were not allowed to come on the farm due to the danger of equipment, log trucks in and out, as well as all the animals.

One spring there was a bad storm that damaged the back end of the house, so action had to take place quickly. With all the help Papa had with him, he kept everyone busy on the job getting the house back to normal. He had it done in only two days by using some of the hired hands. It took too long to cut and shape the many shingles needed for this storm damage. We couldn't afford the time or the chance to have any of the inside of the house to get any wetter, so Papa had plenty of tin to be used and some cypress shingles when time permitted for them to be put on.

With a tin roof, lightning rods had to be put at the end of each gable of the roof and a ground wire running down and wrapped around an iron rod straight into the ground, which prevented lightning from hitting the house. This was called a "ground-wire." If lightning struck it, then the electricity formed by the lightning ran into the ground. .

As time went by, the tin was replaced with the shingles while he had people to do the job. He had everyone working on this project. With a whip near you, of course, everything was done quickly. He didn't like the noise from hail and rain on the tin roof, even though most of us liked it because it made you want to sleep long and hard. Tin had only been put on the back end of the house.

As I grew up, I had even more work to do. I thought plowing with the mule or the tractors was fun. That, I thought, would keep me farther away from the whip. It did part of the time, but his horse could get to the tractor just as quickly. He watched me too much. I knew what I was doing. He was just downright hateful if I did something, wrong or covered up just one plant. Since he was going to stand there watching, I thought he should uncover it himself. He never got his hands dirty except when hog or beef killing time came around in the fall.

He should have waited another week to let the plants get a little taller before he sent me to plow them. There were so many different mechanisms to watch; the plants, dirt coverings, wheels of the tractor as well as the speed. I didn't want the slave driver around so much. He made me nervous.

Tonsils

One December, just before Christmas, a dreadful sickness happened to each one of us. We seem to have a bad sore throat too often for Papa and no work could be done with this sort of sickness. This meant that Papa had to bring in wood for the fireplaces as well as helping Mama in the kitchen while she milked the cows. That had to be something for one to witness to believe. He should've done the milking more often and Mama doing the dishes.

My parents had many different concoctions and remedies for sore throat as well as anything that ailed us. Before the boys went into the service, and while we were all well, Papa decided that our sickness would spread to each of us and that our tonsils needed to come out. He decided to take us to the hospital in Opelousas to have it done. He said this would eliminate all the sore throats that seem to go around occasionally when he needed all of us at once.

The hospital was full of sickness so the doctor had us lined up in the hall, so the nurse just took one at a time in for the surgery. When one came out, there was a bed in the hall for him to be recovering until the doctor finished with each one of us. (Papa didn't plan on us staying there very long anyway). The doctor had all put to sleep with ether except me.

When he got to me, he talked about how huge mine were and seemed to be just hanging in there. I was the only one who was not put to sleep. He took mine out "locally" without being put to sleep. Mine were an inch in diameter and when I had a sore throat, I couldn't talk because of the size of them. All the doctor had to do was jack my mouth open with some sort of apparatus, until my mouth was opened as far as it could go. Next, he mopped my throat with medication to deaden and sterilize the tissue.

He began to sit on his stool beside me to start snipping my tonsils out. This was going to be an easy job for him. About the time he sat down, an unexpected emergency came up. He had my mouth all ready to go, he thought.

After jacking my mouth open someone yelled, "A woman is having a baby on the steps of the hospital!""

The doctor (being the only one in his clinic) had to run and deliver the baby and directed the nurses to finish the job.

When the doctor returned to me, he asked, "Can you still feel anything?"

I couldn't answer him. I was still in the same condition he left me.

However, I was trying to yell as loud as I could, "UUHUH, UUHUH-HH," with my mouth still jacked open to say yes, but he didn't understand.

He should've known to mop my throat with the numbing medicine again anyway. At least I could breathe, but not much more than that. He just went to "snipping" my tonsils out. He put some medicine on my throat then to deaden this area after the procedure and rolled me out. That hurt.

We didn't even spend one night in the hospital. Papa was ready to take us home long before the doctor was ready for us to leave. He wanted us nourished well at home, so that we could get back to work cutting firewood for the fireplaces and splitting pine blocks of wood for the cook stoves. To tell the truth, he was exhausted from doing the work, which couldn't be put off until we got well. On the way home, Papa picked up some ingredients to make "homemade" ice cream when we got home. This was something, which I was anxiously await-ed. I had never had any before, but had heard about it. I was so sore from having my tonsils ripped out that it hurt to spit.

Mine would still bleed. When the ice cream was made, it had a vanilla flavor with an aroma, which was so breathtaking it would "knock-your-socks-off." Some was dipped out into a bowl for each of us, but I couldn't eat it. I stirred and stirred it, thinking that I could drink it, but I just couldn't swallow it. I was the only one who couldn't swallow the ice cream. Then Mama put the remainder of the ice cream on top of the ice in the old icebox. There was enough put back for the others as well. It stayed cold, but not hard, but that didn't matter, I still couldn't eat it the next day.

Mama would save some each day for us because ice cream was about all that any of the others could swallow and it did make our throat so cold that it stopped hurting a little bit. I would have to spit mine out, but as long as it was close to those "snips," it felt good.

However, it took at least four days for my throat to heal enough so I could drink some of the melted ice cream, then it was gone. I wanted Papa to buy some or make another batch so I could have some more since I missed all of it except the 4th day.

He would not do it. He had too much to do. I thought it funny that Papa had his work cut out for him. He had to do most of Mama's work and all of ours except the milking, and Mama did that for two days, then the older boys did it. About a couple of days when I thought my throat was well, Papa had some English walnuts to give us for Christmas. Of course, none of us had ever had any, so I cracked one open, took part of it out and chewed it at least 100 times. It was just like spit, but couldn't swallow it at all. I just managed to mess up some healing that was taking place in my throat. Now I had to wait for that to heal while the others showed me that they could eat most anything.

Rodeo

After all was well the plantation work was about to begin, with disking up and down and then side to side to make sure all the old stubbles turned under the soil. Then some of the white laborers talked to my Papa, saying that there was going to be a rodeo in Lake Charles, La. I could hear him, but I didn't know what a rodeo was.

"Are y'all going?" They asked my Papa.

Without any hesitation, he said, "No, we're going to have our own rodeo right here."

I had never heard of a rodeo. The following Saturday evening, he had all of us rounding up all the steers, hogs, goats and horses out of the pasture and put in the barnyard pen. After all were herded into the pen, Papa called the name of the person he wanted to ride the animal that he was going to let out. This went on for a while and was somewhat funny watching the horses buck the boys off, because Papa put a corncob under the horse's tail to make him buck as he let each of the boys take their turn riding, one out at a time. The boys knew nothing about this until sometime after this home rodeo.

A steer was brought up for me to get on. I wrapped my legs around that steer, holding on to its mane and tail for my dear life. As soon I thought I was going to make it, the tail slipped out of my hands, so I wrapped my arms around its neck. Then I lost my balance and went tumbling as he bucked me off, hitting the root of a tree knock me out. That ended our rodeos.

I don't know what my Papa had for smelling salts (probably some castor oil or the like) but I got over it. It took a while for me to get in shape to breathe. Soon I was able to get up and then walk. I had to be ready to work the next week, so he had Mama put some "rubbing" compound on me and that was supposed to help me get the muscles back in shape.

It looked like "lard" to me, but I guess the old man knew what he was doing, because my back was well over night. However, that did end all rodeos at our house. Each of us had enough of that. The next day being Sunday, there was no picking cotton, but milking the cows, and picking the rest of the turnips and cabbage that was left out of the garden for dinner, had to be done. Now it was "Mama helping time." Evette and Andre usually kept the stove woodpile stacked on one of the sides of the wall near the stoves.

Mama had to keep the stoves with at least enough embers from the previous meal so that she could begin breakfast early the next morning. This also kept the water tank on one side of the oven warm from this wood stove. Mama and Lili used the hot water with lye soap to keep their hands clean.

They would clean everything just in case there were germs, which might have gotten on anything during the night or day. She and Lili had always kept the kitchen as clean as a hospital room. However, she never knew what had poisoned Angie, but she surely didn't want anyone else to get sick like that again.

Once a year, in the summer, Papa would take all of us to church to hear this certain Quartet Singing Group. They were very good, and he enjoyed listening to them. Since he knew all of the singers and the piano player, I got to take a fan up and fan the piano player. Everyone was all dressed up and without a fan or air conditioning; it had to have been 100 degrees in the church. It was a hot summer night, but I had the opportunity to fan that pretty piano lady.

Another time that Evette and I were allowed to go to church was during the time we stayed with my oldest sister, Isabelle. She wanted us to go and be with her two oldest children for them at "Vacation Bible School." This was a week between cotton chopping, gathering and canning of vegetables.

On this, our first time of Bible School, we made religious items from clay as well as learning a couple of songs like "Jesus loves me" and "Glory, Glory Hallelujah." We also learn the "Lord's Prayer" and the

"23rd Psalm." I made a pair of "Praying Hands" for Mama. Everyone who went made some kind of Biblical Ornament to take home. Papa was quite upset because he said that he sent us there to learn from the Bible and not to make "toys," as he called it. Well, that ended the Bible School even though we did learn a lot and made something that made Mama quite proud of us.

Sixth Grade

When I was in sixth grade, the teacher (Mrs. Taylor) would not use the state issued textbook for her reading class. Instead, she chose "The Weekly Reader," which each child paid $0.25 a week. This was required reading by her and no one was allowed to share with those who couldn't buy one. Just how hateful can a teacher be? This was downright cruel. She knew there were many poor people who couldn't afford this.

We were not poor; but my Papa was just not going to spend a dime. However, I thought we were poor like the students on the State Assistance Program, but they were one of the first who paid for a Weekly Reader. They had prettier clothes and neat school supplies. He liked the principal and the school board (who gave him the job), so he did nothing about it. He was a "wimp" as far as I was concerned. This was the only time that he let something of this nature happen. I believe she did this because she remembered me on those fire escapes every year. This might have been the reason for her dislike for me in her class.

From the first grade through the fourth, I would scoot up as fast as I could to the 3rd floor and step out and slide down six flights of the fire escape. THIS WAS FUN! When I got to the bottom, Mrs. Taylor spanked me, and I went right back and did it again getting a whipping each time. A sledge hammer would've been the only object to keep me for doing it. It never stopped me though, until the coaches talked to me. Then I stopped for them, not for the one who spanked me. They had other ideas for me, and I liked what they had to offer.

Now Mrs. Taylor had me and I couldn't do a anything about it. I got hell at school and hell at home. I couldn't help but think of all this in her "new reading class" when she saw my name on her roster. It didn't matter who had done the same issue in class, if I did it, she called me to the front and beat my rear not knowing what I had done. She would just ask if I had any sore places, and then as I showed her my legs from where the whip got me, and she would just say that she was not going to hit there.

She would not have gotten by with this even if I taught there. I would've turned her in. A reprimand would've been derived somehow and she would've had to buy the "newsletter" herself or used the state issued text. I always thought that everyone was afraid to challenge anything she did.

I just knew for sure that Papa would not buy one. He told her that the school furnished the books and that was it. Why did he let this go? All her tests were from the reading of that weekly paper. I am sure it was good, because it had to do with current events.

This was during the end of the WW II, and the news meant a lot to me. I had lost one brother, and five brothers who just got out of the service and two more preparing to go. This would've been one of my favorite subjects. No one was allowed to loan their weekly paper, because she took them up to read their comments. This was an evil trick.

She didn't care about comments. She just made sure everyone passed them to her so there would be no loaning of one. Oh Lord, she was HATEFUL!" I could've read a couple of them on the way home on the bus, and hidden some under my clothes as Evette did when she got up in grades. I would've hidden in the toilet to read have all of them read in a week, I could've passed the final exam. I loved school but none of us could ever bring books home except those darn piano books, when I took those lessons on the tablecloth. Everything else had to be taught at school.

We didn't have the time for it anyway. We didn't have electricity to study at night. We did have a generator for electricity to run the washing machine and to sharpen all the farm tools. However, Papa was not going to use the gasoline needed to run the generator for us to have electricity in the house. Later, one of the boys bought the wire and one chandelier for the living room. It was only used for a special occasion, like Christmas Eve or morning. That meant that you could hear the generator running while you were trying to eat or open "Santa Claus."

Why would Ms. Taylor want to listen to a slave-driving dirt farmer, anyway? Little did she know how smart he was? He had finished the 8th grade and passed the 8th grade exam. She would not have known about timber measurements such as measuring trees for lumber.

She wouldn't know how much timber to cut for building a barn or house or the number of bushels in a wagon of corn if given the measurements, let alone, the farm being measured in rods. He knew music, history and was a very smart and shrewd man and she treated him as if he was just a dumb "dirt farmer." I could've choked her!" I wanted to go to summer school and take the class over. The coach also begged Papa to allow me to live with them. However, he needed this farm hand for the summer.

He was upset with Mrs. Taylor, for what seemed to be her enjoyment of the situation. No one could do anything now about it, or were afraid of her. The principal wanted me to stay with them and his younger boys wanted to play ball with me, but it was too late now; the damage was done and everyone let it go.

She made 13 of us fail when she only had twenty-nine in the class. I made A's in everything else, but 13 made an "F" in reading. That, along with English and Arithmetic, were major subjects. If you fail one of them, you had to repeat the grade. Each of us lived from five to twelve miles from school, so there was not anyone who went to summer school to take it again. As soon as one could read and study these weekly papers, then take the test and passed it, you could go on to the seventh grade.

Blaise was teaching in Baton Rouge, Louisiana at the time and he wanted Papa to let me go to summer school there and live with him or to agree to stay in Villeplate and stay with the principal. He had friends where he lived, and Richet and Annette lived there. Papa was not about to give up one of his "boys," which he needed in the fields and didn't have to pay for the work.

Papa would not have anything to do with it. I hated him for not buying the paper. I was beginning to hate him for any and everything. It was as if he couldn't afford it. He was a wealthy man and pretended to be just a dirt farmer. He associated with the wealthy and all they probably talked about was where to invest the money. He surely never spent more than $1.00 a month on coffee, salt and pepper. He probably bartered for that. I just lost out!"

The next year, the principal put me in another sixth grade teacher's room. That was Mrs. Deaux, whom I loved so much. I made straight A's. I will always believe that Mrs. Taylor was quite jealous of Mrs. Deaux and all of those who were not as "sour-minded" as she was. She never visited or sat around other teachers to visit, as all the others would gather.

I often wondered if it ever occurred to Papa that piano lessons, which I had in the 4th grade, would've cost a lot more than the Weekly Reader. Why he never thought of this is beyond me. I would've enjoyed the Weekly Reader.

Nevertheless, either he would've beaten me to death or I would've wished he had. I should have threatened to tell about Joe. Now that would have "done him in."

I wanted so much to say, "Why in the hell did you make me take piano lessons in the fourth grade, but would not buy this paper for a lot less?"

I struggled to learn as much as possible and listened to the teachers with all my heart. Mrs. Deaux also knew that I couldn't take books home. She just knew how to teach and included the Weekly Reader in her lesson. I did everything that I could to learn as much as possible, from Mrs. Deaux. Now that woman could teach as well as enjoy her students.

Leaving The Plantation?

The next summer Isabelle talked Papa into letting me babysit her daughters. This would mean going to Baton Rouge while she got her Bachelor of Arts Degree. She had been teaching third grade at Villeplate Elementary. She had a Teaching Degree, but it was a two-year plan back then for teachers and she wanted a Bachelor of Arts Degree. It paid a lot more money. I have always believed that everyone shamed Papa and made him feel so guilty for not letting me go to summer school the previous summer. So, he allowed this "slave girl" to go.

While Isabelle was out of school with the girls, she ran the store that Papa had built for her and the little ones, as they came along, could stay in the back room. It had a single bed, a small table and chairs, a play pen, plus a stove. The store gave them some extra income to get by. She was out for each of the three girls and it took its toll on Isabelle.

Well, I was the happiest girl in the world, at that moment, to be having this opportunity to get away from the farm. I was about 13 years old and I had never been away from the country, except to school on the edge of town, and having my tonsils out. This was for nine whole weeks away from the farm. I WAS ECSTATIC!"

On the first weekend, Isabelle took all of us to the "Natatorium" at the college so that the kids could learn to swim correctly. She was a terrific swimmer herself as she was growing up and went to the same college. She wanted me to learn the proper strokes as well as what each of the strokes were called. We were all like a bunch of ducks and loved the water. I was elated to see Isabelle arrive home each day from her classes, so that I could go swimming. This was very different from swimming in a river or creek at a "swim hole."

Isabelle lived on High Street, in Baton Rouge, in an upstairs garage apartment. It had two bedrooms upstairs for us. Isabelle slept with the two youngest girls in one bedroom and Paulette and I slept in the other.

The previous spring semester, the children were in school and she didn't need a sitter. The summer semester was going to be a big problem if Papa had not let me go to help. He did allow it and babysitting was fun. There was a tire swing in the back yard, which was tied to a limb of a tall huge tree. They loved this "tire swing." Once the youngest wanted to have the swing all alone but wanted me to push her without the others getting a chance to swing.

Of course, I told her, "Oh no, you are getting off right now."

I did get her down, but I had to spank her. I kept wondering if I was being just like Papa. Therefore, I had to start behaving differently and with more compassion. That spanking had to stop. She did have a bruise and I did not know if I caused that or not. Maybe she had fallen on the roots of the tree. Nevertheless, a hand spanking would not happen again.

I had never heard of "time-out" at the time, but she did have her sit on the steps and watch the others play for about 3 minutes. I suppose Isabelle was the only one who had ever spanked her, and very little at that. Then Antoinette did the same problem, and I couldn't get her off. Finally, with some threats I pulled her off the swing.

I then pretended to spank her even more. She thought that she got the same spanking. She didn't though. I was just pretending. I wondered if she just wants the extra attention that her sister got? I did learn not to spank with the hand though. I had never been spanked with a hand. My whippings were "killers," I thought.

This was the first, and the last, time I ever used my hand on any kid. We started playing other games that would not cause as much fuss as the swing did. We would play "hide and seek," hop-scotch" board games and read books. Working up challenging activities appeared to work well, especially in reading all the books. Sometimes we played chase just to get outside more. This was the easiest game for me, by pretending that they were hard to find.

The downstairs apartment was much smaller. There was a young couple living in it. Part of the downstairs had a garage for the owner's car. The young man was a mail carrier who had to walk from house to house each day with the mail. I had never seen a "walking postman." Our mail carrier drove through the country roads in my part of the country. What a simple learning experience this was.

One night, Paulette walked in her sleep. She needed to go to the bathroom and went into the closet instead. She had never walked in her sleep before; that we knew of, but I suppose that she was just a "sleepy girl" and went through the wrong door in that small apartment. Of course, there was nothing in the closet to soak up the urine, so it took the path of least resistance and went through the floor.

The next day, the mail carrier asked, "Do you all have a plumbing problem, or did someone spill something?"

"Why do you think that?" I asked.

"Well drops kept hitting me in the face during the night," He said.

I couldn't tell him the truth. I just told him that one of the kids probably spilled their water, which was not far from the truth. We shall never forget this event and I don't believe she has ever done any sleep-walking since. Can you imagine what he would've done if he had known what was dropping on his face?

The apartment had a screen porch with a refrigerator on it. I didn't grow up with a refrigerator. I had never seen one, and knew very little about them but learned about them quickly. It was electric and kept objects cold. This had a small freezer section at the top with some ice trays of frozen water. This was all new territory for me. Oh, I wished that my Mama had one of these.

Once, I was trying to boil some water for some reason, and as I took the lid off, the steam burned the back of my hand very bad. I knew nothing about cooking or doing anything in the kitchen. This was a gas stove, which I had never seen either.

Next, after burning the back of my hand, I thought that I needed to do was to start cooling the back of it by putting it in the freezer section of the refrigerator. As soon as I put my hand in the freezer section, my hand stuck to the top. I couldn't pull my hand away without the skin coming off. I didn't want to lose any skin. I had to stay there until the kids brought me enough hot washcloths to warm that part of my hand so that it could be released from the ice.

"Hurry, hurry with the hot wash cloths," I yelled.

"Each of you bring a couple RIGHT NOW AND HURRY," I screamed.

With this constant hollering telling them to hurry, I finally got it off but some of the blistered skin still stuck to the icy part. When Isabelle came home, she put some sort of salve on it and wrapped it to keep dirt out of it. It got better in a hurry, which was good because I didn't want to miss any swimming opportunities at the college.

When Isabelle finished her classes for the day, I walked up to the college. The students saw the wrap, but I told them that it was just a steam burn.

"The water will be good for it and I'm ready to swim," I said.

I learned a lot more about swimming. Some neat boys and girls showed me how to dive off the three-meter board as well as the high springboard. They wondered how I learned so quickly, and amazed that this short and strong little girl could do whatever they taught.

Therefore, I told them that I was almost fearless about my diving into the camouflaged nets, which the soldiers left behind after the war was over. I told them how we would cut the tree limbs off so we could dive, jump and flip down on the nets.

First, it would be about eight feet on up to about thirty feet. They found this quite interesting and had a bunch who would gather about me to learn more about my upbringing. They couldn't believe what all I had to do as well as what I could do. For once after failing the 6th grade, I felt wonderful with all this attention as well as learning as much about swimming and diving as I possibly could. To get to go every afternoon was heaven to me. This was WONDERFUL and I had the time of my life. Why did the summer fly by so quickly? I knew then that was the college for me and with my sister and coaches, I couldn't have had better role models. I also wanted to be as helpful to others as these young people were who taught me about the diving boards with the "flips" as well as the swan dives. I had to do well and work hard to try to earn as much money as I could and hide it, so I could do all these things that was introduced to me when I got to college.

That was my dream. Occasionally, Isabelle would take us to the ice cream parlor. This was the first time in an ice cream parlor for me. It was exciting to see all the cars and to be able to walk on a sidewalk in a big town. I was in awe of all the traffic and people we saw.

No one knew how proud I was to be in that big city and I felt very important keeping those girls. They were special to me as well. I had never bought nor had an ice cream "cone." I had never seen the night-lights of a city. All the different kind of cars fascinated me everywhere I went, as well as all the people walking back and forth. They were mostly college students, Isabelle told me. All were dressed so different from any I had ever seen. I never thought of the fact that they were "grown-ups" in college and I was used to seeing high school students or "mothers" and older people as well as farm hands or "dirt people" as we were often called. What a sight!" It was entertaining for me to just sit and watch the people go by. This looked like Christmas to me, with all the electric lights shining everywhere; even the streets were lit up. The girls liked this too, but they soon got bored and wanted to play.

On one or two occasions, Boudreau (Isabelle's husband) would go to Baton Rouge to see the family. While he visited with Isabelle, I took the girls on their walk down to the ice cream parlor. That was fun but trying to keep those three girls on the sidewalk and attempting to get the youngest two to hold onto my hand was not a very easy task. The sidewalk was next to the busy street and the people drove faster on it than they did in the country. Paulette was easy to get along with and a lot more fun because of she was not too much younger than I was. In many respects, she knew so much more than I did. She was amused at my excitement. She had seen all this before, but she could cook and iron and I didn't have a clue as to how to do any of this.

The time passed so quickly, that the nine weeks of summer school were over, and the best time of my life was ending. We packed up everyone's belongings and back to the little brown house, we went. This was not so hard to do because the apartment was furnished and all we had to do was get all the clothes and linens packed. Then off to the farm for me, who only had a part of a flour sack full of clothes and a bathing suit which Isabelle bought me. I sure couldn't let Papa see or know about this. I would hell for it and Isabelle too, probably.

After receiving a B.A. Degree, Isabelle was making much more money. Soon, they sold the little "Brown house" and bought a farm near us. Here they had a horse, raised sheep, steers for beef and a cow for milk. They had 100 acres of bearing pecan trees, plus a nice size garden with enough corn for feeding the sheep, cattle and horse. Boudreau would ask one of us to take the wagon with a plow over to their house to do some plowing for him. He had never done very much of that kind of farm work before.

He would also pay me for some help with plowing, climbing and shaking pecan trees. I was just like a monkey, going from one limb to another. After the shaking of the trees, we would pick up the pecans. The young ones would be gathering them while I was shaking, so there was not too many for me to pick up. Therefore, on to the next tree, I would go, and this went on all during the fall, as the pecans would mature.

One child, a boy (Pierre), was born there and then Mama started keeping him while Isabelle taught school. I never heard of an amount paid to Mama, but she saved it until she had enough to buy some special concerns. She hid her money as well. I remember Mama ordering a C.O.D. (cash on delivery) package once from the catalog. She bought some pretty material to make something neat for Evette and me, and seemed to have some left for quilting scraps. She saved the rest for my college fund that she had been hiding. Of course, I had no help, but had to work double time to make up for the time away from the farm chores. These were special favors for allowing me to play softball. I didn't mind this at all, because there was too much of a pleasure in it for me. Mama could see this excitement in me even though she never saw me play any games.

My Mama had never been away from the plantation to go to town except when we had our tonsils out. She had quite a learning experience of her own on that one trip. That was her first time out of the plantation or swamp. Mama had so much to do that she didn't have the time to go places except to visit a brother on Sunday afternoon occasionally. She did the milking for me so that I could have the opportunity to play both basketball and softball. Evette had fewer chores to do than I had. She didn't know how to milk a cow anyway, but became an excellent cook.

Mama watched how excited I would be when the coach and girls came out to get me or help me. Once at a home game, I hit a home run and turned my ankle as I rounded first base. It became "a hobble type run" then and I was barely able to make it to home plate. Papa ran out quickly to make sure that I had not ruined those "New Tennis Shoes." He was not concerned about the turned ankle because he could cure a sprained ankle but the tennis shoes cost money. I was so embarrassed!" He did cure it in about a week and a half. I don't think that I missed a game. This "red oak ooze" (as it was called) baked my foot in such a way that I was able to get back to the fields, quickly. It was some sort of "voodoo" concoction I had to go through, but well worth it to me. This type of plaster or a hot mustard was used to cure most anything. It didn't matter whether it was on the foot or up to the top of one's head; it seemed to take care of whatever ailed us. The acifidity bag, which we wore around our neck for the flu and other sickness, had a dreadful smell. I must admit that I was a great ball player.

Coach and the girls drove twelve miles out to get me. I was next to the oldest one home now and could operate the tractor and all the equipment. There was not much to be planted, but as long as there was a cow to be milked, there had to be corn grown as well as sweet potatoes, Irish potatoes and my Mama's large garden to feed everyone. I didn't mind this, because I couldn't cook. This allowed me to be able to work for my Uncle and the friends of Papa who needed me to plow their big tractors or pick cotton for them on the weekend. They paid me well and I saved it all.

I had to work extra hard and do as many duties as possible after five of my brothers went to war and Ted was in college. I sometimes could sneak in time for a basketball game in the fall or a softball game in the spring. I didn't miss any because the coach and some of the girls would come out twelve miles and help me pull corn. This was quite a learning experience for each of the girls.

Sometimes after school was out, the softball team and coach would come out to camp and fish down on the Villeplate River. I would take a team of mules and the wagon full of kids and the coach. Mama filled a tub with fried chicken, tea-cakes, jugs of water, and peas to be heated on the campfire and some precooked biscuits to warm over the camp-fire. She did warn us that the vegetables needed to be eaten that night. Biscuits could be reheated over the flames like marshmallows. This was another time for one of the best times of life. (However, noth-ing would ever beat the time that I kept the girls for Isabelle while she went back for her degree.)

Papa only went to softball games because they were being played during the daytime and before bus time to take everyone home. Papa made a harder working slave out of me for this favor of allowing me to play on the team. It was worth it as far as I was concerned. I could've quit anytime but was not about to quit playing for one of my role mod-els. Papa knew that I was good in softball. I would pitch about four or five innings without hurting my shorter leg; play shortstop some of the time and catcher at other times. This would happen especially after my pitching arm had formed a corn on it and would bleed from pitching the curve. I had a fastball and a curveball that no one could hit.

This ability was due to my limp, which allowed me to put an extra spin on the ball as I limped out to pitch. I was also a good hitter because I was strong from all the hard work at the farm. I had a good eye on the ball. The opponents didn't like to see me come up to the plate to hit or be at the pitcher's mound. I loved the coach and played in every game in one position or another when I got to the eighth grade. I couldn't work out with the basketball girls when they had practice after school because I had to ride the bus home.

I was aggressive, I worked and played hard, turned flips and walked on the top of the tall, big, 2 x 12 fence around the barn. Boulean didn't even try this. I did everything to get my Papa to say that he was proud of me. That never happened to me or to any of us. I don't know why he wanted me around, especially after the ordeal with Joe. This "play time" helped me release anxieties. Hugging both fans as well as both coaches seemed very necessary to me, whether we won or lost a game. Most thought this was strange except the coach, who was doing the same gratefulness. Winning the tournaments enabled us to go to the State Tournaments and we won State three times while I was in High School. Papa allowed this because he didn't want to disappoint the principal or the coaches. At this time, I was a junior in high school.

The Cow Horn

One night I had a basketball game to play, but couldn't stay in town after school because of all the night work along with the milking of the cows which I had to do after the boys left home except Boulean. The others had been in the service, finished college and married by this time. Boulean and I had it all to do now.

The evening that I had to hurry for the night work, Boulean had gone out "night-fishing." He had milked the Jersey with the sore bag and udders the night before. This was caused from getting into the briar patch. She had messed herself up. All this milk was given to the hogs, or else you let it hit the ground. She had made a mess in the barn, and I had to walk in it. Boulean never told anyone about the cow raising hell as she was being milked or breaking one horn off while he was doing this. Therefore, I ran and told my Mama and she told me how to handle this Jersey cow. She was not my regular cow to milk, and I didn't like it at all.

Mama said, "Just tie her one horn and "nub" to the barn post and to be careful because she was pretty sore and will be angry and try most anything to keep from being touched." I could see that immediately. I could see that in this cow's eyes. I secured her nub of a horn and the one good horn to a support post and then strapped her belly to the planks on the side of the stall. Next, I began to try to milk her. She kicked all over the place and was very angry. She had diarrhea exceeding any normal cow, but typical of a Jersey cow. This was typical of a Jersey, especially when she got hurt or nervous. She didn't want to be tied down or milked and she was letting me know that. As I started milking, she kicked me and messed all over the place.

I began screaming to my Mama, "I can't do this. She is kicking and messing everywhere."

"Ram your head in her flanks so she can't raise her leg up." Mama kept hollering.

Well, I tried and she pulled the other horn off and one plank off the stall wall.

"I can't do this and the team will be here soon," I screamed out again.

Mama told me how to treat the horn, by wrapping it with a rag wet with kerosene, and just try to empty the bag because the cow's bag HAD to be emptied. "Daisy," the milk cow, had already kicked the milk bucket a winding so I looked at that cow that was looking at me.

I said, "You S.O.B.!" I am going to milk you or kill you, so just get used to it."

Mama was still hollering, "Honey, shove your head in her flanks."

"Okay Daisy, you are going to be milked!"" I said as I dove into the flanks.

I went at her so fast, not knowing that she had already flexed her leg to kick me. Therefore, when my head went toward her flanks, my head went under her tail instead. She messed all over my head and I went screaming to Mama with my head hanging way out in front and side of me. She could see what had happened and had prepared for it.

About the time I got to the house, the horn blew, which meant the team was there to pick me up. I don't know who told them that I needed a little time, but Mama was washing me down with that lye soap from head to toe in a wash tub of warm water and lye soap for a bath. She knew that I would need it when I finished that job and had it all prepared. I first had to wash my head in another bucket before jumping into the wash tub.

It didn't take long for the two of us to do this in the kitchen where it was warm. I later thought it was funny. I had short hair, so it didn't take long to comb it and jumped in the car with my basketball uniform in a sack as fast as I could so Papa couldn't see that I wore shorts to play. I took off with the coach and the girls. They loved to come out, because they learned something new each time, and enjoyed my family as well. They didn't know about the kind of troubles one might have when milking a cow.

We didn't have any perfume for me but sometimes someone would give Mama some kind of good-smelling bath powder and she used it on me before going out, but that didn't kill the smell on me. I could not smell the powder, but I think that the odor of the cow mess hung up in my nasal hair.

I knew that all they could smell was the lye soap, but cow mess was not the easiest odor to conceal. However, something worked pretty well in the game, because no one would get very close to me, and I scored more points than usual. I also caused many girls to foul out and we won that game. Winning that was easy. The team and the coach felt sorry for all I had to endure as they took me back home to the country. They also received an accomplished laugh out of it, which alleviated most of my embarrassment. They knew all the challenging issues I had. They knew it was tough. However, I was admired for it. They knew nothing about farming, but they did learn about milking a Jersey cow with bummed-up udders. The cow still had to be milked anyway to prevent mastitis.

I found out that night after getting home that my Mama had gone out and with her soft and tender touch, she would was able to finish milking her. She took that syrup bucket, cleaned it to be used again for something else. She kept milking just that one cow, putting salve on her until all of her udders and bag was well. The hogs were happy until that cow got well. This had to show what an angel my Mama was. I loved her, and she kept us from getting into trouble. She knew also that if Papa found out, there would be a "beating" with most anything to us. She kept the secrets, though. Mamas was wonderful!

We didn't realize that we were so blessed until we were much older. Other kids at school who didn't do farm work or any hard work, made a point of shunning me. Little did they know that my Papa helped put food on most of their tables also? I didn't know about it until I was in college and my brothers told me about all this. My Papa didn't brag about anything like this. These people were hungry and didn't know how to manage a "welfare" check to last a whole month. They would work on the farm to make it until the end of the month, and then we wouldn't see them for at least two weeks.

These kids, mostly kinfolks, made fun of me because they had lunch boxes with "Movie Star's" pictures on them, and all we had was a syrup bucket. It didn't make any difference to us. I can never recall being jealous of them because in some way I believed I knew more than they did and I was happy; while they did not appear to be. They didn't know one anything about hard work, much less farming and making it from one month to another.

These syrup buckets, which we used for our lunch, were the ones, which had gotten bent somehow and couldn't be used again for syrup. Sometimes my lunch would be a boiled egg and a turnip green biscuit sandwich as well as a baked sweet potato.

With the gas created by the boiled egg and a turnip green sandwich, all one had to do to open the can was to gently ease the lid a little with your little finger and the top flew off. It sure had a bad odor at first, but it was not long until the odor drifted around. Everyone knew where it came from. They called me all kind of names, from "redbone to rotten shrimp." I didn't care, I had a good lunch.

It was quite ironic that one of the sons of Papa's wealthy friends would trade me a big red juicy apple for one baked sweet potato or a biscuit. He liked to sit next to me. I was not his or anyone else's girl-friend. He just knew that I would have a sweet potato. Now that was an impressive trade for me. I liked to sit with him because he always had an apple or "store bought sliced bread" to trade for the sweet pota-to. Many were jealous of me for him to come sit with me. They liked him for a boyfriend, but he was not interested.

My Horse

About the only thing that I enjoyed at the farm was riding my horse, as well as any job that had to do with riding him. I had to round up the cows to be milked if they were in another pasture. I trained my horse well, except from jumping or darting sideways from gadgets that rattled whether it was a jalopy or a bucket. Once a year, it was mandatory by the state and federal government that all farmers have their cows "dipped" at a central location called a dipping vat. This held some kind of chemical that would prevent the cows from getting ticks that would kill them if they got the fever caused by the tick.

Many people were opposed to this. I don't know if it cost the owner of one cow or a herd of cattle to do this. It just took time and effort to get one or many cows there. In Louisiana, there was at least one "dipping vat" per Ward or District. The one we had was only a half a mile away from home.

I learned later that it took a long time to eradicate the ticks. The ticks were found in most all southern states. The people who opposed it would even shoot at officers in charge of the inspection or they would dynamite the complete dipping vat.

I had always wished that it had been on the other end of the Parish. This would've given me more time that was exciting by being on my horse and herding the cows. Many people had to travel several miles to this location if they only had one cow. I only wished that they had asked me to do it for them. I also wished that they had asked Papa if I could herd all the cows for any of them. That would've been a great day for me.

Even with the short distance, this was an entertaining time. The whole herd was driven into a pen and then each cow was driven into the vat until they were completely submerged for at least a couple of seconds. They would hold their heads up, but they couldn't get it high enough. The shorter ones and baby's got a good soaking. This chemical also helped to prevent flies and gnats. The flies would lay an egg, which became a nit (or larvae) and then they bored into the skin and became "bloodsuckers."

The Parish Government had this land deeded to them by my Grandpa Thibodeaux for a place to put those vats. The cows had to climb out on some cross bars to aid in their exit out of the vat of chemicals. These bars came out into a "v-shaped" area and this was where the ear was marked with a metal clip which had a number to show that it had indeed been dipped. Then we would herd the cows into the road to drive them home. They didn't care for the dipping so getting them herded back was not a chore, but fun for me. Oftentimes, I was sent to the store on my horse and Papa warned me to keep moving until I got to the store and not to stop any place to visit. My maternal Grandma knew Papa was like that.

She always knew what to do when she heard me galloping up the road she hurried in, grabbed a biscuit and filled it with turnip greens. She knew that I loved a turnip green sandwich hot or cold.

She would meet me in the road and say, "I know you can't stop honey, but I brought your favorite biscuit sandwich when I heard the horse running."

I was moving very slow as I reached down for the biscuit, then threw her a kiss, and thanked her. She was only four and one half feet tall, and was almost that large around, which was not tall enough to reach me. By keeping the horse moving, I bent over as far as I could to get the treat. Then I could then tell Papa that I didn't stop. That's all he had to know. She knew that I loved her, but was not allowed to stop. With that done, she sent me on my way to enjoy my snack.

I hurried to the store to get the needed items and got back home to hear, "Did you stop anywhere?"

"I only stopped at the store where I was told to go," I truthfully said.

Anything to do with horseback riding was fun for me. Riding the horse to the store was usually my chore. One time one of my sisters-in-law, wanted to ride a bit with me to take a bucket of fried chicken to my Grandma and Grandpa on a Sunday afternoon. About a half mile from the house, my horse saw a black lizard run in front of it. The horse jumped sideways and the chicken, bucket and I went flying away. The saddle turned under the horse as I fell off and I took the big spill. My horse tore the saddle into pieces as it tickled his underside. He went back to the house and with each gallop; he tried to kick the saddle out from under him. It was a long time before I got another saddle, but I still enjoyed riding my horse even "bare-back."

Another time I had a spill, was when I was sent to the store, and on the way back home with the goods, an old jalopy was coming down the road toward me. My head told me that something bad was "fixing" to happen and it did. The horse took off into the woods and started under a limb. I saw immediately that the limb was too low for both of us to fit. Of course, I came off the back end with the groceries but one of my shoes just disappeared. The horse immediately ran back to the house.

All was okay after that, except that I was missing a shoe. I couldn't find it anywhere. After I walked home with one shoe on, limping all the way, my Papa asked what happened and immediately sent me back to find that shoe. This time Papa didn't whip me with the whip, he just gave me a kick in the butt which sent me almost on my face. I didn't find it. The next day, some of the others went back to help me find my shoe. It was never found. It could have hung up on the stirrup and lost on the way when the horse took off to the house. This meant another pair of shoes had to be bought.

You can bet that I had to do additional work for that new pair of shoes. My Papa always had reasons to give us extra work. We never let him see us idol but one time that I can recall. He made us go in the pasture and pull "bitter-weeds." No fun there and it didn't happen again. We should have been looking for the shoe instead. That shoe could've flipped up in the tree and hung on a limb. Who would know? We couldn't find this shoe and it didn't matter how many times Papa kicked me.

One Sunday afternoon (during playing time), we were playing on the big swing, which was across the road from the house. We liked to do high swinging. On this particular tree (about 100 feet high) across from the house, one of the boys climbed up and out on a limb, which would allow the swing to be used without hitting another limb.

One had to take the rope, which had two huge knots tied on it your hands to hold. Then to have a thrill, you had to climb another oak tree, (while hanging on this thick and heavy rope), which was 30 feet away, that had its limbs trimmed for an easy climb. Once up the tree, you hung onto the rope and jumped out. This was seeing the world in a different perspective, as well as the tops of other trees.

Sometimes the boys would ride their horse up under the swing to try to knock you off, but their horse would see this coming and buck them off. They finally figured that the horse had more sense than they did. They also knew that I always had some secret tricks to pull on them when the time came to use them for doing this anyway. I would swing my feet up and turn completely upside down and they couldn't reach me. That was the trick planned and practiced if they neared me.

I was overjoyed that Richet, who would never give up, would end up getting bucked off each time he tried to make his horse go under the swing. It would not have been very funny however, if any of them had succeeded in their devilish deed.

Started College: Cost?

I got the attention from Mama when I was plowing or picking cotton for farmer friends to earn money for college. Mama would save what she could for me. There was plenty of time for her to help Evette go to college. She would probably get all cash from Papa. She didn't, but got a lot more than I did.

Mama didn't want me working in the fields. She wanted me to learn to cook and to teach me matters that I needed to know. She wanted me to be a lady. This was before and after I started college with no money for personal hygiene material or other real needs.

She would find Papa's pants on the floor by his bed, and then shake them for coins to fall out. Then she would leave a couple of small ones on the floor for him to see and kick the rest under his bed where he would not find or look for them. She would get those when she made his bed. She always wore a "house-dress" with pockets, and into the pockets, the coins would go.

She would secretly conceal them and send it to me when it was essential. What a Mama I had and she was the best. When I left home, he didn't buy sanitary napkins. I don't know what he thought I would use. Here again, I think that he was showing meanness of me not being a boy, as if I could help it.

You will not believe that my Papa had to send me to my sister's for a while to learn to talk like "educated people." As Cajuns, we never enunciated our words correctly, which ended with an "ed" or "ing." All of those words sounded like an "en," instead. I just picked it up from the close association with my best black buddy in the field and then it stuck with me every day from birth through high school. My brothers didn't pick it up because they worked and played together. The blacks didn't even add the "en." It was just shortened.

First, we had a few purchases to make because Mama insisted that we go to town for a few articles that she wanted me to have. She must have threatened him, because Papa never hesitated one bit. The three of us went to Opelousas, Louisiana. This was Mama's first trip away from the plantation to a store. We had to buy me a pair of shoes (brown and white saddle oxfords-no polish). She had gone to the hospital when we had our tonsil out, but never to a store. She was certainly in awe, and couldn't believe anything like this existed. She began picking out a couple of pair of underpants and a slip and shoes for church. I think Mama was hoping that I could at least get to go to church. I also had to have some new tennis shoes for college. (I didn't need any dresses, because I had lied to my Papa and told him that I had to have "home economics" to finish high school in my senior year.) I did not, but I knew that if he thought that, I would make three dresses. I had also saved some money for two pieces of material to make two "sleeveless jumper dresses" that zipped down the back. That made five different outfits for each day of the school week. I thought I would be "fit-for-the-Queen."

Now to college we all went with all my belongings in three apple boxes. When we finally got to the college, students from all over the country were pouring in. They had lovely suitcases, and my Papa had one apple box of stuff, Mama and I each had a box full. These three boxes held all I owned. My head dropped at my meager belongings because the three boxes held everything I owned.

These boxes contained my homemade dresses, sheets, quilts which Mama made a feather pillow from our chickens, a pillowcase all made from feed sacks, and then the new panties, slip, and new shoes. I didn't have a toothbrush because we always brushed our teeth from a stick from the black-wood tree. I had a box of baking soda, because that was what we all used at home for cleaning our teeth. I had for jaundice and I am sure that they didn't allow me to leave home without it. All I had was open to all.

Mama turned and noticed my head hanging low and that I was quite embarrassed. She knew that I was ashamed of my boxes___just plain old ruff cut wood boxes___of my belongings and people could see what I had. Some would look at us as if we just came out from under a bridge, or some bus from Mexico or the Orient, and some would turn and giggle. Mama stopped and gave me a lesson right then and I never forgot it and have taken heed ever since.

She said, "Hold your head up and don't ever be ashamed of anything you have or don't have. You have done more and earned your way here, and these people don't have the guts that you have. So, get your head up and smile and be proud of who you are!" I'm proud of you and so is your Papa, even though he won't tell you. Those young ladies don't know what it was like to be a slave girl like you were and to get to go to college."

That was the best lesson I had ever learned that truly stuck with me. I saved those apple boxes because they meant a lot to me after that lecture. They were also needed to go home or anywhere when I left for home or spent a weekend with someone. I knew extra clothes were needed and the box held what I needed.

Anyway, I did what my Mama said. I cherished that lesson and never forgot it. Her advice to me that day made me so popular, because I marched like a trooper with those apple boxes right to my dorm room. With that said, they must have thought I was something else, because they elected me president of the dorm. I appreciated this, but it was not long before I resigned, because I saw how much fun it was to be like my friends, such as giggling and talking after "lights out" in the open and screened in sleeping hall. Our dorm rooms were too hot for the summer because there was no air conditioning. The dorm lady accepted my resignation and we were the best of friends all the way through college. She kept up with me, probably because of those apple boxes. I'll have something very special now to teach young students when I begin teaching.

At night, we slept in the neat sleeping porch, which had some electric fans and windows with screens every two or three feet. This was entertaining, cool and enjoyable for me. All could see why I didn't want to be the proctor for these girls. I loved them and it was quite amusing to be on that porch. I worked like a slave to get through college.

I was used to hard work, but this was different. I had to worry about finances, of which I had never had or needed to worry. At the end of summer school, I always worked for different people in the fields mostly for Papa's friends. This was hard work, but I was making money each day that I worked while I was home between semesters. They paid me more than Papa paid for his workers. I was allowed to ride my horse three to five miles to work for them. I didn't mind that, either. I just wished there were more days for me to work and earn more money. This was every year.

I struggled taking as many correspondence courses from two different colleges that my Supervisor didn't know about until I was becoming a second semester junior. She just overlooked it. However, that didn't keep her from having a fit because I was not supposed to work and take more than sixteen hours. I had been taking 24 without her noticing.

When I told her how it was at home and not having enough money for college, she said, "I didn't see, hear or know anything. Just go to class."

Well, right quick I found out that she was going along with it. She was a wonderful, compassionate and thoughtful advisor. Then my roommate came up with something that I thought I would try. There was so much that my Papa didn't know about that I was doing. I wondered if he knew how I was able to go to college without any money from him.

Papa didn't know that I had written the Evangeline Parish School Board for a loan if I promised to teach for them. They gave me $25 each semester that I was in school without interest. Papa had not spent more than $25 the whole time I was in college. Blaise and Ms. Yolanda (the basketball coach) helped a lot, along with my dear Mama hiding money that fell out of my Papa's pants when she picked them up. I did babysit for Richet and Annette who lived near the college.

He also did not know that I had a full time working scholarship in the Physical Education Department, wore shorts every day, had a bathing suit and went swimming most every day. He would've jerked me out of college in a second, and I would've been the number one "farm lady" in the whole country for my Papa. I also know that I would've been a number one jailbird for the rest of my life for killing him.

When I was a second semester junior, I didn't know if I would have the money to be able to prepare for the next year's student teaching classes. I didn't know what to do. That took extra clothes for the high school student teaching in math, and extra shorts and outfits for high school physical education classes also. I didn't have it and no way to earn it.

The Lady Marines

My roommate invited me home with her for the weekend. Unbeknownst to me, she visited the Marine Recruiters while there. She learned that if she joined, she would only serve during the summer. Money was no problem for her.

She wanted to show them that she could pay her own way out there when she finished college. She signed up, and since I was old enough, I did too. We were going to be Lady Marines in Quantico, Virginia for the summer when the spring semester was over. I was ecstatic!" I would make more money in the Lady Marines than I ever would working in the fields

So, the next weekend I borrowed Blaise's car and went down to see Mama and told her what I had done. I also wanted to see if she had found any more coins, which might have dropped out of Papa's pants. I still had the spring semester and that meant more trouble.

I was shocked as I looked down the hall toward the front porch and saw those two Lady Marine Recruiters walking to the front porch. These were the same lady recruiters I had seen the weekend before. Why did my Papa even have to be at home at that time? He could have gone to the bank or visiting anybody. But no, he was sitting on the front porch at the most uncalled-for time for me. Why was he there that time of day, I have no idea.

"Are you ladies lost?" he asked.

"No, we are here to let you know that Jo has signed up for the Lady Marines. We wanted to see her and thank you all and show our appreciation," One of the ladies said, immediately.

"I am sorry that you have wasted your time, but I will see to it that she has this undone!"" Papa said.

"Well, she has signed it, and was old enough to sign it, and that was all we needed." the other lady said.

"We just wanted to meet you and her mother, to thank you for Jo's ambition to serve, as well as to speak with Jo," the first lady said.

"No, I told you lady that she is not going. You can leave now!"" He barked.

Papa kept motioning for them to leave. He had left the polite mode and gone into the "I'm in control of my children mode."

So they turned around to leave and said, "We are sorry for bothering you as well as how you feel about Jo joining

Papa just motioned for them to keep going. He was so rude and obnoxious. Of course, they left, and as soon as they got out of sight, he called me to the front. I was shaking all over as I thought about what Papa did to Boulean (my older brother) for running away from home. I should've just stayed there with Mama and pretended that I didn't hear him. Nevertheless, I went out and Papa was standing up with his belt in one hand and the other arm out to grab me by the hair of my head. He then jerked that belt around and started thrashing me all over the porch. He jerked at my hair and it was short, but still hurt.

Finally I hollered, "You had better give me enough money then to finish college or I will get a job as a barmaid."

As soon as I got that out of my mouth, I thought he was going to kill me. He was hitting me like a boxer in the face, and blood starting running out of my nose, mouth, arms and legs as well as bruises all over me. I kept running around the rocking chairs. Of course, I didn't even know what a "barmaid" was, but had heard that they made a lot of money on the weekend when the army base was near. He slammed a chair, then a rocker at me and then knocked me clean over the swing and the banisters to the ground. He was livid!" I couldn't believe this. He had gone insane. He was angry that he was losing control of me.

Mama went to the porch wondering about all the loud commotion. She immediately saw how violently mad he was and let him have it.

"Sit down and don't ever lay another hand on her again. I don't know what has happened to you, but you keep your hands off Jo," she screamed.

I think at that time he realized just how old I was and he had lost control and could do nothing about it. I was happy to hear Mama threaten him with something. I had wished many times that she would just shoot him or leave him or at least had her way many years before all this.

I went crying around the side of the house to the back. Soon Mama came to me, hugging, cleaned up the bloody places and became angrier by the minute with him when she saw all the bruises. She tried to comfort me.

"What an injustice!"" I shouted loud so that Papa could hear me.

She knew that I was hurt physically and emotionally as she observed the blood dripping from my face, legs and arms. The bruises were packed with cold wet rags. The hugs helped more as well as the lye soap. Mama cleaned the cuts from any germs for sure, which were formed by the belt, his licks and the banisters. The mishandling of me was inexcusable beyond anyone's imagination.

"I'm old enough to join the Lady Marines and Papa can't do anything about it." I said.

Mama said, "Honey, please wait. I know that you are hurt right now and sure, you are old enough, but you are so innocent and know very little of the happenings away from home. You are ignorant of the corruption that takes place out away from the protection of family. You learned and experienced many areas of life for the first time, but you had family ready to help if needed. Please don't get upset with me because you didn't deserve any of the torture that Papa gave you. I hope that you understand that you are not ready to be acquainted with the happenings of being out of state with no family member to come to your aid.

"You know nothing about the evil situations you could encounter. I feel so guilty. You have never known about any of this and it has been my fault. I should've insisted that you help me in the home instead of working like a man in the fields. I don't know everything, but Isabelle taught me a lot that you should've been taught at home. I don't know everything, but could've given you more information of becoming a young adult and more about the dangers out there if Papa had allowed you to help Evette, Lili and me in the house and not out in the field." She pleaded.

Mama was right of course and I was glad that she talked to me. I was not aware that she even knew what she was telling me. She sure knew more than I thought she did, and I knew nothing about all she was telling me. Nonetheless, she had been babysitting for Isabelle and promised that she would send me more money just as soon as she got it.

I said, "Why couldn't he have talked to me some before being so rude and beating the hell out of me? He just lost what little respect I did have for him by talking to those women like that. He has always treated women with the greatest respect. Just as they came up, he met them as if they were the Queen. Then when they began telling why they were here, he went ballistic!" He was cruel and hateful toward them. I hate him for this. How old does he think I am? No, Mama, I worked too hard for him on this place."

I continued, "Just tell him that he had better give me some money or send it to me himself. You have done enough for him and me. You keep your money and buy items like you have always wished you could have. Are you listening to me, Mama?"

Mama said, "I'm not crying for me, honey. It is for you that I am crying. I should've taught you when you were younger. I'm so sorry."

Mama was so upset that she couldn't stop talking and trying her best to smooth issues out for me. It was comforting, and I understood, but it was distressing for me to understand how rude, obnoxious and mean he had been to the ladies as well as to me.

"That's okay Mama. Don't cry for me. I will nullify whatever needs. "Mama, I'll do it just for you," I cried.

I stayed to assure my Mama that I would finish college if it was the last cotton picking thing I ever had to do. But, I'll stay away from that crazed slave driver, though. If I had my own car, I would've left after visiting with Mama. Nevertheless, since I had borrowed Blaise's car I didn't want to drive his car back at night. I slept with Mama that night, woke up early with her and as I started to leave, she stopped me.

"Wait and eat with me, hon." Mama said, sort of begging.

She wanted me to sit down and eat the breakfast she had prepared for us.

I said, "Okay, Mama, I'll just take a biscuit and a piece of bacon, but if he comes anywhere near or around me, I'll leave.

I don't want to see him. He would just get me all mad again and there is no telling what I would do to him right now with the sores he left on me for all at school to see and I'm afraid I go get his gun and try to shoot him in the foot maybe," I whimpered.

Mama continued to weep for me. When she brought the flat biscuit, as I always enjoyed, she gave me $.75 collected from the floor along with hugs and kisses. Papa had given her none for me!" NONE!"

I left crying most of the way back and began thinking of what kind of work I could get to help for the rest of the time in school. I had to work it out, if not for me; it would be for my Mama. I needed to finish before school started the following year because I had a teaching job waiting for me if I could graduate on time. If there had been less control and more giving, I would not have to put up this constant panic and apprehension.

When I got back with Blaise's car, I told him what I had done and what had happened at home. He saw all the welts on me as well as many bruises. Blaise said that he wished he had gone with me to the recruiters. He also planned to file the papers for me to get out of the contract. He was happy that I had changed my mind about joining, and was glad to hear what Mama told Papa after he beat me up. We both thought she should've stopped many thing about 45 years before.

My brother was so angry with Papa for he remembered the whip lashing he received when he returned home on furlough from the service, because Papa thought Blaise talked all the others into joining the service all at the same time. He knew that it cost Papa ten extra hired hands when they left. The tightwad deserved it.

Anyway, he and I worked up some ideas on how I could get by for that spring and summer, and then we would work toward the following year. I thanked him for the use of the car, and went back to the dorm. I told my roommate that I was not going into the Lady Marines, and that Blaise would help me in getting it nullified. I also told her that my folks were quite upset with me, so I decided not to join. She was going anyway for the summer and was sweet to me about not going. I could tell that she was looking at the bruises on me. I didn't tell her about the thrashing, there was no point in it.

With help from Richet and Annette's babysitting jobs most weekends and with help from the coach and Blaise I made it through the spring semester with a breeze. I had some money saved and would work more to get ready for the senior year.

Summer school went by quickly. I went home and worked for the same people plowing this time for them. My uncle had quit growing cotton. The plowing, working at Isabelle's home, and receiving some help from my dear Mama, helped me tremendously before the fall semester.

I stayed away from my Papa. I never asked if I could ride the horse to go plow; I just saddled him up and took off. I think he might have been afraid of me. I was hoping he was, anyway. I rode the horse to Isabelle's and did the plowing for anyone who needed me. Mama fixed my meals. I couldn't have made any of it work without her. In August, she was not babysitting, but she saved what she made.

A friend, Rene and I decided to rent an apartment in town close to the college for the fall and spring semester. Blaise thought this was a good idea and it would be cheaper for us to share it. This would help a lot with the financing. Rene had a car and took me most mornings because she had an early class also. I walked home, because it was only four blocks, which was nothing to hike for me.

I was only taking the eighteen hours during the fall with student teaching in physical education in both high school and elementary school. This was taking most of my time, so babysitting during the week was out for me. I told folks that I could babysit anytime on the weekend. They used me as often as they could.

My advisor was happy with the way all the classes went. Now she had to start getting the math student teaching arranged for high school and elementary or junior high school for me. She took care of me after I told her what I had done, and what all had happened for me to stay in college. She was glad that I did not decide to go into the service, also. One day she called me to schedule a meeting with her. This sounded serious.

She said, "All the courses that I needed for the spring semester would be offered except one. She would try to see what she could do, but it would take both of us working on it. She said that student teaching in math for high school would be offered, but I couldn't take that and the elementary student teaching together the same semester. Some rules had just changed and she had just been notified. Junior high math was not offered at all that summer."

Therefore, we both began calling schools to find out where it might be offered. We began with all of the "sister colleges" of L.S.U. in New Orleans, in Metairie, and in Lake Charles to see if they offered the class. At last, the third one came through. Lake Charles was the one, which offered the class. I called and talked to a Mr. Helms, the president of the college. I knew him, if he was the same one I thought he was, when I was in high school, but had forgotten his name.

One door was shut and another opened. All the hell I went through ending up being a blessing for me!" I was still in a state of shock with this news. My Mama said it would work out. I knew then that she had been praying a lot for me. I began trying to recall Mr. Helms when it dawned on me why his name was so familiar. Not only did I remember him, but he also remembered me from high school.

I called him to find out the particulars about the class when he told me that he remembered me. He was the one I had thought about previously. He was Supervisor for the Evangeline Parish School Board at that time when I was in high school. He had come into our home economics class that day to observe. The teacher was trying to show me how to fry chicken. When he told me that, I remembered and was embarrassed about the teacher saying that I was the only one who couldn't cook in her class.

I talked to my advisor at L.S.U. and she advised me to take the junior high class for graduation in August. She told me where and who to see to pay for cap and gown rental, as well as other fees.

Rene and I continued to rent the apartment off campus. I missed the girls at the dorm, but did drop in occasionally to see my old roommates and to tell them what all had happened. They knew that I was a "tough act to follow,"

I told Rene about the "two math student teaching classes, which they stopped not allowing anyone to take during the same semester. When told her that I found it offered for the summer at L.S.U. Lake Charles, she was excited for me because she would graduate in the spring and both of us would be leaving the apartment. We had a good spring. The finances were okay, I paid half of everything and Rene cooked, and tried to teach me how. We split all expenses. I cleaned and Rene cooked.

I went through the two semesters without hearing a word from my Papa. Mama wrote often and sent me some money. She never mentioned My Papa when she wrote. I didn't mention him either. Maybe one of these days, God will help me forgive him for how he enslaved each one of us as well as my Mama. The spring semester ended with Rene going to her home to teach in New Roads, Louisiana. I was going to Lake Charles to finish for the summer semester. Blaise knew all about the finances and helped me.

Final Semester

The advisor had everything set for me to graduate in August. Of course, Blaise came up with that money. I had a little, but would need some for going to summer school. Blaise volunteered to take me over to Lake Charles to find a place to rent for the summer. Well, that was a breeze because the second place we went was just perfect. It cost $25 for each month for a bedroom and told me to have supper with them. I told them that if I was there that I would, but not to wait for me. I ate a small lunch at the school Student Union. They were the neatest people. They were pleased to help for which I was grateful. Blaise paid the rent for me, and visited with them as I unpacked, then he had to get home.

I visited with everyone for a while, and later went to the college to meet my old friend, Mr. Helms. He had not changed a bit. He hugged me as I entered. I thanked him for the opportunity to do the student teaching. While there, I also asked if there was a chance of being an assistant for any teachers who might need an aid for their classes.

He made a couple of phone calls, and sure enough, Miss Boudreaux needed someone for six classes of swimming and one in dance. Wow!" Mama is still "on her knees." Mr. Helms told me where to go to see her and wished me good luck for the summer.

Miss Boudreaux was a joy to meet and took me to where the classes would be taught. She was happy that she didn't have to go searching for someone to do all this and made sure that I wanted all of the swimming classes and the one dance class. The school was only a short walking distance to each of the classes and back home. She was a wonderful and precious lady who was willing to help any time. There were two classes of swimming starting at six a.m., two more starting at 2 p.m. and another two at 4:30 p.m. each day Monday through Friday. I assured her that I would love to do them. The college paid $.47 per hour. I was thrilled and hoped that six hours a day of swimming would not exhaust me. I couldn't let it happen.

The dance class was beginner's ballroom dance, which started at ten a.m., and I loved it. Each of us had to dance in the "guy's" position for most all the dances because there were more women than men taking the class. I told her that it was fine with me, because that would happen, wherever you go.

The next hour and a half was student teaching for junior high. They were great kids and that class was small. All of them were repeating a major subject, math, just as I wanted to do in when I was in the 6th grade. These were all 8th grade students. I slipped a little algebra in on them and they had fun with it. I certainly didn't dare call it "algebra," though. I knew that they would do well in high school math.

Leaving Miss Boudreaux, I immediately went to the mall to get a decent bathing suit. When I found one, it was perfect; "boy-legs" (they were called then) until I saw the price. It was $75. That would take every cent I had. Nevertheless, it would last me a lifetime.

Next, I went to my "landlords" place, which was two blocks from school. They had two little girls and had planned a family picnic and wanted me to go with them on Saturday. I was excited to receive this invitation. The picnic was to be on the lake and had to be careful with getting mud on it. On Saturday, we went to the lake for the picnic.

What a fun time. Everyone did some swimming, and then I told them that I would be teaching six hours of swimming and one hour of dance.

I told them about the bathing suit but was disappointed that I was swimming in the lake for the first swim. I should not have even mentioned it.

I said, "Oh that's alright. I'll make $.47 an hour and should be doing well for the summer."

The landlord said, "I'll give you next month's rent free if you can swim across the lake."

I said, "You've got to be teasing me, right?"

"Nope." he said.

Off I went doing the entire group of strokes I had learned for speed and rest. I had never been in a lake that had hot and cold currents in it. This meant that it was essential for me to be aware of the possibilities of developing cramps.

I just kept swimming to the other side, picked up a hickory nut, put it inside the top of the bathing suit and got back as quickly as I could. I was happy. In less than one hour, I made $25. I couldn't have found a better deal at a time of financial need. I would make more than that working all summer teaching swimming and dance, but this came in when I was penniless and all at one time. I was ecstatic!"

I couldn't believe all that had happened to this little 100-pound girl. The summer ended too soon for me, yet not soon enough to go to my own graduation. I had told them that I couldn't be there and why. So, most of the fees would be returned to me if I wanted them or I could walk down the aisle with the fall semester graduates. That was what I wanted.

Finished

After all the acknowledgements and recognitions were offered to each of those who had been so outstanding in assisting me, and for all of their considerations, I then had to get ready for going back to Villeplate. The next day I packed and played with the girls and the family for a while. Then, they took me to the train station where I purchased my own train ticket home. I had never ridden a train before and that became quite another experience for me.

When I got to Villeplate, I called my coach who was happy to see me and took me home. I enjoyed our visit so much on the ride back home, that I forgot about asking her to let me spend the night with her. I needed her to take me to look at and give advice for buying a car.

I couldn't think too well for dreading the trip back home to see what my Papa would say or do. She could hardly wait 'til our teams played each other. When we got home, my aunt was there visiting with Papa on the front porch. I spoke as I entered only looking at my aunt,

I ignored my Papa. I had hoped that he felt that I was still angry about the beating he gave me, and I went straight to Mama. Then Mama and I went out where Papa, my aunt and the coach were laughing and cutting up. Papa didn't say a word directly to me. It had been a long time since I had talked to him, and I did not want to be engaged in a conversation with him at all.

As soon as the coach left, I said, "Oh, I wish that I had asked her to take me to Opelousas to buy a car because I already had a job and would need one.

"You won't need a car because they have teacher's cottages there. You can walk. Papa snarled.

My aunt commented to Papa, "Are you crazy? There have not been any cottages there since the depression."

I was so happy that my aunt was there, and let Papa have it. She said that she had a cousin with a room to rent for me and would be teaching at the same school. I had told her previously about where I would be teaching and coaching high school basketball. The next morning, I told Mama that I needed a ride to Opelousas. She immediately told Papa.

My First Car

Papa said, "Do you see that black car out there? It belongs to Ted. You take that and trade it in and I'll take that car for what he owes me."

I said, "That's fine with me if it was okay with Ted."

He said, "I just wrote the debt off in my ledger. It was not any good for him anyway, so take it. That's about as far as it will go without breaking down."

Therefore, the next morning I finally got the car started and drove it straight to Opelousas and traded it in. I knew absolutely nothing about buying a car, much less trading for one. So, since I was alone, "green and ignorant" about financing a car that I had to have. I bought a "stripped down" new car. This means that it had no extras. I didn't know until winter that it had a heater.

They took me, this ignorant "gal" to the cleaners. My payments would be $75 per month for 3 years, and a balloon note of $300 and my insurance was included. I didn't know what that was or understood any of this trade. I just knew that I had to have a car. I think in the long scheme of things that I paid them to take Ted's car for off my hands for $300 and the interest about 100%. The price of the car was $1800. All I was worried about was monthly payment. Well, that was done, and I didn't think that the car even had a heater in it, and certainly no air conditioning, but was fine. They would not have done this to me if I had the coach with me. I had never done anything like this before. Well, I knew that I could do without air-conditioning. I had never been in one with it except Blaise's and the coach's car, but I didn't care as long as I had wheels and it was new, I didn't have to worry about any car problems.

When I got home and got off the dusty gravel road, I just had to clean that white car up. Mama went with me and I took two buckets of water. She was proud for me, but thought it amusing that I wanted to wash a new car. I just wanted something to do and have Mama all by myself.

The next morning as I began to leave, Mama gave me some money to buy some clothes for teaching. I don't know where she got $20 and I didn't ask. It probably came from Papa but she didn't say a word about it if he did. When I left, I went straight to a clothing store, and was pre-pared to pay for them, but the sales lady said that if I would set up a charge account and pay for it at the end of the month, there would be no interest. I knew nothing about this, until the sales lady explained it to me. So, I saved the money Mama gave me. Well, I knew that I was not going to pay any interest, even if I had to do without food for it.

The sales lady said that when the statement came to me, if I could pay all of it, there would be no interest charged to me. Paying all of it was my plan. Therefore, I purchased three cute and cheap little outfits, which were made well and on sale. Even though I could pay for it, that was a great feeling and unexpected.

Unpacking was easy after the meeting and visiting with the folks. They told me that the rent included meals. I thanked them and told them that I would probably need and enjoy some home cooked meals, but not to worry about me if I was not there when they were ready to eat.

When I finished with the car, I needed to pack the apple boxes along with other purchases into the car. It was necessary for me to arrive at the school board office early the next day, and then go out to meet the principal. He had a "father-like compassion" toward me. We had a great visit. Then, I needed to go to where I would be renting (which was my aunt's cousin) and put my belongings in the room.

The rent was again $25 a month. With my car note at $75, plus $25 a month back to the school board (which was loaned me free of interest if I taught for them), and the promise of paying Blaise and Yolanda $10 each, there would be very little money left. When I met the school board, they told me that after taxes, and retirement that my check would be about $198 a month. This yearly amount included $100 year for coaching. I would not have much to live on, but more than I had been having. I would be better off in three years. That was fantastic news.

The next day, I knew what I wanted to do after passing that little creek on the way to my new home. I went to the little shop, bought a cane pole, a roll of fishing string, hook and then found some bait and went fishing at that little creek just to "think" about how my life was changing. This entertainment was all I needed to get away from it all. I needed the rest.

Soon I was "cat-napping" when a fish almost jerked the cane pole away for me. It startled and excited me as well. Beginning to fish then, catching little brim and throwing them back in made a relaxing day for me.

The teachers were to meet the following Monday, but I wanted to go to church the next day. This had been my goal when I left home, finish college and got a job. I had always wanted to go to church, so the next morning, I arrived at church and I was immediately smothered by about 200 students, it seemed, as I parked. The "landlady" had told the people at church that their new coach and math teacher would be there soon. That was why they were out to greet me, and in a very spectacular way. What a welcome!" The girls wanted me to teach their Sunday school class.

I quickly told them right then I couldn't because I needed to be in a class. I stayed for the service and left. The promise that I had made to myself ended that day. I didn't go back. I knew nothing about the Bible, was embarrassed about it, and didn't know how to handle it. Therefore, each weekend afterward, I went fishing or to see Mama or work in the gym.

Monday was teacher workday at school, which meant meeting all the teachers. The principal, whom I had met previously, escorted me around, so that I could meet and greet each teacher. There was one teacher in particular who made sure that I had everything I needed. She was especially in control of the "get to know you." Her name was Marjane and she showed more kindnesses than any of the others. It was very obvious that she was getting too close, and doing so too soon.

The next Saturday morning, I had a "gut" feeling that I needed to go home to see my Mama and Papa. Leaving there before left very bitter feelings about my Papa and I couldn't keep that heartache any longer. Nothing about my senior year was mentioned. That generated the idea that all was forgiven. Forgiveness had to be done. Realizing that he just couldn't let go of his last hard worker was too challenging for Papa. I truly believed all was well between each of us. Mama hugged tight and kissed and Papa just gave a light hug and kiss on the forehead. I was genuinely touched.

CHAPTER 2

The Slave Driver: My Papa: Joseph Thibodeaux

My Grandpa's name was Joseph Thibodeaux." also. He enjoyed talking to me and telling about history. I was the only one who would sit and listen to him on Sunday afternoon. Sitting down with Grandpa though was a lesson of history to be learned. He said that during the 1800's." very few people knew about what was happening in Washington. He knew because he and his brother were eight and six year old "stow-a-ways" on a ship leaving Europe for the United States.

When they were found and taken to the owner of the sailing vessel, they became Indentured Servants for him for ten years. The owner couldn't believe these two boys had slipped away from home onto a ship to sail to a country they knew nothing about. They were treated like family for he and his wife had boys about their age also. He had a huge home and he and wife fell in love with these boys immediately. They had a great life but had to remain there learning everything the Headmaster had to offer for the ten years.

Grandpa was more enthusiastic toward school than his brother Van, who quit after the 8ᵗʰ grade. Both helped the family in and outside, learning domestic chores as well. They were schooled by their owner's "Headmaster" as he taught them about the happenings in Washington. They were taught about why the Civil War happened and that is where Grandpa learned all about the Carpetbaggers and the advantages they received from the Federal Government during the 1800's. He also taught them about the Carpetbaggers and the Southern Scalawags during the Civil War. He said that if they went south and got involved politically that they would have some difficult times, warning them that the Scalawags were southern whites who wanted to gain politically against the northern newcomers called the Carpetbaggers. He said that they wanted to take control of their state and local governments. The Carpetbaggers were given control of the railroads and were given miles of land adjoining them as payment for building them.

Grandpa was schooled through high school subjects within an eight-year period and was taught the courses equivalent to a college degree for the next two years. When they were not sleeping, they were learning every day of the week. He became a brilliant man, learning all the Headmaster had to offer within the ten year period. All were taught leather-making skills gardening, gunsmithing, hunting, types of ammunition as well as what kind to use to kill certain animals. They also learned to mix the powder for rifles and how and when to use them. All the boys became skilled hunters as well as leather making skills.

When their time for serving as Indentured Servants was up, Grandpa was eighteen and Van sixteen and they were allowed to leave. The Civil War was over but they didn't take part in any of the fighting on either side. Both wanted to go south for warmer weather to make their living. They were told how they could manipulate their way to avoid any danger after the war. Having been Indentured Servants for the landowner during the war, their owner thought they would be safe if they did as he told them. He also taught the young men where and what they should do to make a good living in the area both wanted to live. Their "Master" gave those young men leather-making tools and a bundle of leather. Each was given a horse, rifle, pistol and plenty of ammunition to help protect them on their travels southward. Their horses were loaded. He also gave them some money so they could get started without a lot of challenges along the way. For them to be capable of buying plenty of land, he must have given them quite a sum of money, for he loved them and gave to them as if they were his own. Grandpa never told how much they were given and I had learned never to ask.

As soon as Grandpa and his brother left the North, they told the people that they met that they were from France instead of Belgium and soon changed their name to Thibodeaux All along their route, they told about the Scalawags and Carpetbaggers. He told about the Yan-kee Carpetbaggers and the Southern Scalawags during the Civil War. Not many people knew that the Republican party began in the south to try to prevent the freedom of the Blacks. The Carpetbaggers were giv-en control of the railroads and were given miles of land adjoining them as payment for building them.

Grandpa knew what was happening and he wanted to get ahead financially in Louisiana to stake a claim on some land. He and his brother Van made lots of money selling their wares as they traveled.

Soon Grandpa had fallen in love with Lucy who was living on the mountains with her folks where they camped out for some time. Soon he married Lucy and had several children, one right after another as they meandered south. When they entered Tennessee, Grandpa and his family had grown to seven children two girls and then five boys. His family and Van were raided by the Cherokee Indians. He lost most all of his leather and some tools. However, both still had their weapons, money, some tools and their education to keep going. I learned from Grandpa Thibodeaux that our Grandma had been dragged into the woods and raped by one of the Cherokee raiders. From the high cheekbones and skin coloring, I could tell then that it had to be the youngest who was "my Papa." We had Indian blood from both sides of our family.

Traveling south, they helped blacks escape from places where they were mistreated by the KKK. Grandpa offered them a home and work if they wanted to stay with them. He told them that he would treat them well, but he was a hard worker and knew how to get people to work hard. They all loved this offer with help to hunt and feed the families. They all made money bartering and selling leather goods as they made their way further down south with his leather making skills. He was well educated taught them to read and many skills as they traveled with the blacks down south.

When the group arrived around central Louisiana, Van wanted to stay near Bunkie, because he wanted to be near his brother, but not too close. This was a small town and would be north of his brother, who wanted go further south. This was where Van met his wife and soon they had twin boys. Van bought enough land to begin raising sugar cane fields and gardens, but was not as ambitious as Joseph. Van was satisfied with a large nursery, selling to flower shops, stores and wholesalers, and the rest of the land was sugar cane, which was hauled to sugar mills, and made into granulated sugar.

Grandpa said that he decided to go farther south to settle in Ville-plate. The land looked good and he knew that this was the place for him. He was still close to his brother but not in competition for land. Grandpa was a compassionate man, yet he was such a determined individual that he drove himself and commanded the best from others. He treated the slaves well, teaching them to read and write as often as he could. They were satisfied that they could do whatever task grandpa needed with the education presented. Blacks did not to go school back then, and Grandpa wanted them to be capable of learning and passing it onto the rest of the family, along with working on machinery.

If he were caught with the blacks without "ownership-papers," he had worked out a plan with the blacks. They told him that he could be hung by the neck to the nearest tree for having them. The blacks helped him come up with an idea he knew would work. All the slaves knew this and went along with Grandpa that he didn't care if the law came because he would just say that he couldn't remember which ones he had sired. This was all planned from the beginning shortly after being rescued. He taught as much of the eighth grade program as he could to them. They didn't learn that much, but they learned enough along with many skills to help Grandpa and others with most anything needed.

They loved him because he treated them like family. This behavior was passed on to all young babies of the slaves born and raised right there on that farm. When Grandpa decided this was where he wanted to live, he registered 500 acres to begin with as "squatter's rights" and began immediately building a small house for his family and as well as one for the slaves. Then they began fencing his land. He would acquire more as time went by and it became available.

His Master had told him about the open and unclaimed land rich, yet desolate and dangerous land in south Texas. That was where he would begin to start his first farming, and make enough to begin his plantation. He led his family of ten along with all of the slave's families down to south Texas in 1894 when my Papa was five years old.

This trip was estimated to be a 300-mile trip (or more). He drove and worked them very hard. When he found the fertile land he wanted and no one else claimed it, he got "Squatter's Rights" on what he believed was 2500 acres. This was used for all the cotton crops except for gardens to feed the crews and corn for the animals. There was plenty of fruit from the orchards that was already there for their animals to graze on the side of the property near the river.

All the needed equipment was bought at bargain prices by the time they got to Texas. Those people needed to sell as much as they could. It took three months to prepare and plant the seed, as quickly as it was prepared, he said. It had to appear as if one was watching a troop of soldier ants one, right behind the other. Some were plowing and the others planting.

Grandpa told about how hard the people had to work. He had to drive and push them hard and train those with delegated authority how to push their workers. He found Mexicans who were eager to work and they found as many workers as Grandpa needed. Each of those "bosses" rode their horse equipped with shotgun, pistol, lasso and a whip. They were on the horse most all day. He described how well the cotton grew there and the money he made. They also grew corn for all who needed who needed it for their food. They were not equipped with a mill, so the corn was roasted (shuck and all) and eaten right off the cob. Most of the cooking was outside, and there were plenty of mesquite growing near, to use for fire.

The Mexicans were responsible for their own meals and garden and rode horses to stay and work on the farm, never going back. Home was where there was work. Many of their families moved with them to help with meals or work. They camped on the other side of the orchards and had use of some land for their needs. All the families had cattle with them for milk and young steers as they grazed on the fertile banks of the river. Some hurry back to their homes near the border leaving funds for the family. Upon returning, they had javelins' (wild hogs), killed, dressed and roasted on open pits.

Grandpa and Grandma's family and slaves camped out next to the small huts, lean-to sheds and covered wagons near the river. My Aunts and the older slave couples helped Grandma with meals and worked in the gardens and the orchards. They had plenty to feed their hard working troops, which was prepared immediately near the banks of the river.

The orchards were there, which was the reason he chose the site. Some of the "covered wagons" were for cooking while others were for storing basic needs and sleeping.

The Mexican workers were capable of this hard work and were happy to be able get it. Employment was hard to find in those days in south Texas as well as in Mexico. The rivers were near, so plenty of water was at their disposal. For them, home was where the jobs were.

As a slave driver, Grandpa and his hired "delegates" rode their horses all over the land to make sure the work was done and done well. They carried their lunch and water with them because they were on the move over the cotton fields. He was making sure that the shacks for storing the cotton were safe as well as forcing the workers to work harder, without any pity. They were used to hard work, and glad to have a job. He had to have them, he said, because there was more land than he could handle with his own crew and he knew very little to speak their language.

I was so amused at all the details Grandpa had to tell me. He didn't seem to leave out anything, and if I didn't understand how he handled something, I would just ask. He didn't skip a beat. The only issue that I was never able to find out was why they left their country to come to come to the US. I was the only one of our family who enjoyed him as well as having the time to listen.

The slave's families were responsible for working their own group; some were added as they traveled on toward the land around the rich valley land. These slaves were happy for the work as well. After listening to the other slaves, Grandpa said that they even wanted to stay with them; and if they could speak enough English, they came back with them for the work.

A group of the Texans went to Grandpa and wanted to buy his "Squatter's-Rights" as soon as he decided to leave. After three years of farming cotton, he sold this land to them and they became the owners thereafter. He had the land prepared for farming without any prior work needed. He made a "Killin" and left Texas as a very wealthy man, besides the selling of the cotton. Selling the land was lagniappe, which he didn't expect to achieve in the Texas Valley. He could have kept the land, but at the time, the offer was too good to pass up. It was several times more than he made selling cotton to the same ones who wanted to buy the land. He was elated.

When they returned to Louisiana, pushed to the limits, they cleared land and finished the homes for all, then began on all of the barns and other fencing for the animals. Most all of these animals were bought on their return trip. It was quite a cattle drive back home. Grandpa purchased a thousand more acres and plenty of cattle, mules, oxen, and horses to get them started for his dream of the ideal plantation. of which he had seen pictures, read about them and had plenty of money to get it done. The oxen were used primarily for clearing the land of all the timber. They were much stronger than the mules for pulling the stumps out or "grubbing the land." The timber had to be milled and dried as soon as possible. This would be used for homes later and the land for farming.

Now he had as much timberland as he wanted down along Bayou Nezpique. He built barns and a home for his family as well as the slaves, their children and grandchildren. Grandpa hired many people within the area to clear new ground to begin his plantation. This was near the community of Villeplate in Evangeline Parish. These people needed jobs and traveled for miles on horseback, or in wagons to work. Grandpa's boys hated him, because he worked them so hard.

The girls helped my Grandma prepare meals for all of their hired hands. Some of the slave's grandchildren began a huge garden as soon as they returned to begin feeding all of the families as well as some of the workers. The locals took their own meals, but others who came from afar, had to be fed where they camped. Some of the men lived so far away they would camp out in the woods and send much needed funds back home.

These "Yankees" took advantage of the South, treating everyone like slaves, as they cleared land for the railroad. Each group actually "raped" the South of all the long-leafed pine. No reforestation was done at all. The south would suffer in time for the damage done by the railroad companies lack of responsibilities of not planting pine trees for the future. Millions of dollars were made and continued through generations with heirs owning the mills, lumberyards and hardware stores all over the south. The federal government gave the companies the right to own as much land, as they wanted, up to ten miles on each side of the railroad tracks if they would build the railroad track, going south, east and west. The number of miles each company owned varied as to how much land they wanted to deal with. Some took the land long enough to re-sell it.

Finally, Grandpa said, "They hired many cooks and people to move the logging operation along as the plantation was about to be cleared. He wanted to plant sugar cane, sweet potatoes corn and lots of cotton. Most of his land was more suitable he thought for sugarcane, but he had seen the value of cotton and this was rich Delta Country. Again, his "Master" taught him well about what to expect and what to do if he wanted to succeed before the railroads came through.

There were others to cut the trees down, strip the limbs, loggers with teams of mules, horses, oxen and wagons to move the logs. This was the primary way for anyone to get a job during the end of the 1800's. They hired many people (both black and white) for years. Papa learned it well and hated to be treated worse than the slaves were. As soon as Papa thought he could handle this, he was tired of being treated like this; working harder than the slaves. He was not being paid for his work, so one day he grabbed his horse, gun and whip and took off to the railroad company, where he knew there was plenty of "paid" work. He was twelve years old and ready as any older man to handle a job with the railroad company.

He had done the clearing and logging for his Papa without pay, now he was ready to do the same work with pay. The owners noticed Papa guiding them to do their best. They hired him right away to supervise the workers. They were happy to find someone who knew more about logging than they knew. Papa became a "slave-driver." He was given a new horse, saddle, as well as a rifle and lasso because he had learned the Slave Driver method from "The Best," his Papa. He was young, but knew how to work the crews.

He was in charge of many different teams of men and their duties. Logging was a dangerous operation. Many oxen and mules were used to pull the loaded long wagons with flanged wheels over the rails. He taught those skills, and expertise in their work as well as safety.

After several miles, they built a railroad spur veering close to the dumping grounds to hold. These spurs moved the logs to be picked up later for future lumber yards, which would be built later. In later years many mills and lumberyards remain and others added by the heirs nationwide.

It didn't take long until Papa saw that he had to delegate some of the many chores to several responsible men to be in charge of the many different activities, which had to be done. He was pushing them hard as they were doing the job expected. The company could hardly believe this one young man had the ability to run this operation. This made Papa proud, but the job became larger with so many delegated to help, he saw that more workers that are responsible were needed to delegate authority. As each area grew, the extra authority grew.

There were hundreds of workers and many in authority with whom Papa had to meet. He was fearless and tireless. Every phase of the railroad building had to have someone in charge of the labor for that particular job. They would meet for advice when necessary. There was not a lot of whining because these people knew that there were others waiting for their job. Everyone was housed and fed well so that each could do the best job. They had to have many living quarters and kitchens set up in the huge tent-like dormitories. Papa was certainly the man on the horse as the slave driver of them all. He proved that he could be in charge of all these duties, and they paid him extremely well.

The railroad company had to have younger and stronger steers, oxen and mules for the work that had to be done as well as for food to feed the large number of workers and many of them were no longer needed for the section they had worked for so long. They were too old or not needed right now for the trestle areas as soon as the flatter areas were finished. Some sections were to be completed now along the Villeplate River and Bayou La Chigot. The company sold him some building materials, as well as cattle, mules, oxen and lots of the milling machinery, which was needed immediately for him to start his farming operation by Grandpa's slaves until he left the company. No one who stayed had time to spend money. They would send money home by a company messenger as long as they remained working for the railroad.

After ten years, my Papa made enough money to buy all that he needed. The company was happy to sell as much of the river and bayou land as he wanted because it was too much trouble for them. At that time, they didn't want the cypress timber. They didn't know of its value, but my Papa did. He purchased 1500 acres with timber and some adjoining his Papa with most being flat land.

Papa bought from a family who had gotten too old to farm. All this old family needed now was a garden and their home. The railroad company was exceptionally kind to Papa for he worked hard for them for ten years training new ones as others left, and taught other leaders to take his place. This took a lengthy period of time itself, because there were so many different jobs to do in building a railroad, as well as logging the timbers cut along the route. They knew that they would never find another one like him. They allowed him to acquire most anything from them, because they said that he deserved it all. Papa was 22 years old when he left the company with the intention of building his own plantation.

Later, Papa got more logs than were immediately needed and then sold or traded them for other needed items or animals. He bought enough milling machinery from them and material to cut slabs of lumber for building barns and needed sheds. Some of the area was not heavily wooded and this was where the first little "hut" was built for him to live. The hut was about 18' x 25'. My Papa had "Squatter's Rights" for some of his land. Grandpa kept people from using the land that my Papa wanted. Many thought he was so mean that no one wanted to be near him anyway.

Soon Papa was hiring workers from nearby communities, and allowed them the use of the hut which he set up as a dormitory for the workers to stay if they liked. These hired hands began clearing more land immediately. Teams of mules and oxen were used to pull stumps out after some grubbing had been done around them. This made it easier and faster to pull them out. This was referred to as "grubbing new land." Grandpa and Papa, along with many hired hands who Papa had met in the timber business, cleared all of the timber between the Villeplate River and Bayou Nezpique. They then cleared all but 40 acres, which was mostly oak, but was saved for winter fireplaces as needed.

Papa needed the back timber land near the Villeplate River because he calculated that he would need all of this as time went on to build more barns, and a larger home. He took almost all of the cypress trees for milling, which would be needed for buildings as soon as it had dried and cured enough to use. He also bought oxen and plenty of cattle from the same company. He and Grandpa taught his crew how to work on the machines for they would have to be ready for plenty of use. Papa's savings helped to build barns and a huge house whenever he had his own family. Whoever wanted to stay the night to work on the farm did so as all was moving on to completion. The slaves as well as their children and grandchildren helped Papa as well as Grandpa.

This was true as soon as Grandpa finished with them each day. Grandpa and Papa were good to them and they were pleased in return. All of the slaves were glad to have a place of their own and a plot of land to grow what they wanted. They soon had a larger home to live in as their grandchildren increased in numbers. Soon the grandchildren had children of their own as the men and women married some of Papa's hired hands. They all worked and did well for both Papa and Grandpa.

As they married and began their own family, Grandpa gave them timber so that they could run it through the mill. They built their house right there on Grandpa Thibodeaux's property and did it as well as his. They were as happy as the others who lived there also. All became helpers for Grandpa and Papa. All of the wives took the "Thibodeaux" name just as the older slaves did after being rescued.

These slaves knew that they could leave at any time. The nearest town was twelve miles away and those blacks as well as the slaves knew they would be treated despicably. Many went hungry or would do most anything for food to eat. They knew how it was when Grandpa rescued them. They never wanted anything better than to have Grandpa and Papa as their keepers. Grandpa had high expectations of the slaves, their children and grandchildren. These slaves had the same ambitions that Grandpa Thibodaux had expected from each and they were prepared well for whatever tasks were presented.

As time went by and the dream plantation for Papa had plenty of help and all knew what had to be done. Soon, the company Papa had worked for wanted to see him. They told him that the parish school system was looking for a man of means to build a wagon with seats to haul schoolchildren to school. They wanted to know if Papa was interested. Papa was ecstatic. He told him that he was ready for it, because he had two of the slaves grandchildren who would manage all activities that he wanted done. He told Papa to begin getting it ready, because he would tell the school system that they found someone and that he would begin in September, as the school board wanted. These companies had plenty of political effectiveness and power.

Papa was pleased with this news and had his wagon ready to go. The benches were built by Cedric, and he had them well polished up by grinding them with sand and wet rags. Papa began the school drive, picking up eight students, and by the end of the week, his wagon was loaded. He rode one of his horses home with the other one tied behind him. The wagon was left at school and protected by the school master until he returned. The horses needed the rest, feed and water before the return trip for the children.

The school was only three miles from the farm, but had several side roads. These roads had children who wanted to go to school, also. This then, became a six-mile trip to school. The children would study on the way to and from school, so Papa got him some books, and began to study also.

The students enjoyed studying with Papa. My Mama was one of the students on Papa's wagon. She had ridden it every day, and loved school. However, one day in spelling class she misspelled "crochet."

She studied the "Blue Book Speller" well, and was a straight "A student." She had no farming or night work to be done, so she studied all her books well. She would compete with Papa with some of the spelling or other studies. She was so embarrassed by what she did spell that she took off running home and never rode the wagon to school again. All were upset with her for quitting because she was in the eighth grade and could easily have finished. However, this little girl was smitten by Papa's attention that she made sure he saw her every time the school wagon passed by. Papa noticed her all right. Each and every day, he tipped his hat at her in passing. He missed having her on the wagon, and she missed being on it each day. She was just too embarrassed by what she did spell, that she would not show her face at school another day to be teased.

Later, Papa went to her house, and asked her folks for her hand in marriage. Her parents were happy for this union because it was one less mouth to feed. They were very poor and her Papa was disabled from a sugar mill accidendent.

Mama was almost 14 years old when they got married. Little did this little girl know just how naive she was and what she was getting into. Papa was dedicated to do all he could to succeed. She would suffer the abuse without realizing what was happening to her. She had no idea that she was marrying a "slave driver" who wanted as many children as possible to complete his dream. The trauma, and emotional abuse and turmoil continued as the slave driver struggled for success!"

CHAPTER 3

Wife of Slave Driver: My Mama: Beth

INSIDE IMAGE REVISED: LIBRARY OF CONGRESS, PRINTS & PHOTOGRAPHS DIVISION, FSA/OWI COLLECTION, [REPRODUCTION NUMBER, E.G., LC-USF34-9058-C] ; ARTHUR ROTHSTEIN - PICKING COTTON, LAUDERDALE COUNTY, MISSISSIPPI, 1935, and Hines, Lewis W. (1874-1940), Boy picking cotton, ca. 1912, Gift of the Photo League, New York: ex-collection Lewis Wickes Hine, GEH NEG: 30195, 77:0183:0033*

I could write a book just about my Mama. She deserves more than what appears to be these few pages of her. However, she will be the one who stands out above all the rest throughout this novel. She had five babies before she was twenty years old, along with four miscarriages. Overall, she had twelve children and sixteen miscarriages, which I know about. Most of these were in the first trimester.

Papa was a hard, harsh, driving man who demanded, expected and received a submissive wife. Once she loaned his brother a plow and Papa made a nasty "suggestive" comment to her while she was heating grease in the frying pan. She pitched the skillet of hot grease at him and it hit him right on the pants placket. That took care of those types of harsh comments for a long time.

His drive for more children and the traumas suffered during child-as well as miscarriages was too much for Mama. The emotional abuse to her and as well as the cruelty to the children was so disheartening to her, but she was not to interfere. Mama was unaware of many things until the damage had been done. She wept often but privately. The triplets were the third live births who were his pets for quite some time. They didn't get the whippings that the rest of the siblings received. Of course, they were 14 years older than I was. I am sure they were punished as they grew older.

When the school closed near home, a new one was built on the west side of the parish. However, the school board needed someone to buy a bus to pick up children to go to school in Villeplate on the east side. They would hire someone else for the west side. They asked Papa if he wanted the job and told him that there would be two different routes to run loading the bus with each one. He told them that he did and had the means to buy a new school bus. Then he made the 2nd round to a saw mill town and loaded the bus again. This not only gave him more income, but a bus, which could be used to haul everything from hired hands, to cotton, syrup buckets, watermelons and soldiers when it was not used for school children. .

Ted, one of the older boys who used the bus to haul hired hands before Papa had to leave for school. Ted left at five in the morning to pick up the hired hands who were primarily blacks. These people were happy to have a job and were excited that someone would pick them up and take them to the job. Papa left at seven o'clock each morning and Ted had to be back before Papa had to have the bus for his school run.

Each time Ted went in to pick up workers, there were more gathered up to work. Soon it was standing room only for them for the twelve mile trip back to the plantation. They also enjoyed working for Ted. Soon Mama began trying to cook for the many hired hands, until Papa saw that it was impossible. He hired Lili, who was one of the slaves grandchildren to help her in the hot kitchen. As time passed and the plantation grew, so did the responsibilities in the kitchen. Then with Lili's help, (Mama's side kick), they were capable of cooking for all those hired hands after getting another old wood-stove. There were at least 60 from town that Ted picked up in the school bus as well as ten others from the community.

This was the most hired hands Papa had at one time, but that did not last long when they saw how hard the work was. No wonder Mama never complained, she didn't waste her breath talking. She just grieved and hummed a song. Whatever she hummed, Lili hummed the same one.

Evette, the youngest girl, who spent most all day hauling in stove wood for the two wood stoves. Other than Mama's helper and Evette, I was the one person she most wanted around her. She begged Papa to agree for me to help her and learn to cook and be treated like a girl and not like a man. I could also help Evette with all the wood that had to be brought in. Papa told her that he was not about to consent to this slave girl going anywhere except to the fields. Jo would not be bringing in firewood or vegetables from the garden or any other place for anyone. He made the decisions each day where I would be working and what I would be doing. Mama kept begging for me, and Papa kept refusing. He needed his "slave girl."

Mama's pet projects, which took time at some point during the night or day, were the little chicks that Papa would buy. These would help in some way to feed the working crews. Mama would raise them until they were good layers and good for dumplings when they got old, because they had to be boiled to get them tender. The others would lay eggs and Mama would mark rings around them and put under several hens until the hens had about eight eggs under each one.

A hen would use its "God Given Sense" to turn the eggs during the incubation period. This was amazing! Sometimes the hen would lay her own egg and Mama would send one of us to check each "set'en hen" and take the unmarked egg. Each one would have the same number of marked eggs under her to hatch. Once she sent me to get an unmarked egg from under the hen and she pecked a wart off the side of my face near my eye. I didn't get the eggs after that anymore. She could just as easily have pecked my eye out. I was glad to get rid of the wart, but this was too close for comfort.

When the hens had too many eggs, they had a natural instinct to "set" on them until they hatched into little chicks. She only left her nest to get water and some grain. That hen took care of those chicks and the male chicks were so pretty with different colors. No one ever told me that it depended on the color of the rooster. Mama knew how to tell the sex of the chicks by looking under the wing. The male's row of feathers were longer under the wing and the same length while the female chicks row of feathers under the wing were of different lengths and shorter.

The mother hen had enough to do with eight chicks if they all hatched. The hens were up and down all around the sides of the building with their boxed-in-shelfs of straw nests Sometimes a chicken snake would be around to get the eggs and all the hens would give out a loud cackle when one came slithering around. If one hen started the cackle, the news spread quickly of the danger. You can bet that someone heard them and killed the snake. I always relied on someone else to take care of that job. I would not do it.

The chickens which were fryers were "white-leghorns" that Mama raised from chicks. Papa would buy twelve dozen at a time to be put in 4 coops. Working with the chicks helped relieve Mama of stress. She enjoyed her little chicks. The coops were built up off the ground and were 4' square and 2' high, with an inch of sand on the flooring. The end was covered with hardware cloth for the feed and water.

Under the sandy flooring was room for Mama to have kerosene lanterns or lamps keeping the sand warm for the chicks in cool weather. A small opening was made for the chicks to run out on the uncovered area for water, feed and sunshine.

Mama was proud of her little chicks and didn't allow anyone else to do these chores. This was one of about four chores that Mama enjoyed doing alone. She would make sure that there was clean water and feed. Soon the chicks were ready to roam. Out on the ground they would go for their own "pickings." Then Papa would bring another batch of chicks. There were several of these batches to be raised and it didn't take long for them to be ready to leave the coop. Each one was needed because it took a lot to feed the noon meal.

Besides loving to work with chickens, Mama also learned how to make lye soap from Grandma. Mama made this soap using different levels of heat from the firewood used around two wash pots. She would put hot embers on or shove some back if it seemed to get too hot. It took all day to make the wash pots full of soap. This was done in the fall when there was no cooking for hired hands. The rest of the family would be harvesting fall crops except the young ones who hauled wood for her. This would've been impossible for her to do while the planting, picking, chopping, and canning was going on with the hired hands.

The soap was a mixture of lye, water and animal fat. She was the only one who knew how much of each ingredient, would be needed. Mama had a special technique to use, or the soap would become a gel instead of getting hard. She never allowed us to help her in any way with the soap, not even to stir. Evette and Andre piled the wood used to heat these wash pots. She wanted us to have a different life than hers had been when we were out on our own. I don't know how she could tell, but she could. Her Mama taught her that there was a certain time and way to stir as well as the amount of heat needed for the mixture. Papa made a big spoon from a cured cypress board, two-inches thick and four feet long for her to use in the stirring of the lye soap. This was quite a handy "tool" for her to use.

He used a drawing knife to plane it down to the right length for her short body to reach over the hot mixture. He shaped it like a huge spoon, handle and all. Papa used "home-made" carving tools and a sharp curved rock for scooping out the end of the spoon for holding some of the soap from the pot. An old file was used to smooth the edges. Cedric used his trick of a wet sandy rag so there was not a rough spot on it. It was skillfully made. That spoon intrigued me so much while watching Mama using it ever so gently. I knew one day that I wanted the spoon as a keepsake. She kept it in her hands during the entire process without leaving the pots. She would scoop out a little, inspect it and back in the pot, that little scoop would go.

When all was done, Mama let it cool by pulling all the hot embers away from each pot. The next day it had cooled just enough for a sharp hatchet and a big butcher knife to cut it into practical sized bars. The soap was made every third or fourth year. The soap spoon was never used for anything else other than in the making of lye soap. Then it was kept in the loft of the shed where Mama kept the entire container of extra soap.

This kind of soap kept us clean for bathing, washing hands, hair and dishes as well as all the laundry which was washed and hung out on the line. The lye would kill any germs. This was shared with several of Mama's folks as well as Papa's. All the soap making was done before any hog killing was done.

With all the soap making finished, it was time to prepare for hog killing. The smokehouse was checked closely for cracks. If any were found, they were chinked again to prevent the warmth in the smoke-house from venting outside as well as preventing varmints from enter-ing.

Small hot embers readied the smoke house in a dirt pit on the floor the day before hog killing. It would be full of warmth and smoke by the time the sausage links, hams, shoulders, loins and ribs were strung from the ceiling of the log house. Oak and hickory wood was used to create the smoke as well as the aroma and taste that hickory added.

Everything and everybody was scrubbed well with lye soap. Raw pork would contaminate anything quickly if it was not cleaned up, cooked or smoked. The next day, all were ready before the light of day to have the wash pots full of boiling water and ready for the hog killing to start. The weather had to be cold enough to work with this hot and "nasty" job as well as keeping the pork from spoiling.

Next, the boiling water was transferred to the barrels which were placed in a slanted hole so that the hogs could be dipped and turned easily until each had soaked long enough to loosen the hair of the hogs for scraping. Two hogs at a time were dragged out onto a platform to be scrapped. The scrapers (butcher knives) were previously sharp-ened to be ready for the hogs to remove the hair. This enabled Papa and the boys to get the hogs perfectly clean before dressing them.

Once the wash pots were emptied, they were quickly refilled for the next two hogs. The same chore was repeated. Then all the hogs were cleaned, butchered and cut. All were involved in this job along with Papa. This was one time of the year that he got dirty and nasty. All the women were ready for cutting strips of pork for grinding up sausage meat for cooking, or done in patties. When the patties were done, they were packed in huge crocks with sea salt; and then stored in the smoke house. All the pork was salted before hanging to aid in the curing process. The sausage links were hung from poles across the smoke house. The hams, shoulders, ribs, loins and bacon were wrapped in thin cheese-cloth before hanging them. Some people rubbed syrup onto some of the pork before salting it.

Papa never kept a big fire, but just enough to have hot embers burning and smoking day and night. This chore had to be done within the day that the hogs were killed. Usually four or five hogs would be killed before the five boys went into the service. This is how all pork was cured. This smoke house was only used for curing pork. All remained in the smoke house until it was gone. Smoking usually took about 3 weeks. It had a wonderful odor that was recognizable, as people would drove by.

Another hobby which Mama enjoyed was quilting. She worked so hard but somehow she found time for her hobbies. The four 2" x 2" supports, called quilting frames, were made by Papa and the boys. The "bracing bit", operated by hand, spun around making each hole-opening six inches apart all around the frame.

The hole was then heated with a hot rod making a smooth opening for the rope to prevent "raveling." These ropes held the quilt in place very taut by a cord tied opposite each hole. She took scraps of a dress or shirts and pieced them together by hand for many different quilt patterns. She placed the colorful pieces in a way that was attractive. Most would've thought she was an artist. The lining was from white feed sacks. Mama used our own cotton, which she made into fluffy batting, and then it was placed between the top, and the feed sack lining.

Each stitch sewn went from the lining through the cotton and up to the top and back, with thousands of tiny stitches. God only knows how many stitches it took for each quilt. Her thread was strong, and the quilts were to last for a very long time.

She didn't allow us do this either and she never tried to teach us because we had too much to do. Each night before going to bed Papa and three boys would roll this frame down so that Mama could quilt for a while. Then roll it back up before she went to bed, to prevent hitting anyone's head on the frame.

I believe Mama spent quiet time with her silent praying. There were no quilting bees at our house because she wanted to be alone. There would be plenty of people around for other chores. These were her quiet times. This was always done in the wintertime when there was not a lot of cooking going on. Most everyone was in bed. The fireplace was keeping her warm as she busied herself quilting tiny little stitches for each pattern. Mama was the only one who knew how to "cord" the cotton into 3" x 8" flats, which were about one half inch thick when fluffed. My Mama was the sweetest to each and every one of us. This was true of Lili also.

I had never heard either say an ugly word, or ever complain about all the work. However, she did it with a smile. She wanted piece at all times. Often, if she needed to go somewhere to release anxieties or cry, she would walk down to the swim hole at the river, sat on a railroad cross-tie, and weep and pray. That was at least a mile there and I remember seeing her coming up through the pasture with a stick and as song, as if she was leading the choir.

Now I have to show my Mama's compassion. I can remember getting only one whipping, (or preparation for), from my Mama. This happened when I had stolen a whole pound of sliced dried apples. To keep anyone from finding out that you had stolen something you had to either eat all of it or bury it somewhere so that an animal would not get into it, because then you would certainly be exposed.

I didn't know that these dried apples would swell three to four times their size after eating them uncooked. I just knew they were good dried and I didn't care for them cooked. I also knew they would find out when Mama was preparing them for tarts or a cobbler. That would be awhile yet before that happened, I thought, so I had time on my hands to prepare for a lie of innocence.

Well, I hurt so bad with a stomach ache because I had eaten the whole bag and put the wrapping in the stove to burn. It was not long before I was rolling all over in the ground in the back yard, which was nothing but dirt and sand. Thank God, Mama found me.

After she felt my stomach, she knew what to do and ran everyone off. This was on a Sunday afternoon, and once all left, she made me go behind the chicken coop and stick my finger in my throat. I threw up all the apples and my lunch. She was so angry that I not only stole them but that I also had eaten every one of them.

As sick as I was, she made me go get a switch from the privacy hedge growing by the smoke house. I knew never go and get a little switch; even though Mama had never sent me for a one, I got a real big one. She took me into her bedroom and told me to drop my pants and to lie down on the bed. I turned around to look at the switch to see if she had broken some of it off.

As I did this, I saw my rear end in the mirror of the old dresser by her bed and I giggled. She looked also to see what was so funny. Then she started laughing and couldn't begin with her intentions of whipping me. We both just lay down on the bed and laughed. Mama would not tell anyone what had happened and of course, I certainly did not.

When we met her out in the pasture as she approached us, we asked where she had been. She would tell us, but being young, we knew nothing of cross-ties, and we just called it the "tie-tie." As I grew older, it hurt me to know that she had to have gone through a living "hell." I hate the thought that after so many brothers to play with, that I thought it was fun to work in the field.

The boys were the only ones who were old enough to play with me, so I followed them to the field. It was fun for a while. When it began to be no fun I should've "pitched a fit" to stay with my Mama. If I had rebelled at that time, I would've gotten a good whipping, but I got'em anyway. I would've grown up as a lady and I know that I would learn how to do all that she did. As hard as I worked in the fields, I am sure that I could've been a hard working helper for her.

Ahh, you can bet that anytime Papa went to town, Mama sent me on the horse up to her Mama's with a pot roast and vegetables from the garden as well as eggs and syrup. She found a way to help her Mama.

The verbal abuse as well as the abuse to all of us, was more than she could handle. I know God listened to her prayers. To have gone through all the miscarriages, and losing a young lady and a young man, was the toughest she was dealt, and I am sure she is comforted by her Maker now.

CHAPTER 4

The Thibodeaux Family

Isabel

Mama was fourteen years old when she got married, and had her first miscarriage two months later. Eight months later, Isabelle was born prematurely the following October. She had diphtheria as a young baby while my Mama was pregnant with Angie. The doctor quarantined the place and no one was allowed near. In those days, if someone was not expected to live, a photographer was brought in for a photograph. Since he was not allowed near, my Uncle Duran, who lived there to help my Mama, was taught how to use the camera. My Uncle (my Mama's brother) helped my Mama day and night while Papa worked the hired hands. No one could leave, if the person had been within 100' of Isabelle.

The doctor told them to put her in a keg of oil to prevent the skin from cracking open from the extreme high fever. As the fever rose, they had to bath her in cold water from the "spring fed" creek to bring the fever down. This was a continuous job for my dear Mama and Uncle Duran. As soon as her cool down was over, back in the keg of oil she went.

Uncle Duran built a frame to fit around Isabelle's neck after being put in the oil keg. This frame allowed her to lean her head over to sleep for a while, until the fever went back up. They continually kept a cold cloth over her head. This didn't allow much sleep time, because the fever would rise so high again. Then it was back into the tub of cold water, along with splashing it over her head and face. Feeling the top of her head was the only way they could tell if the fever had dropped at all. This went on 24 hours a day; taking turns to get just enough sleep while Isabelle was in the keg.

Angie was born the following September. Then, Mama had three miscarriages after Angie was born, each during the first trimester. Her body was just worn out. She had her hands full with five babies and four miscarriages   I think Papa was trying for several sets of triplets with each pregnancy. My Uncle was a bachelor and stayed with Mama often. Papa paid him well to stay there to help while he worked the hired hands. I always thought a lot of him, but he should've shot my Papa for putting Mama through this trauma. I never understood why she put up with this.

Isabelle was always good to me as I grew up. She left for college two months after I was born. She was one of my great role models. She kept me from getting many beatings by the slave driver. She gave me opportunities that I would never have had before graduating from high school. She married Boudreax, after her first year of teaching. Later she had three girls; Paulette, Antoinette and Bernadette, and one boy, Pierre.

Angie

Angie was the next baby born eleven months later in September. She died of food poisoning when she was sixteen years old and two years before I was born.

Triplets: Tray, Ray and Jay

After four (first trimester) miscarriages, Mama had triplets, Jay, Ray and Tray. They were called this until they joined the military, when a middle name by their choosing was done. The triplets learned to work hard while they were young, and as young teenagers, they were partial to me. Angie had died and Isabelle had left for college. I was the only girl left and was entertained by each one of the boys. Tray and Ray was Mama's big helpers, while Jay was Papa's helper. As the rest of the boys grew up, they were extremely jealous of the triplets because they were the oldest and whipped less.

Jay served in the Navy for four years on a destroyer in the South Pacific during WWII. Jay married Linda from CA. Once when Jay came home on furlough from the Navy, and brought a burlap sack full of almonds in the shell. I had never seen any before, so this was quite a treat for us. I even planted one. I put it where no one would bother it.

That "sucker" grew up tall, just like a long switch and I cut it down. I could see me being the one getting the whipping with that tall switch so I was happy to chop it down.

One day I saw Jay put a big matchbox on top of the chifferobe. As soon as all were gone, I climbed up to see what was in it. This chifferobe was homemade, and all that was needed to climb it was to open the doors, climb the shelves until I could grab the top and hold on. That matchbox was filled with pennies. I was just seven years old and only took five pennies, and then I climbed back down. He put them there in front of me, so I thought he purposely did this for me. In about a month, I took five more pennies. Each time, it still felt full to me as I hung onto the shelves to get back down. This went on for months and the box still felt like it had plenty of pennies.

Once when I got to school and while Papa was making his second load with the bus, I slipped down town with a hand full of stolen pennies and bought some paste. I had eaten all of my paste. I don't know why, but after that, Papa made me take a flour and a water mixture. The kids just made much fun of me and I couldn't stand it any longer. I kept climbing and feeling, and the box felt as though it still had a lot of pennies in it. Another day I got five pennies, went to town, and bought me some candy. Pull candy from syrup was the only candy I had ever had. This was so different and good. As I walked back to school, I saw some flowers and picked them for my teacher.

"I don't take stolen things from people. I passed by when you picked those flowers so I know that they were stolen." She said.

Oh God, that hurt! It broke my heart! She was one of my favorite teachers at school. Her name was Mrs. Deaux and I loved her, but I learned a big lesson also. I didn't take any more pennies either because when I looked again, they were just about gone. Boy, this was scary. I had used so many and didn't realize how fast that box was emptying. I never told a soul that I stole them. Jay knew that I saw him putting them there. Maybe he planned for them to be used for little things that he knew I would need. He knew that I never got any money for my hard work. I never asked him about them, and I sure didn't tell him that I stole them. However, I never looked back to see if they were gone and someone else had taken them. I didn't want to know. I was feeling sick and guilty about all that I did.

My brothers and my sister-in-law told us later that the groups from our farm, plus hundreds of others, were shipped to Bristol, England. Many Brits were already bombing and being bombed when the U.S. got there. They told Ray that the Queen served as a truck driver and worked in the factory just as others did and wore a ladies uniform.

Ray and a trainload of young soldiers were shipped off to Bristol, England, with bombing going on there. One of the boys was sent to Africa, two were in the South Pacific, and one in the Atlantic, serving in the Coast Guard. All who were shipped to England were then shipped to Europe and killed by the hundreds as they climbed the beaches of Normandy where their bodies now lie buried. The platoon that Ray was with, marched as long as they could. They made it through France, but he became deathly ill with pneumonia.

Ray, along with many others died in a snow covered fox-hole. Those boys didn't have a chance with the kind of weather they encountered. Others marched on through it for hours, day and night until final victory. My Mama was torn from this loss, and especially after losing Angie. I was still the "Little Crip," but still remembered the fun I had with Ray. He and Ted were two of Mama's big helpers in the kitchen especially during canning time.

Tray married a friend a mine and built a home near her folks. He had 3 long chicken houses to raise baby chicks until they were old enough to become layers. Once after a truck load of 35,000 baby chicks were delivered, all were excited and ready to get these little chicks to be layers, and get the nice check for all the hard work. However, three days after the delivery, all the chicks died. They did nothing different, and called the delivery man and told him what had happened. They had to have been diseased when delivered, but the bosses claimed no fault. Their dream was shattered.

Then Tray began lay ministry and took some classes at the Baptist College. He also studied and met with other ministers and became a substitute for any who could use him while they were on vacation. He also went to Nursing Homes to give a short service and visited the sick.

Blaise

Blaise was also a hard worker and was always trying to "prove himself" and show how strong he was to Papa, though he never received praise for it. Papa never praised him or anyone except his hired hands. That made all of us angry with Papa. Blaise was the shy one of the bunch. Mama had 2 miscarriages between the twins and Blaise. When he picked cotton, it was always a sack full. It always weighed more than the other boys, except the one day that I beat them all in total weight. He was strong and had to lift the heavy sacks of cotton for Papa. He would throw them up in the bus for one of the others to empty. He served in the Navy in the South Pacific also and his ship was damaged during the fights to knock out the Japanese suicide fighters before they could bomb or shoot them. After four years, he was so happy to be discharged.

He went to college on the G.I. Bill for those who had served in the war. He was quite athletic and played track and field sports as well as football. He excelled in them all. Papa always believed that Blaise talked the others into joining the service. With them leaving home for the service, he had to hire ten extra hands to take the place of the five boys. They had to work harder than the hired hands.

He was very angry. Blaise never came back home until he finished college and was teaching at the Athletic Department at the Baton Rouge High School. Blaise was responsible for student teachers in the physical education department at L.S.U. He was in his 40's before he married Micheline who was nine years his junior. She taught in the college where they lived. They were never capable of having children of their own, so they adopted one girl and two boys.

Ted

Ted was everyone's favorite. He didn't fight, but would sing a song or make up a song to the agitator. He was much like Mama in that respect. There was one miscarriage between Ted and Blaise. He worked hard with the hired hands, picked them up in town and brought them immediately to the plantation. He enticed all to work as hard as they could.

All of us loved him. He would work, sing and teach them a funny song as they continued to pick cotton or chop the weeds away. He kept them and the rest of the family in a good mood. He would sing mostly spirituals in the field as loud as the blacks sang them right along with him. Every day, Ted would make up some funny words that would rhyme and put them to music. Everyone got a big laugh from his antics. The blacks had never heard it before, so they would ask him to sing it almost every day until they learned it. We would also sing his songs when we did the milking or playing. He was just a lot of fun.

Late on Saturday, Ted would take the bus to Camp Claiborne; fill it up with soldiers from the Army Base who wanted to go to the Villeplate bars. Those people would get so stinking drunk that on the way home, they would throw up and many would lose their coins and sometimes a dollar or two. The next morning I would clean the repulsive mess out of the bus and kept all the money found on the floor of the bus. I didn't tell anyone except Mama about the money. She kept it for my dream.

I never dreamed that I would find any money when I volunteered. Now there was more money for Mama to store up for me. I was doing it for both Ted and me. Camp Claiborne not too far from our farm and the Commandants found a perfect place to bivouac. The land across the road from our house with 40 acres of thick woods was perfect for them.

This was a great "thicket" where they could hide, and not be seen by aircraft, while the war games were going on. These soldiers from the Blue Brigade would practice fighting with the Red Brigade in east Texas. This camp was the 82nd-101st-Airborne Division. They were often visited by Patton, Bradley, Eisenhower, Krueger and McNair. My Papa was excited to meet some of them. Many Army officers present at the maneuvers later rose to very senior roles in World War II who spent part of the time in McNary, Louisiana. The Generals commandeered my sister-in-law's parents dairy barn near McNary. They made a "Country Hotel" out of it for the wives and families to visit. Her parents also had a grocery in the town of McNary in which the Generals frequented quite often.

Annette met all of them, but being so young with no brothers in service, she didn't think much about these important people then, but remembers them dearly now. They were just costumers, like the others who came in to purchase something. She and I played on the same softball team. She was two years older than I was, but she was a good teammate and strong from a very different type of farm and store work. Those in command knew they would have permission to bivouac there on our land. The soldiers would march back and forth for miles until dark.

If any planes were heard, they darted into the nearest bunch of trees, corn patch or bushes. During some of the march, which would be lunchtime for us on the farm, Papa would agree for us to draw buckets of fresh water, and run to the road for them to have a fresh drink of water. They were so appreciative. Sometimes they would throw us coins that we tried to give back, but they would not take it. There was always a filled bucket coming when one was emptied. We felt that this was an honor for us, and prayed that our brothers were treated as well, wherever they were.

Sometimes the soldiers would walk along the road to the field to see what we were doing. Upon returning, they would have some cotton and would sit to pull the seeds out to fill a pillow or something, or maybe just to reminisce about home and loved ones. I had thought that they didn't even know what all grew in those fields, much less why we grew it. They were from all over the U. S. and saw things and people work that they knew nothing about. Patriotism was high on our list even before the boys left to war. The soldiers were well respected any place they were seen in passing as well as at home.

Every morning before school, we Pledged Allegiance to the Flag, then we sang war songs to keep our service people in our minds each day. We prayed for them and kept up with the war as time went on. There were many lost that were related to someone at school most every day. The songs were sung each day at home as we did our chores and thought of our brothers in service.

Scrap iron was melted down to build planes and tanks. All students took scrap iron on the bus. This was collected from all over town. Those who picked it up said that our school always had some of their largest loads. Men were joining in to fight from all over the country and women served as well in many capacities. They worked with machinery, meal preparation and factories, helping with the building of everything from nuts and bolts to planes and tanks.

I was even wishing that I were old enough to join up. This was when Papa fed many people and some lived with us because their husbands and sons were called to serve. They needed a place to stay and worked in the fields to earn money for needed items. We were blessed to be able to feed them and house some of them. They would work in the field and have the boys double up in their beds before they joined up.

I was always concerned about Mama worrying about the boys who were in the war at the time. Many friends nearby were killed and some were cousins and close friends. Mama was blessed to have eight boys in the most strategic areas and all but one to come home. The boys would write home, but they wrote on the front and back of a piece of paper. We couldn't understand any of it at all. For security reason, the government cut some things out because they mentioned something about where they were. There were so many holes in it by the time it got home no one could understand what was said. At least Mama knew they were alive somewhere at that time.

The soldiers didn't know that the war was over until Papa told them and they saw it in the paper. You could've heard them whooping and hollering for miles. They were so happy because they could soon go home. Then they got all packed up to leave, and gave everything from the kitchen that could be given to Papa, as well as all the tarps and camouflage hanging in the trees, and anything elsewhere, which they didn't have to turn in to the base when they returned. We were especially happy to have the camouflage nets hanging in the trees.

They were strong because we tested them out before jumping into them from the trees. We climbed the trees, cutting limbs that would be in our way down and jumped up and down turning flips as well as practiced diving techniques until we got near the end and flipped over. The swan dive was the safest to practice because you could see the net sooner and flip before landing.

This was for training and preparing for me to go to college. The shenanigans we played were endless. Everyone who knew about them wanted to come and play with us. That was like Christmas to us, every Sunday. Of course, I had no idea what gymnastics was until I went to college. The tarps were of multiple use for us: from threshing peas, covering the house after the tornado, used as a tent when camping out down on the river or for shade from the hot sun.

When Ted did have to go into the service he stayed in the States. He griped more than anyone in the family about the war did. He was a physicist and did Statistical Research for the Army. He planned statistical research for the top brass during the war. He did not like the fact that they were leaders and didn't know how to plan, yet was in the position to do this. He was not allowed to leave for 2 years. He was needed on base and was on call every day. Ted also taught algebra, geometry and trigonometry to soldiers in training.

Thus, the reason he didn't like it. The first five boys stayed four years in service, but Ted was drafted for two years and that was all he was going to stay. He wasn't allowed to come home because they needed him every day. He would write, though, and send presents.

Ted was a teacher, and principal for many years then retired from the Louisiana Education System. He moved to Birmingham and entered the U. of Alabama, and had almost finished his PhD in physics. He was brilliant in many areas, and he spent a great deal of time on his research.

Then one day his wife said, "Ted, you can continue to go to school or stay married to me, but it will not be both."

Well, since Ted was never a fighter, he dropped out of school. I was so angry with her, along with the rest of my family. She was, and is, the most hateful, selfish and ignorant woman I ever knew. She tried to control his every move.

Ted said, "Okay, if I'm going to have to stick around; it will be on a lake. I know of a place I want and I'm going to buy it."

She was not a happy camper with that, but went along with it. To stay away from his having fun, she got a secretarial job paying a little of nothing. She would not allow him to drive to see me, nor allow me to go see him. He would sneak into town to see me and we would have a great time visiting, and singing "cotton-patch" songs.

Ted had many doctor visits, but came to see me each time, and his wife knew nothing about it. She was jealous of me for she was not willing to work as hard as I did to go to college. Sometimes Ted would call me and say that the "coast is clear" and I would hurry out to eat, out on the lake or just anywhere that she would not see us together. He told me more about my family that I never dreamed had happened. He told me all about his and Papa's vigilante group and the KKK. I knew that he was very close to Papa.

If it had not been for his wife, Luanne, he would've been the Executor of the Estate. Having said that, I knew that there would've been equality in the distribution. I never understood how he put up with her, but he loved those 3 boys and the daughter. She was the PRIMARY REASON he was not chosen as the Executor of the Estate. All are grown now with families of their own.

Ted was one of my two best buddies and died too young of kidney failure. The other one died of renal failure. It was the saddest times that I had to go through in years was in losing both of them. So much that I did learn about the family came from Ted, Uncle Duran and Grandpa Thibodeaux.

Richet

Richet was always in trouble fighting with his younger or older brothers. He was two and a half years younger than Ted. Papa tried for triplets, I guess, twice again. Mama lost 2 more babies. One happened in the 2nd month and the other one was after the 5th month. Oh God, how could she keep up with all the work she had to do?

Richet was a hard worker and very aggressive. He was always sneaking a smoke with rabbit grass or some kind of weed. His dates as well as the other boys were done on horseback. I am sure that he lied about his age to join the service because he went in with the other brothers. Richet was tired of picking cotton and tired of getting the whippings from jumping on every log truck that came in for timber. He was just tired of it all and when Blaise, Jay, Tray and Ray said that they were joining the service to fight in the war, he was ready to go also. During the wartime back then, you didn't have to prove your age nor get permission from your parents, however, if you weighed enough they took you.

Richet and Annette (his first girlfriend) have one daughter and three sons. I baby-sat for them while I was in college for much needed funds. All of the children are grown with families and grandchildren of their own now. Both are retired and both enjoy life by traveling, playing bridge or being with their families. Richet never came home on furlough. He enjoyed traveling out west when the ship came in. He was in the Navy and served on a Destroyer Escort in the South Pacific.

Boulean

Boulean was an exceptionally hard worker. He worked as hard as any of the siblings, but hated the farm work. He disliked school and had to wear his overalls, which were dirty from morning chores. Mama was sadden when she found out that he didn't dress in clean clothes each day.

He said that he didn't say anything because he had to hit the field every day when he got home anyway. He would always have things ready for me after I went in to put my overalls on. That is when Mama would slip us a "goodie," which was a biscuit and jelly or a hot baked potato with butter. This was a secret, which she did often. That sweet potato was hot and when I put it in my overall pocket to hide, my leg got blistered each time. It was worth it though until I got to the barn because I didn't want our secret to be seen.

I had thought that since none of us was allowed to bring our homework home, Boulean never had the opportunity to learn just by listening to a teacher who sat at the desk to teach. He needed his books to study and had the same teacher who required the Weekly Reader as her primary text for teaching reading. He needed more time and attention from school, because no one ever tapped his abilities, Therefore, he was bored of the hum-drum every day. He knew that he was going to fail the class. This would not only mean a whipping but another year on the farm. One of his friends, who rode Papa's bus, was in the same dilemma at school as Boulean. His folks had a large farm also and he was a hardworking boy and hated farming as well. Whether he got the beatings and whippings that Boulean got, I never knew.

One day he and his friend ran away from home. They were gone two weeks before being found. Boulean had sold his baseball glove that he got for Christmas so that he would have enough money to ride the bus or hitch a ride. The friend sold something else for trip money. After getting back home by the sheriff, Papa took him along with the cow whip across the road far enough that no one could see what he was going to do. He literally beat him almost to death. He didn't know when to stop. When Boulean fell to the ground, Papa quit whipping him. Papa must have thought that he had actually killed him with that whip.

Boulean was dripping with blood, and had dirt all over him when he returned. I often thought about Papa running away at the age of twelve years, and never went back to see his Papa for ten years after working for the railroad. However, messages were sent to Grandpa Thibodeaux. His Papa didn't send a posse search team after him. It would not have done any good. Papa would've shot'em. Boulean was older than Papa was when he ran away. I doubt that it ever entered his mind.

As soon as Mama saw Boulean, she began yelling at Papa saying, "No one should be beaten like this. You had better not ever whip one these children like this again I don't care what they do; never do this again to any of them. Do you hear me?"

The closer the time came for the end of the next school year, he knew that he was going to fail, so Boulean and his friend ran away again. He and I had to do too much by ourselves. The runaways were found north somewhere and brought back again. He was tired of doing all the work left for him after the other boys left. He received another whipping but not near as hard as the beating before. Working every day in the summer heat with sweaty and filthy clothes kept the wounds from healing, as they should.

Mama kept washing the area with lye soap to keep it from getting infected, but the sweat and dirt still got in it. If he had done this to me, I probably would've shot Papa. He got by a shooting, so I felt that I could. I wanted to shoot him when he was beating on Boulean. I think that it sure would've been self-defense. Papa knew that he had better not whip him as bad as last time, or Mama might have shot him.

I have always wondered why Boulean did this again, and In December of that same year, he ran away again, and couldn't be found. He was old enough then to join the Army. He was in Boot Camp when he wrote to Mama and told her what he did, why he did it as well as where he was. He was soon shipped overseas. He didn't write home very often, but when he did, it was addressed to Mama. There was no wonder how he still felt about Papa and I think Papa finally got the message as to why all of Boulean's mail was addressed to Mama.

Boulean's time was spent in Italy and Southern Europe. When he got out, he married a girl five years his junior and bought some land from Isabelle and Boudreaux one mile for Mama and Papa. He built his own house, and after a hurricane blew Papa's house off the back foundation, Papa decided that he was going to have one built down on the ground. He got Boulean to draw up the plans and build his house. I think at that time, Papa considered this an apology.

Boulean was one of the Co-executors of the Estate with Blaise. I believe that Papa was trying to say, I am sorry for beating you so hard and often. He didn't apologize but I think that Boulean felt that this was his apology.

Jo – See CHAPTER 1

Evette

Evette was three and a half years younger than I was. You are guessing correctly if you are thinking about more miscarriages. Yes, my poor Mama had three between Boulean and me and two more between Evette and me. Each of these happened during the 2nd trimester. Then Lili, who helped with the cooking, stayed pretty busy with the cooking on the old wood stove, and Evette stayed busy hauling the wood in for Lili. There were quite large groups to feed. Evette didn't work on the farm except two times with me, after all the boys were gone. Her job was the kitchen and helping Mama and Lili

Once when Evette and I were digging sweet potatoes, and the other time was just before I went to college. I was plowing sweet potatoes, and Evette was turning the vines. Papa went berserk with each of us this day. This was mentioned earlier. Evette knew how to handle her

Papa. That long dark hair and those big dark eyes got his attention. She was the biggest tattletale I ever knew.

I thought that since I was going to get a whipping anyway, I'll just beat the tar out of her for tattling. This worked for a while, but she would still holler at me so Papa could hear about me not doing the dishes correctly. He would tell her to go in the living room and I had to finish the dishes. I was not supposed to do any dishes. How did this come about? Evette was supposed to do all the dishes. I had cows to milk and she didn't even know how to do that.

The only job that she could do was to help with the cooking and boss people around. Sometimes she did have to pick vegetables out of the garden for Mama. She also had to shell peas, butter beans and help clean up after Mama canned sweet corn. All of this has caused poor relations between the two of us. As Evette grew up in high school, she needed me. Now things should be different. We played basketball together when I was a senior. I knew the coach and the girls well. They helped me in the field and she couldn't. However, she was smarter than I was because she would sneak books home under her clothes. I NEVER told on her.

She was allowed to wear her uniform shorts home, but I didn't have that privilege from Papa. Do you see the partiality being shown here? I was a senior and got the coach to try her out with me and she did well. After that, I felt she owed me. No more, tattletale remarks from her because I did a big favor for her that year, and she was great for the team.

Evette went to college the year that I graduated from college and while I was teaching at my first school. Yet one month I was beginning to think that I would starve because I sent her $10 from my first check. I don't know if she even remembers it or not. She cleaned house at the barber's home when she didn't have classes. He had a shop at the "Student Union" on campus. During the Christmas break, she went home, and her fiancé was with her.

She went straight to Papa and said, "I am not going to go through the hell that Jo did to go through college. We are going to get married in January."

"Well, okay then. Are you sure that's what you want to do?" Papa asked.

"Yep," She said without hesitation.

Well, that was the way Evette was. She didn't "hem-haw" around to get her point across either. She just announced it out loud, so that there was no question as to whether she was serious or not.

After she left home, there was no one to help Andre who was 4 years younger, so he couldn't do too much of anything. Evette didn't learn to milk, so he didn't either. And, yes, there were 3 more miscarriages between Evette and Andre. They were all in the 1st trimester. Mama's poor body just couldn't take it anymore. I know that I would have met Papa with a shotgun by then, at least.cc

Andre

Andre was my other buddy after being in the service. He was eight years younger than I was, and knew nothing of the hardships that came years before him. However, Papa was still trying to get him some playmates with Mama having 3 more miscarriages between Evette and Andre. Then after Andre was a year old, Mama had one more before the old doctor came and told Papa that if she had another, it would kill her. Her body had suffered enough.

That's when the doctor was called by my uncle. The doctor took care of Mama with 3 nights in the hospital. She needed blood and I volunteered to donate. They asked if I was eighteen years old and I lied and said that I was, "almost." I didn't care; I loved her and would have told that lie many times if needed, but I needed my Mama to live.

She had gone through enough hell, and if one lie would help her, then I was going to do it. I shall never forget this first time of donating blood.

Now Andre was not taught to do anything except a little work in the garden or ride the horse to the store. They didn't need him to learn anymore of what we all did. The farming, as the rest of us knew it, was over. Andre did help Mama a lot, took his books home and did well in high school.

Andre was never involved in sports. He was only eight years old when I left for college. We didn't do much work together except shelling peas or the like. Papa had gotten rid of the tractor and all but one of the mules, and he tried to teach Andre how to plow the garden. He had to learn to do a little of everything except milk the cow. Papa gave his mule to Boudreaux if he would prepare the garden for him. Well, he could not plow any better than Andre could.

Andre would gather up eggs, but he never learned to plow well, nor milk the cow. Sometime Andre did some household chores. By the time he was in high school, Papa had had running water in the house, electricity, and a black topped road. He would help Mama round up the milk cow and feed it. Andre was the youngest and most spoiled. When Evette left home, for college, he sure was a loner. He also helped Boulean, as needed, to build a bathroom on the old home.

Papa would even loan him the car to go see a girl. He and Papa did go to the big city of Alexandria. Andre hated those trips because he drove so slowly. Papa couldn't parallel park and knew very little about the city. He did know where the funeral home was and always parked there and walked where he needed to go. Andre would fool around until Papa finished with his business.

Once Andre was mowing the yard, after the new house was built, when he saw something in the small culvert, which kept water from running down into the portico. He reached down and found a bottle of liquor. Wow, that's a good way to pay for mowing. Oh, he was thrilled.

Not thinking about another chore when he finished mowing, he took several "swigs" of that, and shortly Papa told him to take the ladder and get on top of the shed to nail the tin down. He didn't know that Andre had gotten into his liquor. This tin had been pulled back from the windstorm. Andre got all the material and while on top of the shed he got so dizzy that he rolled off the top. Mama saw him roll off and ran out to check on him. He was so intoxicated that he never suffered the first scratch.

When Andre graduated from high school, he went straight to college. After two years, Uncle Sam found him and drafted him into the army where he served in Vietnam. He was a "Combat Medic in the army which had to be a living hell. I believe that all who served there thought it was also.

There was a movie made based on his unit, but he would never watch it. He lived it! The rescue helicopter could never drop down very low for the medics to get their equipment out; they had to jump out in a hurry so that the helicopter could get the hell out of there before it was shot down. Andre and his helpers were trying to keep a low profile to get to the wounded as well as try to kill those who were trying to get them as well as the wounded. The medics would use their bayonets to keep from shooting to prevent the enemy from finding them by the noise of their guns.

Once Andre was using his bayonet, but that didn't do enough, so he ended up trying to beat the stuffing out of them. He was tall, strong and good-looking, but was wounded several times. Once he was wounded with shrapnel in the face. When the chopper came back to get them, medics had to work on him and one of his friends. They had to get them to a medical aid station to be patched up and ready for action again. He was not just hiking through the "Agent Orange"; he had to wallow in it. During this time, Mama didn't hear from him for a long time. Finally, when he was able to get a note out, he told her that he had been playing football during some off time and turned his ankle. She was excited then that he was doing fine. This news made her feel so much better. She knew so little about what they went through.

Andre ended his career in two years with two Purple Hearts, two Bronze Stars and one Silver Star. He was recognized many years later, for all his service and was presented an award by the governor at a large meeting of service people from the state in Baton Rouge, Louisiana.

Shortly afterward, he had cancer.

He asked the doctor, "Could all this be caused by Agent Orange?"

The doctor said that they claimed, "No!"

Cancer finally got to Andre, but he died of a stroke from some sort of blood disease. He was only 69 and had so much to live for. His children were wonderful to him and with him. Andre was my best friend and brother, and I enjoyed each telephone visit with him.

Being a medic ruined his hearing, but he would try to call occasionally. He couldn't hear half of what I would say, but would laugh before I had finished the sentence.

I asked him once why he laughed before I had finished what I was saying.

"Why Jo", he said, "Everything you say is funny, so I just started laughing."

He and Nicole couldn't have children and began adopting. They adopted one son and a daughter, and then Nicole got pregnant with Jim. He was spoiled. He became a professional student, so he could live with his Dad. He worked just enough to have a car and enjoy the girls.

The army paid him a stipend as long as Jim stayed in school because Andre was disabled after he got out of the Army. Jim found his Dad the day he died where he fell over on the sofa. This devastated him because he was just with him watching a ballgame on TV and went to get both of them a sandwich. He was the only one not adopted.

Andre always said that he couldn't remember which ones were adopted anyway. They were all very special to him. They all loved their parents and visited often. Lendeux, the oldest, served in Afghanistan.

When Lendeux returned, he married a gorgeous girl and had his first beauty of a daughter. The second adopted child, Lisa, married a handsome young man and had the only grandson, which was a joy for Andre. She then she had a beauty of a daughter.

I told Andre a lot that he did not know about the farm, as well as that which Ted had told me before I was born. There were a lot of things that I had wanted to know for each of them, but I just never got the chance. The last time I got to see him, he flew over here where I lived, but knew nothing about the town. Ted picked him up at the airport and knew the town and street, but that was all.

He said, "How will I know where your place is?"

I said, "I will move my car, and there will be something in my parking place that will remind you of home. Well, it was ironic that we use to call the home place "Kneedeep." I took a huge refrigerator box from a dumpster and placed it in my parking place. Then with a large marker, I wrote "Kneedeep" with an arrow and number of my apartment at the time. When he and Ted saw that, they knew exactly where I lived. They both came in laughing about that unique idea. We had a blast!

CHAPTER 5

Planting and Chopping Time

During the planting season, the farm was like a beehive with workers everywhere. The hired hands would be there with some plowing, while others were tilling and planting. Into the ground went the seeds of watermelons, peas, cotton, corn, peanuts, Irish potatoes and sweet potatoes. Most of the tomatoes for canning were in a different field of 15 acres. No one knew where the different groups were working unless they were in the same field working together except for the slave driver on his horse going from one field to another.

I plowed and worked primarily during this time planting everything that Mama wanted in the garden which was about three acres. There were some tomatoes for daily use, straw berries, sweet peas, butter beans, some Irish potatoes, pole beans, bush beans, and onions to name a few. We did have cabbage, mustard and turnip greens in the spring and in the fall.

We had this garden to grow a few of everything grown in the fields for Mama to use during the day if she needed something nearby, or to be near for Sunday meals. In late August just as they had been picked over, we turned the stalks of tomatoes over with a turning plow while the tops were still blooming and this method gave us tomatoes until frost.

Watermelons were planted as early as possible because Papa wanted the first load into town to sell. The blacks were always having a celebration on "Juneteenth" (June 19) and if we didn't have those "black diamond" watermelon seeds in the ground early, then we did not get a good pay-back. This day in Louisiana was well celebrated by the blacks back in those days.

Papa would soak these seeds for two days to get a jump on them sprouting. Planting the seeds had to be handled with care because the seed was very tender from the soaking. Then a team of mules would be hauling barrels of water. As each spot was planted with three or four seeds, another would quickly pour a half cup of water in the hole to give them another boost. This boost helped to get the melons ready before anyone else. Another one of us would carefully tap the dirt over them. Then we went on to the next hole.

This was a continuous and a very tiring operation and the old mules knew just when to move forward. When ready to pull and very large, the bus was loaded and each sold for $4 or $5. As the days passed by and the melons were smaller, they were sold to people for $.10 each in the fields. That went fast because many people came to fill their automobile with as many as they could. They took them home to re-sell them.

Sometimes when the melons were for us, Mama wanted to make preserves from the very thick rinds of these melons. We usually just burst them in the field, grabbed the center and ate the best part of the melon. I was grown before I ever cut one for myself. For preserves, mama cut the melons in very thin slices and with the thick rinds; they were cooked, as any preserves would be done.

Some people were always trying to steal watermelons because they were too lazy to work and raise their own. Papa happened to slip up on some once by riding the horse right up to them before they could get out of the field. He always had his equipment on his saddle. Papa had another idea for them that they would never forget. He made them eat every one of them. He kept an eye on everything and everybody.

When they said, "We are full."

Papa said, "No, there's more; you pulled'em, so finish'em!"

You know that there were some sick thieves. I doubt that they ever stole another melon, especially from Papa. They probably didn't even like watermelons after having to eat all of those.

They were like some friends of Papas; back in the 30's who were stealing melons. The irony of it was that they grew melons at home; but it was more fun when one would get into another field. Once the brothers were trying to get them over the fence so that they could take off with them, the owner of the field shot his "shotgun" at them. At that long distance, he meant to frighten them, but one pellet hit our friend on the flap of his ear.

The bullet pellet cut a "V" into our friends ear. The ear never grew back together like the other one. Everyone called him "swallow fork" from that day on. Swallow fork was the name of a "Parish Courthouse

Registered Mark" for the owner of hogs. No one took another's animal, because the owner knew his animals by the registered mark in the hogs ear. Papa could always find his hogs. He knew when they came for feed if one was not there. Papa missed one in particular one day because it had "stocking-legs." Papa got on his horse and rode exactly where he figured he would find it.

These people didn't have much other than a garden and were too lazy to work. They claimed some sort of disability and got on the Huey Long Welfare Program. Papa found the hog all dressed and cleaned. He first found the ears of the hog they killed and that told the whole story. They knew it also. He told them that the "under-bit in one ear (which was a 1 inch slit on top), and a "swallow fork (a V) and an under-bit" (another slit on bottom) in the other was his registered mark and everyone knew it. The man saw the whip and rifle and was glad to obey Papa's command to keep from being killed. Papa would not have killed him, but he didn't know that.

Papa was somewhat glad that he had gotten there just at the right time. It had been killed, gutted and ready to be cut into sections. Papa told him to wrap it up with flour sacks, sheets or something so that he could take it home on the horse. He did that and threw it up on the horse for Papa.

The man apologized to Papa, "Saying that it would not happen again."

Papa raised his hat off his head as a manner of acceptance, and rode off with his hog that caused very little labor to prepare the rest. The worst part of hog killing and dressing had all been done. Mama and the rest of us had our work cut out for us. (My Papa believed that this family would steal anything because they were so lazy and jealous). These people didn't ever work for Papa or anyone else. They got whatever they didn't have by stealing. This hog was killed when it was hot weather, which meant that it all had to be cooked immediately. The rest was all put in the oven to cook over night. It was too soon to be killing and smoking the meat. It took almost all night to finish and clean up. The hired hands had pork most every day. Some was given to Mama's folks, but it had to be eaten within 3 days.

The next day was for more planting. The rows were so long, that we had to have sacks of seed at each end of the rows. This was done ahead of time to prevent wasting time

Many of the hired help lived in the community and helped with the planting. After about three weeks, it was time to bring in the whole bunch of hired hands who knew how to chop cotton. These blacks loved Ted and he had fun visiting with them. The bus would hold just so many and it was full of those who needed a job regardless of what it was. Therefore, Ted would go into town, filling the bus with hired hands to chop as much cotton as they could.

All of the ones who came had been there before, Ted thought, and they began the spirituals right away. I chopped right along with my buddy. I still had a limp, but I was doing a good job. I didn't tire easily because I could chop from the right or left hand. Soon my Papa spotted a new one and asked him if he knew how to chop and who used him before. Ted had not noticed him.

"I knows how to chop cotton. I done it lots of times." He said.

Papas said, "Then get to work and let me see just how good you can do it."

It was noticeable immediately that the young black didn't know what he was doing and had never done this before. Now, my Papa would help anyone who needed work, but this kid was not going to work for him. Some of the other blacks tried to show him how to do the job, but he ignored them. He would still miss the grass and chop the cotton down too many times.

Therefore, Papa told him to give the hoe to him and the young man made a move toward him in a threatening manner. Some of the blacks started after the kid to stop him.

Nevertheless, the kid had gone too far. He raised his hoe and began mouthing off something. Oh boy, this would not do with Papa on the horse with all his equipment, and this kid didn't know this boss at all. The rest of the blacks were hollering for him to put the hoe down. He didn't until my Papa popped the whip in the air. This frightened the kid and he put the hoe down.

Papa said, "You had better hit the road now and don't come back. If you start now, you might get a ride or it'll be night before you get home. Don't stand there and look at me. Hit the road "cause I'm not changing my mind."

He said, "Yes sur."

The others knew what Papa expected from his hired hands and they would've supported him if the young man had tried to get any uglier. Papa had never had a situation like this before. Soon they all went back to singing the spirituals that they always sang, whether they were chopping or picking cotton. There was one special girl with whom I always tried to stay very close. She taught me a lot about the life of blacks as well as how to sing those spirituals right along with the rest of them. She became one of my best buddies.

Papa had a musical field. We were with them so much, that much of their dialect "stuck with me," and my speech was similar to hers. Everyone picked at me about that. I was with her so much that I just picked it up as a kid. That was how we became so close. Picking cotton was usually the same crew, plus some extras who were not very good at chopping cotton, but made more money by picking. Choppers were paid by the day, and pickers were paid by the pound. On picking days, the bus would have so many on there that it was standing room only. As soon as any of the hit the field, they learned to put green leaves in the top of our their hat for insulation. As soon as we could get near another tree, we replaced the leaves that had become wilted by the time we got to them.

On Saturday, it was time for another family job, because it only took ten of us. The sweet potato beds for growing the "slips or short vines" had been planted. It was 50 feet long by five feet wide. The vines needed to be at least eighteen inches long, and cut into 14-inch lengths. These were called "potato slips." The prepared ground was made into rows; then the plow had a three-foot board attached to make the top of the row flat on top. Twenty acres were allotted for the field. The potato slip had to be laid precisely two thirds of the way across the flat surface and exactly twelve inches apart. This was so that the one behind you with the shoving stick would push the little vine in the center of the row. It had to be shoved in the cent to prevent the cultivating plows from digging them up or covering the plant if it had not been a precise measurement.

After the slips were planted, we hauled barrels of water from the bayou to do the same as we did for the watermelon seeds. It would be fall before these potatoes would be dug. All would be used at one time or another. Every day, at least one potato was baked for each person. Sometimes a hired hand would ask for an extra one. There were plenty and they could be stored for a long time.

By this time, the cotton was growing and becoming more mature. Papa kept a close watch for the buds developing.as well as an eye on the time that the dew formed on the cotton. Of course, this depended on the weather, as to whether it would form at eleven p.m. or 2 a.m. We had to be ready to hit the fields before the boll weevil got to the bud or bloom. As the buds began to form, it was time to poison cotton. Nine of us each had a pole cut from an iron-wood tree with a floor-sack full of cotton poison tied at each end.

This pole had to be strong enough to hold a sack full of poison, and long enough to reach across two rows of cotton as the horse walked down between the two rows. This was quite a laborious job of riding a horse while bouncing the sacks of poison with your arms up and down as the poison dusted the cotton. The slight speed of the horses kept just enough draft for the poison to spread on two rows for each one dusting. The moon gave us enough light to see and the horses knew to stay in the middle of the row.

At the end of the row, we turned for the next eighteen rows. This was done until the dew had dried. As long as it was wet, the poison stuck. We continued this, each morning until the entire fields had been dusted. If it rained, then dusting was re-done immediately after the rain had stopped. This kept some strong muscles on each one of us.

The boll weevil would get into the bud of the bloom or the bloom itself. The male boll weevil fed on the bud, bloom or the boll. The female would eat, but would also lay an egg in or on the bloom, or she punctured inside the boll and laid her eggs. This egg developed into larvae, and ate while inside the boll. This ruined the boll of cotton whether inside or outside the boll. Afterwards, the larvae became another "boll weevil."

Anytime the cotton crop was bad and the price was too low to sell, he stored the cotton in log cabins in the field. He showed the boys how to heat an old hoe in the fire to straighten it out and then shove the hoe up the sapling and peel the bark off. Many cabins had to be built quickly, so the bark remained on the log. Papa sold many saplings to the creosote plant for posts as well as logs, if the cotton price was too low.

CHAPTER 6

Harvest and Canning Time

Late May and early June was also time to pick blackberries. The black women did this and they were my responsibility, and one was my closest friend. We all worked together all the time, but she was good at all the work. I took the wagon of women with two long 2" x 12" rough-cut boards down to the bayou to carefully place over the briars after the ones in front of the large patch had been picked. I didn't want to break the briar plants, but with a syrup bucket tied with a rope around our waist, we could pick with both hands. We walked up the boards, picking berries on each side. You had to have good balance to do this. Usually that was my job and some of the younger blacks and my buddy. We had the most musical bayou in the country. Each worker was paid every evening, after work by Papa.

Papa would come down on the horse, bring lunch for each of us and as usual, it was fried chicken. Everyone enjoyed that. While we were eating, Papa took the wagon with all the berries back to the house for Mama, Lili and Evette to wash and prepare them for putting in canning jars for cobblers or jelly.

Then he would bring the wagon back to where we were picking, get on his horse and leave. Later, if there had been at least three sunny days between berry-picking times, the berries that came in late had to be picked by me. I did keep my eyes open though. Since I was alone, I didn't want to see Joe nor his bones. When I finished I had quite a load of berries for Mama.

Picking other types of berries or figs required ones who could climb. The climbers were Evette, Boulean and me. One tree was the "sloe" berry, which was like a crab apple that grew in the swamp. We would climb up or pull a limb down and pick those for jelly or jam. They didn't make good cobblers or pies. We also had huckleberries and gooseberries, which grew wild in the sandy loam areas.

Figs grew behind the barn in a very fertile and heavier soil. I was not allergic to the "scratchy" leaves. I didn't mind this because they were good raw and I ate my share and more. Everyone else was allergic to the milky sap from breaking a leaf or the fruit after it was picked. The leaves left a rash on the others if they climbed the tree, similar to poison ivy, but I was not allergic to either.

Pears were grown in large trees near the barn. I was the one who had to be very careful climbing these for the fruit because the limbs would break easily when loaded with pears. I was small, agile and not afraid of heights. Other fruit trees were just scattered about. We had plums, peaches and satsuma trees. Sometime we would sneak out through the weeds to get a pear.

This was usually before they were ripe and the wind had made them fall. Often we would get a terrible stomachache. Once you were caught for stealing and got a whipping, you didn't try that very often. Papa could see those weeds shaking and knew there was not an animal in the area. I don't know why we never thought about that. Therefore, he knew immediately what was going on. As tasty as they were, it was well worth the whipping we got.

I never cared for cobblers and pies because I preferred the raw fruit. They were made with biscuits sweetened for crust from "rock sugar" because Papa would not buy extra sugar for anything except enough for Mama's coffee. Therefore, since he and I didn't care for the pie or cobbler, Mama would give me a "flat" biscuit (or flat bread) made on top of the wood stove. All it needed was patted down on top and flipped over. Sometimes Mama would slip me a hot sweet potato with real butter on it after a meal. She knew that I didn't like the sweets.

Mama never used curse words, but Papa, on the other, used all of them in front of us and to us. Oh, he was mean! I hated him and wished many times that he would just die, or that I would. That was terrible to say, but I did feel that way. I knew that the boys hated him because of the whippings and too much work. The work never ended!

I would hear the boys say, "Oh, that old SOB's going to kill us with all this work."

For meals, all the hired hands were on their own for breakfast or supper, unless they lived with us or were sharecroppers. They would be helped out sometime because they were all working and didn't have time to cook from scratch. The ones, who lived with us during the depression and the war, would always help Mama with the canning. Naturally, they were fed three meals a day.

Some people, even the blacks, knew that Papa was mean to us, but never to them. They had to know that he was mean. They saw the whip come down on us and see the signs of a beating on our legs and arms. We were never allowed to put our hands on our butt to protect it because people could see licks given to us.

We still did it anyway because it hurt. He dared us to tell or show anyone our bruises or licks from the razor strap, whip, switch, belt or whatever was the nearest for him to use and many times he would just kick me in the butt. I just never understood why the boys never got the boot on their butt. If we did put our hands behind us that would just mean extra licks. Of course, we were afraid to tell because somehow he would find out.

To me, that shows that he meant to be mean by daring us to tell anything or show his marks. I think he was sometimes ashamed of himself for pushing us so much. Shortly after the tenant homes were built, Cedric decided that he wanted to live in town. This was about twelve miles from home.

He had gone with Ted to take the "town hired help" home one evening, and I suppose he felt that he would like that kind of life for a while. He never remembered much about the rescue, which Grandpa and Van did when he was just about five years old. So, getting to town seemed like a new venture that he needed now that most of the farming was waning. We never saw Cedric again and missed him. We didn't know if he left Villeplate and went to another town, or got into trouble and put in jail, or what. The people who worked for us said that they never saw or heard anything from him after the day Ted took him to town.

He had saved his money, because he never needed anything to spend it on anyway. He could have anything he wanted or needed. Grandpa and Papa paid all the slaves and their families but not as much as the regular hired hands, because housing and food was furnished for them. Cedric and Ted were very close and Ted was most disappointed when he decided to leave. No one had seen him, so we thought he might have caught a bus or the train to go up north. He could've been sick and would not tell anyone. It bothered Papa and

Ted because he had no papers on him for identification. However, during and after the war, it was easy to get papers by saying that he was Cedric Thibodeaux. Ted and I always believed that he was sick and wouldn't tell anyone.

In farming corn, the cream corn had a white cob and was for canning or "corn on the cob." The other field was the feed corn and had a red cob. This was made into cornmeal or grits. The cob however, was ground up for nubbins which were easily chewed by the hogs or the cows when used while we milked them.

It was planted in a different field and was used for seed corn, the cattle, hogs, chickens and other animals running around. We always hoped that all corn would grow quickly and be tall enough before a hard rain came because replanting would have to be done. Enough kernels from the red as well as the white corn were saved for seed for at least 3 years, and then Papa would buy new sacks of seed.

For canning, the corn had to be harvested first while the stalks were pretty and green, as well as the corn shuck. This corn had the white corn cob. Mama had to have many helpers for the canning of corn. It had to be gathered and shucked and cleaned from its "silk" while fresh. We never pulled more than Mama could handle in one day because it would sour. This was continued until Mama had all that she intended to use. We always kept some out for corn on the cob for that day. We could always go back and pull a dozen if we wanted it.

It was a painstaking day in the kitchen for canning anything and especially corn. The ear of corn with its many kernels had to be sliced very thin, making two or three slices down the ear, and then turning the knife sideways to scrap the cob for "creamed" style corn. It was a mess to clean up after this job was done, due to the splatting while "creaming" the cob. This corn fed lots of hired hands. Mama and Lili had skilled help for this with only two boys helping. The rest were not a part of that. The rest of us were gathering it. Ted and Ray were Mama's heavy lifters for the two "doubled pressure cookers."

After Mama ran out of jars, she used cans and the cookers held four layers of the cans of corn, because they didn't require a "screw-on" lid. The cans had a special lid, which was heated and sealed with a machine, which "crimped the can together with the lid." This was my "get to be with my Mama" job to do the turning of the crank and making sure, the lid sat on the can correctly. One would place a hot can of corn on the machine, another would have a hot pot of hot lids for me and I turned the crank. Another would take the can of corn and stack it out for the cooker. This was a continuous job with the canning of corn, peas, butter-beans, snap-beans or whatever was to be put in cans for the pressure cooker.

Beef was never put in cans but would be put in jars as beef stew. The pork and beef were always done in the fall of the year. It was not as hot in the kitchen for this as it was for the vegetables. Ted and Ray had to be extremely careful with the hot glass jars to prevent breaking them. I remember Mama saying that she always had a thousand cans of corn, and peas, but a forth of that in butter beans and sweet peas along with as many as 500 quarts of beef stew in thin gravy.

Summer-time was hot enough in the kitchen, without all the canning going on. This took a lot of time to prepare when canning. All of the rest as well as some of the local hired help was in on the gathering and shelling of peas, beans, sweet peas and shucking corn. My Mama and Lili had to have been "hotter than blue blazes" from all the heat. There were plenty of windows and doors to open for cross ventilation, but it still was very hot for them cooking over these 2 wood stoves all day.

I wish that I could have relieved them. But, that was not about to happened. One day after all the plants grew up to a good size where there would not have to be any re-planting, it rained for several days. The Villeplate River came all the way up to the first hut or barn built. This was built up off the ground for flood protection. It was the first house Papa built to begin the plantation, and where the first five kids were born. There was not much work going on during the flood time except being able to milk the cows and feed the others. This gave us time to get peanuts to parch them, make peanut brittle or pull candy.

This was great to be able to sit down and enjoy the floodwater while we could, because when the rains were over, there would be plenty of work to do. This happened just as school was about to be out. All the schools were closed in the areas due to the flood. The Nezpique River, creeks and bayous were flooded and no one could get across. However, for me now, it was the haunting fear of Joe being washed up by the flood somewhere. An alligator came up near one of the sheds. Then I thought that as large as the gator was he probably ate Joe for a long lasting meal. Farming was what Papa knew would be the way to keep Ted out of service because he was too old to farm himself. I wanted him off that horse and working. That would've kept the slave driver off my back for a while.

Even with Ted being exempt from service, Papa was still the slave driver but Ted ran the farm as well as some of the slaves. The primary difference was that Ted was not a SLAVE DRIVER. He also said that Papa had too many acres to farm and the same number of hired hands after buying Grandpa's place. If Ted had gone into the service, Papa would not have much of a farm because most all the hired hands lived in town and had no way to get to the farm.

We would've worked hard for Mama, for sure. Nevertheless, she would not have sent me to the fields. I would've learned to cook, sew and learned all about the troubles that young girls got into. As it was, I only heard of trouble, but never knew what kind or why.

Papa said he didn't have time to go get the hired help. That is why he talked Ted into staying home and helping with the farm. I never knew whether he was paid a dime or not. Next, it was time for me to plant peas. I had to take a sack of peas over to the north forty to plant where I had previously prepared the soil. With a hoe over one shoulder and a sack of peas on the other, I was off to the field by myself. As I turned in the bend of the spring creek, I thought that I saw someone following me. All I could think about was Joe. It was darker here at the creek with all the trees, and I began to get scared. Papa had broken his own oath for me, not to go anywhere alone unless I was on my horse.

I threw that hoe and sack of seed peas down, and took off to the house limping as fast as I could. I told Papa that I thought Joe was back and he was probably following me. He didn't believe a bit of it and sent me back with a few licks of the whip. Mama said that Papa followed me but stayed back enough for me not to see him, just in case there was someone and if it were one of the KKK men or anyone else, they would be facing his gun. I had already looked behind me, saw no one then picked up the hoe, and continued to the gate. I climbed it again.

Of course, some of the peas spilled out so I had to go back down to pick them up. The ones, which scattered took up too much time to pick up so I just dragged my boot over them and covered them up, not thinking ahead that they WOULD come up. Of course, every one of them came up and I was found out! He also knew that I had climbed the gate or this would not have happened! You bet I caught it with a good whipping wrapping around my back and another one for crying, spilling the seed peas and climbing the gate. Why he never said that climbing it would make it sag, I don't know.

It was 1 1/2 miles to the pea patch. I had previously plowed the old vines under because they left plenty of nitrogen in all of soil for the next year planting time. To plant, one would make an indentation with a hoe and drop about three or four peas in the hole and drag some soil over it, and then tap it lightly with the hoe. This was continued each evening after school, or on Saturday until the ten acres were planted. It was always dark when I returned home. On Saturday, lunch and plenty of water was brought to me in the field. My Papa didn't do anything but ride that horse and push everyone a little harder. He came to where I was so that there was no wasted time for me to go home for dinner. They would only need to be plowed two times. These peas were for canning.

CHAPTER 7

Small Harvest Jobs

Mama had two large wash pots, which were well used for most anything. One of the uses was for cooking figs. Together, these pots would contain up to about 100 pints of cooked figs. They were delicious with biscuits and were used primarily by the family. Sometimes a jar would be given to friends and of course, Isabelle always got her share. It was a trade usually for some of her Japanese persimmons, pecans, or mutton.

Collecting honey was done in the wintertime. During the summer especially, bees were out collecting nectar from the flowers. They used the nectar from blooming plants in the garden, trees in the swamp, the blooming weeds, and sometimes the bees were carried to other places for different flower nectar.

Papa had several beehives. He always used a little bit of honey to get the bees started, from a barter. Sometimes the boys would find a bunch of bees in a split tree in the swamp filled with a huge hive of bees. They would put on a thick rag for a scarf, with netting over their faces and wearing thick clothes and gloves, they would steal honeycombs from the bees and put them in a bucket. This is where the bees would stay in the cold weather or at night. We would all get together with banging bells, pans or anything to make noise and the bees followed the noise straight to a beehive. It was strange to see them follow the noise. I don't recall any selling of honey, but it was given away to friends, with or without the comb. I can remember chewing on the honeycomb for a long time. When Mama would give us honey with the comb, she would always ask us to save the comb for her. She washed the wax, cleaned it from all the honey and then melted the wax to sterilize it to be used for several different special effects. Wax was used for sealing jellies and jams, after they were put in jars. When the jars cooled, the hot wax was put on top of the jelly or jam, which sealed the jars. After a short time, this would get cold and harden. It completely sealed the jellies and jams. If Mama had some wax melted that was left over, she would make a candle for overnight camping at the river. This also kept the mosquitoes and other bugs away as well as varmints from coming around.

CHAPTER 8

Sugar Cane Harvest

We planted our sugar cane to be used for the hired hands and for us. It was a necessity, because we had syrup every day. Since there was very little of the "Blue Ribbon" cane grown it was great for "bartering" for different items, which Papa needed.

This field was harvested after a good frost. It was necessary to evaluate the taste of sugar in the stalk by peeling and chewing some on subsequent days after the frost. If a freeze was predicted, we harvested the cane immediately. This one crop needed very little work and attention. This was an annual plant and weeds were pulled out once a year, while the plant was still small, but required nothing else until after the first frost came.

The sugar cane was first stripped with cane knives that looked like a "machete" with a very sharp hook at the end of one very sharp side. The foliage was stripped off all the way to the bottom of the stalk and the hook at the end was used to snap the blades off. Then another cut the top of the stalk as well as the bottom and laid it down on the ground. After the cane had been stripped, cut and laid down, all would begin picking the stalks up and loading them on the sugar cane wagons. Then Ray would take off for the mill on the tractor to have the belt hooked up to the flywheel, which turned the grinder. He also made sure all was ready for us when we got there.

These wagons had curved sides or "ribs," which fit into slots on the wagon to hold them tightly to the wagon because of the pressure put on them by the cane stalks. The cane was piled up high along the ribs until each had all they could handle. There were three wagons loaded at a time and then pulled by a team of horses seven miles to the cane mill for making syrup. The owner of the mill was told in advance, when to expect our cane because he had to have the "kettles" ready with very hot fires from the oak wood and pine knots.

Ray was in charge of shoving the stalks into the "grinder," because he knew the danger of getting your hand too close. As soon as we arrived, Ray began immediately loading the cane into the grinder, for the juice to follow a tray to flow to the kettles. He did this until the last stalk of our cane was finished. The juice went into huge vats where the heat would begin getting the juice to a boiling point removing the water from the cane. This was enjoyable to watch as each stage was processed. The first stage, before it began boiling, tasted very good and was called "sugar cane beer," and if one had too much, it would make them drunk.

Then all of it had be at the boiling point and thickened slightly to go to the next stage by a slot. Each vat was stirred for a time, and then released for the next vat.

That vat was watched closely as the juice continued to thicken and turn golden. There were two more stages of scraping the bottom of each kettle with this long and wide spatula, which prevented the juice from burning or getting too thick. Each stage required the release and the filling from one vat to the next. This was a very hot operation for making the juice to the consistency desired for syrup.

Papa had the empty buckets ready for us as soon as the syrup had reached the last vat and ready to open the spigot to release the syrup for the buckets. These buckets were extremely hot, and carefully loaded into the school bus. They were loaded in such a way with blocks between several rows of buckets to prevent them from sliding, as the bus would make a turn in the road or to stop. Ted and I were first for grinding, then we would leave for the house for the boys to begin filling the wagon up again. This kept me from being on the road alone. The farm bell was rung to signal for help to load the wagons as each came back. This was also done when the bus loaded with the cans of syrup arrived, and all helped to store them.

All wagons were timed to be there for the next load ready for Ray. The mill kept cooking our syrup until the last wagon was done. He couldn't wait for a wagon, which is the reason we rushed back with an empty wagon, to get it filled and back to the mill before Ray ran out of our sugar cane. Papa made sure that all was done in a timely manner.

With our syrup, we could also make "stretch-candy" and "peanut-brittle." The stretch was usually done in the wintertime or on special occasions. It made great gifts for teachers, especially. During this time, we would all be in the kitchen visiting Mama and watching her as she made it. The syrup from the cane was an important staple food for us. It was the only sweet food we received each day.

We always had at least 100 buckets of syrup stored in a separate and dry shed to prevent them from getting any moisture, which would cause rust. The foliage was raked up and burned to prevent rot, mold or mildew. The flags did not make good compost. The cane came up every year without planting unless there was a heavy freeze, which ruined the roots. Then we would get new stalks of cane, laying two or three down lengthwise and covering them up. The sugarcane bower "bug" damaged our crop so bad that we had to stop growing the cane. There was no known way to rid this bug. This all happened about the time the hired help no longer worked on for us.

CHAPTER 9

Potatoes

Digging sweet potatoes was the PITS! You got absolutely filthy as if you were a mole under the topsoil. A plow called the middle buster was used to plow straight down through the top of the row where the potato vine was planted. This made the potatoes roll up out of the ground or just under the top. One of the boys had previously dug the potatoes up so that they would be ready for us as soon as the syrup making was over. Now to keep the farm running smooth, we began with these sweet potatoes, many times after school. It helped a lot if the rains would come and make them more visible. After the potatoes were gathered up in the center of the row, another put small heaps of potatoes into a burlap sack. This took a strong person to lift these sacks. Then off to fill another burlap sack. This continued until the last one was sacked.

As soon as possible, the sacks were tied and put onto a slide, which was pulled by a team of four mules. When the slide was filled, I drove the team home, pulling a slide full of sacked potatoes. One of the waiting boys took them off the slide, and back to the field I went. This part of driving the team of mules was fun for me. This field was one half mile away. Nothing except the garden and one patch of cotton was planted very close to home. Pasture land was all around between the fields. This left plenty of room to prevent cross-pollination. As you can see this took a lot of teamwork with the boys and of course the Slave Girl "Jo."

The potatoes were stored in different places. One of the places was a squatty pole barn, built just for sweet potatoes. The pole barn was cinched with a prepared mixture of mud and straw, by cramming it in between the poles all around shed. This cinching kept out the rain and wind as well as much of the cold weather as possible.

The burlap sacks of potatoes were each scattered on top of thick layers of straw. Then another sack was emptied on this layer of straw, and so on until the shed was filled. Next, a thick layer of straw was put on the top and sides to help prevent freezing. The burlap sacks were stored in there on top.

The rest of the potatoes were put in "potato pumps." These were made by digging a hole (or crater) about six feet deep below the frost line and four feet wide. After piling the dirt over on the side, the hole was filled on the bottom and sides by a thick layer of straw. Next, the potatoes were poured in carefully. This packed the straw down and another cover of straw was put down. Then more potatoes were put in until there was a good cover and another layer of straw.

This was repeated until the hole was ready to be covered with a very thick layer of straw. Then all the dirt that was piled up from the "dig" was put top. It formed about a three-foot high mound all around to prevent any freeze from affecting the potatoes. The mounds were called "potato pumps."

There were several of these potato pumps, and they were used first, because they were out in the elements. Often the rain had taken its toll on the mound, and had to be repaired quickly. There were enough potatoes to feed anyone and they were used every day in one form or another, mostly for baking. With all the people Mama had to feed, there was a great need for them. Papa knew what he was doing when he saved all of the pine trees around the barns and sheds The twenty acres of potatoes were done several evenings after school.

After the sweet potatoes had been planted and laid by, it was time for the Irish potatoes (Russet). These had to be cut into sections. Each section had to have two or three "eyes" or buds on it when all the potatoes were cut. Lime was put in the sack with the cut up potatoes and was shaken so that each part had lime on it. This was to keep worms, or bugs from getting on them when they were planted. We only raised enough Irish potatoes for our family and for special occasions. Some were given to friends and some were probably used for barter.

Irish potatoes had to be harvested the exact same way, but stored differently. They would rot if stacked on top of each other, or would sprout again if they were placed on dirt. Therefore, they were stored in the barn in a floored room. Those on top of others were used first.

Sometimes Mama would go to the field to check before the harvest to see if there were some small potatoes to cook with snap beans. Often she would pull some dirt back to see how large they had gotten; and gather the largest ones so that each of us had some to mix with the beans. What a thoughtful Mom she was.

CHAPTER 10

Papa: The Tyrant

In spite of all the hard work we did on the plantation, Papa was the most atrocious man in the world as far as how most of us felt. The following will show just how mean my Papa was.

One morning as Papa was to make the school bus run, both Boulean and I had a harder time getting the milking done and cleaned up for school. We had not quite gotten all our school clothes on when we heard Papa pulling out in the bus. We knew that he left at seven o'clock sharp, but we had no idea of the time. None of us had a watch. The ones were on the mantle in the living room, and Papa's watch,

My Papa didn't wait for his own kids. He started the bus, and let it idle a bit. Boulean and I had dropped the milk off for Mama, hurrying to put our school clothes on, but he left. There was no time to clean up, so I am sure that cow mess was on our shoes and we smelled dreadful with the milk and crud on our hands. The cow's tail had slapped us against the head so that our hair was a mess and smelled as well.

Off and running, we went to try to catch the bus with all our might; it appeared that we couldn't make it. However, we didn't dare give up. We just knew that he saw us in the rear view mirror, but no, he didn't slow down. Going up the hill to the next stop, Papa had to slow down. That gave us a chance to try to catch up. We finally caught up to the bumper and held on to it until he came to a full stop. This first stop was about one half mile down the road. These schoolchildren belonged to the sharecropper.

Papa would NEVER do this to any of the other students who rode the bus. They would've turned him in and he would've lost this job. We were very angry about this hatefulness just portrayed by our Papa. We wished that someone had passed to witness this bizarre behavior. However, it didn't happen; no one else saw it unless it was the sharecropper, and he wouldn't dare say anything.

I asked Boulean while hanging on the bumper, "Does he hate us? Why did he do this? How did we know what time it was?"

Boulean replied, "He was just a mean SOB; that's what!"

I said, "Well, I'll bet Mama didn't know it or she would've made us just stay at home. I wish now that we had, because we will get a whipping anyway. We would've enjoyed staying with Mama, at least until he got home. I think Mama would've run interference for us. Don't you?"

"Yep," he said.

Then with the stop, we ran up to get into the bus. Papa cut his evil eyes around at us and we knew immediately what that meant. We knew that a whipping was coming when we got home. Why did we take off running? I should never have left. We could've stayed at home with Mama until Papa came home.

As it was, all I had to think about that day at school was the bad whipping I would get when I got home. We knew it was going to happen. How stupid we both were to run for the bus. If the principal had heard about this or one of our teachers, he would've lost his job on the spot. In addition, just as sure as the world turns, when we got home he said to wait by the side of the bus. He jerked his belt off, beat us on our back and rear end and told us to move our hands away from our butt and he hit us more. If we cried, he beat us for crying.

He repeated, "Now you know that the bus leaves at seven o'clock sharp."

I said, "Well, how do WE know what time it ever was? We don't have a watch and never know how the darn cow is going to   act. Why don't you try to milk her sometime? You'll see."

Well, I asked for it and got three whippings. One licking was for the bad word and one for missing the bus. Last, I thought he was going to kill me, for suggesting that he try to milk the cow. I could barely walk, but got to Mama. She was quite angry toward Papa when she saw me, and helped me to the kitchen. Mama wondered why I was not with Boulean when he came in. Boulean's rear end was so use to the whippings; he was able to walk away when Papa finished whipping him. He wore overalls which helped some for him. I was the next one to get it. I had to wear dresses to school and that was another reason the whipping hurt so badly. The whippings left plenty of marks on me. I had them on my arm, legs shoulder and rear end. Mama was SO upset. If she had started at Papa, she probably would've shot him.

She cleaned me up while Boulean waited for me. That was a real "3-in-1" whipping.

I told my cow, "If you ever mess with me again, and cause me to miss that darn bus, you'll just not get milked as well and your bag will start hurting and wish that I was here to finish that job. I'm glad you keep secrets or I would be crippled for life."

One afternoon, a young man who rode the last run of Papa's school bus, operated the door for Papa so that people could get in or go out without bumping someone. He was on the same run to go home that I rode, because it was the last "run." I was exhausted from running for the bus because I had been in the library studying. This young man and I were in high school, but not in any classes together. He was very courteous. When I approached the bus, he stepped out.

I thanked him. He acted as a gentleman should to allow me in without bumping into anyone. My Papa got very suspicious. As soon as we got home, he told me to stay out beside the bus. I didn't know why, but soon did. He jerked his belt off and beat the hell out of me because he had made up his mind that this was a boyfriend at school. Wow, I was one child who would not think of getting involved with a boyfriend.

"Oh, God, how can I convince you that he was just being courteous?" I said.

I was shocked and hurt. I never got him to understand that it was not true. I held my hands behind me and he beat me more. I cried, and he beat me more for crying.

I had not completely healed from the last whipping. He certainly didn't want me crying loud enough for Mama to hear. I often wondered if he was not a little afraid of what she would do to him with all her help.

Another time I caught it, was in the fall and not much was going on with the farm. Papa wanted me, (who had never ironed a single piece) to iron his khaki pants that Mama had starched. She didn't have time to iron them until she returned. Why me? Where is everyone? He left also and while he was gone, for some reason and I was alone. I had the iron going and thought about the radio.

I wondered if I would be able to turn it on. I had never used the radio before. I jumped in and got it set up with the large battery and was enjoying that radio. I was alone for a change. The only time it was turned on was for Papa to listen to the Grand Ole Opry on Saturday night. Papa had it down low to keep the battery life lasting longer. One had to hover close to hear anything. It was not worth it to me.

That particular day, I turned the radio up where I could hear it without hovering over it. I was enjoying it and trying to keep an eye out for Papa. Oh man, I saw him coming and turned that radio off as fast as I could. I put it all back along with the battery and had that old iron going "lickety-split." Now this was before electricity in our house, so the irons had to be heated (4 at a time) on the wood stove or in front of the fireplace in the winter-time. I was glad that I had not left for an iron, because Papa came in and the first word out of his mouth was about the radio. I know he had not seen it. Why did he think about it? Why did he even suspect it? I had neither taken, nor listened to the radio before for pleasure.

In addition, I didn't EVEN listen with him on Saturday night. I got to thinking that he had been hiding behind a tree watching me. He was good at watching, but staying out of sight of others. We knew this, but that didn't occur to me that day.

He asked, "Have you been listening to the radio?

I said, "I've been ironing your khaki pants like you told me too."

Well, it never occurred to me that the darn radio got warm when it had been on. Next he did was touch the radio, and found that I had been listening and implied lying about it. He got the cow whip on me and it wrapped around me so many times that I was beginning to bleed where it cut like a knife. Then when he saw what was happening, he grabbed his belt. He was a ruthless tyrant!"

He said, "This one was for lying to him, and this is for using the radio.

"Yesss sirhhh." I cried.

I had to finish the ironing and trying to keep blood from getting on them. I was ironing wrinkles into them. I tried the other clothes later on in case I was ever told to do them, but they didn't look any better after finishing them. I just didn't know how to iron.

Finally, Mama came in from some place to see what I was doing and what had been going on. I said nothing and neither did Papa, but he knew that she was not happy. She also knew that he had used a

"SHILLELAGH" (anything used for whippings) on me. I ran in crying. She was outraged! She cleaned me up, and then went to talk to Papa as I went outside. I wished that I could've heard what she said.

With school going on, we had some kind of farming to do whether it was for planting, tending animals or harvesting, I was ready to do it. My arms, hands, back and butt hurt so bad it hurt to expand my chest to take a breath. I wondered why God didn't just take me out of this misery. I heard Mama say a few things before I left out. I wished that I could have stood there and watched his expressions as she raised cane.

I did hear her say, "She works as hard as the blacks and the boys and you whip her harder than you would an animal. I want that stopped right this minute!"

She was mad!

I know she felt sorry for me, because I was not being raised as a lady should be. She didn't get to teach all the things to me that a young naive girl ought to know. I just worked in the fields just as hard as the hired hands.

Sometimes Cedric would be near and he didn't like to see this either. He would often be on the back steps ready for work, but would ask if he could help Mama and Lili in the kitchen. Many white people on "State Welfare" also worked for cash if they ran out of money for the month.

The Slave Driver always kept a pistol in his holster, a rifle, or shotgun as well as a lasso and a cow whip on him when he was on his horse, because something was always going on in the different fields. This was necessary because some were KKK members, or in case there was a worker who might try touching me, or arguments, or fights between others. All were afraid of him even though he was extremely well kind to them.

One day I had picked so much cotton so fast that the burs had stuck me so much that I couldn't even feel the pain. My fingers had become numb. However, the next day was quite a different story. The pain was too excruciating and I couldn't do it or tolerate the pain any more. The heat was so oppressive and that alone didn't help my situation, especially wiping my sweaty face with sore fingers. Not working was enough reason for him; I got a whipping anyway. Oh, I knew that he was the meanest Papa in the world. I usually got a kick in the butt; it was faster, and showed less immediate damage. Later in life, it was a cruel mistake.

Mealtime was an unpleasant time. When the hired were all fed, Mama and Lili put the serving bowls filled on a table on the back porch where workers helped themselves and sat out by a tree, benches between porch columns or on the edge of the porch, swinging their legs down. There were people everywhere for at least 30 to 45 minutes. Family meals were eaten in the dining room. Our dining table was a long "harvest table" with enough benches for ten. Meal time was not a time for talking or joking.

CHAPTER 11

WW II The Boys Joined Up

The boys signed up ready for war. In fact, as soon as the four old-est boys decided to join the service, because they were old enough, Richet who was along with them lied to get in by saying he weighed enough. He did but for sure, he was not old enough. Richet was six years younger than the triplets and 4 years younger than Blaise. He just said he was going anyway because he was sick and tired of the plantation. They hitched a ride with the mail carrier to get to town. I think they tried to talk Ted into joining so the farm would fold. Then Papa would have to leave us alone and for one time we could help Mama.

All five of them were sick of farming and working their butts off. With Papa buying Grandpa's place, they knew that they would never get to rest.

We all got whippings with the cow whip, but Richet got so many whippings that his rear end was as calloused as Boulean's and mine. However, I couldn't get away. They were all signed up, but had to wait about a week to show up again at the recruiting office. They got some-one to bring them back to the house and rode back again with the mail carrier. Gosh, I missed my brothers. I cried and cried about them leav-ing, but didn't blame them at all.

Before they had to leave, they decided to help with planting five acres of peanuts in that "special place." This was the only plot that peanuts were planted due to so many stumps in the patch, which was never "grubbed." However, the boys were not there when it was time to pull them up and build shocks for them. The peanuts would be ready in September. Well, the war had been going on and five of my eight brothers were gone.

I never did mind planting, plowing or pulling up peanuts. After they were ready to be pulled up, they were put on "shocks" which we built with some post and cross bars nailed to the post. These made a base for the peanuts to prepare for harvest in three days. The foliage had to be dried on these shocks in the sun and then put in the barn. The same type of drying had to be done for the hay also, or it would create enough heat to set the barn afire. This was called "curing the foliage" of the peanuts or the hay before baling.

Soon the peanuts were ready for roasting. These were sent to friends or the friends were invited over. Isabelle's family was there if we made peanut brittle or pull candy. These were planted, plowed, pulled and harvested by us for our pleasure. We loved roasting them or eating them raw. I could make brittle sometime and that made great gifts for the team girls. They loved to come out to get me or help me out in the field pulling corn, and the coaches did also.

I only had to watch Mama once; when she took a spoon of the syrup after it had boiled a while, and allowed to drip to see if it formed a tiny thread. If it did, it was ready for candy making "pull candy" or peanut brittle. I knew that I could surely do that, and I did. First cooking job learned.

Before they all left, we made peanut brittle and pull candy with the syrup. The kitchen was full of girls laughing and cutting up. I wished that they could've stayed the night because we had plenty of beds and food.

During basketball season, the team would come out and help me pull corn and do other chores. They would never milk a cow, though, because they remembered what happened to me. The coach would visit with Mama and Papa while the team helped me. This was the only way that I could play basketball at night or go to a tournament. Then I would often have to spend the night with the coach. Papa allowed this, occasionally. I was shocked that I didn't have to come home. That was a 26-mile round-trip to make just so I could play.

Another learning experience for them was how we kept our milk fresh. Fresh milk had to be put in the coolest place, which was the deepest part of the deep well by ropes. Mama would put it in gallon jugs with very tight seals or lids and lower it down into the well. Each had a mark on them as to which was the freshest or oldest. The oldest milk was used first. We got drinking water from the shallow part of the well. These jugs were 150' deep for one, and a little more shallow or deeper for the next ones. Milk that deep down in the well, kept it as cold as if it had been refrigerated. We had to do this quickly to keep it from spoiling. If any of the milk soured and turned to curd, then we churned it. This made butter and had lots of buttermilk. Sometimes this was done purposely because we needed the butter, and all loved the buttermilk.

Milk and corn bread was enjoyed by most for supper. We had plenty and Mama didn't need to cook a big meal for us to sleep on. That was the reason we had so many milk cows. I milked along with six brothers at least two cows each until five of them left home and then Mama helped some. Ted took hired help home and Boulean and I had to do more cows now. Soon, Papa sold a couple of milk cows because we didn't need as much milk.

The hired hands were not allowed to milk the cows. Mama knew that we used a bucket of water, lye soap and a drying rag to keep the milk cow's bag clean. Boulean and I didn't think my Papa had ever learned to milk a cow. He had two sisters who were much older than he was and they did the milking as well as some of the slave women. Papa was just the BOSS, and everyone knew it. We had lots of milk mostly from those mean Jersey cows. The other cows had beautiful steers used for beef. Papa bartered his bulls to get the best jerseys for good milk cows.

"Crowder peas" were grown by most, but we grew "Purple Hull" peas. Papa made sure that we picked all of the dried peas. This was the only time when an allergy or something would strike me. I had done everything with peas from the preparation of the soil, planting to picking and shelling them, so there had to be some weed growing with the dried peas that smothered me. I was just about to pass out when Papa noticed that I was not picking dried peas, but was grabbing my throat.

He asked, "What in the heck is wrong with you?"

I whispered, "I don't know, but I can't get my breath."

Next, I saw the horse coming, and I thought he was going to check me out. He just wrapped that whip around me a few times and that surprise got my breath back rather quickly.

I began trying to hold my breath as long as I could, and that seemed to help some. I couldn't believe that I would get this whipping from a man who was allergic to everything. He was allergic to ragweed, goldenrod and all kinds of wild weeds that bloomed, yet just beats the tar out of me for being allergic to something in the pea patch. In addition, he had medicine for sinuses, hay fever, laxative, headaches, and Lord only knows what else he took. My Mama never took any pills. She never complained and never took any medication if she did feel bad.

After all the peas were picked, they were put in burlap sacks, taken to the barn yard at the center of the barn hall and placed on the tarps left by the soldiers. Then each of us would step and stomp on these trying to stomp enough until we thought they were separated from the shells. This was not a bad job. We just did an "Indian Dance" to crush them. Then, I would climb barefoot up the ladder to the first "lean to" and climbed up the "gambrel roof" edge and on to the top of the old barn. This was a tin roof, and with the load I carried up there with me, I had to use my right hand to hold onto the edge of the tin roof and the sack of peas with the other until I got to the top.

I was the only one who could or would do this. I was never afraid of heights and had great balance. Once at the apex of the barn, I put my feet on opposite sides of the ridge. I then held the crushed peas out to fall on the tarp and the wind would blow the shaft away. This was called winnowing the peas. If there were peas which didn't get smashed enough, the same procedure was repeated until all of the dried peas were clear of the shell. These peas were for seed, as well as having dried peas for a meal. Then they were soaked overnight in hot water then cooked for the next day's meal. Thank God, the wind had blown strong enough to blow the shaft away, each time, but left me on the top of the barn. This barn roof was very tall with a huge loft. Being so high, I had to look out to see if Joe had been resurrected at some time, and was coming after me.

Each time that I slid down, it was fun until I hit a place where the nail was or the tin had been turned up from a storm. Then you would get sliced down the center of your foot or a toe ripped opened. Each of us would climb up as high as they felt safe and slide down. Mama would just wash our feet with lye soap and then put iodine on it. With horses and mules, it was a miracle that we did not get tetanus.

CHAPTER 12

Papa, Friends and Ted KKK

Papa didn't talk politics to anyone except a very few people he knew well, and their thoughts were the same as his. They were Mr. Hebert, Monsieux, Shehee, L. Fontenot, J.Boudrieux and Ted. Along with my Papa, they formed a vigilante group who kept the Ku Klux Klan from marauding against the blacks or raping the women.

In order to stay ahead of the Klansmen, they had to infiltrate the meetings, by wearing the white headgear and robes. Ted kept a sack on the horse to stash his disguise as soon as he finished playing the mole. Two or three would take turns being the mole and each time they rode a different horse. Papa and Mama sometimes took trips on Sunday afternoon to Uncle Levi's and Aunt Annie's house. They went to visit primarily so that Papa could visit about the Vigilante Group actions. Sometimes we had the opportunity to go and play with their children. Those memories will be cherished forever. The men and the women visited separately. The women knew nothing about the men's KKK infiltration. This was my Mama's brother and sister-in-law. These seven vigilantes straightened out the sorry group who lived near us. They would ride sometimes for miles to catch the KKK around their fire talking about where and what they were going to do next. Mr. Hebert usually found out from friends who he knew were in the KKK and kept all the others informed. The Klan didn't know who all their members were. No one could afford to look suspicious.

Many of Ted's own siblings didn't know about his or my Papa's role against the KKK, and were never informed. It was top secret for many years. Had they or any of the members of the vigilante group been found out, they would certainly have been killed or burned out. My Papa truly believed that they suspected him, but couldn't prove it. They did however, burn Papa out at three different places and times.

CHAPTER 13

Wood Cutting

Several years had passed when Papa got a tractor with a belt to turn the flywheel of a huge ripsaw for cutting the fire logs into different lengths. This saved a lot of time, because previously it was all done by a "cross-cut" saw. This required several of the boys swapping off. I wished that we had gotten the tractor years before. The mules would first pull the prepared logs up to the cutting place. It took at least two people to lift the log and keep it sliding up to the saw. This was "back breaking," even with a tractor. Two more would be taking limbs off with the axes and two others to chain up three trees together for the mules to drag out of the woods to be sawed. All the mules and kids stayed busy. Now with the tractor, this was just a 3-week job in the fall instead for 2 months with hiring extra help with more cross-cut saws to use. This was our only means of heat. After the wood for all the fireplaces were finished, the pine logs from the back woods, was done almost the same way. The difference was that the tree was much taller, larger in diameter, and were cut in about 15 inch blocks to be split with an axe, and often using a sledge hammer and a wedge. It took a team of mules to pull one log to be cut. Those huge trees were needed for the 2 wood stoves for Mama and Lili.

Then the younger ones, using a mule and slide took the pile of cut wood for the fireplaces to the house and stacked it neatly in cords. However, with our fireplaces being of 3 different widths, it took different lengths of logs. The kitchen fireplace took the 4 foot fire logs. The living room took the 3' length, and the rest of them were for the bedrooms, which took 2' to 2.5' lengths. They were used less in the wintertime unless someone was sick. This meant that the slide needed to have the same length of logs on it to know which "stack" to unload them.

There were too many trees in the way to take the tractor in this area, when we finally got one. With five boys in service, we had to have the tractor. Just to have a common dumping place for the tractor to pull up to the band-saw was great. Some of the team of mules had been sold by then. This probably was used to help pay for the tractor.

Sometime during real cold weather, the boys cut some fresh wood for each of the fireplaces because they had more sap in them and these gave out more moist heat. This was the kind of sappy wood, which was on the big fire when I was burned so badly. The fire just lapped all around the log once a lot of old wood had been burning first to make it steaming hot to warm for the house.

Evette was most useful in getting wood for the two old wood stoves used more when the hired hands were there. This was pretty much a continuous job for her as well as Andre when he got old enough to help. She also learned to cook and iron and do things in the kitchen that I never learned to do. At least, Mama had a little extra help for her and Lili. Evette didn't pick nor chop cotton or milk the cows, but she did plenty for Mama and learned a lot. She did the stove wood hauling. My job was out in the fields.

One night, someone burned the corn shed as well as the addition which held the tractor and all the equipment. The main shed was burning out of control by the time one of us noticed it. It had to have started underneath the building and ignited by some kind of fuel. The fire was getting bigger and hotter quickly. It was dark and late and whoever started this had slipped off in the back so they would not be seen. If Cedric had been living there then, he would have heard them and saw the fire earlier. He would have shot them. His camp house was near enough to have heard the dogs or animals squirreling around making noises. There would be no corn after this, but Ted ran out to save the tractor and the equipment.

It got so hot while Ted was getting the tractor out, that he took chains and a rope to pull the equipment out as fast as he could. None of the fuel was in this building. If it had been, most all the machinery and perhaps the house as well as the big barn would have been gone with this fire. All our fuel was kept in the garage near the old "T-Model." It was a blessing that they didn't know that. None of us told things of that nature, because there was rationing of fuel along with many other things. Our business was kept to ourselves. All of the plows, wagons, harnesses, and other equipment were kept in the big barn where the mules were. We were thankful for that. The big barn had a tin roof and the embers from the fire were not blown in that direction. The wind was blowing directly toward our house, which had the tin roof replaced with the cypress shakes.

Now we had to keep them from burning. Papa was drawing water from the deep well and filling the washtubs for soaking quilts to place on the cypress shakes to prevent them from burning. Two tubs were placed on the block in front of the well for easy filling. When a quilt had soaked up the water, I ran up and down the ladder with the dripping quilts.

Mama, Evette and Andre were on top of the south side of the house all ready to receive the wet quilts and spread them out quickly as I could get another one up the ladder to them. Then I would hurry down again for the next one. The cypress shingles were soaking the water out of the quilts rapidly. It seemed as though none of this was happening fast enough. The large embers from the burning corn-cobs were hitting the wet quilts. They would scorch the quilt before anyone could get to it.

The shucks were flying like a burning bird, but by the time the wind had blown them to the roof, they were just hot ashes. As long as they were not hitting the rest of the roof, we would be fine. The burning cobs were heavier, so they landed in the pasture. If the wind had been stronger, we would have lost the house and surrounding sheds, even though they had tin roofs. Just landing on the sides of the buildings, the cobs would have caught the wood siding on fire.

However, we did put the last quilts on the east side where some of the shucks were blowing onto the roof. Then the handy use of brooms to sweep some of these out into the yard was faster for us than re-soaking quilts. By keeping an eye on the rest of the house, the brooms were the swiftest way to sweep off the stray embers. There were not very many hitting the other side of the house. As soon as the large embers hit a quilt, it was swept off quickly. All were working hard, running from one side of the roof to another

I knew that Mama was in great shape for her age, but running all over the sloping roof certainly surprised us all. Papa drawing water as fast as he did surprised each of us also. Soon we were able to stop, and leave the wet quilts on top of the house. However, pulling a wet quilt off the cypress shakes would have torn them or pulled some cypress shakes off, so that was the reason to use the big buckets of water. Handling the buckets of water was more demanding for going up the ladder, than the wet quilts. Holding a bucket full with each hand was easier than just one. I balanced well, but would stopped a second if I needed to. Each would grab a bucket when I got near enough to them, and then it was just poured on the quilts. This gave them a good soaking. Now, more running up the ladder with buckets of water was needed. The last ones took care of the job. They just poured water on the quilts, which were spread all over the roof.

I had no idea that we had so many quilts. However, when you consider the number of beds we had and maybe needing two quilts for each bed in the wintertime, it was more understandable. This was the only time I had ever seen my Papa working so quickly and without any help. He had to draw that water with ungloved hands as fast as he could. Those tubs had to be filled quickly for soaking the quilts. I am sure he was worked like a slave in his younger days, but I wanted to see this done. He had no choice. He was too old for the roof and riding the horse every day did not give him much physical exercise. After the plantation was on its way, about all the work he did was to be the slave driver. Driving the bus was not exercise. He was just getting older.

This ended the farming, as we had known it for years. Ted decided to go to college, hoping Uncle Sam would not find out that he was not farming anymore. Hired hands were hard to find now because they were getting old now. As soon they found out that they could get on the State Welfare, they did so. Someone got a "kick-back" from them to get them on and they were too naïve or frightened to tell them that it was against the law to pay someone for this privilege.

Ted and Papa believed that it probably was an appointed "police-jury-men" who was in charge of checking the qualifications of those who applied for the welfare program. Many were blacks who gave the fee, as well as some lazy and ignorant whites who got on long before they were old enough to qualify. This cheating went on in each of the parishes. The politics in Louisiana during this time was very corrupt, and kept the elected officials in office due to the welfare program.

The ballot boxes on election day were stuffed and this was rampant throughout the state. Each parish had several jurymen for that district, depending on size and population. Some would do most anything to get a little extra money, even if it was illegal. It was also illegal to pay the political appointee a percentage for this appointment.

The hard working blacks were good people who worked for Ted, but they were getting old now and could get more money for doing nothing every day, and just were not physically able to do the picking or chopping cotton in the heat as they could when they were younger. They took the welfare even if they had to pay some bucks to get on. I felt that they had earned it by this time. They put in many years of hard labor working on the plantation for us. Most of the others who got on were what I called "leeches."

Ted found out, but did not report the blacks who had worked so hard for him. He was not about to turn their name in, because they would end up getting killed. Ted and Papa guessed correctly and knew that the "leech" would do anything to get ahead, if it did not require physical work. They stole as much as they could get by with along with this fraud. No one would turn them in, so the scandal continued.

Ted loved school, worked his way driving a bus for the city. He was brilliant but no one saw that drive in him to learn as much as possible. However, just as he finished his last semester in mathematics and physics, he was drafted. He didn't get to stay long enough for graduation exercises. His diploma was mailed to the farm and saved for him. He was never shipped out over seas. The army needed a physicist, a mathematician and he did statistical research for the TOP BRASS on weekends. That is why they kept him there. The Generals and Colonels had finished college but had long forgotten all the mathematics or didn't know physics at all. Their trigonometry and calculus had been forgotten if they had ever had it. Ted never enjoyed being in the service. After his two years were up, "he hung it up," as the Cajuns would say.

CHAPTER 14

Free Time on Plantation

Sunday afternoon was when we had free time. This only lasted until time to milk cows as well as other chores. Some of the free time that I remember which has not been mentioned before and was great fun was playing marbles.

We played marbles often. In the marble game, you drew a circle about four feet in diameter in the dirt. (Dirt was all that was in our yard due to all the activity, which was in operation all the time.) Then sixteen feet away a line was drawn, which was called the "lag" line. Each person had to lag (pitch) their marble to see who was nearest the lag line. This determined who went first to shoot at the marbles put in the middle of the circle.

The idea was to knock all of your opponent's marbles out of the ring. If you did, you kept them; they were yours. You kept your turn until you (missed) or were not able to knock one outside the ring. The next person does the same until he loses his turn. The one who received the most marbles won the game and got to keep all the marbles that they knocked out.

Another fun game was walking on "homemade tom-walkers" or stilts. We got them from an ironwood tree usually, and looked for a good fork in the limb. It had to have some distance between the fork and the top, which needed to be long, strong and sturdy, and the bottom was the length of your choice.

We got on these barefooted to prevent ruining our shoes or boots. Since we could run on a gravel road, you know that these stilts didn't hurt us because we had worn calluses all over the bottom and sides of our feet anyway. We would have races, play catch, jump the ditches and kick the can. This was great fun for me because I was more agile and smaller than the boys were.

Another fun time was called "squirrel and dog." This was a made up game of ours and I doubt anyone else ever played it. The "dog" would hide their eyes to the count of twenty-five and the squirrels would take off down to the end of the pasture where the pine trees grew. I was the only one small enough to use a sapling. The boys needed one bigger than a sapling. The idea was for the dog to try to tag them in the tree.

To prevent from being tagged, you would swing the pine tree back and forth enough to propel you to the next tree. You had to hold on tight or slip down or be caught by the dog. The dog would do the same leaping from tree to tree. I was usually the last for the dog to try to tag in the tree. I could use the little saplings that grew close together and the boys couldn't. This game was always done in the late spring while there was lots of sap in them and they bent easily for the sway. This was surely a dangerous sport, but fun.

The boys would swing all the way down toward the swamp. Once Richet had his tree swinging well because he was about to get caught and had to get all the way over to a larger tree that he didn't want to be in, but he had no choice. He made the leap all right, but it knocked the breath out of him and he slid down, skinning his stomach with abrasions all the way to the bottom of the tree. He was caught, but that ended the play for that day. He even peeled some bark off that tree that stuck to him and shredded his shirt. We got him home where Mama fixed him up with kerosene to get the tar and bark off, lye soap to get the kerosene off, and clean the skinned up places on his arms and torso. He was "bummed up." This was fun to me because I had no one else to play with, so they allowed me to join in.

Usually the boys went fishing on Saturday night and they would always catch a large number of catfish, bream and bass. These were all brought home during the morning early enough for the morning chores. On one of those fishing trips, Ted and Boulean cleaned a place for me at the mouth of the bayou and the river so that I could invite the softball team fishing. After being cleaned from all the brush and briars, I took Ms. Sandris and the team fishing several times. A great time was had by all. A little fishing, swimming and wading was done also.

Ms. Sandris was also my math teacher, and a great one at that. No one ever left her classroom without learning all the mathematics she had to offer. She was a great role model. This began from the time she observed me growing up in elementary school, and helped me tremendously as a cripple. She encouraged me to work out with the softball team. She took care of the fire escape problem fast by having me as "bat girl" and warming up in running with the girls before they played. I was the smallest, but strong as an ox. No one except the coaches saw this in me as I grew up. This was a blessing that I reaped and it paid off in the end. When I graduated from high school, I just wore a cotton heel-pad that Mama fixed to build up my heel, and no one noticed a limp. I walked just as normal as anyone.

On rainy days, we wanted to whittle items for Christmas gifts. We made all kinds of toys, sawed and whittle for a gun rack for Papa. We also made some items for Mama such as a back scratcher and spatulas for use in the kitchen. These same things were made for Lili also. You can now see some of the uses for the pocket knives, which each of us had.

Football was one of the favorites. Some of the cousins would ride horses over to play with us. They needed me to be the center but not to do anything but center the ball for the quarterback. Richet played this spot most every time. We only had one goal post, so we just played from the fifty-yard line.

We played with a syrup bucket as our ball, and that put some hurt on you if you didn't catch it just right. Once, after centering the ball for Richet, he threw the bucket to Jay who was being rushed and the bucket hit him in the head, and fights began. The game was over and no score kept for that game.

One Christmas had to have been a good year for cotton, logging and the bartering, because we were so excited over all the Christmas gifts. Even though we had wrapped gifts, the paper was smoothed out and saved year after year. The little cedar tree was decorated with sweet-gum balls, carefully wrapped with foil found on the road from old cigarette packs. They glisten from the fire in the fireplace. That was all we had to decorate the tree, other than little whittled out ornaments covered with foil, and gifts for Papa and Mama and Lili, which was stuck neatly through the branches. They were surprised with the back-scratchers, kitchen utensils and gun rack. We had some rather novel ideas for items to whittle or saw up for Mama, Papa and Lili.

A time that I shall never forget was when Richet received a "real" plastic football as a gift to be filled with air. Richet was so excited he could've wet his pants and began immediately pulling the stem out so he could blow it up. He pulled too hard and pulled the stem all the way out. He was devastated over this and began tearing up. Mama saw him and immediately grabbed the torn football and stuffed the football with cotton (saved for her quilting) and sewed it up. That worked. He was happy and so were the rest of us because the stuffed football was better than the air filled one anyway. The rest of us received gifts of marbles, apples, firecrackers and a coconut which was immediately given to Mama for a coconut cake.

I was about seven and Evette was three and a half years old, when each received our first dolls and a buggy. These dolls would cry when turned upside down. This had us pondering what was going on in these dolls. We got these gifts from Santa (whoever he was), before he ran out for the first time. We had never seen a doll, much less one which cried, or a buggy before. We started trying to see why these dolls cried and began to pry into them up before the dolls were ever put in the buggy. We had hard surfaces along the trails which we would push each other in the doll buggies. The buggy couldn't take this for very long. We couldn't tell the buggies apart so we rode in them and of course, we tore them up before the "torn dolls" ever got in them. Both of the dolls were as good as gone!" We never saw anything from Santa after that except fruit and marbles.

Grandpa taught the boys how to build a cart to be pulled by our goats. The goats were used primarily for keeping the fence line clean from grass or for "bar-b-que". They had homemade harnesses so that we could pull on the reins to train them. The goats didn't like these wire bits, so this made them easy to train. This was fun for all the young folks.

Then he taught the boys how to build a cart for the steers to pull. Grandpa's plans were drawn for a larger cart and much stronger. These patterns were copies just like Grandpa had remembered from the one he brought back from Texas. The harnesses had to be larger and stronger as well. Hard work was used here for this job. A great time was had by all. The boys had a grand time with the carts and steers.

We just rode the horses, slid down the tin barn top, or staying balanced, while walking on the 2" x 12" barn fences for fun. These large and heavy barnyard fences were to keep the Brahma cattle or the wild horses from jumping out from the perimeter of the barn pens. The boys trained the wild horses. They would jump the fences if left out in the pasture. Therefore, they had to chain their harness to one leg. This prevented them from jumping at all. I probably could've ridden one of them if he had the chain on. They still had free range for eating and drinking. Some of our best horses for riding were mares and much easier to train.

However, it seemed that each horse that I enjoyed riding was a male and sometimes quite "skittish." I had made a point to "knee him" in the belly so he would not take a deep breath. Then the girth was tightened so that I would not be thrown anymore if he tried to dart sideways, anymore.

CHAPTER 15

Country Jealousy

One of first reasons for this jealousy was because Isabelle was sent to college during the depression. The local people had no ambition for being educated, much less going to college. Many of them were welfare people, but Papa worked them and paid them just like the all the rest

The blacks were never jealous. They were prepared and eager to have someone who cared enough for them to make a twenty four mile round trip to pick them up and take them to the job. This went on day after day and year after year.

The next reason for all the people who coveted what Papa had was the amount of land he owned, and also added to it by buying out the heirs to Grandpa's plantation. Then, to find out that he had the first gasoline powered generator, when gas was rationed just made matters worse. They had to have found out by working for us and seeing it in the back shed of the wash house which only had a bottom "half-wall." This was where the wringer washer was kept, and of course, they had to noticed that. This building was 40' long. A lot of equipment was stored here as well as the lye soap in the loft. There were tools that needed sharpening or clothes to be washed each time the generator was cranked up.

They were so full of envy. They couldn't stand it. Someone had to do him in. After Papa started farming the land and having cattle in Grandpa's old pecan orchard, then Grandpa's house was rented. After those people moved out, the house burned. Why was all this happening? Mama didn't have the time to spend scrubbing all the clothes on a washboard. That was why Papa got the washer at the same time as the generator to run it. She had to get this done and out of the way, so that she could cook for the large crew, and help Lili who took over most all of the cooking while Mama did the washing. Mama and Lili worked diligently with each chore.

We worked hard for all we had. We fed many of these people and sometime they would work for us, if they felt like it. My Papa watched them like a hawk because they would steal any and everything they could get their hands on. That was one reason Papa stayed on the horse and had his rifle, pistol, whip and rope. He would have used it on anyone if he thought any needed it. Some of them were KKK people and Papa knew them, but never allowed anyone to know who they were; nor that he and Ted were part of the Vigilante Group. He made sure that I was in a different field from them also. Ted knew where to put them as well.

They didn't work too often. It seemed as though they only worked to find out or see what was going on as well as where everything was. Papa had them led away with some of the blacks who knew to keep that bunch away from the barns. Cedric was great at directing the group so that the women would not be bothered.

With all this being said, nothing was ever mentioned about how our help was treated; or how often he gave produce to others as well as hiring anyone willing to work. I thought we were poor people. These local folks had "store-bought" clothes, nice shoes, and hats and lunch boxes. They even had "store-bought" sliced bread. We didn't have all that. Papa only bought items that were needed and we went without these needless items.

That generator was used as one would use a plow or tractor. It was a tool! We had the kerosene lamps just as our ancestors had. It took gasoline to run the generator and since Papa farmed and drove the school bus, he was able to get plenty of gasoline and oil or tires as needed. It was rationed for all others.

My Mama had been using a big block of wood to "beat" the old overalls and then a rub board to get the dirt out of the clothes during potato digs. The washer was a "God-send" and came with the matching tubs.

Cedric and Ted built the long bench that the tubs set on so Mama didn't have to bend down to place the clothes after they had gone through the ringer. This gave Mama the opportunity to save many hours as well as her back. The two wash pots were used for boiling water for the washer to do the laundry, cooking figs, lye soap as well as boiling water for scalding hogs after they were killed to scrap the hair off. These were multipurpose pots used for many very different things. Everyone had an old wash pot to use for something.

Our clothesline consisted of four wires about one block long, there were four posts to hold four lines of clothes. These held the slave's, their children and grandchildren's clothes along with our clothes, or anyone living with us after we got the washer machine. Mama had plenty of help but made sure the pieces were organized on the line. There were usually three or four helpers for Mama on washday. They share-croppers had the use of the machine, but hung their clothes on their own line for accessibility.

Each post was well braced and poles from the "ironwood tree" were used to help prop the lines high enough to prevent any from dragging on the ground. When all were dry, sheets were used to spread on the grassy area for gathering clothes, and sorting them for each person. All overalls went in one sheet except Evette's and mine. The slaves sorted theirs on another sheet. Towels, washcloths and dishcloths were put in another sheet, shirts and so on, until all were bundled up and taken to their respective places to be folded. The boys and I didn't fold clothes.

That was for Mama and her helpers to make sure they were clean as they handled them and left them on the bed for one who would be wearing them to put where they belonged. They made the beds, and then placed the clothes on it. We had no closets at this time, but a homemade table for most folded clothes in each room and nails in back of the door for hanging clothes. The line was well organized with work clothes separated from the sheets, towels, school clothes and dress-up clothes.

One could always tell when a new one was born because the diapers (flour sacks) were hanging altogether. Later, when times were good and Mama had to order cotton sack material, she would also order several yards of "muslin" and make her own diapers. Mama did the wash on Mondays if it didn't rain, and she used a "bluing" to help clean and brighten the clothes. The name, "Blue Monday" came from the "bluing" used in the cleaning process. Most all households used it in washing clothes, whether they had a washer or not.

We were lucky and happy when Papa got the generator. The generator started with a crank like the car had. We had a large number of hired hands then. With the soldiers in the front 40 acres, Papa might have even gotten it from the Unit Leader. He was impressed by the work that went on at the plantation, and had never seen anything like it, and likewise, Papa was impressed with the set-up the soldiers had.

After the war was over, the army didn't need a lot of material and food, along with tarps, camouflage nets, and some machinery and tools were given to us. I know that we were given a lot of food, such as onions, sliced bread and different fruits and nuts. That was like Christmas to us.

While Isabelle was out of work with babies, Papa built a store in Eunice, Louisiana to help them and maybe help himself. During this time, the store must have made good money because there were only two places to shop; the other store included the Post Office in the small town. The store kept Isabelle and family financially stable. After a year, Isabelle went back to teaching and Boudreau ran the store. Before long the store in Eunice burned.

After the store burned, there was nothing left but ashes, broken jars and lids scattered everywhere. They only sold groceries: no tools, shoes or clothing. There were people who were assumed guilty of burning the store; but this couldn't be proven. I always thought the old man who stole the hog, burned us out because Papa caught him "red-handed" with the hog. The store was too far away to keep a watch. Who would think that someone would burn it? Papa just "sucked it up" and went on with his business. However, it did mean less income for my sister, her husband and their kids. Her husband was able to go back with the butane company shortly after that. The property that Papa bought from all the heirs of Grandpa's was used for corn, gardens and the pecan orchard for pasture. I didn't mind, because I didn't have to put up with listening to my Grandma raising hell at Mama. Keeping Grandma part-time was the primary reason Papa got a good price for the land. However, it was a living hell for my Mama. She had enough to do and this was going too far, unless he was going to hire someone to take care of HIS Mama. Grandma Thibodeaux was senile and had no control over bodily functions.

There was an old man who lived nearby that would make our mattresses. He had plenty of cotton for ours and was allowed to have enough to sell mattresses to others. That was one way he made a living. He also made some furniture. Papa bought a chifferobe which he made. It was nine feet tall and eight feet wide. It took all the boys to wiggle it into the living room. That was the only place that had enough room for it. The living room was 20' x 20'. The boys room was the same size, but it was full of beds. It was well made and very heavy. It held extra quilts and had a small section for hanging clothes. Mama kept extra feed sacks and flour sacks in it along with some of Papa's outfits. There were several shelves for shelves for Mama's uses. Evette and I didn't keep anything in it. Our clothes were hung on nails which were driven on the back side of the homemade door. We didn't have many clothes, but the ones we did have were clean and ironed for school. The rest were folded and put in an old apple box stacked behind the door. The boys had nails on the back of two doors for their clothes as well.

We were one of just a few cotton farmers who raised cotton nearby. In the winter, we had the feather mattress switched to the top of the bed. Mama had picked the soft feathers underneath the neck of chickens after killing them for meals and saved the feathers in a sack until she had enough to fill a pillow or a mattress. She knew that they would always be needed soon.

Soon another storm blew up from the Gulf of Mexico. It took off a half of the back end of the house because it was tall enough under it for a five foot kid to walk under the back two sections. In this storm, the kitchen, dining room and two bedrooms were scattered everywhere. Papa immediately had all hands busy with the building. This time he made it the same height, but was a 40' square divided into four rooms.

All was finished on the outside and the roof first. Then the kitchen, dining room and two bedrooms were section off and sheetrock used on the walls instead of cypress boards.

The old man who made mattresses and the chifferobe was asked if he would like to finish the inside with the sheet rock walls and build the closets between Mama and Papa's bedroom. He did want the job and needed it to supplement his income. He was hired immediately so that the rest of the hired hands could get back to the fields. .

Late one evening after the old man left along with all the hired hands, Mama had time to check the building process. When Mama saw how Papa told the old man how he wanted the closets, she knew nothing about it until they were almost finished. They were only six inches deep on the inside. She was devastated. She couldn't store quilts and would have to hand her clothes on a nail or hung sideways. She was not going to have this. She had labored too hard to put up with this, so she got the crowbar and began tearing one side of them down. Papa heard the commotion and began jerking the crowbar from her. Unbeknownst to him, the boys were right there behind him. They picked him up by the arm pits, and dragged him out to the pasture under a pen oak tree and sat him down. They addressed the situation, and told him that if it was to be done, it would be her way. However wide or deep she wanted them, that would be the way they would be built. That was all it took, and he added the closets just as she wanted them.

Now she had a place to hang plenty of clothes properly as well as storing quilts and some dressy clothes which belonged to each of us.

I remember when Grandpa died that his funeral was on the front porch and the yard in front of that large plantation farmhouse. It was full of people, both black and white. I found it quite amusing when he told me the story of getting kicked out of church. It made him furious, because they were just racing home. The "powers-that-be" thought it was a bet, as in gambling. Nevertheless, he bought ten acres for a cemetery near the church where they had been going. He saved three of those acres for the Thibodeaux family and their heirs if they wanted it.

He specified that it couldn't be used by those who were responsible for having him kicked out of the church. That was where almost all of the family and others were buried. Upon returning from his funeral, people assumed that he had buried his money under the blocks and piers of the house. They had dug under each one to no avail. They left very disappointed. This shows another means of theft and jealousy.

People who did have an old car were jealous of Papa when he bought the new "stripped down" car. They never admired him for his work ethics, hard work and diligence. My Mama's folks were quite different. They were not jealous. They were saddened by the fact that neither my Papa nor the family ever visited with them very often.

I think the only time Papa went there was when he asked for Mama's hand in marriage. Papa thought they were just lazy. He didn't care if they thought he was cruel to work each of us like a bunch of slaves. They didn't have the funds to buy the property like Papa and his Grandpa Thibodeaux, nor had the opportunity for an education.

Mama's brothers would've liked to work for the railroad if they had known about it. Some did work for Papa on the farm, though. Some of Mama's siblings worked for Papa and I worked for some of them for college money. Another was a blessing for my Mama was Uncle Duran who stayed while Isabelle had diphtheria. Uncle Jeremiah and Ike did well. Nonetheless, people didn't have the unmitigated drive to succeed as Papa had, and he would've had not been for the suffering of all that my that Mama bore.

CHAPTER 16

Hard Work Went for This

As mentioned earlier, when I realized that I was not about to stay on the plantation and was going to go to college like most of the others, I started saving all I could. Mama had been saving by kicking money under the bed, which fell out of my Papa's britches. If he never looked for it before bedtime, she kicked it under the bed. Then later she picked it up and hid it. She "baby-sat" with Pierre, Isabelle's only son, and saved most all of it for me. I never knew how much she was paid but I did reap that for personal hygiene and more.

Each time when we finished a farming job, I would ride the horse to Uncle Levi's house, or some of Papa's friends to see if they needed cotton picked or plowing to be done. I could use their tractors or mules. They along with my Mama always knew that I wanted to go to college like my coaches and older sister, as well as six of my brothers after they got out of service. I wanted to be a teacher like my coaches who helped me emotionally and physically when I was crippled.

I loved them both and wanted to double major in both subjects and be a role model for others someday. They were wonderful to me and I hoped that I could do as much for my students when I became a teacher as they did. I was so determined to make it, and planned to work my brains and farming ability to do it. I believed that we all had our Papa's desire to succeed and my Mama encouraged it to the end. A few items had to be purchased before leaving for college. Mama strongly insisted that we go to town and purchase some underclothes, 2 white blouses, tennis shoes and a pair of heels for church.

Plantation life was over for me. I believed that I could do anything if I wanted to bad enough. The environment in which I grew up was done. Had I only one dress and had to wash and dry it every night I would've done it to reach my goal. I was going to stick it out. My Mama knew that I would do it. It didn't matter what I had or didn't have, and no matter what other people thought of me, I was going to college. When I was on the way to the campus with Mama and Papa, I knew that I was well out of my "comfort zone." This plantation culture from which I was raised never made it past the depression years of the 30's. The people I would meet would be able to tell that I came from the swamps. They would know that I would have to claw my way out of the darkness of naiveté. I was determined to break this chain of ignorance.

Most of the people where I grew up succumbed to the norm. At the time and place, most from the plantation territory either married too young, or had to get married, and some just had babies before finishing school with different fathers. They would continue the "give to me" attitude, which most "welfare" recipients received. This attitude was "widespread" in the country, perpetuating the cycle from one generation to the other.

CHAPTER 17

1st Teaching Job: 1st Day

This first day was a teacher workday at school on Monday with the principal escorting me around to meet and greet everyone. All seemed pleased to meet me, and one in particular made sure that I had everything I needed and had met all the teachers. She was especially in control of the gregarious, "hail-fellow-well-met demeanor" which I thought was out of my comfort zone. Her name was Marjane.

Marjane Moureau taught across the hall from me and persisted that I meet her nephew, Jean Fromond. She, along with her siblings and her friends at school, made sure that I met him. On my free hour after school started, I ran to get a biscuit (which was my free breakfast) from the lunchroom, and there was Marjane and some of the other teachers, with Jean. She could hardly wait to introduce me to him. They didn't like the girl with whom he had been engaged after he came home from the Korean War. Jean worked offshore as a "Seismic Exploration Agent" with an oil company at this time.

He was with his Aunt Marjane each time he came home from working in the gulf, which was every two weeks. Their antics were as foolish as elementary kids, waiting to see if I would soon be there. I was embarrassed, stunned and was not impressed at all with their launch to start a relationship.

Marjane and others, as well as one of her cousins who was a state trooper, did all the research on me and my family to find out if I was good enough for their family. They even had the audacity to tell me this. I was not only shocked, but also angered at this statement. After the research on me, the family was persistent to push this relationship. I was scared, and each weekend that he was to be home, I went fishing on a little creek near home. I found this place before school started, which was just a few miles from where I was renting from the first grade teacher at the school.

When I returned, which was late, the 1st grade teacher said that Marjane, her sisters and friends had been desperately trying to find me.

They were upset because they couldn't locate me. I told her to tell them next time that I was not in the habit of telegraphing my "whereabouts" to anyone when or where I was going.

The next day was Sunday and I went to church. When I arrived, I was met by so many wanting me to teach their Sunday School Class. I certainly did not expect this situation just because I could teach school. I went to learn the Bible and was shocked when they approached me with this issue. I stayed for the service and never returned. I broke my own promise by not going back and joining an adult class.

Upon my return to school, the group came at me again because I had missed a chance to be with Jean. They led me to believe that a lady my age of 22, who was not married, would be shunned and thought of as being "gay." I was not sure what they meant by that statement, but was soon told by others what it meant. I wanted to be single like her from the beginning. Why did I not say something when they said people would say ugly things about me if I remained single? Why, Marjane was at least 45 and had never married. Why is she allowed to say this to me? Why did I sit there and take this, without anyone having the audacity to ask her why she never married?

I had never dated any one person, that turned me on and these conversations certainly turned me off. I needed to make a living for a while instead of turmoil and uncertainties. I was hurt with what they had said, but I didn't know how to handle it. I was so ignorant about this because I had never heard anyone talk like this. Are they manipulating me against my interest? I thought about this quite a while, but still didn't know anyone with whom I should ask.

I didn't want to be with Jean or anyone. I didn't know how to handle the family and their friends who were pushing this relationship with him. I was teaching there and knew that somehow it had to be handled gracefully, with dignity, and certainty, and be sincere of my feelings.

I started buying cereal for breakfast instead of having a biscuit each school morning. I didn't care for cereal, because I didn't like milk on it, so I used water and sugar. To me, my hands smelled too much like those cows that I milked every morning before school. This cereal cut into my budget, so I just ate it twice a week before school and neglected the coffee break. I thought this would cut down on the gossip also and the visits with Jean. The next time I saw him, I had the girls basketball tournament. I would not dare tolerate the girls knowing that someone was interested in me.

He would go to the game and I ignored him. Finally, by mid-October, they came up with a way that we could be together. Someone, whom they all supported, was running for President and they needed some help sealing envelopes to be mailed off for this campaign. Of course, Jean was there. If I had any idea that he would be there, I would've turned down the invitation. They had us over to visit for anything and everything. It became a chore that they needed help on something, or I was invited for a meal with the aunts or his folks. This was easy for them to take turns because Marjane lived with her sister, so each would ask me at different times and with different emotional needs and ideas. They would not leave me alone. I caught onto what they were trying to do with me, but I still didn't know how to deal with the situation without being downright offensive or unpleasant. I wanted so much to talk to someone I could trust with this, but didn't.

After all, this was my first teaching job and I needed encouragement and praise for doing a darn good job as a math teacher as well as coach. We were winning all the games and I worked out more than the team. They couldn't believe that I could work out with each group running plays.

Two weeks later, I went to see Mama and Papa. Andre was the only one left of the siblings still at home. I was determined to "get lost," and I did not care about being with any of them. Evette had started at LSU-Lafayette and was working her way through school, just as I did. It was challenging for me, but I needed to do this for my peace of mind. I wanted to talk to them about what all was happening at school; and thought they would have noticed that I was bothered by something. I needed to tell them what was happening. I was too embarrassed to bring it up because I didn't date in high school. I wanted to tell them about Jean and regretted many times that I didn't have the intestinal fortitude to talk to them about him.

I felt very relieved for having gone down, especially this time. I believe that I had at least, ended the bitterness and sadness that Papa had for me leaving home. I was rather late figuring this out. He was just not brought up that way and neither was I. I know that he could see the love that Mama and I had for each other. There was a bond that we had long before as a youngster. He would try to reach out for the same hugs, but they were not tight hugs as my Mama's hugs. I knew that he meant them to be the same. I felt sure of that.

Again, back at school, the group wondering where I was over the weekend and chastised me about the gossip that would start. Marjane had her troop of teachers with her at all times, and it seldom had to do with pleasure of visiting me. Other times it was an invitation to morning biscuits and coffee. Each of them made sure that others were around listening to the conversation and each time Jean's name was brought up. This had to be their reinforcement schemes.

Why would people care whether I was 20 or 45 years old? So, still ignorant about it all, I began seeing Jean almost all the time at school because they had him quit his Gulf job and got him a job at a well-known family store at Joli Vean's. He was "Head of Furniture and Appliances" at the store. The store opened at nine, and he was at the school by eight. Can you see the "CONTROL" coming through? This was becoming another type of slave driving, but I believed it was the lack of control with her tongue instead, and my lack of guts to put a stop to all of this.

I had high expectations of myself working harder than any one. Why am I letting these people intimidate me? I prayed asking God what to do and didn't know how to pray. I asked for any kind of help. I knew that I believed in Jesus Christ and I needed Him, but lacked the daily fellowship with Him. What was wrong with me? What can I do to end this right now?

Why did I forget about going back to church? Someone would've taken a different approach toward me. I should've gotten involved at church, that would've stopped this, eventually, and God would've listened to me. I know that someone at church would have helped me.

I was ignorant about dating, because the only real dating I had done in college was with groups playing golf, fencing, swimming or gymnastics. It was always fun for and not romantic. I was not interested in becoming romantically involved with anyone. I was taught to be "afraid" of boys away from home. Having said that, I had major jobs to do which I knew I would thoroughly enjoy. I wanted to be the best mathematics teacher, and coach as well as having my girls, not only win most all basketball games, but all tournaments.

I was having fun and enjoyed my math classes scoring higher than ever. We even went on to win the State Championship Tournament. I knew that we could. All this passing time, I had only been on "coffee-break" five times, and only eight minutes each time at most, and there was always other teachers and of course, Jean.

Where could I have gone to get away from this? Should I go to Baton Rouge and talk to Blaise and Richet? Should I go to see Isabelle or Mama? Oh, God, help me! All of these questions haunted me so much that it kept me from sleeping. Soon, I developed bleeding polyps. At that point, Mrs. Cooper, the school secretary, gave me the name of someone to see and it was Dr. Bill. He was wonderful. He was so compassionate and I was happy with the referral.

He suggested that getting pregnant would help this problem. Oh God, I thought to myself, he must be related to the Moureaus. I liked this doctor but I wanted to slap him for saying that. I told him that I was not married and that was not a possibility. So, I ended up having to have a D&C.

On his day off, Jean would be at school to visit with everyone and of course to see me. I had only been on a date with Jean and his FAMILY for five or six weekends and a couple of nights in between with work for their candidate as the family was politically active. Each of these times was with one part of his family or another. I drove to wherever I was supposed to meet him, even to meet his parents. I never thought of these as true dates. A group of family members or someone else was always with us.

Sometimes a date with Jean would be to go to a basketball game; he drove his car and I rode in the bus with the team. I insisted that Jean stay far away from me, so I didn't consider that a date. I had a team of girls playing their hearts out. He did follow me to the house where I rented but he couldn't get out and I made sure that I didn't wake anyone up. Many times, they would still be up to hear about the score if it was a home game. I saw the lights on in the kitchen, so I knew they were up.

I left him sitting there and just hollered "Goodnight."

So that certainly was not a date. They were always anxious to hear about the team. What a team, and I was so proud of them. They played their hearts out. I was so excited with them, that several times I thought I would wet my pants when we won against my former coach and role model. She took it like a pro hugging me tight.

I was especially proud of one player in particular. Before I tell you about her, I must tell you this story. I was able to repay a special favor, which I received in high school from a very special teacher. I needed glasses, but told her that I couldn't get them and why. She said to go to see if her Daddy thought that I needed them and she would take care of the cost. I was so appreciative; I didn't know what to do. I got the glasses and Papa said nothing. It certainly made a lot of difference in my study habits as well as being capable of reading the blackboard. The teacher said that I might one day have an opportunity to help another in my lifetime and I did. This same thing happened to this basketball player who kept hitting the same spot when trying to make a goal. Her Papa also told her that she only wanted them because "so and so" had them. The same thing that my Papa said, she did need them and I paid for them, a little at a time until I paid them off. I later found out that he gave all at half the price.

Now back to the special student who had the same issue with getting glasses. I allowed her to pick out her frames and told her that this was a special secret between the two of us. This opportunity made me feel grateful that I could help someone else for the same favorable act of compassion, which was once given to me. After Sharon got her glasses, she began making almost every basketball shot go through the hoops. She was the top scorer after receiving her glasses. Now, at last she could see well.

CHAPTER 18

Who's Naive? The Puppet?

I had mentioned earlier about my Mama knowing very little about how naïve she was at just shy of 14 years of age. She had no idea of what she was getting into by getting married so young. Well it may be hard to believe, but I had more education, was just shy of twice her age, teaching high school math and coaching and was more naive and ignorant about what I was getting into, than my Mama was. Jean was "pushy"; none of the group seemed to have any self-discipline. Jean appeared to lack the ambition to succeed by goofing off all the time, but my Papa had both and plenty when they got married. However, I lacked the courage of seeking help and I needed it, BIG TIME. I had never had a date with just the two of us. This relationship situation went on from mid Oct through December 10th; just about 2 months "to the day" of meeting Jean for coffee breaks with him and the crew at school.

When asked to dinner one night by his parents, I drove there. I noticed several cars there and wondered if this was just the group again. I began dreading it as I got out of the car and Jean met me out front. Jean popped the question asking me to marry him. I could not believe this. I did not know Jean. We were never alone. The teachers at school or his family were always with us. He never picked me up. I always drove to their place in my car. What is going on here with this group? Someone is pushing him into this and wants it done quickly. Well, I was in total shock, and all that I could think about was all the things that everyone would say about me, if I didn't get married. That was stressed many times. Well, not just that, but what Dr. Bill had said didn't help out one bit. His talk to me about the bleeding polyps frightened me.

I remembered having trouble in college with bleeding polyps. The Dean of Women even had me in the College Infirmary. She called my brother, Blaise and told him that I couldn't go back to class without a letter from a doctor. I had passed out in history class seven times. I sure didn't want to pass out in any of my in the math classes or with the basketball team.

In thinking about the bleeding polyps, I felt that I had to say, "Yes."

Oh Lord, I hated that I had said this. I had been trapped, and I knew it. I felt like the untrained mule back on the farm with the chain from his leg to the head harness. I did not know what to do and was frightened to my wits end. I was some kind of a "down-right-scared" gal.

He gave me a large diamond ring. I almost fainted at that moment. I couldn't help but wonder what it cost? I was not going to wear it in public for sure. I didn't want anyone to know about it. I had never seen one that large. I allowed him kiss to me, but not on the mouth. I didn't even know how to kiss. This was the first time. I had never kissed a man. Mama and Grandma were the only ones I had ever kissed anyway, but not in the mouth.

Wasting no time though, after popping the question, and the "yes" answer, Jean then took me down to Mama's and Papa's IN HIS CAR, and I ran to Mama while he asked Papa for my hand in marriage. I didn't say a word on the way there. I was almost in tears. He talked, but I never answered a single question. I just shook and was so angry with myself for saying "Yes." I didn't worry about what Papa would say, because he had told the Lady Marines to hit the road. I just knew he would do the same thing with this situation.

Since Papa never approved of anything I did, without consulting him, I thought surely he would tell Jean NO! On the contrary, he said YES, because he knew Jean's cousin, the Moureau state trooper, and thought a lot of him. Jean had to bring this up (like a carrot) because he knew that Papa knew his cousin. What a thoughtless reason! He never made decisions like this by knowing someone's "kin-folks." I was so upset with him and myself for not telling him to think about it for a while. This would give him a chance to talk to me privately. I was distraught! I could not believe this.

We didn't stay long there, because Papa's answer was all Jean needed to know, and he was ready to leave. If Papa had said to give him a couple of days to think about it, I know then that I would've made a special effort to get myself right back down there the next day and give both of them a good talking to about that family. I wished many times that I had told'em about this and the "shenanigans" they had pulled and pushed for a wedding to take place as soon as possible in front of Jean. At that point, I was so angry, I didn't care about school or anything other than thinking, "what am I going to do now?"

Oh God, it bothered me because Papa didn't hesitate to tell those Lady Marines "NO!" He showed them the road without any hesitation! I was upset with myself for not telling Jean to just go home; leave now. Papa will take me back. Then I would have talked to Papa. He would've taken me back to get my car, and I would have bid "adios amigos" to all of them right then and there. Next, I would've called the principal and told him what had happened. I'd tell him to get a substitute for me and hire another teacher, because I was leaving for good. My thinking always seemed to be 20-20 hindsight.

Jean hurried back to give them all the news to get the wheels turning. We did not talk on the 24 mile trip back either. I didn't know or care what he thought about me not talking. I wanted to get in my car, go home and not go in for supper. I think Jean felt that I wanted to go home also. His folks were having us for that bloody steak that they were so fond of for supper, because they were waiting for a YES ANSWER THAT WE ARE GETTING MARRIED. He drove faster on this trip than I ever drove. He was in a hurry.

I was so upset that food was the farthest from my mind. I wanted to go home, but all ran out to meet us. I didn't want any more gagging of raw meat. But, before the dinner began, they had the wedding date set, right then and there. Jean had Papa's approval and they took control of the rest. The dinner was set. They had to feel like a "YES" answer. I was sick of all this. This was rigged from the beginning with Marjane. She told Jean what to say, and how to talk to Papa

I didn't want to eat. I nibbled on a little but I kept going after fruit salad. After cutting two tiny pieces of steak, and a few vegetables, I had enough. It was time for me to go. All the rest were talking about "stuff" that I didn't know or care about. Then Jean's Dad slipped something in my hand while everyone else was talking about the wedding. I looked at it, and thought it was the most precious gift he could have given. In the box was a gorgeous wedding band. He knew I guessed, that as country as I was, that the diamond wasn't for me. He whispered in my ear, "Just don't let the sun go down on your wrath." Well, I knew that if I wore anything, it would be that wedding band. It even had my initials inside and it had belonged to Jean's great, great grand-mother. That band was 7/16 if an inch wide. His Dad cared for me. He probably knew that Jean couldn't afford the ring, which went with the ROCK. The big engagement ring was the one he had originally given to the previous girl. I don't know if Marjane was paying for it or not. She took control of everything else. However, she did not take control of the other girl. She got rid of all of them.

I didn't know where all this was happening. I soon found out, though. None of the bunch had ever met anyone in my family, except Jean; when we went down to see Mama and Papa. They were the only ones he met then. How did they find out who all was in my family and how to get in touch with them? A week after talking to Papa and Mama, Jean and his folks had me over again for a steak dinner. Again, I drove THERE, so that I could leave as soon as I could. Why didn't I have guts enough to do something immediately?

I figured out why they were in a hurry for the wedding, because the day after the wedding was the beginning of the 2-week Christmas breaks. This meant "honey-moon" time. I wanted to wait until school was out. I knew if I could put it off, I would have time to run away, join the service or something. You can bet that there would not have been a wedding until I made the decision and not someone forcing me and planning all of it themselves. I needed time to know him, and love him without people pushing me into this so quickly. This happened to be a "big deal" dinner planned. Why couldn't we have chicken? I could al-ready imagine the blood running from the middle of the steak and was about to get sick. I had knots in my stomach just thinking about it. For sure, this steak looked the same as before. I am glad that I took many of the side dishes and ate the edges of the steak. Someone besides me could have the red part. Jean's Dad noticed that I was going back for fruit salad again, and he kept pushing that toward me. I winked at him for catching on right away. He was a true sweetheart. However, this particular "steak" dinner was a special one so that I could meet Jean's sister, Denise and her husband Mac.

They stuck with Jean and I stuck with Jean's Dad. His Mom's cooking was sure different from my Mama's cooking. The kind that I grew up eating was cooked all the way through and was never served with blood running out when you cut it. I thought that I was going to vomit each time I thought about it.

I would chew, gag and secretly put it into my napkin when no one was paying attention. When that meal was over, I went to the bathroom to flush the meat out of my napkin. When I returned, I sneaked the napkin onto the counter. If this had happened two weeks before, I would've taken off running. I would not have stopped until I felt safe from them all. Then the "not so funny matter" began to happen.

Jean's Mom asked, "Jo, what is your PATTERN?"

Well, that was a mighty strange question to ask me, I thought. I didn't make the dress I was wearing, but_.

I said, "Well, I had a pattern for a regular skirt and ahhh wraparound skirt, and ahhh----?"

"MOTHER, it is all the same as mine!" Denise SHOUTED.

An interruption before I could finish? Why on earth did she do that? I was gonna tell her about my dresses. I didn't know what kind of dresses Denise had. Surely, they were not like mine.

Denise and Jean had heard just enough of the conversation to interrupt and to tell their Mom that my "pattern," (whatever it meant) was the same as all of Denise and Mac's patterns. They had the feeling that I had no idea of what their Mom was asking.

"Oh!" She said.

"Those are lovely patterns!" She said.

Well, that ended the "pattern" questions on the spot. There was time yet to figure out what prompted that conversation. For "God's sake," what blame pattern does Denise have anyway? I was very curious then to know what in the "sam-hill" she was talking about. Why didn't I just start running away then? I don't know. I drove there in my car and Jean lived there. What was keeping me? I knew that I didn't belong in this "controlling" group who was running and ruining my life. That was happening all around me. I just didn't know just how "cotton-pick'en" stupid I was until a much later time.

I kept my prayer vigil though, asking God if he would please help me here. Well that prayer was not meant to be for me this time. They were in a big hurry for all to happen nine days after popping the question for me to marry him. The wedding was for the 19th of December. They were afraid that if I went home for the holidays, I would talk too much and all would be called off. You can bet that their fears were real and correct! I would have talked for a long time. You can bet on that!

While in town, I went to the department store and since it was wintertime, I bought a $25 suit, a flannel gown with a "Peter Pan" collar with long sleeves and elastic at the wrist, and it hung down to my ankles. I thought that it was pretty and that was just what I needed rather than the feed sack gown. I did not know what to get.

I had pajamas and a gown that Mama made out of feed sacks, so it's that or the flannel nightgown. Why not this? I purchased a couple of pair of undergarments and went home. I wondered as I was going back home why I had not gone to the library in town to look up how to prepare yourself for a wedding night and married life. I knew that I needed a book for a long time. Then I would be free as a bird. I was so frightened with this family, yet I never permitted them to know how controlled I felt. Oh, for sure, that was my mistake. I just knew that if I left them, I would never get a job because they knew all the lawyers, superintendents and principals statewide who had the power to "do me in."

I had debts to pay immediately if I didn't keep my promise to the school board. They loaned me money to go to college to teach for them. I believed that I had to do this. They, not my Papa, were in control now. I had to take anatomy in college, but they didn't teach what to do in this situation, nor about sex and marriage. I had never slept with anyone other than my sister and niece. Evette and I (even as kids) were never allowed to see each other in the nude. And, that's not all; Jean was not going to see me nude and LIVE TO TELL ABOUT IT!" We all grew up in "a different" world from any of these people.

I know that I had "too much pride" to tell or ask questions: Why I had finished college and should know everything. No one I knew ever talked about any of this sort of situation. Rene had been married before and she never talked about sex and such. When we shared an apartment, she had regular dishes. Embarrassed? Why no! I didn't know enough about all this to be embarrassed about cooking or anything else. I was just angry because I didn't know how ignorant I was. I made A's in college. I loved learning. I loved teaching.

Woe now, Marjane and a lot of family and friends and teachers began having wedding showers, one right after another. This happened immediately after learning what "my pattern" was. I was in total shock over this. I never had anything, and had not needed it and didn't want it, and last, but not least, I would not know what to do with it. I am glad that I didn't ask what their "shower" was because I didn't know. The only time I had heard of a "shower" was when we had a light rain. Oh my, they would've died if I had asked what it was!

I should've asked, after all. That would've ended everything. Then, instead of always asking God for help, I would've been thanking God for all the help. That would've been a rather reasonable question from me. Did it ever occur to them that I stayed on the plantation and worked like a slave? However, they would've seen how ignorant I was about this; and made me get lost. I had my ticket and LOST IT! I have no idea how many showers they gave, but there were many. I didn't know the name of what all these gifts were I didn't know what or when anyone would use it. I opened a small package and there was a "glass" in it. I had never seen anything like any of this "stuff."

I didn't see any of this at Jean's house either. I didn't know that it was crystal, nor why anyone would ever use a strange looking glass. I was given a complete set of eight different kind of glasses, and at least that many different shapes and sizes. Marjane ran the "show" in telling me when to begin opening presents, as well as an "urge to say my WOW'S, OH'S and AWE'S THAT IS SO LOVELY" messages. She told me that I "did it well." Oops, I should've left one or two out. Maybe I could've gotten my ticket home. I screwed it up by "doing it well." Oh, she was so pretentious! OH, what can I do? I thought.

Sometimes at home, there would be a pretty little cup and saucer in a big box of oatmeal, which Papa bought occasionally. I wished that I had told all of them right at that moment that I didn't know what any of this was, and had no idea what to do with it. It bothered me to no end because I did not tell them.

I was so frightened. How did I get through college without knowing some of this? All I could think about were the obligations to the school board, the principal, Blaise and the coach. I had to pay all those people back immediately; or so I thought if I didn't teach for the parish. I believed that my Papa would've paid all of this off and I could've gotten a job elsewhere; but the "puppet" didn't tell Papa or Mama. That was all running through my mind. It was many years later before I finally told some of the siblings about all this, and they would've helped me, and was quite upset because I didn't tell them. I had "too much pride" to allow anyone to know how ignorant I was. I had high expectations of myself. I was a taskmaster, not a show off, but I had accepted this; now I have to take the punishment that goes along with it.

I could see that I was talking to God only when I needed him, or when in a bind. I should've gotten quite, still and listened to see and feel His answers. I needed to thank God for so much, and all I had been doing was asking for help. I was so ashamed of myself, at this point.

The showers kept happening. There were two of sterling showers. WHAT A TURN OUT! WHERE DID ALL THESE PEOPLE COME FROM? NONE OF THEM WAS ANY OF MY FAMILY! They wouldn't have known what was going on either. I had never had, seen or even used "sterling" as far as I knew. Therefore, when directed by Marjane to begin opening things I did so. Here, I received a five-piece place setting for eight people, plus serving spoons, soup dipper, meat knife and fork, plus a heavy wooden block of steak knives with so many other large knives that I could've gone to war with them. Next, there was a pie server with a plate. Then there was the silver tray with a tea and coffee server.

I didn't know what I would do with all this. Why would you use this and what would one put in it? At home, we slowly dripped coffee through a sack, similar to a sock. They probably had never heard of that. Since they have been running all of the business, where would I put it? Am I going to live in a place where I would need all this? Most of all, I wondered where I would live? Had they picked that out also? No one ever mentioned it. Was I supposed to ask and show my ignorance again?

Then, there was a shower for tablecloths, napkins and linens of all sorts. They were for a long table, round table, square table and "or any other kind of table." Each one had a linen "runner" for the center. What was this far? This blew my mind. They also gave bed linens, (some were satin), quilts, bedspreads, towels and washcloths. Also, many fancy pillows for the bed or sofa were given.

I had never seen one on a sofa except where the showers were given. I had been use to flour or feed sacks for towels, washcloths, sheets, pillowcases and homemade quilts and some mattresses as well. I couldn't help but think that these folks had never seen anything made from a feed sack. This made me wish that I had worn one of my feed sack dresses to all the showers. I still had a couple of them. I wondered what they would've said to me. Now, my question would've been, "which "outfit" would I sleep on?" Why were all the "ravels" around the bedspreads and the towels and washcloths? My Mama didn't have one like that, and none of the people where I visited had them. If Mama's had ravels, it meant that they had been torn or ripped, but not evenly around.

Anyway, one lady said, "I gave you that!"

Now I was country, but to me I thought that was out of place. Each item had a name-tag on it. I would find out, without calling out the name of each one who brought a gift. I did my "thanks'," without looking at them. I didn't know who all these people were anyway.

You know that MARJANE told me what to say, and when to say it with her "throat-clearing" noise, or a bump with her knee or elbow! We sat together on the couch, and used the coffee table to display the gifts. I was hoping that all of this was over and a lady said that next would be one at her house just for utensils for the kitchen. Oh, my God, what else could I need? I had already received all types of items such as knife sets, ladles, copper bottom pots, pans and sets of sterling utensils. Oh Lord, I had no idea what to do with those were either, because I couldn't cook. I also got many electric items, such as a mixer with a bunch of different size bowls. Another gave me a hand held mixer. Mama and Lili used the same old eggbeater and a fork or spoon to mix things together. What is going on with these people? There was an electric coffee pot and slicing knife, as well as so many "gadgets", which I had never seen or used before and didn't know what any of them were. I also wondered why anyone would want or have any need for need that many different knives. What a show!

My Mama only had 2 butcher knifes for beef or pork after they had been killed, and she and Lili were the primary "cutters." She had one knife for slicing a watermelon or cake, two small ones for slicing corn off the cob when canning and two paring knifes for peeling potatoes and such. That was it. I don't know of any others she might have had or needed. Our meat was cut up in mouth size pieces of stew meat or you used your fork to cut it smaller. The smaller knife also cut our meat into smaller pieces, but Mama did that. We didn't have a knife at the table. We only had one piece of flatware. If we had soup, we had a spoon; a regular country meal, we used a fork. We all kept a pocketknife, but it was never used at the table.

I was so happy that I kept the name-tags and didn't lose any of them. I got so tired of writing those "thank-you-notes" as neat, meaningful, and thought provoking, as I could've gotten them. I wanted to sell some of this to pay for the note-cards and stamps. Now, I wished that I had enough money to pay the School board off and go join the service right now. Just run and keep running was about all I could think of. However, I had to think of my Mama. Or, I also could go back to the farm. I do know that I would've skipped a few days of school, or maybe be fired. Maybe the farm was not that bad after all.

CHAPTER 19

Got Married

The wedding was held at his Aunt Gezelle and Uncle Firmin's home with his folks and mine attending. You should know I would think by now, that I didn't plan any of this. They even planned for Evette to be the bridesmaid, even though they had never met her or any of my family. They made the decision as to who would be in the wedding with me as well as where it would be held, got the cake, refreshments and the minister. I still don't know how they got in touch with all my family. I am sure all this was a good idea, because those questions would've been like the one about the "PATTERN" to me. I had never been to a wedding. I would not know anything about inviting anyone. I had been to a couple of "drive-in" movies, in my brother's car, which showed a segment about a marriage. The trunk was filled with friends from college, who pinched coins together for me to pay my way in. I have always felt guilty about that. However, there was nothing about setting up a wedding, and if there was, I missed it during one of our laughing spells. Nevertheless, I never went to a movie on a date, unless it involved a group. I couldn't afford it, and I wouldn't let anyone pay my way, anyhow. I had been to one theater, and 2 drive-in movies. Someone should have told me to study about all this. They had to know how ignorant I was.

They planned it all, but it didn't stop there; they planned everything from then on as well. (There will be more about this later.) Ray, Jean's best man and Evette, my maid of honor, made me feel comfortable because they could tell that I was nervous. Ray had been Jean's friend since elementary school. He was a handsome young man with the best of manners, and very elegant. I wondered why I didn't meet him at someplace? I didn't know about the writing on the car, or why mine was hidden. We started for Bay Bridge, Louisiana, but stopped at a cheap little motel on the way. Here the shakes began. I wanted to run up the road to the service station and bum a ride home, but we were in my car. I was so nervous that I had forgotten that!" I could take mine, and he could call Marjane to come get him. Oh, Lord!" Do I have to go through with this? That would not work right now.

I went on into the bathroom and put my flannel gown on. Jean had already gotten into bed. I had rice all over my little suit, my hair and my paper-bag of clothes by that time, shaking like a leaf in a tornado. I didn't know what to expect. I must say I didn't get anything out of it, even though all was done in five seconds. He went to sleep, and I pretended to be asleep also, wondering IS THIS ALL IT IS TOO IT?

From there, we went to Bay Bridge and saw my second movie, a musical. That was ALL that I enjoyed. After the movie, we went to a fancy restaurant and had something I had never had before. I don't remember what I had but it was not steak, but had sand in it. I just finished it with a spoon as if it were soup. Jean ordered the meal for me.

He had steak, and I was so glad that I didn't have that. However, after the gritty meal I had, maybe they would've cooked the steak for me without blood running out. Needless to say, that I didn't eat much of that and certainly didn't chew it with anything. I didn't know what to do with all the forks and spoons and a knife on each side of my plate.

Therefore, I watched Jean as well as some other folks in there and made it. I did eat the bread and salad and talked about the different students on the basketball team.

One day I will have the intestinal fortitude to tell his Mom that my meat needed to be almost burned. We came back the next morning after a night in the same little "joint," and I fell asleep FAST. It was a short honeymoon for me because it was Christmas break from school and I told Jean that I had to move all my belongings into this tiny apartment behind Jean's Mother's house after he finally told me where we would be living. What a SHOCK!" The apartment had a tiny stove and a bath without a tub or shower. Why was this set up for a young married couple? This was a play-house, with a tiny bedroom without closets, a stove in a 3' X 8' closet to live in. I didn't expect it. Well, I later found out more than I wanted to know about all of this marriage. Jean, his Mom as well as aunts now tell me that he couldn't afford anything else. As big, a rush as they were in, you would have thought that the town was running out of apartments. He couldn't afford any of the apartments that I had assumed we would have lived in. Jean's Dad suggested that we take the front bedroom in their house. He was the only one who was so sweet, kind and considerate.

Then all the "sweet and kind conversations" were over. The sharp tongue began after about 2 weeks, and I was speechless by this sudden change of events. I didn't want to stay in his Mom's house any longer and listen to his Mother every day after school and her stinging, sharp tongue. It didn't take very long for that to start. I do not have the vaguest idea why all the changes of attitude. The "nice expressions" to me had ended abruptly. Maybe this was her way of disguising her embarrassment by their rush for a wedding, and her son's lacking financial planning. I didn't know what her problem was. I just hopped on the bed in the "play-house" (no room for a chair) as soon as I could and began grading papers and preparing lesson plans for the week or stayed longer at school if I needed to be alone. I worked in the gym after school as late as I could before going home. The principal told me that the janitor would do all that.

He was a love, but he didn't know that I wanted to be the janitor of the gym instead of going home. I should have gotten on the bleachers and graded papers. Maybe he would have joined in some conversation with me and told me about a lot that I needed to know, that he already knew.

In fact, I almost drove off many times before I found out that I was pregnant. We finally moved into the main house and stayed in the front bedroom until school was out. When I knew I was pregnant, I knew that I had to do something or I would leave, pregnant or not.

Therefore, I did find a tiny apartment upstairs behind the store where Jean would be working. At least he could walk to work when he changed jobs and sold his car or it was repossessed. This little apartment was a bigger midget than the one behind his folk's house. The living room, bedroom and dining room were all one room. However, it was three times the size of the little one behind his Mother's house.

The living room, bedroom and dining room were all one room. However, it was three times the size of the little one behind his Mother's house. The kitchen was open to the living room. I couldn't cook, so that was fine with me. I did get some courage to talk to the doctor. He just repeated the fact that he needed to talk to Jean, but Jean would not go. I certainly couldn't make him go to either talk or listen to the doctor. Jean told me that there was nothing wrong with ME.

My doctor repeated this many times, that the one he needed to Jean, but Jean was so perfect and was not about to show anything was different about him. Surely, he knew that I would have to be out of school a year if I got pregnant. We needed the money. What was his problem? Now, I was beginning to wonder if my Papa killed Joe. I needed Joe now. I would've told Joe, but I was so afraid to tell my Papa. Both would've died in jail if either of them had known what was going on in this family.

CHAPTER 20

I Am What?

I was pregnant. I guess Jean told everyone that I couldn't eat well, was throwing up all that I did eat, and couldn't stand the odor of a cigarette. Marjane told all the friends at school and they were ecstatic. One would have thought Jean was pregnant. Now the showers started again and this time I knew what a shower was, but not what not what to expect.

These were for needs for the new baby. There was a baby bed, stroller, bassinets, diapers galore and many baby clothes. There were toys that the baby would've had to be at least four years old to play with. However, in time they would all be used. They gave at least three more showers. One would not tolerate another to get ahead. There were baby bottle steamers and bottles, a little bathtub, wash cloths, receiving blankets, an iron and a box filled with a mixture of different kinds of baby food wrapped very pretty with a bow which had a small box in the middle. I couldn't imagine what this could be. I had never seen a gift wrapped with a gift in the bow. I opened it and there was a sterling spoon and fork for a baby. What an unique idea! You would've thought that Jean was having the baby with all the excitement, or that I had hung the moon. I finished teaching that year and only began to show a little by the time school had ended. I only weighed 100 pounds, and I could tell that it showed on the side of my waist. I just bought a "Mitie Blouse," as it was called then. You were not to tuck it in and it covered my sides. I had never seen a pregnant lady in my life other than my sister, Isabelle, but I just thought she was fat. I didn't know that she was going to have a baby. She knew not to say the word, "pregnant." It was a forbidden word, I guess. Later, Evette told me that she was pregnant. If she had used the term, I would've known what they were talking about. I didn't know what kind of clothes to get for being pregnant.

Jean's Mother, who had taught home economics for a while, could make anything, and began making me maternity clothes. I had never seen one. I didn't know that it was a special outfit. This was the first time that I thought she liked me. We went down to see Mama and Papa. They noticed immediately when they saw me.

CHAPTER 21

She's Beautiful

Two weeks before Christine was born, I had the flu, which was rampant that year. I had to be rushed to the hospital from the little apartment with an extremely high temperature. When we got to the hospital, they saw immediately that I was pregnant and were beginning to take me to the delivery room.

Jean said, "No, she has the flu and has high fever. She's not ready for the delivery room yet."

It was not long until Dr. Bill, got all settled in with me along with another doctor who worked in the same office building. After a week, he had me well and sent me home. I wished that Jean had been there before that, because I would've made sure that he talked to the doctor. I think that I probably had the flu for two weeks before anyone thought about me going to the hospital.

I never understood why the hospitalization insurance, covered the flu, but not the pregnancy. If I had known that, I know that I would have waited before Jean got anywhere near me. Otherwise, maybe if I could have waited at least four months before being married. Now really, if that had happened, then there would not have been a wedding. Moreover, God only knows what would've have happened to me if I had waited four more months, but I do know that if there had been no help in getting the group to leave me alone, I would have run away.

Anyway, you had to be married a year for the insurance to kick in. Christine was born on November 28. What a huge surprise this was to me. A beautiful girl and she was mine, with the curliest long hair, which made her look much older especially with the lovely olive skin. I was glad that finally I had something of my own. Maybe now they will leave me alone since I have a family. I named her after a friend I knew in college and my mother-in-law (Lou). Little did I know then that she would not be mine much longer?

I didn't know how to hold her, but I had to learn quickly in order to nurse her. This was something that I had never seen done before except from materials at Dr. Bill's office. Just those pictures were frightening to me. After about one week, I was dismissed from the hospital with many gifts that were sent to me for Christine. All of them were addressed to "Miz Lu" or "Miss Lou" as a "nickname," but I was thrilled with the name and maybe this would give me some "points." Wishful thinking, but it didn't happen. Now the work began trying to learn to change diapers and to nurse a baby.

Then I had to learn to how to wash diapers. Washing diapers was done in the commode and the lavatory was used for rinsing, then boiling to make them sterile. We didn't have a washer or dryer; however, we later found that there was a washer in the complex. Jean found out about it, and then I strung a clothesline across the one large room. This worked for me and they dried quickly. I did the folding and pressed them with my hand to make it smooth and looking ironed. I had to do most all washing and drying on weekends. I kept busy because I would not let Jean near me because I had Christine up against me. I wanted him as far away from me as I could. I didn't want to get pregnant again. I didn't believe in being submissive and obedient as my Mama was. I was happy with just Christine now. She was my refuge and I wanted her all to myself. When it got warmer, I wrapped her up well and took out in the stroller looking for another place to live. I enjoyed these walks with her. She was mine and I did not take her to his mother's house at all. In about four months, I found a larger apartment with at least a separate bedroom for storing all of the shower gifts, and a kitchen and eating area. It had a place for a washer, which Jean got at a discount by working at the store where the BOSS got him a job. We had a yard outside that already had lines for clothes. I used this when the weather permitted so that the electric bill would not be too high. I didn't know that he couldn't afford any of this rent. Have I ever gotten myself into a big mess?

Soon he bought a black and white television from where he worked. I had never seen or watched a television before. I don't know why he got it because it was snowy and hard to watch. Therefore, it was only turned on when Jean was home. He had no control over spending. I had my check divided into twelve months so that helped until summer. I didn't have a job until I was out of school for a year. That was the state law.

Now all the money went into a joint account. I didn't write the checks and Jean was the designated "bill payer." I had hoped that there was enough money for us to get by, so we would not have to move in with the "boss." She was certainly one who told you what to do and when to do it. After we moved in with Marjane, we didn't have to pay rent. This was the first time, as far as I knew, that she found out that I couldn't cook.

This became a big problem. She asked me to fix a baloney sandwich. This package of meat in the refrigerator had baloney written on it, and I thought it was raw meat slices of some sort. I had never seen any like this before. I began trying to cook it in the iron skillet. It began curling up all around it and I didn't know what to do. I held it down with a spatula, but it just curled right back up. Next, I cut all around the circumference of it with half-inch slits and it flattened the meat out. Then I flipped it over and finished browning it. Marjane had a fit. I never understood why, because she was much older than I was and didn't know how to cook either. She was a pure, first class fake.

Soon, she wanted me to begin preparing something for her. She told me to go to the kitchen, turn the mixer on and put a stick of butter into the bowl. I did exactly as she said and in the order given to me. This instantly flew all over the kitchen. After cleaning that tremendous mess, I called it quits. Someday, and somehow I would have someone to teach me how to cook. Some of the recipes made it and some didn't, probably because I cooked everything on high. Well, what do you do if you don't know what medium, low or simmer meant on a stove like the one I had never seen before?

CHAPTER 22

Anger!

The anger began shortly after moving in with Marjane. Jean had bought so much in material things that we couldn't use or need. In addition, to make it worse, he told me nothing about the financing. My siblings thought that we were "rich" and made plenty of money. He had a problem of boasting about money that we didn't have and when he did, he didn't know how to handle it. Why I didn't tell them differently? He would've told Marjane that I contradicted him.

I could've handled it and we could've made it on our own if I had handled the money, and dared him to buy anything unless I told him to do it. Since I never had money before the teaching job, I made it through college on little. We didn't need all the furniture and electronics he would purchase. I knew that this FAMILY HAD CONTROL OVER me. I did tell him to stop buying all the items purchased because we were still paying for the hospital bill each month. Joe would've gotten him in the back and given him a Thibodeaux lesson without a second thought. Gee, I thought about Joe so often, because he would've done most anything to help me.

Jean said, "Just don't worry about that. All's good."

I said, "You are lying to me!""

The next year, someone else had filled my old teaching job and the school board had an opening at Opelousas High School for me. I truly believe that God took care of that job for me. He closed one door and opened another. This was a very prestigious high school where I taught Algebra I and II, as well as a senior math for 12th graders. This was a business math. This class had several students who were older than I was. They had run away from home and joined the service during the Korean War as soon as they were old enough. After they got out, they wanted to continue their education. Many went on to college. I was extremely proud of them. They were great role models for my classes and others as well. There were some wonderful teachers there and we became great friends.

They didn't permit just anyone teach at that school, but of course, all of them knew Jean and all his folks. She didn't tell me that she mentioned anything to the school board, but I would be willing to bet that she did. Having all the bosses telling me what I should do was nerve shattering. Jean never backed me up or told them that this was our business. He owed them too much. After one year, I loved the school, but I hated living with Marjane. I was ready to pitch a tent. Evidently, he didn't have the intestinal fortitude to do anything about it because later we could afford the rent somewhere. I had money then and wanted out.

His aunt claimed that she wanted us with her because she was afraid to live by herself. Here, she became the "controller" of everything. What was going on? Had I married an idiot? I couldn't understand why he didn't stand up on his own two feet and tell them to leave us alone? I was becoming hopeless. Why did she build the new house?

Christine was a year old and into all the paraphernalia on the coffee table in the "boss's" house. I taught her to not touch anything because, "that belongs to the LADY," and spanked her hand as she would reach for something. She learned right away to obey. She was the most obedient 1 year old there ever was, because everything "belonged to the lady."

I was getting enough of this and could not handle any more with her not knowing how to cook anything, and wanting me to cook for her. I was getting out of there somehow. I had thought about a divorce at that time, but I remembered someone back in the country who had divorced, and was ostracized by the whole community because of it. I dealt with it by biting my tongue and praying for guidance.

I needed Evette and she would have taken care of the situation without any hesitation. I just had not told her about all this mess. She would have taken care of each one, beginning with Jean. She would have cleaned "house." That is exactly what would've happened. I would've been cleaned up for sure, but I didn't have any idea how many she would've taken down with her. As much as I was going to "conquer, overcome circumstances and adversity to succeed," I was nowhere near it. I had "clawed" myself into a new world for sure, but all the intestinal fortitude had vanished. I have certainly regretted many times that I didn't tell her. We were very close then also, because she had a little boy 2 months after Christine was born. Evette would probably have had all brothers in "combat" with each one of them. How I wished that I had talked to her or Isabelle and the situation would've been under control two years earlier.

Sure, I wanted to move out of Marjane's house, but we didn't have "neither a pot nor a window to throw it out" much less a down-payment on a house. I was afraid that I would have a nervous breakdown. I was glad that Marjane had given Jean her car when she bought a new one. Now I could have MY car back and do what I want.

Finally, I went down to see my Mama to talk to her about what to do. She got Papa into the conversation. Can you believe this? I had the nerve to go home for help. I just didn't tell them enough. That was my defeat.

I wanted to say, "Just let me move back here for a while."

He could tell something was wrong. Papa said that we needed to get out of town. They didn't feel that they could even visit me while living with her, and I never asked them to. I wished then that I had told them everything a lot sooner. Was I afraid he would shoot someone again? You bet!" On the other hand, I was too afraid of getting him shot by them.

After the visit there, I had driven a long way out to the town of Lafayette where the principal, who had once been my high school chemistry teacher, to see if he needed a math teacher. He was glad to see me and took off from school long enough to show me this little 25-acre place with a neat red barn and cottage and if I needed a math job, he had an opening. There was a complete change of attitude at that time. I was ready to take them on. When I saw that newly painted white frame home, and the owner's would finance it I was in "shock and awe" for sure. I knew that I had enough guts now to get away.

They wanted $1,000 down on $10,000 for the house and land. There was one more trip that had to be made right then. I drove back down to see Mama and Papa and had Christine with me. Five years had passed since I lived there and the old home place looked strange when I looked out and saw nothing but pine trees growing where I use to chop and pick cotton with all the hired hands. I also remembered old

Joe, and wondered where he might be, if Papa had not killed him. If he were still living, he would've taken care of all those situations I had. He and I both would probably have ended up in jail. Joe liked me and would've done anything for me. He just lost his mind that day in the field. I hope now that he lived over it and I could get him to help me. The control would've ended shortly after his arrival.

I finally told Mama and Papa more of what was and had been happening in my life and that I needed to get out of that house. I told them that Jean's family members were ruining my life. They couldn't believe that I had been putting up with it. However, my Mama got my Papa to do something he had never done. That something was loaning money to me. Maybe this was his way of the "pat on the back" for good hard work.

He wanted me to be in control, and keep Jean's family from controlling me. I told them about the house, the job offer as well as how far and how much the house was. Papa wanted me in a house of my own. He was willing to give me the $1,000, but I don't want a "give-me," I wanted a loan to pay back soon. The only problem was that it was 40 miles farther from them.

CHAPTER 23

My Papa Did What?

Papa, who never loaned money to anyone that I knew of, loaned me $1,000 for the down payment on this home, which was a long way from Jean's family to let them bother me. I was so excited. The next day I went to the school board to find out if they knew of an opening for a math teacher at Melville High School. I couldn't tell them that I had "a jump on the situation" by going out, and talking to the principal before talking to them.

They said that there would be an opening for a math teacher in the fall. I then told them that I would like to have it because I wanted to buy a house, which was one mile from the school. They said it was mine beginning the next year. Maybe they sensed my anguish as well as recognized that I needed to "get the hell out of Dodge."

They all knew Marjane, and knew how she pretty well tried to control the issues at the school board. This house was on the edge of the Parish line so maybe they would not know how to get there or even want to. God found me at last, I thought, not knowing or realizing He had been there all the time. The school not only needed a math teacher but the principal was very eager for me to teach for him.

The next task was to tell Jean that I was moving. What a surprise this will be to his folks because I had not told them about buying a house, or getting the new job? I didn't ask them for money and this was going to be MY place. I didn't care if they ever found me or not. Next, I talked to Jean, and let him in on it because it was about 24 miles more for him to drive to work. I told him that he could stay with his Aunt Marjane or his Mom if he wanted to, but I was moving into this house and had the down payment. Wow, it felt good to say that. I am getting "an attitude," which I have needed for a long time. I had to keep it going. This move would also put me 50 miles away from Evette. She would not get to go out, or I would have to tell her more than she should know right then. I was in control, I thought. At this time, Jean's folks knew these business people who had given Jean the job back as the furniture and appliance manager. This was a well-established family store. He could get furniture and appliances at cost. I didn't want him to tell me that. I could sleep on a pallet on the floor if I had to.

I did lead him out to see the place, and he was excited to have a chance for a house and that lovely "big red barn on the property" just swept him off his feet. He immediately told his Aunt Marjane that this place was something that he had always wanted. I often wished that I had not taken him out to see it. Hey! What was going on here? She gave in and offered to help and I told him to say that I didn't want help.

We did, but I was not going to take it from her. Jean did get some old living room furniture that his Mother had stored in that "play-house" we lived in before Christine was born. He had it put in while I was gone. We did have enough furniture to last us forever as far as I was concerned. I didn't care what it looked like.

It was not built of cypress boards and we didn't have the homemade cotton mattresses and feather bed, but it would work out fine for me. I could have gotten furniture from my folks, but didn't have a way to haul it. When school was out for that year, we moved into that house. Our marriage saved for the time being. Working for Joli Vean (the family store) and with Jean becoming the head of the furniture and appliances, he made better money than he ever had and he got a nice commission. In one month after moving into the house, I paid my Papa back by consolidating our credit. I didn't know anything about what that meant, but if he was making enough money and could pay my Papa back this quickly, Whatever it meant, I was all for "consolidating" the credit. I thought that maybe the store had given give him a big bonus.

I was able to pay the school board back $150 still owed to them. I even finished paying off Blaise who gave me about $200 when I was in college, plus the use of his car, $50 to Ted and I also paid Yolanda, my coach who had given me $300 altogether. However, even though she said she didn't want the money back, I insisted that she take it. I expressed my gratitude, and let her know that I would be hurt if she didn't take. I told her that I kept a log of who I owed and how much. She had felt sorry for me because she knew how "tight" my Papa was.

My first thought, was that now I could run away, if I could only find a job where they would not find me. That is my dream. Maybe I could now talk to the coach. She had been so helpful to me. Each time she went to the college to see all of her old basketball players she would do things for us and take us out for a sandwich or something. She knew that I was having a taxing time and had nothing, so she slipped $20 bills to me each time she went up to see us.

She was one of my role models, but I never thought how she could afford to do this. She gave of and for herself. However, I was glad to get all these people paid back, even though I had never heard of "co-signing" for anything nor consolidation. When I did find out, I was furious! This made me so angry to find out that Jean couldn't borrow money on his own. This was brought on by Marjane. I had borrowed money before and I didn't have to have anything "co-signed" before the first teaching job. They had never seen me before. I told them where I would be teaching and who the principal was. I paid for those 2 little cheap dresses the next month.

I loved this little white cottage with three acres in the front of the house with a white fence to a small creek and a neat white "storybook" bridge across it. Up the crooked little lane was the house surrounded with the white picket fences. It made my day. It was a "storybook place" for sure!

I was so thrilled! This place was real! In addition, all of it happened because God gave me the courage to do something with the "controlling people" and my Papa and Mama came to rescue me after all. The Lord gave me the audacity to forgo the pride and accept financial help from Papa for the down payment on the house. All the "consolidation" was Jean's problem, not mine.

This house had a telephone, but it was a "three-party" line. It rang two quick rings for us. This was aggravating to hear the other rings during the day when I was there, but that didn't last too long. All I was interested in was having Christine all to myself. I was not that anxious for school to start since we were alone all day. School would start in September and I would be at work. I could put up with that. All party-line users knew not to make calls at night. It was necessary to let people know that we had this type of phone line.

Not too many people knew where we lived anyway. I didn't answer the phone even when it was our ring. I didn't want to talk to Jean's family, Jean had no reason to call and Papa was too tight with his money to call, so I just didn't worry about it. I had Christine and we played dolls, sang to each other and I read to her. I could read the same book to her and it didn't bother her. She knew if I skipped a page or read a sentence wrong. She was smart and knew that I had made a slip-up and corrected it right away. She could ride her tricycle in the house and run into furniture if she wanted to.

I kept saying, "Oh Lord is this real? Am I finally able to get away from another type of slave driver? Thank you, Lord for all these blessings." I just wanted my Mama and Papa to see this. I had worked very hard to make it like "my place." Therefore, it was not too long until I called them. It was long distance, but I didn't care. I was in "hog heaven."

"Hello!"" Papa said.

They didn't get a phone until after I left for college. It was a party line also, but different from ours. For some reason it didn't ring unless it was for them. If someone wanted to call out, you picked up the phone and if you heard someone else on it, you put it down.

I said, "Can you and Mama drive up? I will have a meal ready for you. I know you will be surprised so, just follow the signs. When you see the school, check the mileage, and the house would be exactly one mile from there on the left side. Look for the one with the white fences. You cannot miss it."

Papa said, "Oh, yeah, we'll find it. How 'bout it if we go up on Saturday?"

I said, "Yes that'll be fine, I'm so happy, Papa."

They came and were surprised that I had fixed a roast with all the trimmings. Mama was proud of me. They knew some of the financial problems, but not all. If Papa knew about all of the problems I had been having, he would've taken care of Jean and his family.

If it meant staying down at the farm and teaching at a different school, he would've worked on it immediately. He had some "pull" with the school board also. He and Mama would've kept Christine. However, this was the happiest summer that I ever had during married life. I wouldn't have any money, though until school started. I had Christine all alone now and that was all I needed. Every third Sunday, we would drive into town and then to the farm to see both Grandparents.

That was enough for me at his folks and I always had a reason not to stay too long because I had other things to do. I could spend a week back home. This didn't go over too well with them Jean's folks, but I didn't care. I was running things now and it felt good. I reckoned that I had begun to be the boss. Knowing how my folks felt, maybe I could do this. I told Jean that they were coming, so he worked every day that the store was open. He had to, because we had to have the money.

When school started, we had enough money coming in to hire someone to keep Christine while I was working. She was wonderful, and her name was Mrs. Bobeuf. She was more than a babysitter; she cooked and cleaned the house every day as if it had never been cleaned. She was grateful for a job and loved Christine like her own.

She cleaned the blinds everyday as well as the rest of the house just as if the President was coming. She had supper cooked when I got home. I didn't tell Mama that Mrs. Bobeuf cooked the roast and I just mashed the potatoes and bought the canned biscuits and vegetables. She probably knew, but didn't want to embarrass me by mentioning it. I wanted to ask her so many questions, but I knew that anything that I might bring up would hurt her feelings because she was unable to teach me growing up. She just never had the chance.

CHAPTER 24

Trouble? Where?

One day, soon after school started, when I got home the babysitter told me that Jean's mother had driven out and taken Christine home with them. She was afraid to tell them not to until they called me. I wished that she had, because I would've run home and made them leave after playing with her, but not take her home. Well, this brought on a fistfight, because his Mom cried and said that Christine was the only grandchild they had and they wanted her at least once a week. Jean knew about this ahead of time and never told me one single word about it.

He gave in to them because he said that he had to drive to town anyway, and could drop her off, and pick her up after his work and bring her back home. This meant that I didn't get to have her when I got home on Tuesday after school. I could recognize the warning sign. I wondered what would be next.   I raised unmitigated cane because Jean didn't tell me of the scheme they had planned without consulting me. He just walked off as if he didn't hear a word I was saying. Therefore, now his Mom had her on Tuesdays. She bought Christine everything you can imagine. She was given 47 cute little dresses that were never opened. This made Jean happy because his Mom was buying items for Christine by keeping her. I resented the notion of buying love.

Christine loved her Grandma Fromond because she now has to see her more often and Grandma did everything for her and bought her anything she wanted. Her Grandma would put her up on the kitchen counter and teach her to do little things. She would have her get a spoon or something else to make her feel needed. Christine enjoyed licking cake from the mixer batters and scraping the bowl. Soon the one day, became two days of going with Jean to town and on to Grandma's with Christine.   Then the principal wanted to use Mrs. Bobeuf those two days to help him if I didn't need her. That was fine with me, because I am sure, the lady needed the work and there was no babysitting for her to do and I could save that money.

My Mama lived 40 miles northeast and seldom saw Christine, much less becoming more acquainted with her to show her love also. She didn't have a dime to give anyone and always felt sad that she could not enjoy her more often. She wanted the same affection from Christine that Jean's Mother received. She believed that she was smarter than any of her grandchildren. Both of them were in awe of the child reading before she was even in kindergarten. None of the other children did this. They just didn't read to them as I did. They knew that she read to the boys when they came along and that they began reading before starting to school.

They felt so "left-out" and Mama would try to make Christine something or save a piece of candy or fruit, or biscuit; just anything to show that she loved her also. They lived too far to have the closeness that Mama and I wanted Christine to have with them. Equally, Christine wanted to see them more.

In only 3 months, Jean just had to have a tractor, and bought it at a time when finances were being paid off. I had no idea where he got the money, but I was beginning to see that the controller had something to do with it. I just know he told her that he had always wanted one and now he had a place to use it. Of course, she would please him, get him in a financial bind and I would be in another bind. Then he just had to buy some little orphaned bull calves to put on little "farm," as he called it. He had to have a little bit of country and knew nothing about it.

I said, "Jean, the grass is for the calves, not for the fun of using a bush-hog that you know nothing about."

He didn't know how to use a tractor with the bush-hog. I had to show him, and do most all the work. I could have shot myself for teaching him. He didn't know how to do anything except drive it. At least it was used once. I ended up doing all the work after school while he was at work in town. Jean would get off work anytime between 6–9 p.m. He enjoyed the auctions on Saturday like a kid. He made people think he had the money to buy all he wanted. The little calves were brought from the auction by a friend with a truck and cattle trailer. This, to him, was better than having one million dollars and made him feel so "wealthy."

However, he never fed or did anything with the calves. The "puppet" is feeling the change. Well, that meant that the calves had to have food, and no mama cow to feed them. Therefore, we had to buy these buckets with an udder at the bottom of it, which was similar to the udders on the mother cow, and then a mixture of powdered milk and water to feed these little calves. This was just about more than I could take. He never fed them because he had to leave for work too early.

He didn't want to be all messed up with this smelly job. How did I end up with this? Why did I take it or just leave one day while he was gone? Why did I not tell him to move in with his Mom? Jean was never satisfied and had to have more. He was driving me crazy! I told him that if he had that kind of money, that we needed more furniture to get by for guest who might come by after school. I also told him that I didn't have time to feed the calves.

That went in one ear and out the other. Soon I got some new and some used furniture from the store and some more from his folks that had been stored in the attic of the "playhouse." We finally got a dining table and chairs at that time.

After 2 weeks with the calves, we began losing them. A neighbor's dog was killing them by grabbing them in the neck. It had to be a "hog-dog." I knew it because that was the way a hog-dog was trained. It was not long before we both saw the dog jump over the barn fence. Jean grabbed the shotgun and shot him. The dog made it home before it died. Well, that ended messing with the calves. That dog got the last one. Now, he didn't need the tractor. We had bush-hogged the 25 acres of pasture and had it looking very "clean-cut."

Soon, we had to let the housekeeper go, and then Jean's car was repossessed. Next, he had to sell the tractor and we were about to lose the house. The two days a week keeping Christine while I taught, had now become five days.

Jean knew I was angry when I asked, "Whose child is she, your Mother's or ours? I don't like it at all! Why in the hell did you get the tractor, calves and all this stuff? You knew all this was going on and never said a word. I got this place so I could keep away from your family. Papa helped me with this and he is going to be angry if he discovers what has been going on with you and your family. My Papa would kill you if he knew all his money had been squandered. Maybe I am the one who needs to shoot you!

"Where is all the money going? Are you gambling? Do you have another girlfriend? We had plenty and now nothing. Why are you losing your car for non-payment, but you bought the tractor, calves and have taken my car? This does not make sense to me. You are gambling, or playing around. I'll get to the bottom of this when I talk to Papa. He loved this place and so did I. You can live with your folks, but Christine is staying here with me. If I have to sell this place, I'll take her to the farm and teach where Isabelle is teaching. Are you listening to me?" I was yelled.

I've yelled and should have a long time before now.

He never said a word. He just shrugged his shoulders. I knew that he was up to something when all the "farm stuff" started coming in. For five months, I had to ride in a carpool from school into town (24 miles), walk 2 ½ miles, crossing over a long bridge over the river to get to the store where Jean worked. I had no transportation. I tried once to take "my" car; picking up Christine and driving back to the store or home without Jean. He could "bum" rides for a change. But, that sure didn't work.

Then I had to wait for Jean to get off work before we could go home. That gave his Mom fits, she lit out after me and I just couldn't handle her without knocking her out first. This meant that Jean took Christine to his Mother's house every day for babysitting now with my car until I got back into town. I knew that I had to grin and bear it or tell my folks. That would have brought on a kill'en.

Why, I could've walked home, but that was exactly what his Mom wanted me to do! It was a shorter distance to do that than having this 2 ½ mile walk to the store. This would lead to her keeping Christine every night and I could see this trying to happen. I was not about to agree for her getting away with all this. This was tough on me since I walked with books and papers to grade and had to wait in the store for closing time.

Next, we drove to his Mother's house for Christine while I stayed in the car for a way to "stay sane" and then drive home. This was so humiliating for me, because she had a tongue like no other. Jean's father was the most precious man I had ever known. He was nothing like my

Papa. Why couldn't Jean have the compassion and responsibility like his father, I didn't understand. The companionship was forced upon him. There was no wonder why he got "skunk-drunk" when he got home. His Mother had no compassion for me. If she didn't like what Christine had on in the morning she would change it. One day during the when I had to bum a ride to town, it had snowed so hard and so much that the principal let school out early.

It was exhausting for my 24-mile ride in and then 2 ½ mile walk and crossing the snow covered river bridge just to get to the store and wait for Jean to get off work. This made me furious with my teeth chattering and grinding as I carefully walked over the bridge and then to the store. Soon it began snowing harder. I had no cold weather shoes, boots or clothes for all this.

They closed the store and Jean and I went to his Mother's house so that we could quickly pick up Christine   Jean goes to get in this English Sports car.

I asked, "Where is my car and what have you done with it? Did you wreck it?"

He still never said a word. By that time, we were at his Mom's house.

As soon as I walked in, Jean's Mother lit into me about dressing Christine in pants, which she said were boy's clothes. I told her that she had plenty of them for this cold weather. His Mom had taken her red corduroy cowboy outfit and boots off and had put a dress on Christine. I immediately grabbed her, put her red outfit back on and prepared to leave for home before it got to snowing any harder and before dark. Jean's Mother said that we were not leaving back out into that bad weather and that Jean and I would sleep in the front bedroom. She was in control and planned with all energy she had to force us to stay. She couldn't hold her tongue. She wanted Christine; she didn't want us or especially me. I had to stay with "the package" and she was not part of it. I was determined to leave. Jean said nothing. I began to see what I was going to have to do or put up with her until I was able to get away.

Well, all hell broke loose because Jean traded my "paid for car" on an old English tiny convertible, which he financed and the title to my car was at home. Now how this could happen without somebody forging my name? Well I was determined to arrive home right then and this car mess could be straightened out later. He got a little money for my car, on the trade, and I got nothing. I wished that I had thought of going to Evette's to get away. I didn't take time to think or I would have left in a second. I could have taken off in it with Christine and left him with his Mom. I wished that I had thought of the basketball coach. Jean would not get back to my house, for sure.

Then Jean's Mom said, "You all are going to STAY HERE!"

I said, "Oh no!" We are going home right now; and Jean you had better get into the car immediately!"

Jean had never heard me give a command performance like that. He put his coat on and all wrapped, for the ride back. His Mother was screaming for us to get back in the house. I told Jean that this was one time that he had better listen to me or I will leave with her right then. He got in the car and we began the snowy ride back home. As we got out of town, we were making our own tracks with this narrow car. Other cars had slid into the ditches. This little car was piling up snow on the front like a bulldozer. I would jump out, wipe the snow off the wind-shield and jump back in. I kept getting the snow off and Jean driving through it, making his own tracks. With God's blessings, we made it, but we had to bundle up in bed. The butane was freezing and the heater barely light up.

You must know that this was the first time that I had a cross word with any of the people who were running my life and ruining it. I was proud of myself for once, but I know that God had to have given me strength and His blessings to do something. After nine months, Jean had accumulated so much debt that we had to have another "bailout," which I, once again, knew nothing about.

He was always buying things and surprising me with little gifts, which were truly bribes to keep me from "killing" him, I guess. I couldn't understand the debt, and I didn't buy anything but lunch at school, which was only ten cents for teachers. Nevertheless, in less than two years, we had to sell that "dream house." You know now that the "fami-ly" was happy. It was as if all this was planned again, and I knew it. I had fixed it up nice and the house sold for a good bit more than I paid for it. We only had to pay a mortgage ($9,000 minus the payments and interests). This was "my bailout" money and not his folks. I sold it and the buyers got their own financing for $12,000. I gave Mama $3,000, and hid the rest. Jean knew nothing about this money; this house was mine, as well as the profit. Mama had enough for me that soon I could run away, if it came to that.

Jean had made good money and Marjane call the debt off which had cosigned. That presented a situation where we had to move back. I felt sure "the controllers" all got together and planned this out, and they got their way. I was so angry! Now they could deliver the tongue-lashing with me right at their disposal. I was glad that I gave the profit on the house to Mama. I had no idea what would happen next. I still taught out there and now I had to "bum" a ride the other way. How embarrassing can this get? I made up excuses and was about to run out of them right away.

Jean did everything possible to keep me in his favor, and guess what? I think he "drugged me." I was pregnant and didn't know it until I went to see Dr. Bill. Oh my God, how and when did this happen? I would have to tell the principal.

Finally I said, "Well, I'm pregnant and need to be near Dr. Bill. All of the teachers accepted that, but the principal was very disappointed that I had to move and would not teach for him. He was grateful for the time that I taught there and so was I.

CHAPTER 25

My Paradise?

My Papa had killed before and he would surely kill again if he had known what was happening now. I will have to let him shoot them or tell him a lie. I don't like to lie to my Papa. Oh, I wished that I had told my Papa a long time before now. God only knows what he would've done. I don't remember telling him anything about us moving into town, other than I was pregnant and needed to be nearer the doctor. What a wimp, I had turned out to be again. I was moving near Evette. Maybe this will work out just with an unexpected twist after all. Having Evette near will give me the mental strength needed as I had before. That will work well after all and Mama was happy that I would be closer for them to visit. That would be better than killing Jean and going to jail.

After the sale of the country house, we were able to buy a house close to where Evette and her husband, Arnaud, lived. He was a "full blown" Cajun. We visited often because her son was near Christine's age. I was pregnant, which meant that I couldn't teach the next year and had to dip into my hidden savings a couple of times. However, Jean had to come up with a down-payment somehow. I have no idea where this came from.

This was a neat little brick home in a subdivision where most of the people were military because it was close to the Air Force base. During this time, Jean was still working for Joli Vean and getting a larger commission than he had been getting, as well as a monthly pay.

He knew that he had better make a lot, I thought, because I would not have an income. I had to talk to Dr. Bill and he repeatedly, told me that he had to see Jean. How many times will he say that? I wanted Jean to do the calling, but he would not. I was ready to leave and be a pregnant "runaway" with a child. Now that would've made the front page of the morning newspaper. They were ruining any relationship with Jean that might have been tolerated for a while. I got up early to have the house clean at five a.m. wherever we lived.

I never knew when his folks would arrive or just drop in. Poor Marcel Sr., had no say so in anything either. If Jean's Mother said hop, he hopped. I was very fond of him, saw his distress and could only offer compassion. No wonder he stayed inebriated as quickly as he could after he returned from work.

I couldn't cook, but I could clean. The family never had a chance to say that I was not a good housekeeper. All were "spic and span" clean, beds made, dishes washed and put away. Jean's Dad would not hurt me anyway. He was kind and sweet and I kept wearing the ring "HE" gave me. I'm sure that he wanted to tell me several times to leave Jean, but he never had a chance.

The only escape he had to prevent hearing the tongue-lashing to him and to me was to get "skunk-drunk." Everyone made sure that he was never alone with me for him to tell me anything. And the problems with Jean kept happening. When his Mom wanted a surprise visit, he had to drive her wherever she wanted to go. Many times, they would pop in when no one was there. How? Why, Jean's Mother made sure that she had a key to every place we lived. I certainly didn't want her watching me trying to prepare a meal. She was an excellent cook, but I was not a cook at all. I was never taught.

I would ask and it was all in "ambiguous terms" like a dab, pinch, to taste, smidgen or just a "little bit" and I just kept making too many messes. I wanted precision in good "measures!" Once I was making pralines as I saw his Mother do. I had the recipe and it looked like hers. Then, shortly after I beat it as she did, it looked so much like the consistency of buttermilk that I immediately thought that something was wrong and if she came in and saw this, I would get a lot of lip. Back again, I went for the shovel to dig a hole, poured it out and covered it completely as if nothing had ever been there but grass. I had to learn to cook before the yard got any sweeter.

This happened several times with pralines. Another time was after watching her make a pecan pie. When the timer went off I took the pie out and my pecans were sitting on the bottom. Who ever saw a pecan pie with the pecans on the bottom? Therefore, while it was hot and before anyone saw it, I went out and buried that pie somewhere near the pralines.

CHAPTER 26

Rawhide! Round'em Up!

I was about seven months pregnant and Christine was waiting for a baby to come. In no time, a hurricane blew up the Gulf. It lifted the back end of Papa's house up about 14 inches. Papa told the Lord that if he would allow everyone live through this time, he would build a house closer to the ground. Papa kept his Godly promise about having a house built closer to the ground if God would spare them from the hurricane. It was tiny compared to the size of the plantation home. They didn't need that huge home anymore. This one was a three-bedroom, one bath home with a living room, kitchen and a dining room large enough for a double fireplace. It only took about two steps to get into the high end and one for the low end of the house.

It seemed as though Papa had to see someone else take over the pastures and one field. Jean approached him about putting some cows down in the country and leasing the land from him. I don't know how Jean made him think that he was in the money now. This did excite Papa. He was bored after staring out into the land, and seeing what used to be planted there. Therefore, he leased the land to Jean for $1 a year. Jean had the auction barn bring his cows down first. The next was a load of hay and a big brahma bull. As soon as the bull was allowed out, he went running down the pasture in break-neck speed. As soon as the bull heard the cows "mooing," he stopped so quickly that he created a cloud of dust. That bull was glad that he had company.

"Where did the money come from for all of this? Are you aware that I need a car?" I asked.

Jean didn't say. He would never tell me anything, just a "wave-off."

I said, "You had better tell me or I would tell Papa more than you want me to tell.

He still waved me off. Oh gosh, that made me angry.

I could've shot my Papa for leasing this land to Jean. He just did this I think, to keep his mind occupied. However, he didn't know anything because I had not told them about the mess we had been in and it was getting worse. He probably thought that I wanted all this. Now it was too late to tell all about the mess.

I said, "Jean I think that I might just keep Christine here since I'm pregnant and can't teach school next year anyway. I'll pack enough for us tonight so that when we come back tomorrow, they could enjoy Christine every day for a change. I could still get her enough books to read each week."

I said, "The Bookmobile comes to Papa's or nearby out in the country. Christine would have access to all the books she could handle. She, Papa, Mama and I could each check out six books at a time and order books she wanted to read. If I wanted to stay, they are for it.

There was no response___Just a wave off. I was the one who was stupid! I talked when I shouldn't and didn't talk when I should've. I should've kept my mouth shut that time. Jean didn't even come to pick us up. He went straight down to the country from work. He knew that I had everything packed for the next evening to stay down there when we went down. That was a daunting idea though, but it didn't pan out.

However, all of the BOSSES would've been down there to get Christine back up there in a "New York Minute." If they had gone down to get her, my Papa would have had a lot to say before he ran them off. I had no idea how they "swindled" me out of a car or who forged my name and signed the papers for my car, which was paid for, when the title for it was at the house. I would also ask what happened to the little sports car that he traded my car for and why and how Jean ended up with this piece of junk he's driving now? That would have ended everything, I think. Why won't he tell me? This is my fault. Again, hindsight is 20-20.

Oh, Papa enjoyed this show immensely that Jean was delivering at least once a week if not every day. Jean was having a ball at the auction barn in town and going broke without a second thought about it. He put cattle down on Papa's place to make others think that he had hit the "Jackpot." What a mistake this turned out to be. He knew nothing about raising cattle, but he needed a new toy to play with all the time that I was pregnant. He also wanted to have the first melons and get richer. He had heard my older stories of how the watermelons sold quickly and for the highest price, if you got them ready by June 19.

He didn't know anything about farming and had never planted anything in his life. He didn't feed the orphan calves, and now he has a herd of cattle. I have wished many times that I had not told him anything about the farm. I couldn't help but think of this so many times. Darn, I was stupid and afraid of his family.

I asked, "Do you know what a watermelon seed even looks like?

Again, no answer. I wondered if he had given the first thought of how he would sell them if some did grow. He had no truck, just a used car, which barely made it back and forth. If he raised any watermelons at all, he couldn't haul more than a dozen. I know that I married an idiot, but just let it go. I was not confident that his folks knew about all of this.

How, I wished that I had told Papa and Mama about all the troubles back when I borrowed the $1,000. Papa should've figured it out by now, since I had to borrow money to put down on the house and we had already lost it in no time. They could see that I was pregnant and should not be doing this work.

We planted the watermelon seeds, though, in "peat moss" cups and covered them with plastic to keep them warm so that they would get a "boost" in growing time. Next, Jean just had to have another tractor.

He did not need this tractor any more than the last one he bought. This one with all its tools could've planted everything from a mustard seed to a coconut. He didn't know one tool from another. All he needed was a turning plow and a mule. He didn't need to mow the pasture; the grass was for the cows! This was just like a new toy to him. Why can't Papa see this?

I had to do the plowing anyway while I was seven months pregnant, but soon Jean would have to learn how to do it with my instructions. We both put the cups of watermelons out in the field and they began to grow. It was all we could do by living in town, and hurrying down to check on the cattle and watermelons. That was a 52 mile round trip to the country and back home.

All of this had to be in God's plans. About the time the watermelons had a 4" growth, there was an early freeze. I was elated, but we had never had a freeze that early as far back as my Papa could remember. God was with me and I felt it. There was my help. That was the end of all the watermelons. God knew that I didn't need to be doing this and knew that I would be the one who did all the work. He had not thought about preparing any soil for the watermelons. If I had waited a week, we would have nothing to plant due to the freeze.

Getting ready to have a baby in 2 months didn't bode well with me in the farming any more. Thank you, Lord for taking care of this big mess. After the freeze, he didn't need anything and getting rid of equipment was much more risky and frustrating than buying it. Jean was now forced to sell all the cattle to whoever would give him the best price at the auction, and they would have to go to the country to get them. He didn't seem to care. His folks never scolded him. However, they would chastise me if I mentioned that he had no business messing with his "dream-world." Papa thought it was all because of the freeze and ruining the watermelon patch. It was not. It was finances again, "ALWAYS FINANCES!" I know that I am losing it for not telling them everything I know. I should and then move there after the baby is born and well enough to make the move. I wanted to leave now! My folks will understand this now.

In November, it was time for Marcel to be born. Evette ended up taking me to the hospital because Jean was working. On the way to the hospital, a man pulled his car out in front of a motorcyclist and killed the man. The people kept driving for about two blocks. Evette took my maternity jacket, which was yellow, and started flagging down traffic so they would not run over the man on the highway.

I kept my eye on the car, which hit him, noticing that they exchanged seats, so I was able to tell the police, once they got there. The first cop called in another one to handle the road while he escorted us to the hospital because Evette kept screaming that I was having a baby. That cop got all the information he needed and the other one led us on to the hospital. Evette stayed at the hospital until Jean could get there. Through all this excitement my contractions stopped. The doctor had them take me back to my room until they started back.

It was not too very long until Marcel was born November 17th. This child was named after his Grandpa Fromond, nickname and all. However, he was not readily accepted as a grandchild with Jean's Mother until he was much older.

Christine was her love and the only one as for as she was concerned. Finally, after Grandpa Fromond accepted this little boy, he did something so that his first and only grandson, at the time, would be proud. He quit drinking, smoking, and he joined the church straight away. He tithed and worked as often as he could toward painting, maintenance and building projects.

As soon as Christmas was over, I wanted to talk to Papa. I told Jean that it was ending. I was sick of the finance problems and his folks treatment of me. To make up for all the finance, and mess, he promised it would not happen again. You would not believe all the loving that went on. Has he drugged me? Why did I agree to this? I still thought that Dr. Bill had me fixed up, but it didn't work. I needed Dr. Bill to have someone check out my sanity now for sure. Here it is February and I find that I am pregnant again.

We had an interesting time with the getting library during the summer for Christine. Marcel had lots of baby books, which kept us both busy reading to him. He began noticing if you skipped a page and went to another, just as Christine did at that age. These will be smart, but very poor kids who loved their Dad. It was nearing Christmas and I saw that we would never make it on his salary alone and I am becoming distressed over what and how we would make it with three kids. We had to move again. The expense for the house was too much.

The house sold quickly with the air force base being near. We arranged with the buyer to rent the house from him until after Jean-Paul was born. They were quiet kind and considerate and I was thankful for this. We made some profit and I held onto that and gave it to Mama again to hold. Mama and Papa came after Marcel to keep until Jean-Paul was born. It was time any day now. On a Thursday evening while Jean was working, I felt the labor pains coming. I called Evette again, and she rushed me to the hospital where Jean was waiting. This didn't take long. We got there just in time. I was in the hospital only four days and the following week, Mama and Papa returned with Marcel. He had forgotten everyone and was so startled with a new baby, and didn't recognize me. I didn't expect that to happen. Marcel was only 14 months older than Jean Paul. I kept telling Jean-Paul to say, "Hi brother Marcel, I love you." I had to get him use to his little brother and me. It was as if he had forgotten where he was supposed to be. That blank stare bothered me.

He needed this affection and it was not too long that he accepted this little brother. After pretending that Jean-Paul was telling him "hello" along with many other expressions, he began remembering who we all were. In no time at all, the people who bought the house needed it immediately and we had to move with the baby only four weeks old. I did the packing with as much ease as I could and Jean had two of the delivery men from the store move us into this cold barn of a house on Florence St.

Jean had found a house that was cold but had space heaters, which we had to burn day and night. With two babies and Christine, we had to try to stay warm. That four year old became my "maid" and running here and there to get items for me. What a sweetheart she was and of course she was so motivated to help in any way to show how "grown up" she was. She was enthusiastic over being old enough to help her two brothers and me.

There were no "showers" for the boys as there were for Christine, but there was plenty of "hand-me-downs." Jean's Mother kept begging for Christine to stay with her, but I didn't allow it. I needed that little girl more now for help and she gave it on her own accord. Much was voluntary and predicted when I needed something, or the new baby (Jean Paul) for a bottle. Along the work she did, she also found time for her reading and read to Marcel. She would read or play with Marcel, who was keenly aware of all the excitement. This became a gamely action, which she cheerfully enjoyed and so did he. Jean-Paul was so tiny, he was not aware of anything other than something to eat. Those little diaper tops had been handed down now from two babies and still in great shape.

I wondered why I was not getting over this delivery as quickly as the other two. Well it didn't take long to find out. Darn, I can't believe that I am pregnant, and having excessive cramps. He must have given me a "knock-out" pill again. I remembered nothing. I called my Mama and asked if she would come and help me. Evette had her hands full. I couldn't bother her just about this. She had two of her own now, and they needed her. I needed someone with plenty of experience, and my

Mama had plenty of that. Both Mama and Papa came immediately. Mama wanted to stay with me, so Papa did some business in town and went back home. I made Jean stay at his Mom's house, so that there would be room for Grandma Thibodeaux: my Mama. Jean would call or come by to get a list of needed items for us. His Mom, who was an excellent cook, would send food over by Jean.

In less than an hour, I began bleeding all over the bed. I had a miscarriage right there. Mama knew exactly what to do and took care of soiled linens as well as the mattresses and me. She was an expert in that area. Christine gave Mama her undivided attention in giving help to her, Marcel and bottle fed Jean Paul. A new brother, a Grandma with us and a sick Mother needed all the help she could give.

Mama was amazed at how smart and helpful Christine was. My Mama truly adored that child. I don't know how I could've survived without either of them. After 2 weeks, all was well and comforted, so Papa came to check on us and Mama returned home. I would truly miss her with that kind touch, comfort and love which I so desperately needed. My doctor had me go in for a "D and C." Trying to negotiate some normalcy, I tried to cook a little with Christine's help. We did fine until Jean brought home some shameless news about finances again.

I had told him that I was going to move in with Mama and Papa and he could do what he wanted to do. He couldn't take it, but I don't know what he did when he left. About that time, Jean's Mother walked over to find out what all was going on. I am sure that Jean told her about Mama coming up and about the miscarriage. However, it was after she knew that my Mama had left that she made this appearance. She had to be ashamed of Jean, by not coming to see her. She had only met her at the wedding. I couldn't believe how unashamed her actions were.

Since Jean had to stay with her for a short time, his Mom knew when to come. This was cruel and remarkably, he finally realized some of the problems, which he had brought on us. The finances were very bad and I had no job again for another year.

CHAPTER 27

Not Again!

Now we would have to move back into the Moureau house for a while again. This was the barn, in which we were in first for three months and then for four months before moving here. This house was old and would make good firewood. It appeared that varmints had been living in it before we first had to move in it, and now it is in the same condition again. I couldn't tolerate it again. It was in shambles.

I would handle it though, but I am concerned about the kids. I believe their Dad had just LOST IT!" We were the only ones who had lived there for three months and I'm sure it had been vacant for at least thirty years or more. There was no telling who had lived in it. Jean wanted to declare Bankruptcy, but I would not go for it. It was critically important to me that we were not going to declare Bankruptcy or go on Welfare. I would pitch a tent first. The Thibodeaux barn was cleaner than this. I had to clean that barn out and teach school. It was cold and creepy. It was big, and the layout was appalling. For sure, no one came to see us there! Even his parents didn't ever come. Marjane was just spitting distance away and she never came. Maybe she was too proud to know that her "favorite" had to "stoop" pretty low to have to live in this rattrap. I should have them come out. The more I thought about it, I decided to call and Grandpa Fromond answered the phone. Wow! What a surprise that he was the one who answered the phone.

"Hi, Pawpaw, why don't y'all come out for visit and see what we are living in?" I pleaded.

Since it was about Christmas time, they did come out. It was clean, for sure, but to move from a $300,000 home which sat 200 feet away to a house that would make good firewood. What an embarrassment!" It certainly was to Pawpaw. He just hugged me and whispered how sorry he was that we had to move into this shack. She didn't see or hear this conversation. She visited with the kids, and in ten minutes, they were gone. Oh well, I wondered what she thought. Jean acted like "business as usual."

I didn't have to worry about cooking something and his Mother seeing it. I don't think that I did any cooking besides scrambled meat helper with some different mixes and I knew how to cook eggs and make toast. Eggs could be boiled, fried, scrambled, to eat as is or made into sandwiches.

I learned to use tuna fish with the boiled eggs and add chopped baked potatoes and apples to stretch it into extra meals as well as for the added nutrients. We had plenty of peanut butter (bought by the gallon) and jelly that Mama and I made. Now, where would everyone sleep? We stayed here about four months. I couldn't stand it anymore. My anger was about to erupt, but it didn't happen around the kids. If it ever did, it would be as I LEFT with them.

Jean found a house near Christine's school that rented for $100 less than the Betsy house and we had lived rent-free for four months. I ate very little except at school. I just made sure the kids had plenty of food. Jean could get his when and where he wanted. We moved to this less expensive rent house as soon as it was ready.

This seemed like a dream for me; to be settled for a while in a decent house for a change. Christine loved her teachers, who were my friends as well. She was in the fourth grade. I drove myself to school at Miller Junior High and took Marcel and Jean-Paul to school in town. When Jean-Paul was in kindergarten, he was reading to everyone. He did homework right along with Marcel.

Marcel was in the second grade Jean's Mother had to pick Jean Paul up at noon from kindergarten because he was a January baby and had to stay in kindergarten another year. Then she went back to get Marcel at the end of the school day. She had fallen in love for the boys by then just by being with them more. She needed this time with the boys as well as they did with her. However, they never took the place of Christine. Jean Paul was already reading Marcel's books and he was just in kindergarten. Marcel read books for fourth and fifth graders from the library and taught Jean Paul some of them while in the 1st grade. All the children loved reading. I knew that they would be smart, if this excitement continued.

Now the fun began when I had to go to Jean's Mothers to pick the boys up and then go home to grade papers and rest. This place we were renting now had a small barn and a tiny pasture on it. The first thing I knew, Jean bought a milk cow to put in that barn. We only had about three acres and Jean thought that he could milk a cow?

I said, "I hope you have learned to milk a cow, because I have other things to do."

Why, he could've tried that on most anyone's farm, but no, he had to buy his own cow. The cow lived on that small pasture for feed, and he thought that was enough for one cow. Oh God, what was lacking here? Jean needed to be committed to the Insane Asylum, which was on my way to school. He couldn't milk that cow and had never done it before. Maybe I needed to be committed first.

His folks were so proud of him with all this ambition to learn new things. Therefore, that was another job for me now; milking the cow, straining the milk and cleaning up everything. There was feed and a churn to buy because he thought he wanted to churn and make butter, and I made sure he did. Now the troops came to chime in.

"This is a great learning experience for you, Jean and I must say, for the kids," Marjane said and his Mom nodding her head in approval.

They thought that he did all the milking and to keep the kids from hearing me embarrass their Dad, I said nothing and neither did they contradict him. I had to do the milking and they did use all the milk that poor old cow gave, which was only about 1/2 gallon. She was old and probably didn't get enough feed. Oh, I was so angry about this "so called experience" he and his family wanted him to have. I began to hate them more and starting to hate to see Jean's face.

His experience was to watch the work, which had to be done. They thought that he did it, but never did anything but buy that milk cow, deliver it and churn. If that was a real farm experience, then I was a fool. I should never have let that cow stay there one night. We would've been better off financially to give her to someone.

However, I should have told his folks, "He needs to share these experiences with all of you and enjoy paying for it, or actually doing them when he does not have time to do them. This would be quite an experience making you all happy with all of his undertakings, as well as adventurous ideas for each of you, because I was taking the kids and leaving." Why didn't I tell them that?

CHAPTER 28

`Something's Happening?

I could smell it like a rat. I felt that something was about to hap-pened. The boss was around and there was whispering. I understood the part that "she'll never leave with the kids, for sure, so let her threat and see what happens." They already knew that I couldn't cook and had plans if I threatened him again. Therefore, it was not long until Jean sold the cow because he saw that it was too much trouble, he claimed. He knew something else also, but he didn't tell me. In two more months, he had to tell. We had to move again when school was out and move back to the Moureau home again with no rent cost. I wished for a gun so bad not knowing, which way I would point it.

I said, "I will not do it again unless we put it in some kind of order so that it would be habitable. This was worse than the barn back at Papa's. I would rather live down there than here. In fact, that's where I'm going with the kids until you have enough money to support us. I can teach somewhere down there."

Wow, that didn't take long for action to take place. The building ma-terials, even used, began coming in. There were nice used windows from the Realtor friend's jobs as well as new sheet rock left over from another job and I had my summer cut out for me. First, to the library we went because the kids could do no part of this and they enjoyed reading. Christine had some required reading for the next school year, so all of that kept them busy while I hung sheet rock, built upper and bottom kitchen cabinets because there were none except what was under an old metal kitchen sink which was rusted and leaked. I even put "bottle glass" panels in the top cabinets, which made them look nice, especially after I had painted all of the rest of the woodwork. The bottle glass was out of style, but they served for this purpose.

I was not a carpenter, but sure knew measurements and lived in homes and remembered how the hinges were supposed to be hung. I enclosed the back porch so that there would be another entrance to the only bathroom without disturbing Christine and her privacy. I could only help Jean with the plumbing so that the washer and dryer could go to the back porch. The boys got the living room for their bedroom and Jean and I got the storage room which was next to the kitchen. The dining room became the living room. We enclosed the front porch with all those leftover windows and this became the living room.

Christine got the main bedroom, which was at least 20 by 20 feet. This house was free rent so we could relax a little. This material saved a lot of money, or we couldn't have afforded the remodeling job. Jean gave me $200 for paint, plywood and hinges for the cabinets and the rest was donated material. I wondered why no one came around? None of the bosses came to see us at all until Christmas time and Jean's Mom and Dad came out for the first and last visit. It might have been the feeling of guilt for discipline that Jean didn't receive as he grew up. Maybe it was guilt for Jean's upbringing.

She couldn't keep up with our business here. We did take the kids to both Grandparent's house a couple of times. Jean had been study-ing real estate again when he had time while at Joli Vean, (back to the old job). He was smart and renewed his license. He did some listings and selling after work again. Then he left Joli Vean's store again, and I thought that was a big slip-up, because he was making good money. I wondered often, if he just couldn't stand to live without a crisis as it seemed that this was a challenge, which he enjoyed at our expense and the "Puppet" cannot do anything about it.

Jean's Aunt Marjane decided that she would just give him the old Moureau home. Maybe she could see or hear me working my butt off, and decided that it should be ours now. Jean didn't have very much time to work on it. I knew that it had to have some work done before I was going to live in that barn again. Hanging the sheetrock was quite a chore, and sometime Christine helped me balance it as I climbed a ladder to seal up the large cracks in the board ceiling. I learned to hammer with each hand and used my head to help keep the sheetrock in place, using it also like an extra hand. I never wanted to do that again. I listened carefully to all the gossip about keeping the kids, if I left. They had to be dreaming, because that was not going to happen.

Jean had to tape the sheet rock cracks and seal it properly. He also worked with the electricity because I didn't know how, but watched so that I would know a little if ever I needed it. Keep in mind that I taught school except 5 summers. First, one was The Paradise home and I played with Christine all summer, next was the camp house where we read books and skated every day, and this barn that we just remodeled that summer. There were 2 other summers that I was out for the boys while pregnant and the first one was the first pregnancy with Christine. I never got to rest. Once Jean called the house to talk to me and Christine answered the phone. He needed to talk to me right then for some reason.

She said, "Mom's on top of the ladder with a big piece of sheetrock and she cannot come to the phone."

Well, he didn't mind me working, but didn't want me to hang sheetrock by myself on the ceiling. It was agonizing, but I did it, and didn't answer the phone. Now, I did tell him that he could do the "finish" work on it and paint it after he came home. He did it, too. We had barely gotten everything done when Jean had an offer on the house. That was probably the reason for the "unanswered" phone call. I couldn't believe this was happening now.

It was at least more comfortable, warmer, it was ours and he wanted to sell it? I couldn't understand it. I was teaching at Miller Junior High and he was making good money back again at Joli Vean's. Why take any chances? I could handle this. Finally, we had no issues with finances. Well, we had only been there for five months when it was sold it to his boss, Mr. Guideaux,

He got it for a steal at $8,000 as well as the commercial lot. I didn't know that he agreed to let the commercial lot go with the sale, which was stupid. It was worth more than the house. Anyway, that was when he had the money to buy the Linda Drive house that he had listed and sold to himself, so I guess HE did come out better for this sale anyway, but we still had a mortgage on it. We had only been in that house on Linda Dr. for two months and then the Moreau house burned to the ground. I always believed that this was purposefully done for the insurance money by someone. I don't know if Mr. Guideaux sold it or owned it when it burned.

We had no house note, until he bought this nice home in a great neighborhood with a big house note. We didn't need this nice home.

We were out of debt and he couldn't stand it. We were both working now and had a wonderful chance to put some money in savings for something that might come up. The house is very nice and we were in it quickly. The next school would be Capitaine Elementary that was near the house. Christine would be in the sixth, Marcel the third, and Jean-Paul in the first grade and they could ride their bikes there. Jean Paul was a January baby, which meant he was a lot older than the other first graders. He already knew how to read all the 2nd and 3rd grade books. He did all the homework that Marcel had in every subject, I knew that first grade teacher was going to have a problem. It was 2 weeks after moving there when the principal paid us a visit and asked if we would mind if Jean Paul was moved to the 2nd grade. I knew he would miss out on some "sit and stay" disciplines and writing skills. He did assure us that he had talked to the 2nd grade teacher who said that she would take care of that.

I did agree and was disappointed that there were no plans for a student to progress at their own rate. However, the (1st year) first grade teacher had 36 students and handling one who was that advanced was more than she could handle. The new teacher was wonderful with him and did allow him to excel as fast as he wanted to go.

They had many friends in this new subdivision, and enjoyed them all. It was a very nice subdivision and Christine was thrilled with her private bedroom and bath. It was the fourth bedroom and Christine claimed it immediately with the private bath. She deserved it! We lived there a little less than three years, which was the longest time at any residence.

I was still teaching at Miller Junior High at this time. This job only lasted five years because Marjane was a member of the school board, and the integration of teachers being moved to other schools instead of students to meet government demands was going to be put into place in 2 years. Beginning the 3rd year teaching there, the principal, Mr. LaBeaux came to me almost in tears and said that I needed to call the school board to see what had happened to my check. It was only $2.25. He and I just knew that there was a big error.

I called and had the biggest shock of my life. They said that the Internal Revenue Service would be garnishing my check for three years. When I asked why, he told me that the taxes had not been filed and that since I was salaried, IRS had the rest of my check and our bank account. They couldn't get Jean's check because he was on commission, but they did get the bank account, every last dime. However, people on commission couldn't be garnished, but still owed. He couldn't put money in the bank because they could get that. I didn't know what to do. I was so embarrassed and Mr. LaBeaux just hugged me when I told him that it would be worked out.

He said that he would give me money to help out, but I asked him to pray for us instead. That not only made me feel a little better, but also kept my mind off shooting Jean or myself. I kept wondering why this "reckless action" didn't come about until we moved into the mortgaged home. I know now that IRS would have gotten the house but did not want one with a mortgage.

I finally made him answer the questions, "I just didn't and that's all I have to say."

Taxes were automatically taken out of my check. I actually had claimed "0" dependents so I could get a nice "windfall" back from the government. I had purposely chosen "O" dependents so that if anything happened, I would have money coming in to pay it off. It was a good that I didn't have a gun at that time.

I found all the copies of the tax forms in his Dad's desk, and showed Jean that all was done correctly on my part and signed with W-2 attached that he had never filled out his part out. I also him how much we would have gotten back because I claimed no dependents. When asked why, he just shrugged his shoulders and left the room. Now I found out why we had to sell the neat home on Linda Drive that all of us enjoyed so much. I drew out all my retirement money and teaching for $2.25 for 3 years plus the bank account.

"Start talking, buddy, and tell me what you know about this?" I asked.

He said nothing and I was so angry I could have shot him, but we had to help after school at part of the building business. I was tired and had papers to grade as well as lessons to prepare. The kids had homework for the next day. How could he have done this to us? He deserved going to jail to keep us from going any further into debt, or the

Insane Asylum.

I threatened again saying, "From this day forward, you MUST NOT build another house. Do you understand? I mean it or I'll leave!" What a useless threat he thought, until I told him that I would move to the farm. Where are the bosses? He knew he was good at selling and listing but promised never to build another house. I am glad they tolerated him back in with the furniture company. I don't know how they put up with him leaving and hiring him back. I believed him because he knew that I was serious. My Papa would stand behind me if I went to live there. His folks would run into trouble for sure if they bothered me. I was going to take the kids to the farm if he had not agreed.

I was going to take the kids to the farm if he had not agreed. Mama and Papa would visit and have money if I needed it and I did at the time. I only bought necessities. The retirement money, 3 years of teaching and the bank account paid it off. This would hurt my retirement. In fact, my retirement check would be about $1000 to $1200 more if it had not been for that. Everyone at Miller was friends whom we enjoyed. So, what was I to do now? I resigned at the end of the 7th year because I was not assigned to teach school in a black school. Marjane didn't care whether I would reap repercussions from gossip or not. That particular year, they had the teachers move to black or white schools instead of the busing of students. They did not assign me to a black school. She had to be a party of this decision. I knew that I would not be a party to this. All would say, that's political pull you have there lady, and lots of it. I wouldn't do it. I resigned.

During this time, his precious Dad died and Jean was supposed to have flown to Shreveport, but later, I found that it was to Missouri. He Dad was my sweetheart in the family and he was dying. That was my first death to witness. I had to take care of that business after summer school. This was my afternoon chore.

Later during the summer, I was asked by the children's pediatrician, Dr. Denier, to go to the private school as assistant principal. He was president of the board of the Lafayette Private School. I took the deal making much more money and had the kids follow me there. They got in with my teaching two classes to pay for their tuition along with being Assistant Principal. I did not know that the teaching two hours of mathematics, was paying for their tuition. This was music to my ears. My salary was great, and Mama kept the savings buried until I needed it. That was great for them and for me. I was making good money and it was all mine!" There were excellent teachers there because they didn't want to be transferred to the black school, and the private school "had the pick of the litter" for teachers as well as students. .

At the private school the kids excelled in every way. Christine was even allowed to take Algebra I in the fall and finished Algebra II the second half of the year. The next year she took geometry the first half of the year and a trigonometry the second half. This would make it a breeze for her when she did take pre-calculus the next year. This was not allowed in the public school system. Then during the summer, Christine went to the Baptist College near home, and took "The Bible as Literature," and aced it. She loved school and could have gone all year long if given a chance.

She was given credit for 2 of her high school classes which was history and an English class by taking this six-hour class. I taught at the private school for three years. At the end of my third year, the board fired the principal and asked me to take the job. I knew that the board would run the show, there was too much school politics and I didn't like it. I didn't want to be in a position to do anything that these people knew nothing about. I refused, even though they offered a greater salary than the previous one. I couldn't do it even though and we could've used the money.

I could've paid the retirement money back. The majority on the board thought that you only needed to add one teacher if you added another grade, such as, 9th grade, 10th grade, and so on. I saw that Doctor Denier needed a better understanding.

I said, "In elementary school, the teachers are qualified in each area for the lower grades. That's why you could add one grade and one teacher. In the upper grades, the teachers in two specialized in two areas. We were fortunate to have these certified teachers for the school here. We have math teachers capable of adding the 8th grade, teaching Algebra I, Geometry and Trigonometry, another in science and chemistry, and an English teacher, in Latin Debate classes. Keep in mind that you got the cream of the crop to add the eighth grade for those kids who were smart to take upper math and science classes."

"I see that you finally understand, right? The same laws apply to all upper grades in high school. You can't get a teacher qualified in each subject for all that should be offered in high school. You need a qualified teacher for each subject to be certified by `The Private School Organization,' and besides that, the state would not qualify these kids when they left for college. You need to talk to the board and get them to understand this. They would be a part of something that I know will make you look like a blooming idiot when these students needed to go to a college."

I sure wish that I could've sold the silver, crystal, and china then to pay IRS, but it stayed packed. I didn't use that kind of fancy stuff, didn't want the polishing job either, so it just stayed packed. I had NEVER unpacked any of the nice items during all this time! Jean could not stand it without a crisis, so he chose to build houses again, as well as, sell them. Was he greedy? He built houses in a black neighborhood: eight of them. Most of them sold, but he didn't make any money. In addition, the bank took care of him. The rest were repossessed.

I said, "You promised that you would not build another house. This must mean that you want us to leave or you are losing your mind or testing to see what I'll do. Which is it?"

As usual there was no answer from him; just a "wave off. He also hired some Cajuns to build and they wanted to be paid on Thursday. I told Jean that they would not be back on Friday if he paid them early, but he didn't believe me, and sure enough, they didn't show on Friday. I was so angry that he didn't listen to me. This meant that I had to help after school as well as the kids working some in cleaning up the lawn. I was climbing the ladder with roofing material, because Jean was not physically able to do it. I didn't like the grit in brickwork. He and I both operated the table saw. I knew for years that I was the one who was stupid for not leaving a long time ago. However, Mama kept reminding me that it was against God's laws.

However, I also knew that if I left, they would see that he kept the kids. Where could I have run with these three kids without being found? I should never have shown up. The kids and I both had our own work that had to be done. The next day, the only one working was

Jean. When I got out of school, I had to help him. I knew he was not physically able to do the work. The kids helped some by picking up more scraps of lumber on the lawn. Jean lost money on every house and the last one had to go back to the bank. They didn't mind though because Jean had already paid 20 percent of the loan in order to get the loans to build the house.

The bank made plenty and they knew that these would sell soon, especially in that neighborhood. Jean didn't receive any profit from any of them. After this episode, I DARED him again, to think of building another house. Well, I didn't know that he had a pre-sold house going on in Low Bayou Park.

This was the only modern house in town, at the time. It was pre-sold, but the people made so many changes after most of the house was completed that Jean couldn't possibly make any money on it. Finally, they even changed their mind on buying it. They kept promising him that they would make a down payment, but didn't. This was a demand by the finance company required before they could get financing. He just pretended that they did, but he did it for them. How? I have no idea.

Therefore, since it was the only modern home in the area, the only way it would sell was if we moved into it and I decorated it to show its beautiful features. It had a fireplace, three bedrooms and two baths with an open floor plan which appealed to many women. There was none like it in town. Finally, that little house sold, but not before the boys left their bikes out behind Jean's truck and he backed over them. What a mess and a promise to buy two more bikes. He let the house go for a smidgeon more than what was owed on it. I was livid! Then we had to pack for the next house.

However, I did put my foot down. I told him that I would not put up with him building another house again. He could see about going back with the other Realtor to see if he would take him back or find something else or move in with his Mom, because she was alone now. Otherwise, I was leaving him and taking the kids to the farm, because there was a job opening where my sister taught. He believed it, I thought, but I don't think that I had thought it through and through. I was giving too many threats and no actions. That was MY biggest mistake from the beginning.   Therefore, they took him back and he sold cancer insurance on the side. We had it, Isabelle bought it and he sold a lot at staff meetings after school. Well, now you see the power that his folks had. He went to all the schools in the parish. as well as others because Marjane knew everyone.

CHAPTER 29

Where?

During this time, Jean's Mom had to be put in a nursing home. This was what she wanted to do, because she knew that she couldn't live alone any longer. He did make good money from just listing and selling real estate as well as the cancer insurance. Where was the money going? I still thought he was gambling, but maybe he had a sweetheart somewhere who never had to raise cane with him. Let me know and you can have her. I will be eager! I was at the point that I didn't care about that, but the kids and I needed a home. I was sick of all this. Maybe he was paying his aunt back. Hell, she caused all this mess, why should she be paid back. I kept my money to pay late utility bills. I had to have a telephone. There were many necessities for the kids and auto payments to get everyone to school. I was working but it took more than my salary.

The Fromond home was furnished, and would need some remodeling before it could pass "muster" with us after living on Linda Drive. Jean's sister came over and got what she wanted that would fit in her car, and we sold the rest. I kept all the profits from that, which I sold and made Jean give me his. I told him that Christine's "loft" needed a lot of work and the back porch needed to be turned into a laundry room. We had to have the junk cleaned out and torn down with the little apartment scraped and hauled off. I cleared about $3,000 to give to Mama to bury. I had enough to leave anytime now. Just wait, I thought, for the next crises.

So into the Fromond home we moved as soon as possible. This meant no rent or house note. She was excited to have the loft, and she needed this privacy. This was her "Crow's Nest." I kept some money and gave my Mama the most. I had enough to leave now and go anyplace where I could not be found.

Since Jean's Mother had a piano, I decided to give each one of the kid's piano lessons from our camping friend. Can you imagine three in this house taking piano lessons without me losing my mind? I wanted them to and they wanted to take them, so that was it. We had no rent to pay then. I told that if they started that they had to finish the year. They did quite well, but Christine did the best. I wished many times that she could've started many years before. It was a huge house, and since we didn't have a house note, Jean jumped at the idea of buying a motorhome. When I saw it, I thought I would just die.

I asked, "Where did you get the money for this?"

He said, "Well, I have the house and no house note."

"Well," I said, "Just where is the money for paying for the motor home, boat, 1 car note, food for us, as well as fuel and utilities?"

He just said, "Don't worry about it because all is alright."

I asked, "Did you rob a bank or something? Do you mean to not worry until we have another crisis?"

He didn't even listen or answer me. He thought he was "for one time" doing everyone a favor and I was "madder than hell" about it all. That was why so many of my in-laws and siblings became so jealous of me.

I said, "I don't like any of your favors, because they have made us move into the Moureau house too many times and now it's gone and we would have to pitch a tent.

As we began to leave for the trip, the engine would not start. He tried a stupid act of starting the engine by pouring gasoline into the carburetor, which blazed up. It got some of his eyelashes, some of his hair, and blistered his hands, though. We were just darn lucky this time because the engine was inside and between the driver and front passenger seat. There was only one exit, which was behind the passenger seat, and the passengers in the rear had to exit on the side from it also. This could have blown all of us to "smithereens."

I held onto the money though that I had not given Mama and hid it in my toiletries in the suitcase. I was so frightened because I could just see us getting out west somewhere and running out of gas or food. I lied to Christine about not having money, but I mentally excused myself in that these plans had to be made. I had no idea of how much money Jean had. He thought that we used all of mine in remodeling his folk's house.

One frightening part of going on a trip in the early 70's was that gasoline prices had doubled and many "Mom and pop" gas stations went out of business. The only ones you would find open were on the freeways. Their prices were even higher, if they could ever get fuel delivered there at all. That was, where most of my "Fromond estate" money went on the way back. I knew if we got out there, we had to get back. He picked a bad time to go. A year sooner would've been great, but we had nothing. A year later would've left Christine out and I was not about to allow her to miss this. If anyone goes, she is going also.

This meant that I had to do all the driving. Having said this, he did not think about having a cut-off valve put on to prevent the original tank from overfilling. We were running out of gas before we got to Houston from Villeplate. The new tank was much higher and the gas was just pouring out. This meant finding an auto parts store to get a "cut-off valve." We did find one and began with the cutters for the copper line adding this new piece. This prevented the wasting all that gas. I had to do the work with the kids handing me tools as I needed them and the guys in the parts store told me how to start and end. Jean's hand could not have the gasoline on it at all. The motorhome gas filters had collected most all the "trash" left over from the welding of the new tank. It had never been cleaned out from the welding dust. That should have been cleared before the top was welded on.

Therefore, while we were at the parts store, I bought a dozen of these filters, because I knew that I could not buy them in the desert. With the main part of the motor inside the motorhome, we had to take a cover off and change the filter each time the engine started sputtering, which happened quite often. I had never driven anything in a large city, much less a motor home. For me to drive the motor home all through Dallas and on out toward El Paso, was quite nerve racking, tense, and very tiresome. Christine helped me to get in the correct lane ahead of time by being where she could see the signs before I could from the driver's side. She was my co-pilot while her Dad slept. This made driving a lot easier. If she had not done that, I would never have made it through Houston, much less, Dallas. This seemed so much wider than Papa' bus, but it was the same except in the front where the bus engine was all outside. The bus engine was outside and stuck out which made it seem more narrow. I had driven that many times for hauling cotton.

We spent the six weeks traveling all over the west with the boys having a friend go with them so that Christine could read and not be bothered. We passed through Los Vegas, Nevada, and obviously, the kids couldn't gamble, so I took their coins in and to play the slot machines and won a few nickels for each. A nickel at a time was all I risked, and never lost a dime.

The only painful happening, other than Jean's burn, was when Marcel got his fingers caught in the crack of swinging glass doors in Reno. He was not aware that these were very tall glass doors, because the entire front was glass. When someone went in, his fingers went into the crack. The owners of the casino were out to him immediately. However, when I heard the scream, I knew it was one of mine. After winning some coins for each of them, Marcel's hand began feeling much better. They would've paid damages, but I couldn't do that. Marcel's fingers got well in no time. It was just the tips which turned blue, but his winnings helped the pain, and he just forgot about it. Most people would've taken them to the cleaners, and they would have paid it, big time. I believed that somewhere and sometime the Lord would've taken it out on us. I just didn't believe in doing people in like the ones who sued us when they ran into and killed the horses.

I think that in the end, all had a good time and saw sights that they would probably never see again. Next, Jean wanted to go to Florida with the camping crew. Can you believe that Jean got some more money from Marjane for the trip to Florida for two weeks with our camping friends? We cleaned up all the clothes and replenished the motor home with supplies.

We joined a group of camping friends with campers and motorhomes in a caravan to Panama City, Florida. This was a lot of fun and cost much less, stopping in New Orleans, Biloxi, and Mobile where all of us got on a submarine, and then to Pensacola and on to Panama City for fun on the beach. I had never been anywhere from the farm except to college and where I taught and the special 1½ day wedding trip. This time, we used Marjane's money left over for groceries and gas to star, but I stayed frightened not knowing if we would arrive back or not. I can truthfully say I was never relaxed when we traveled anywhere. Jean would often run out of gas on the paper route. I knew that he would take chances on anything and everything.

I never knew how much money Marjane had given Jean. She certainly was not going to tell me. This trip was only two weeks, but I thought, that we had been to places that one would only dream of having. They did have a wonderful time. Probably the most exciting for me was going through the submarine in Mobile, AL. The kids enjoyed seeing the ocean again as well as playing in it.

CHAPTER 30

Jean's Mother Died

Jean's Mother died that year while in the nursing home and it was a terrible time for Christine emotionally. She hid in what was Grandma's closet to cry her eyes out, until there was not a tear left. This was her love and she just died. How was I going to handle all this? Christine loved her more than she loved anyone. Thank God, Grandma Fromond went to the morgue earlier and picked out the same casket just as Grandpa had and had it all paid for in advance, or Grandpa might have done it before he died

Next, the new school was beginning and the summer had ended. Now Christine has to go to Opelousas High School after leaving the private school. This was just for one year. Christine was to begin this last year here and could walk to school if she wanted to. She went to this prestigious school (where I had taught when she was just a baby) and excelled in everything. She loved her teachers as well as her classes. She took advanced placement classes, but never dated and I didn't know how to bring the subject up. I kept thinking that I should, just as my Mama was going to do for me, but never did. I did talk to her about other dreadful things like the period every month, when I thought I was dying.

She and a nice looking black boy were co-valedictorians. They had to practice after school quite often and he would bring her home. This was when I really got concerned, but said nothing. They both did well at the high school graduation, and Christine had a "commanding performance," all with a standing ovation. I was so proud of her. I still had to handle her like "eggshells." She was quite fragile as far as being in a close relationship with the boys, her Dad or with me.

CHAPTER 31

Christine's Off To College

Soon Christine was to go off to college. I thought that now I wanted to show Christine more attention after losing her Grandma. She needed it, but she seemed to resist any attention from anyone. This hurt me, but I did not think about how long it took to grieve "her way" for her grandparents. I was never that close to mine, so this took a long time for me to understand. I loved that child dearly. The bosses took her away from me and I resented it. I was happy that she had a great role model in her Grandma Fromond, but I must say I was hurt most of the time because she bought her love and it stuck and we never had money except the one Christmas when she got the new bike and a pony. I had prayed that she would grow up and never know how I felt about their closeness. She needed her Grandma and she needed Christine.

Off she goes, majoring in Biomedical Engineering with an academic scholarship. I don't know when I have cried as much as I did when she went off to college. I cried every day and night. Her love was for her Grandma Fromond. After a semester, Christine changed her major to medicine, which killed us financially because she lost her scholarship. That, I felt, was my fault because she never knew that she would lose it if she changed her major. She had never had money to learn to budget because we never had extra money for anything, nor did I have openness with her to talk about problems and how to deal with them in college. She never told us that she was the only female in a "man's" field, and that the professor teased her about her braces. She was not used to this type of behavior from anyone, much less a professor in college.

She went on into the medical field, enjoying her classes and working free at the school's radio station. She was not allowed to work in town or anywhere that alcohol was sold, because she was not old enough. She was only sixteen when she entered college. This meant that we had all the finances to pay.

The next surprise from Christine was when she moved out away from her roommate into a private room. This roommate was an elementary school major and kept her "litter and refuse" (as Christine called it) all over the floor and Christine had enough of that. So, into a private room she moved instead of telling the girl to clean up her rubbish.

Jean wanted to sell the house, which was his now. He did get a great offer. Then he was ready to buy some acreage from Isabelle and Boudreau out a bit from Lafayette, and build a new house. None of his family was aware of anything that brought any problems. You can see, I hope, why it was so daunting to show much affection toward the kids. It was like a "tsunami" all the time. I was always faced with turmoil of some kind or another in trying to deal with Jean.

The boys were occupied with each other, and they never noticed any lack of attention. I buried my problems going to night school, as well as teaching. I never had any "say-so" on anything, so we did build, and it was beautiful. However, the buyers for the Fromond home wanted it immediately and the new home needed about two months of finish work done to it. This meant that we had to move into a rental for two months, which was near the Junior High that the boys attended, and Christine was in college. I was always ready to pack and move overnight, if needed. That was just the way it was.

The boys stayed in the same school until we moved into the new house. Christine stayed in her private room until we moved into the new home. In two months, we were ready for it. I was a professional at packing and moving. I had this place ready to leave over night because I never did much unpacking of anything. The boys had to prepare for moving to another school named Grand Coteau High School. I was still teaching at Baker Street, the black junior high, for which I volunteered after leaving the private school. I was not about to go to a white school with Marjane as a school board member.

The principal, who was black, was thrilled to have me and I was excited to have and learn more about him and the students. He was a wonderful disciplinarian. He appreciated all the new white teachers and gave us the latitude to teach as hard as we wished because the students were not used to having someone who cared about them. Jean and I invited the principal and his assistant to come out and have supper with us. This happened after Jean got out of the hospital with pneumonia. They had a treat of barbecued chicken, sausage, and vittles from the garden. The kids and I worked hard to grow many vegetables in the garden.

Then the house problems, with all the telephone calls that Jean would not return were haunting me. I would have to deal with that as soon as I could figure it out. I did worry about Jean not taking care of himself. Jean just would not do what the doctor ordered. Again, he ends up in the hospital again with pneumonia.

"Well, there are other families who do the same as you. That's why the hospital was always so full every winter," I sassed back.

I always believed that he needed this attention from everyone at our expense. It was the lack of thinking about his job, my job and the children. They needed help with chores, rides to school and time taking changes to him in the hospital. He was wonderful with the kids, and they loved him. That was what mattered to me. They were not old enough to see the aloofness in his demeanor to me or anyone else. That was why he always grabbed the ticket at a diner to pay for everything. He was a show-off trying to impress people. Money just burned a hole in his pocket until it was gone. It was then that we found out the extent of his health problems, and realized that open-heart surgery was required.

CHAPTER 32

St. Luke's Hospital

The financial worries had to be put on hold until Jean had the surgery. As soon as he got out of the hospital with the last bout of pneumonia, the doctor had made the appointment with Dr. Cooley and Dr. DeBakey in Houston, Texas. There was no backing out now: he had to go. This was a life or death situation now. If I had to knock him out and put him in the car, I would've done it in a "New York minute." I had to do all the driving because Jean was not able to drive at all. He slept most all the way, so that he didn't have to answer any questions about all the calls that I wanted to know about.

I had never driven in a large city by myself and I was scared to death. I was given a map on how to get to St. Luke's Hospital and it showed that I was to make a "U-Turn" as soon as I saw the hospital. I later learned that there was a turn lane with lights called "U-Turn Street." I didn't know what that meant other than to make a U-turn right in front of the hospital. Of course, I went up on the curb of a one way street, over the grass and down the curb on the other side.

It was a wonder that the oil pan was not punctured or that the police officers was not after me. I probably would've passed out. There was no help from Jean; he pretended to sleep right through it all. Anyway, we made it there and I was allowed to stay in Jean's hospital room. Thank God for that. I didn't have any money and I don't think that Jean had no more than $50 for gasoline.

It never occurred to me that I might have to stay in a motel. If I had to do that, then I would have had to sleep in the car, and without any fear. I couldn't afford to have "FEAR" at this point and decided not to worry about it. Whatever was going to happen would, in some way or another. That was the kind of luck I had been having, it seemed.

The next morning, Dr. Cooley came in with his twelve "brothers." They called them this because they were doctors, but learning new skills from all over the world. They observed him as he talked to me about what he would do. He sat down with me on the bed, and had a model of the heart and colored pictures of the heart and explained how each part worked normally and abnormally. He showed how Jean's heart worked with the defective mitral valve. He also explained how he would repair it, instead of replacing it, by using a "patch." He carefully explained as the group watched his patience with me. They were in awe of his mannerisms, and my understandings with the intent of my interests. Dr. Cooley continued showing how the valve was like the fins of a fish with many little hairy like particles used to close the value after each pump of blood into the system. Jean's valve leaked a lot, which meant that it was not pumping much blood at all. Therefore, his body lacked the needed oxygen.

If the brain didn't get enough blood, which carries oxygen, you couldn't think rationally. Maybe that was why he never made good decisions. He performed the surgery right away. I slept in Jean's room in a bed just for me. I was certainly grateful with that plan, because if it had not been there for me, I would've had to sleep in the car. The next morning Dr. Cooley sent for me, and escorted me to see Jean in the recovery room. I saw him with a ventilator in him, as did everyone who was in there from open-heart surgery. All were purple-like in color. I was heartbroken to see the 18-month old child in there, who also had heart surgery. None of the patients could talk to anyone. Each was still on a ventilator. Jean didn't know that I was even in the room.

Then I was escorted out and back to the room. I read material that the doctor left. I then slept right on through the night, praying that all would work out and that there was enough money for gasoline to make it back home when Jean recovered. I needed that sleep of about of about fifteen hours.

The next morning Jean was brought to his room with a "heart-shaped pillow." I couldn't believe that. Dr. Cooley had said that the next time I saw him that he would be walking into the room. I didn't believe him, but kept it to myself. He was supposed to cough and used the pillow against his chest all the time to keep from hurting so much as well as not to pull on any stitches. That same day he had to walk down one hall and back. There was a little cardboard "torso" on the door with a "head" to add to the torso as soon as he walked down that hall and back, he could add the head. He would later complete all the limbs to show that he would end up walking 2 miles.

I was excited that the Dr. Cooley noticed me encouraging Jean to get all the pieces added to the torso so that we could get home as soon as possible. I made sure that he walked every time he woke up. I needed to get home and he needed to get well. He walked the two miles, plus an extra one while I filled out insurance papers. He finished his "torso" before the others finished the first mile. They needed a "slave driver" pushing them also. I would not permit him to stop. I had to go back to work when I got home and he had to wait on himself. Then it was time to return home.

The drive home was quite tiresome. I was so glad to get home because I had very little to eat while Jean was in the hospital. I did have $50, and I saved it for gas. I had no idea how much it would cost for gas and I would rather starve than push. The money he had given me would get us home if I were thrifty. When we got home, the kids were thrilled and I was very much impressed with all that Christine and the boys had done in taking care of the house, the meals and going to school.

They had done an extraordinary job with all tasks. They had never had a responsibility like this to take on before. They were terrific! They had seen hard work done and they did this all by themselves.

Now, back home, I had to take care of some needs for the kids. Each one needed a haircut. I had a clipper set and I had never taken them for a haircut. I learned to do that right away because we couldn't afford it. I will never live down Christine's haircut. I was doing a neat job with a "pixie." She had worn this style for some time. This time she moved and I kept trying to correct it. It got too short. She wore a bandana to school until it grew out. Not many people were use to a lady wearing a "do-rag" to school back in that time. It was cute, but her bangs were only about one-half inch long.

That was not the only reason why she wore the bandana; I held her head in my arms to "steady" her head, and shoved the clippers too close to her forehead and the marks of the clippers left the "tooth marks" there. The bandana had to cover this mistake also. Shortly after this, eleven tornadoes hit our area. One in particular did rip our house, but not as bad as other homes. It took out my sister's pine trees, which were next door to us. That whole area looked like a war zone. Thank God, the Mennonites came and helped us because this house was going up for sale. We had to hurry. I knew this would have to happen soon.

CHAPTER 33

Will They Understand?

I suppose that never having had money, growing up working my tail off through college was always on my mind when I had to buy something. I knew that I had to have the money in my pocket as well as the correct amount before a purchased anything. The kids needed some understanding of all this.

I tried to explain all this to the kids that when I first started teaching and managing money on my own that I didn't buy anything if I didn't have the money for it. I always operated that way. Just teaching school was $2800. Coaching was an extra $100 a year, however, that only lasted one year because the law requires you to be out one year for the pregnancy. They had a many questions, which they needed answered. I told them what the principal saw me filling my tank up with gasoline from the station where the school coaches bought all their gas, he made me put in on the school charge because the school paid the coaches for their gas. I told them that this was like Christmas to me . I had budgeted $15 a month for this "God Sent Gift." My take-home was $198 a month. This gift was a little better than 7.5 percent of my salary and it meant a lot to me. I had been driving my car to the basketball games, when the boys team had the bus. The principal knew it and didn't want that to happen again.

They didn't need to grow up as ignorant as I was. They also needed to understand why I couldn't enjoy spending or having fun, except with them because of the finances. I had to tell them that I had never dealt with anything like this that I couldn't handle.

I also told them that I was not paid at home, but worked for others to earn money for college. They were amazed that I would take off on my horse and go plow or pick cotton after their Grandpa's farm work was done, then hurry back home on the horse.

They also needed to know why they were asked to document the phone calls that their Dad didn't return. Jean didn't know this. The kids took care of it not knowing what my I had planned.

CHAPTER 34

Found A Big Problem

Now, I knew that it was time to take care of finding out about some problems that had to be going on. The lady, who kept calling without getting a return call, told me what her problem was when I invited her down to talk to me. I told her that Jean's aunt had died and I promised her that we had a death in the family, and she could show me the problem after the funeral. She was satisfied with that.

Well, it was the "boss" Marjane with cancer. Christine and I had been going to her house and giving her morphine shots every day. We were taught how to divide the buttocks into quadrants and to give the shot in a different quadrant each time. However, she died after 2 weeks.

After this funeral was over, Aunt Gezelle was to take care of her estate. This included her and Jean as her heirs. It didn't include Jean's sister (Denise), I didn't know why, and did not ask. Nevertheless, Aunt Gezelle didn't share the estate at all. If she can live with that guilt on her heart, that was fine with me!" Jean never questioned her as far my knowledge of it. I never dreamed that this lady, who was in church every single Sunday, would do something like this. She never failed to shame us when we didn't go or take the boys to church. This would cause one to wonder if she practiced what she preached.

"Have you been watching Bonanza and not going to church?" She would ask the kids.

"Yes, mam", they would always respond.

"Well, I don't watch that because I'm at church," she said cynically.

Hey, she will get her "comeuppance," as Mama would say. Annie, her only child, would get it all. This meant the house, investments, land, life insurance and all. But you know, that's all right, I had gone through with nothing before, and I knew that I could do it again.

CHAPTER 35

No, They Do Not!"

The kids had no idea why we had to deliver papers before work every morning until it just about did us all in. It was a fun ride for them on weekends, and they could help, sleep or just enjoy the ride. This was all going on when the two of us were holding down five jobs. This was worse than the farm. I just was not getting the physical beatings, but the abuse and the control I was under was doing me in. None of the bosses came to see us when we were going through this, but they kept in touch with Jean. He didn't tell them what we were doing to make ends meet, though. He was too proud.

Soon Jean was driving before he was supposed to drive. He would drive to town each day, (he said), would be gone most all day, and never took care of his phone calls after I got home. I thought at first that people were checking to see how he was doing, but it was not that at all. When he came home, he still would not tell me where he had been. I would give him a list of calls that needed to be made. The children and I took these calls. None of the calls were returned by Jean.

CHAPTER 36

A New Boss

All was going to change now. There will be no more holding down five jobs. Now it was time for my actions! I was not going to put up with any more of Jean's shenanigans or his folks again. As my Mama would say, it was nigh time" that I did something. The strange calls that had been coming would be answered by me. The big boss was dead and now I am not afraid of anyone. First, I must call Mrs. Defoe, the lady whose calls were never returned. When the contact was made, I asked her where and when would be the best time for her. She met me in town. I had called Jean's last living aunt to go with us. She needed to see where he had screwed-up again. Mrs. Defoe led us to a subdivision out near the airport. We were led to the house and found out that Jean had five houses unoccupied out there and one of them was hers. This was where he had been driving every day. It was north of town, which was an extra 25 miles.

Aunt Gezelle said, "He needs his throat cut!"

I wanted so much to say many things, but I did have some respect for the lady who had this problem. I felt her pain. These houses couldn't be finished because there was no water, no electricity or gas for them. The man who sold Jean the land told him that all the utilities were there. He had no document to verify that the man was telling the truth and just took the man's word as his bond. He took Jean "to the cleaners as well as the kids and me" and the people for whom he built those houses.

I never asked how much he owed them. I just couldn't do it. However, Jean might have done as he did with so many of the ones that he built and went under. They probably had never given him a down payment. He had to give these houses to the bank and we had to sell that lovely home in Lafayette. This just about killed me. I didn't know what to do. I believed that I was going to lose my mind over all this. However, I knew that if I was going to be the big BOSS, I had to show some action and do it fast. I knew that much for sure: Not to just straighten myself up but get on my knees and just pray and pray. I believed that God wanted me to keep these kids aware of some problems, and that together we will work with this issue somehow. His car had to be re-possessed and he took mine. I was teaching in a black school and hitching a ride for thirty-five miles back and forth to school. I couldn't even contribute to the other teacher's gas bill except with vegetables from the garden. Christine was still in college and working there at school and living at home. The kids and I had had a beautiful yard, garden with vegetables to fill the two large freezers and trying to enjoy our unusual but lovely home.

There were plenty of vegetables though, for the neighbor who gave me rides to school where we both taught. There were no other homes like this house. It had a gambrel roof with a front and back porch was sixty feet long. However, we had to sell and had not even been in it for six months. The people who bought it knew we were in a bind some-how, and we barely broke even. We sold almost everything, saving for the condominium we were to rent (as far as Jean knew), that was the part of the money that Jean kept from the "estate sale."

I insisted Jean pay for this move. This was where I saved more money in the freezer. He never knew how much money I had taken in. We had many valuable family antiques, which sold quickly, I ended up with better than $15,000, I only showed him $2,000 and about the rest of it, he knew nothing.

I ask Jean to give me the rest of his money received from his sell-ing, to pay off the people he owed. I knew it would burn a hole in his pocket. He did give me some, and that was how I took care of some of the unfinished business. However, $15,000 went in the freezer like a piece of wrapped up meat. He didn't know how much I made with all the antiques. Someone stole an antique 18th Century spindled rope bottom bed. This was valuable and neither of us sold it. We kept it in the attic of the garage in Jean's area of selling. Nevertheless, he said that he didn't see it leave. Maybe he lied as I did, but I just didn't care. I think someone just walked off with it in a truck. I was in charge inside and the buyer paid before the anything was taken out of the house.

It was not long before I found that the truck had been picked up for non-payment as well as the boat. The kids and I got to use the boat more than their dad did. We would miss it the most. I had taught them to water ski, fish, and just have fun out on the creeks and lakes all around on weekends and after school. I had hoped that they would at least remember some fun times that we shared. I enjoyed the boat with the fishing while the kids studied and got all their homework. Then the water skiing began. I would not let them give up. They had to "hang on" until they got those skis up. Christine was just about to cry when I made her go two more rounds. Then I felt that she was glad because she got up and found it lots of fun. She was happy then that I had her stay and stick with it.

CHAPTER 37

$15,000: From the Freezer?

Now with money hidden, it was the time for renting the condominium in town. No one knew about it and it was kept in my secret place in the freezer. It was stored like any other package, so I knew that I would be the one getting food out and that piece would not be touched. I was ready for the divorce then and Jean knew it, but other issues had to take place first.

I had been teaching at the black school for almost three years and taking off only when Jean had the surgery. I was only out about eight days, all together, and had saved enough days for an emergency and of course, that did happen so often, it seemed.

Mr. Brussard was a great principal, but he just had too much to do that kept him from seeing that the black teachers were not teaching. When the white teachers came in, they started from scratch. With the aid of the "Federal Title One" materials and teaching aids, we divided the kids in groups. I divided mine into seventeen groups. I was glutton for punishment. They had tape-recorded lessons with workbooks to go with each tape, a teacher aide and room-to-room tables and chairs. Each group was working on a different area. Four were working independently and several were in groups of two or three. I was the slave driver here. For sure, they learned more than they ever had in one year with each group. I was proud of these kids and so was the principal (Mr. Brussard).

When (HEW) Health, Education and Welfare came from Washington to the school board office, they wanted to see and observe the use of all the "Title 1" material. They wanted a good look at the parish to justify how all the Title I materials sent to them were being used and the superintendent knew exactly where to take them. He knew that he could bring all of them to my class. I just wondered when they would come. In no time, they were there, all sixteen of them, including the superintendent and his assistant. None of them were afraid to come to see my classes, because he knew what to expect, because there was no doubt that I was a good teacher.

I met them (unannounced) when they arrived. I had no idea that there would be sixteen of them checking me out. These folks were with H.E.W. and I was not sure what they were going to do, observe or ask for a meeting with me. I was not aware that they were checking me as well as the students out.

When they told me who they were, I invited them in to visit with any child and ask them or me any questions if they had any. They could tell that I was a "pusher" for those students to learn because I expected it from each of them. Each student answered questions when asked, and continued back with their work with enthusiasm. All noticed the excitement the students had with their work.

Some were listening to lessons on tape with a head-set, and work-book. The visitors were pleased to see this eagerness going on as well as the Continuous Progress Program, which I wrote and managed in my class. I gave the superintendent a copy and he was quite delighted and impressed.

I happened to have black triplets in the class that they were visiting. One was at third grade level, one at about fifth, and the other at about sixth, and I was actually teaching eighth grade math. These were precious kids. I found that I had to separate the triplets, due to the smartest one doing the work for the other two. This had probably been going on from the beginning of their school years. I never put my butt down in a chair while I had students who wanted to learn and this was true in all my years of teaching. Who could sit and just watch the students. I was a taskmaster, tapping for the most that I could get. These kids gave me their best!

CHAPTER 38

Summer School

Again, I had to teach summer school. We needed the money. When did we not need it? I only missed 4 summers teaching summer school. The principal was quite happy to have me. School only lasted each day until noon, and then I commuted about 60 miles to the college for graduate school with the same teacher with whom I commuted to school. (I only needed that one summer to finish the courses. I had taken more than needed while I was there for I had another goal in mind.) This would put me in for a higher pay-grade for the next year.

The black kids worked hard for me. They wanted to learn because they told how the black teachers sat on their butt and let them clean the chalk boards. I felt sorry for these precious kids. They told it all. After each chore, the teacher would have them clean the erasers and then the classroom; just "busy" work to keep them busy or out of fights and out of her hair.

You can bet that they worked as hard and as long as they could at each activity, I had to tap their capabilities. They enjoyed someone who really cared. I often wished that summer school had lasted all day with the enthusiasm and excitement they exhibited.

The day that summer school was over, I had to go into the hospital for an emergency hysterectomy. Thank God that I did have insurance for most all of this and was able to pay $5 a month for that, which the benefits didn't cover. This was 20% of all cost. It was paid as quickly as I could. With the extra money from having a Master's Degree, I was capable of paying off a lot of Jean's indebtedness. I insisted that Dr. Bill take all the cash for his part. I did not touch the "freezer-money" because it would be quite an alert. Shortly after getting home, I received a call from the School Board Superintendent of Baton Rouge Parish. He said that he was in need of a math teacher. He told me that my Superintendent in Evangeline Parish had highly recommended me as a fine teacher and if I asked for a job, to "grab me."

They knew that I was commuting to finish my "dream." At the state meeting, he was told about my use of the Title 1 material that I coordinated, as well as how I started it. I carried up there with me carried up there with me it. He needed me and wanted me, if I was interested in the job. I was so excited that I didn't know what to do. Now I could get out of town, and be nearer to the school and save on many commutes.

I accepted the job without any hesitation and believed that it was a good decision.

CHAPTER 39

Another Move: Baton Rouge

Now with money hidden, it was the time for renting the condominium in town. No one knew about it and it was kept in my secret place in the freezer. It was stored like any other package, so I knew that I would be the one getting food out and that piece would not be touched. I was ready for the divorce then and Jean knew it, but other issues had to take place first.

I had been teaching at the black school for almost three years and taking off only when Jean had the surgery. I was only out about eight days, all together, and had saved enough days for an emergency and of course, that did happen so often, it seemed.

Mr. Brussard was a great principal, but he just had too much to do that kept him from seeing that the black teachers were not teaching. When the white teachers came in, they started from scratch. With the aid of the "Federal Title One" materials and teaching aids, we divided the kids in groups. I divided mine into seventeen groups. I was glutton for punishment. They had tape-recorded lessons with workbooks to go with each tape, a teacher aide and room-to-room tables and chairs. Each group was working on a different area. Four were working independently and several were in groups of two or three. I was the slave driver here. For sure, they learned more than they ever had in one year with each group. I was proud of these kids and so was the principal (Mr. Brussard).

When (HEW) Health, Education and Welfare came from Washington to the school board office, they wanted to see and observe the use of all the "Title 1" material. They wanted a good look at the parish to justify how all the Title I materials sent to them were being used and the superintendent knew exactly where to take them. He knew that he could bring all of them to my class. I just wondered when they would come. In no time, they were there, all sixteen of them, including the superintendent and his assistant. None of them were afraid to come to see my classes, because he knew what to expect, because there was no doubt that I was a good teacher.

I met them (unannounced) when they arrived. I had no idea that there would be sixteen of them checking me out. These folks were with H.E.W. and I was not sure what they were going to do, observe or ask for a meeting with me. I was not aware that they were checking me as well as the students out.

When they told me who they were, I invited them in to visit with any child and ask them or me any questions if they had any. They could tell that I was a "pusher" for those students to learn because I expected it from each of them. Each student answered questions when asked, and continued back with their work with enthusiasm. All noticed the excitement the students had with their work.

Some were listening to lessons on tape with a head-set, and work-book. The visitors were pleased to see this eagerness going on as well as the Continuous Progress Program, which I wrote and managed in my class. I gave the superintendent a copy and he was quite delighted and impressed.

I happened to have black triplets in the class that they were visiting. One was at third grade level, one at about fifth, and the other at about sixth, and I was actually teaching eighth grade math. These were precious kids. I found that I had to separate the triplets, due to the smartest one doing the work for the other two. This had probably been going on from the beginning of their school years. I never put my butt down in a chair while I had students who wanted to learn and this was true in all my years of teaching. Who could sit and just watch the students. I was a taskmaster, tapping for the most that I could get. These kids gave me their best!

CHAPTER 40

I.R.S. Again

Soon Jean came in, and we were alone. The kids were playing football and Christine was still at the college. This was a good thing, I thought, so now I could talk. He opened the side door by the kitchen and all the papers were on the bar. Oh God, did you know that he was nothing but a lot of disappointments? I was just shaking all over. He kept walking away as soon as he saw the big yellow envelope and the contents spread out on the kitchen bar. I immediately moved them to the dining table.

I said, "Stop! Look at me and explain why we are getting all of this again. He would not stop walking away from me. He went to the living room where he had the printer."

I began following, screaming, "Have you lost your ever-loving mind? Where is your money? How much do you have?"

He said, "I used mine for the moving expenses."

I said, "You are lying to me! What have you done with it? It didn't cost that much to move."

I began screaming at him, "I have been the STUPID ONE! LISTEN TO ME!" It finally dawned on me that YOU have had a mailbox ever since we've been married. We never lived in one place long enough to have home delivery. Oh, God, how could I be so stupid? You have been getting these notices all the time from the post office, and I was just too dumb to think that you would purposely do this to the kids and me. DON'T TURN AWAY FROM ME! Now I am quietly asking you to answer me."

I never stopped, except to take a deep breath. I have been wanting this conversation for a very long time.

I continued, "I think you are in shock that I finally found you out. Right? If I had not gotten home before you, this would've been hidden. Right? Answer me! This is what you did the first time and trashed it. Why, for God's sake, why? I have never talked to you like this and never screamed at you, and should've a long time ago. Should I call

Papa now tell him about what you have been doing for more than 20 years? You know that he would kill you or you would wish you were dead by the time he quit giving you a beating with his whip. I ought to shoot you right now! However, you are not worth the bullet. Tell me, did the kids or I ever get a letter or card for birthday or Christmas? Did, you trash those too, huh? DID THE "BOSSES" KNOW THAT YOU HAD NEVER FILED AN INCOME TAX RETURN? THEY PROBABLY DID, BUT THEY WANTED ME SO THAT MY RICH PAPA WOULD PAY ALL OF IT, RIGHT? THAT'S WHY THEY WANTED ME FOR YOU TO MARRY AND IN A GREAT BIG HURRY! All but your Dad pulled these stunts to get me. You should have gone to jail a long time ago!"

"I heard you all talking about me threatening you, and that is exactly why you did what you wanted to do. I knew that they would tell the judge, that I couldn't cook, and that's all the proof they needed. I could leave then, the kids were older and they enjoyed them. I could leave then and none would care the least bit. However, they would never have gotten these kids. No one would have found me. I'm sure that you never thought about how you or your folks would take care of them with your track record. How and when would you find time to discipline, educate them or give the love they would so desperately need? You would never have thought that far ahead. Right?"

"Oh God, I just wish that this had dawned on me years before, because I would've left you and had a wonderful time and your family would not bother us or see us again. You have always had a P.O. Box. I set this one up because we just moved here. Do you remember the conversation about talking to the kids if you screwed up again and you said you would? You WILL tell them about this, as well as the last neglect of the IRS when they came after ME before. Also, be sure to tell about how they took my salary for 3 years, except for $2.25. That was not all I had to put out (or go to jail), I gave up all of my retirement money and all of the bank account. Can you imagine the principal, who was almost in tears, delivering me that check? Now again, I find that the fall that I took then was not enough for you. You just decided, "by-golly" that you were just were not going to file those tax returns and hit us all again. I believe you would kill me if you thought you could get away with it. If Marjane was still alive, you could've gotten by with it.

She would've seen to that. I can just hear the excuses you would give to the kids. You are above the law and the kids and I take the fall. Well guess what. That is not going to happen to us! I would like to retire one day, but I'm sure that you could care less about whether I ever retired or not! I'm not through yet!" Don't you dare leave! Listen to me! I am leaving you and will file for a divorce tomorrow!"

"This is a heck of a time for this to happen now with Marcel and Christine's birthday next month, then Christmas and Jean-Paul's birthday. We cannot afford to mention a divorce until after all this takes place. If you want to leave earlier, then you can go ahead, but the proceedings will begin tomorrow. I don't believe the children would live over a complete separation after just moving. They are in a new school, new environment, and birthdays and Christmas coming up. I am staying here until that part is over. Are you listening to me? You can leave, but I'll tell them what has happened and that this is not the first time, or I will make you finish telling them. Do you hear me? I'll show them my paper-work, signed, and tell where they were put and what you have been doing with everyone's mail. In addition, you had better not leave out an issue or I'll jump in and tell a lot from day one to the end, as well as what happened with the service records. Is that what you want? Just don't leave anything out!" I yelled.

"I'm listening, I'll wait and talk to them when you tell to tell them," he said.

"I don't want anything said until after Jean-Paul's birthday," I said.

"By the way, did you and Aunt Gezelle plan this trip to talk about the printing press in front of the kids, to see what I would do? She certainly did not know how to find this place. You really told a pitiful story for them to hear. You wanted to put me in another bind, didn't you? ANSWER ME," I SCREAMED.

Jean finally said that he would tell them after Jean-Paul's birthday. I know he was still in shock that I had found him out. He didn't say a word. He turned to leave, but he stayed part of the time at the house working with the printer.

I immediately called the board office and asked for a substitute for the next day. I needed a personal leave day and told them that it was an emergency. I told no one of my intentions. I told the kids to get their

Dad to take them to school and that I would be back late in the afternoon. They never asked why, but I think Christine felt something was wrong.

The next morning, I took off for Villeplate for the attorney. I went by Jean's Aunt Gezelle's house and showed her the papers from the IRS.

She just about had a fit and said, "You ought to cut his throat."

I jerked around and said, "Well, I have heard you say that before, but of course, none of you ever chastised him about any of his wild ideas. I am going right now to see an attorney to file the papers for an immediate divorce. I am sure it will not be contested. I should've done something more than twenty years ago when all of you pushed me into this marriage."

As I left I hollered, "I know that Marjane had put Jean's name on her "Will," and we have not received a dime from it. Should I mention something to the attorney about that while I'm there?"

She screamed, "No, you can't do that. You've got to consider the kids."

Yelling back said, "Oh, you don't understand. I'm doing it FOR the kids. They are to stay with me. All of you made him think he could do no wrong, and now, 20 years later, we have nothing, lost everything and now I'm the boss and you can take him back. He is out!"

I said that so quickly that I couldn't believe it came from my mouth. I love those kids, but I should have had more control and shut them up from the first day of school. My not being married, and what my students would say, was not the issue at all. They wanted a naïve country girl to take care of him. I should've kicked his butt out, shortly after getting married when I saw what I had gotten into from the beginning. I left her with her mouth open and decided not to say anything to the attorney about Marjane's Will. The more I thought about it, he could've gotten it and never told me. That was probably why her mouth fell open. I also thought that it did happen because he needed that money for those unsold houses. He had never asked a buyer for a down payment. He might have used it to put down on the financing of them, because I couldn't believe the bank would finance anything with his record. Or, perhaps he gambled it away.

I finished with the attorney and began the trip home. All the "what if's" are over now and I am so relieved. As soon as this school year is over, I work for my PhD somewhere. So, on the trip home I picked up some chicken, fries and soda pops for dinner knowing all would be hungry.

I got home before the kids got in from school. Jean was nowhere around. When the kids came in, they began looking for a snack and could barely wait for dinner. Since Jean was not there, I gave them half of a peanut butter and jelly sandwich to satisfy them until supper time. They began their homework as I looked at plans for teaching the next day. It was overwhelming to try to think, and I knew that I had to pull it together. Soon, I calmly told Christine as soon as she arrived to go ahead and set out the food. I couldn't eat a thing. I took a pop and sat with them and listened to them tell about school as each would chime in with exciting or sad happenings.

Soon, it was time for more studying or going to bed. I cleaned up and told them that I had to hit the bed. I assumed that Jean would come in late, work with the printer, and sleep on the couch. He knew not to get in the bed with me. All heck would break out for sure, if he did.

All I could do was think about what I would keep when all of this was over. I had nothing except some books, clothes and an 8-year-old car. He and the children knew nothing of the hidden money. I had to be careful going to my "underground-bank" for fear a neighbor would see me. Since it was near the water-tower air-conditioning unit, I felt all was safe. Shortly in late October, Jean got the letter from the attorney and he acted as usual, just aloof, went straight to the printer and began reading. He might have been in the library studying about the printer and the other needed items he wanted.

From that day in October, Jean slept in the living room on the sofa, long after the kids were in their rooms and asleep. I had no idea what he was even printing, and never looked or cared. He had bought several extra things for the printer. He must have enjoyed every second he spent with it.

That was his escape from the realism and problems, which he had created. I don't know where he got the money or why he needed all this extra equipment. He was the one studying it. I was not. I feel he had studied enough to merit buying the machine.

I never uttered a word to Jean and continued as if nothing had happened and the visiting for me was with the kids. He was always gone, or working with the printer. That was not out of the ordinary happenings. Time was slipping by quickly. The first two birthdays and Christmas went on without a problem. I got him two shirts, and he got me some jewelry. The kids only got things that they needed. The boys did get a pocketknife and clothes and Christine received a gift certificate. Jean thought that I had charged for all the gifts and I never told him any different. I assumed he got his aunt to give him some money for gifts.

During Christmas break, the kids and I had gone to see Papa and Mama. I told them about the divorce and that the kids would not know until after Jean-Paul's birthday. Mama gave me the hidden money which Papa new nothing about. She kept her secrets and I kept mine. I insisted that Mama keep some of the money for being my banker. She didn't want it, but I knew that she could use it to buy some things that she had always wanted. It was amusing to see her bury it also. I knew that she would have a chance soon, because I would drive down to get her and have a great time shopping.

Next, it was time to celebrate Jean-Paul's birthday. He got clothes as usual, because he was quickly growing out of his and they were similar to the birthday gifts for Marcel. I was always careful about their gifts at any time. Many gifts were shared.

The day after Jean-Paul's birthday, Jean tells the kids to sit at the table. He needed to talk to them. I was in the kitchen to see and listen. I couldn't believe that he was going to do this the day after the child's birthday. Yet, better now than for him to just take off and have me handle all of it. When they all got in, he did exactly that. He had remembered all of it. It was intense, engaging and blaming his actions as inconsiderate, unpardonable, and lack of care and discipline. He only looked at them when he asked them in to sit and as each sat down.

He concentrated on touching each finger as he listed each fault as well as all the "stupid things" he did so that nothing would be omitted. I was so "awestruck" from watching their expressive question of "WHAT?" I couldn't remember anything but that. The shock on the kids' faces was embedded in my mind as a tattoo, and I knew that I would never forget it.

The next day, Christine and I went to see Andre about his old car. He told us the story of the car: They gave him a price $200 less without the trade-in, therefore, he drove the car up in the country and into the woods and left it. When I asked Andre about buying it, he said that we could have it if we helped him get it home. It had to have $100 worth of gas and belts. After all the regular maintenance, Christine helped us clean it up like new. Soon it needed struts and ball joints. It did last about six months and Christine was glad to have some transportation. She named it "Ole' Leaping Leaner" due to the leaps when she started or stopped.

We got that done and I kept the rest of the money tight. No one knew where it was. It stayed buried as my Papa used to do. Christine's car had lasted longer than I thought it would. It took Christine through the spring semester.

I had made friends with the English teacher who was going to type my manuscript. She happened to have a small car for $500. Christine loved it and the teacher needed the money. I knew that this car was in great shape with low mileage and Christine had to have something. However, she needed it then, so I got it for her. I felt she was safer with that car. Christine might have thought that I had some money hidden when I bought her the little used car, but neither talked about.

CHAPTER 41

A Break In?

I know that Jean had gone through the house while I was in Baton Rouge. He had gotten into my jewelry box. He took all the gifts, which included all that he had given me a month before for Christmas. He took the diamond that came from the engagement ring; It had been made into a drop for a necklace. I couldn't in good faith, wear it, with all that had been happening for 20 years. I put it on when it was made into a drop, and put it up and never put it on again. I didn't feel good in it while going through hell all the time; broke and wearing a big rock didn't match my style. I wanted to sell it.

Maybe this was where he was getting the money to buy the extra things for the printer. He had purchased several pieces to do extra work. He had gotten all the sterling and had been selling it all this time. He made good money for that because it was never used and still in the cases in which they came. I never wore jewelry and that was why I didn't notice it. I had never used the sterling silver and other fine crystal either. We never had the money to put anything in it for its use. I would not know how to use all the utensils, crystal, silver bowls, for I didn't know how to cook anyway. It was fortunate that Jean knew how to cook, or we never would never have had a fine meal. I'm sure his Mother taught him.

I was pleased that he got something for it though, because it was wrapped, all would've ruined in 20 years from not being polished often and that would've been a misfortune. I was pleased that now it could be of use to someone. I'm glad that they stayed in felt cloths within the original crates to prevent them from tarnishing; I just wished that I had thought about selling all of those valuables a long time ago when IRS garnished my income. I certainly would not have needed to withdraw all my retirement and lose all but $2.25 of my income for 3 years. Jean sold it at the time when silver was at its highest value. His family and friends gave it to us. My family had never seen it and never contributed any of that.

I kept the gold wedding band given to me by his Dad and not by him. His Dad, who cared for me, gave me the band to me to keep. It never belonged to Jean. I later gave it to Christine. The ring had been made into a Mother's Ring with three prongs to represent the three kids birthdays.

It was decided between the boys that each of us needed someone with them. Therefore, one would stay with me and one would go with his Dad. Jean-Paul went with his Dad and Marcel and Christine stayed with me part of the time. Jean-Paul was still angry with me about returning the knife he had taken while with me at the grocery.

Back before the divorce, he went with me to the grocery. On the way out, there was a neat little pocket knife, which he picked up and put in his pocket. Jean-Paul was about twelve years old and knew better than to steal. When we got home, he took it out and began to do something with it. I asked him where he got it. He immediately told me that he got it at the grocery store. When asked if he had paid for it or if it was on my ticket, he told me honestly that he just took it. I immediately took him right back to the store to return it. Of course, he didn't want to be embarrassed but I made him tell the cashier what he had done. She tried to get me to allow him keep it, but I would not.

I thanked the lady for her kindness and told her "No, he will return the knife."

Even though Jean-Paul apologized all the way home, this was his way of getting even, I thought. He was the first of the two boys to bring up the subject and made the decision of who would stay with whom. I didn't interfere with their decision-making and neither did their Dad. Jean came back a time or two, in a borrowed car, to pick up some things, but Jean-Paul was never with him. Therefore, I knew that he had his used car repossessed also. To help him with his finance mess again, he wanted to sell the printing press, which I paid for by borrowing the money from the school board. It was in my name, but that had never bothered him before, so he wants the money for it. Blaise made an offer to the school board, since they needed one, but Jean would not allow him to sell it. He didn't trust him. Why did he think that he was in charge of it anyway? I borrowed the money for it so that he would have a way to make a living. Now he wants to sell it and keep the money. He was told that he could have all but $1500 which I paid and he could have the difference. They were going to pay $2,000 which would not only pay for the balance on the loan, but I would have some extra cash that I could use. He thought that he would get all the money and it was in the house, on which I was paying the rent.

I should have given him $500 and told him to get out, because I was going to allow Blaise to sell it if he was not going to try to make a living with it. All the kids were hearing this and waiting, I guessed, to see if there was going to be a fight over it. They knew that I had borrowed the money from the school board, but they said nothing to their Dad about it either. I was surprised that they never said a word. I had often wondered if they were still in total shock over all this. It seemed to me that they could see this coming.

I said, "My life and sanity were worth more than $1,500 so, I told him to get it and get it out of the house now!"

I could've put my foot down, but there were two children sitting there with their mouth open just waiting for fist to fly, I guess. I would not let Blaise, Richet or anyone who was trying to help us, do anything about it.

I would say anything that would harm their relationship with their Dad. Later, Jean had someone help him move the press to Villeplate, where he met and started dating Claudine. I never had any idea what he did with it or any of the other valuables that we had for a long time. Jean and Claudine later married. I knew that she would not put up with his "new wagons." She would also make sure that he didn't squander any money.

I was glad that they were together and that she would take care of the kids when they were around because she had seven of her own and was nine years older. I was hurt about Jean-Paul leaving. Both boys needed the discipline and I was afraid that Jean-Paul would not get it. All the kids were smart, but Jean-Paul scored the highest on the I.Q. test, Marcel was next highest and Christine's was just under Marcel's. I knew that the boys could get a scholarship, just as Christine did, and go to college. All the kids were brilliant. Then he was gone. I didn't know when I would get him back or whether Jean would see to it that he got his education. The boys had a better chance of a full scholarship because their Dad was on Disability Insurance. It upset me that he didn't follow up with the plans with the boys discipline as well as education.

CHAPTER 42

Taking Fellowship for LSU

I had taken a trip to Baton Rouge earlier to move some things to Isabelle's, but this trip was to see the major professor at the LSU main campus to show him the unfinished manuscript which he liked. My fellowship was for $9,400. I knew that I could not live on that, and take nine "unnecessary" hours." I would be expected to take over some of his classes and "publish or perish," with his name as publisher and mine as co-publisher. Time would tell. Some students in other states had entered suit to stop this because it was unfair.

I also went to see Isabelle about putting the washer and dryer into her garage to store until I returned for an apartment. While there, she mentioned that I should fill out an application to teach, just in case some shocking news came about. I did fill out one for Baton Rouge High and one at the East Baton Rouge Baptist College. I had dug up the bank can and turned it over to Isabelle to put in a special account. I kept enough for us to live on and hid it in my lingerie.

After that trip, it was all I could do to stay focused on going to school at night, as well as keeping Marcel and Christine in school. As soon as I got back, I gave the owner of the home a "one month moving out date." Soon the packing up began and we started moving. Marcel stayed with me in a cheap apartment until school was out. After two months, when Marcel heard that Jean-Paul was having a good time while living with his Dad, and Marcel was having to live up to getting his homework and on a "curfew". So Marcel asked his Dad to come and get him. I couldn't interfere with this. It would never have worked out!

Therefore, Jean came after him as soon as school was out. I told him to take all the furniture because I was going to move into a college suite with Christine. He did want it, but would have to come back with a truck to haul it all back because he would need it and was pleased to get it. I told him not to put it off at all or I would be forced to give to it all to Salvation Army. Jean actually met a deadline and picked it up.

I moved into the dorm as soon as the public school was out and got a suite. Christine and I lived there, all through the summer months. I was beginning to see that this would be too much, and I didn't want any finance problems and couldn't afford to stay there. However, an obstacle became a blessing when Blaise and Michele decided to go and take advantage of their fellowship in Seattle, WA.

He worked out a deal for me to rent their house while they were going to the University of Washington for their Doctorate Degree. I was to pay $200 a month to keep their house, cat and yard up for the next year. I was glad to get out of the suite at the college as well as that "upstairs" apartment for more reasons than one. This was cheaper, but I had the to keep the house, yard and cat. This was not fair. We had to store our furniture with theirs at any spot we could find. They left all their things except some clothes. Some had to stay in the open carport. Papa was upset because Blaise was charging me to keep his house, cat and yard. He felt Blaise should pay me to stay there.

It helped a lot to have Christine living with me because she helped with the typing of my manuscript. I know that I would have met my deadline, but it would have taken many nights staying up. I rented a typewriter and Christine already had one.

With the two of us typing, it didn't take long to get all the work done. The manuscript had to be typed on 50 percent cotton paper. One thing that I enjoyed while living at my brother's house was the lake that was behind it. I would go set hooks before school started and when I got home I would check those hooks out. I always had enough fish to keep us with plenty to eat. I didn't know exactly how to cook them though, until a friend told me about grilling or baking them. Christine helped some because she learned to cook from her Grandma Fromond; however, I am sure that I kept her busy typing. I paid Christine $.50 per page and she needed the money. The final typing would be $1.50 per page.

All this time was spent on working on my manuscript, which was now finished; I was accepted by "thirteen" universities for a fellowship. I had already taken the one in Baton Rouge because my oldest sister was living there at the time. Isabelle said that I needed someone close to me while I was in a muddled state of mind after the divorce. She had to know that I was hurting. What a terrifying event this was for me, leaving my kids back in Villeplate. It was quite unnerving and I would cry myself to sleep every night that I thought about them.

When the divorce happened, no one at school knew about it. I said nothing and no one asked. I did tell them that I was living in Blaise's house while they were gone to the University for their Doctorate and running "trout" lines before school each morning. At least they knew that if I was not at school by seven a.m., that someone needed to drag the lake. They assumed the whole family was living there.

The school was so large and by having a dual campus, no one kept up with anyone else. Therefore, if anyone asked the kids anything, they just said we were living at his Uncle's house. I began noticing that Christine was not going to be as close to each other as we had been. It bothered me, but I left it alone. I felt as if she and the boys thought all of the problems that caused the divorce were my fault. They would have to be the ones to decide if they wanted to have any relationship with me. I left that issue up to them. I was happy that I did.

CHAPTER 43

Dissertation!"

Papa gave me a special gift of $2,500 to have my manuscript published. In about five months, I paid him back with part of the money that I had hidden down and away Now that "bank can" had long been dug up and emptied, and I gave the money to Isabelle to put in a special drawing 18% interest or more at the time. I told Papa that I was so pleased about the money, but told him that it would be repaid as soon as I could. I had enough, but was concerned that something might happen. He reminded me that he gave it to me, but I told him that I appreciated it, but I had to do this on my own. He said that he understood.

On the way back to Lafayette, I had planned to stop in and chat with Richet. Before I got there, the motor of my car just died right in front of an automobile dealership. The motor in the car was ruined due to the lack of oil. I was so thankful that it didn't happen on the highway on the way driving back and forth. I was also glad that I didn't give it to Christine instead of the little car. I said to myself, he told me he had changed the oil. Why did I begin to think he was telling the truth, is beside me? He had no job, I paid for everything and he still didn't change the oil. I should have done it myself, which I had always been doing.

Anyway, the manager (a friend of Richet and Blaise) made a deal with me to trade my car in for a pickup truck, which I would needed. This meant an added expense, but I had a new truck which had a cab cover and a trailer hitch for moving the washer and dryer as well as everything else I owned. At least the printing press was paid for by then.

This didn't have a bad effect on my going to the university as I had thought. There was a great job open for me in charge of student teachers at the college. That was what I worked so hard for because I had student teachers who had to be an embarrassment to the class, the college supervisor, and to me.

I couldn't live on $9,400 with this truck note at that time. I had seven hours more than required, but at the time, taking over their class, grading papers and "publish or perish" with their name first and co-authored with me was over. Rules changed, and I was grateful for that. So, I had to take at least 9 hours to be a full time student. This was a loss of help for the college professor, and soon I received the PhD. That was my last degree dream.

Soon, I got a call from Christine. She was on her way to see me. Now THAT made me happy. When she got there, I could've "squeezed" her to pieces. She seemed to be proud of it also. She was staying the weekend. She rested from the long drive, and then we went to a Mexican restaurant for dinner that I had talked about previously. This was her first trip to see me after I moved.

After getting back home, we visited about my school and the boys, and then watched a game show and went to bed. She looked at the Dissertation all bound and pretty as she flipped a few pages.

"I remember typing these pages," she said.

I couldn't have done it without you, sweetheart", I said.

The next day, she got a long distance call from the paper mill, where she had applied for a job as a Project Engineer. They wanted her on Monday morning. Wow! I was ecstatic as well as proud of her with all she had been through and managed to help me with the typing. Going through the divorce was traumatizing enough for her. She was happy, but kept her distance. I knew that I should not press the issue at all. With hugs and kisses as she left, I was thrilled. She had a safe trip home and went to work making twice my salary after 22 years and a PHD. I was so thrilled, and she deserved it all.

CHAPTER 44

Christine Meets Gene

I dedicated one hour each afternoon after school running in the subdivision. One day a man was running also but in the opposite direction. This went on for some time, and when he stopped me, he said his name was Gene. When we finished running, we visited for a while on my front porch. He began arriving about the same time so that he could run with me. As time went on, we became good friends, and learned more about each other. He was a very interesting guy. He was in great shape, weighed about 150 pounds and worked every day on construction and demolition with heavy equipment.

He told about his two years of medical school and having to drop out to take care of the dairy farm which his parents had. After they passed away, he went back to college and found that he had to retake so many courses, that he dropped out and got into heavy equipment operations. He actually taught me how to operate these machines, from a track machine with a ram, a backhoe, bulldozer and more, which he was using at the time widening and tearing down overpasses. I wanted to learn all I could about this machinery. He wanted a closer relationship with me by inviting me to go to church with him. I did go church with him and we became closer friends. We worked out, went to church and out to eat once in a while, but not as often as he wanted me to because I insisted on going "Dutch." Marriage was on his mind, but not mine.

Once he was trying to put brakes on his truck while I was running and I stopped to watch and help if he needed. I helped a little by having some tools and the tire ready for him as he was finishing up. This friendship went on for four years. We never got "involved" romantically but he surprised me once after a run and asked me to marry him. I told him again that I enjoyed him and was unequivocally not interested in marriage, but wanted to keep the relationship platonic. I told him that if he couldn't handle that, then the relationship was over. He was satisfied with that. He was quite knowledgeable about many things of which

I knew little to nothing about using. So, we just became the best of friends.

One Christmas while Christine was visiting, Gene saw me working on her headlights and came over to see if we needed help. Christine liked him from that point on. She had heard me speak about him often. She was quite interested in meeting him as much as I had to say about him. I had told her that he was interested in marriage and that I wanted no part of that.

He came over to watch the installation of the bulb and was impressed that we knew what we were doing. After an overnight stay, she had to leave. Shortly I realized that she had forgotten all of the gifts for herself as well as those for the boys who were in Villeplate. I immediately started to load everything into my car when I noticed that I couldn't back out.

I said, "Gene, hurry and move your truck so that I can get out with this and try to catch up with Christine and give all this to her."

He said, "Let's catch up with her in my truck."

I got all the presents into his truck, and we took off on the route she and I always took to go to Lafayette and back on our visits. Knowing that she would have to stop to get gas, we took off. Speeding down the highway, we didn't find her so we turned around and finally we saw her coming up a hill soon after turning around. We flagged her down, gave her the gifts and sent her on her way. Gene noticed that he didn't have his driver's license, so I drove his truck back, and stopped by the gas station near home and filled his truck.

Gene tried to keep me from paying for it but I didn't allow it. He was in love again, right there. I had to remind him of what I had said. He was very nice, a gentleman, and an alcoholic who had been sober for 13 years. I still didn't want to get married. I realized that he would continue bugging me about marriage since we lived so close, that I decided to build a house and had a great deal with the price, interest rates and all. In 3 months, I had a new house just outside the city limits. He would go with me to see the progress on the house during the building. He came by every evening and we ran for an hour just as before. Soon Gene was not able to run because he had a bad toothache "he thought" and was seeing the dentist every afternoon.

CHAPTER 45

Cancer? Me?

On a routine visit to the doctor, a lump was discovered in my breast. Scans and a biopsy indicated the lump was malignant. The doctor suggested a mastectomy was needed immediately. When I learned the length for recovery time, I told the doctor that the only days I had for this was the Christmas Holidays. This would give me 2 weeks and 2 days to recuperate and that was my chance that I was going to take for this, yet I was quite apprehensive about it. Teachers only received 1 sick day a month each year and they were only given one month at a time.

I chose to have a lumpectomy instead, and could recover during the Christmas Break. He assured me that he would check on my condition often. This wasn't too painful. I just prayed that it would not spread, but he said not to get my hopes up because it would surely spread to the other breast as well as back in the one which had the one lump removed. He encouraged me to learn to crochet because I would not be able to use my arms away from my body if it did spread. If that happened, I would have to have a bilateral mastectomy. Since it seemed that I always had to have something to do, I learned how to crochet to crochet at a Sunday School party, and began crocheting as if I was driven by some unnatural force. I felt sure the doctor knew what he was talking about when he said the cancer would spread and I was extremely anxious about it.

I knew that by then my yard would become overgrown and would need mowing. Living alone with few funds to spare I would need to do this myself. I also knew that I needed to work on my lawn mower. I enjoyed working with small engines. I recovered well, and began a new semester. One weekend I got some diesel fuel and took my lawn mower apart, soaked them and cleaned each part. I put it back together with a new filter and spark plug and it started in one turn of the motor. I practiced squatting down with my arms glued to my sides and raised up as quickly as I could to make sure it would start. It did start each time, and then I began trying to mow the yard as if my arms were glued to my sides. This was my practice before surgery. I knew that I would be able to mow my yard just before surgery and then two weeks after surgery. With a tall fenced-in yard, no one could see me and I could've cared less. I enjoyed mowing.

The doctor called after Christmas and repeatedly in February to see how I was doing. He couldn't believe I had crocheted so many different items, as well as working on the lawn mower. I was the slave driver at my own work or play. This helped me recover quickly. A visit with the doctor on spring break required lab tests and scans.

I learned that I would need the bilateral mastectomy. This frightened me, but I still couldn't take off work, and certainly didn't have the funds and could not go in debt. I would have to face the consequences now, whatever they were until school was out. The doctor was anxious about the three month wait, but I had to take my chances. The only person who knew about all this was my very close friend who taught the same courses as I.

As soon as the last week of school was approaching, he cautioned about waiting any longer. Cancer spread fast and plans were made for me to enter the hospital on Tuesday afternoon for all the "pre-op." Then, on Friday, I went for surgery like a trooper. The surgery was over in no time. I refused the chemotherapy or radiation. After the surgery, my math buddy was there to help me sit up and grade papers. She also entered them in the grade book for me and turned all this in just in case someone wanted to see them. What a precious friend I had!

I learned that the insurance would pay for 80 percent of implants and none toward prosthesis after the surgery. I would need two sets if I went with the prosthesis. Considering all of this, I chose the implants which they would cover. Counselors and therapists at the hospital told me that stress was a contributor to cancer because the human body's immune system was weakened, and I had certainly had my share of stress.

So it went and four days later, I could be released from the hospital if someone was there to drive me home. I lied to the staff and drove myself home in my pickup. I recall how very hot the temperature was that day. Nevertheless, I was careful and being extremely independent, I didn't want to depend on my friends. I thought that there might be other times, in which I would need them in a more serious situation.

I prayed to God, thanking Him for my recovery and asked for healing. I had read "Jabel's Prayer" while in the hospital, and believed in it. The hospital and the surgeon again waved their 20% that Blue Cross was not paying. These were truly God sent gifts. I was so determined to get well as soon as possible and take some computer classes to aid in my teaching. I took the classes in two weeks, and mowed my yard in three weeks. It was so warm and dry that the grass didn't grow very much anyway.

I didn't tell my family about the surgery until August. That gave me time to get better and then drive over. When I went home, it was two weeks before Papa died. My parents had never heard of such surgery as I had with implants. A new lesson was learned by them that day. I was thankful that I made the decision to go home. After enough rest from driving, I went to my daughter's and was able to see the boys. All were concerned because I had not told them about the cancer. I just said that there was nothing they could've done except keep me good company. I needed them right then but was slow and afraid to show emotions toward them too quickly. However, they didn't hesitate with their compassion and love. I made me feel so much better.

I was disappointed in how permissive their Dad had been with the boys. They had tried all that the other kids were doing and wasted their God-given intellect by not finishing college. They had time to finish by then with no cost. With Jean on disability, they also could've gone to college with no cost by living at home with money left over. Each of them would have gotten a "dependent's check" until they finished school or until their 25th birthday at that time. They were their Dad's dependents and as long as they were in school, they would get this stipend. They had time to get a medical degree or any area of engineering, because they were brilliant, the money was there and time, but they were not encouraged by their Dad, and were not disciplined in keeping their study habits as well as curfews. There were no limits, and for sure, they have suffered the consequences. Nevertheless, the boys have to live with those choices. I was saddened when I found out that Jean didn't give them their checks. He kept them at home and fed them, but he gambled the rest away.

My return trip home was extremely tiresome. I felt that I needed to stretch my abilities and build my strength before school started back anyway and this had to be a good a time for it. In addition, I had school the next day. I always got up early and was at school at 5:30 to help any student with free tutoring. Many always needed help from someone's class as well as my own. I was very glad that I had the option for the zero hour class at 7:00 a.m. and had the two hours free in the afternoon to take the classes for shop, small engine repair and auto mechanic. The principal had no idea how thrilled I was as an early riser and was not apprehensive about the zero hour classes at all.

I enjoyed them and they were quite a joy!" I did not tell the principal that, though. The other teachers were happy that I chose to take the early class, because they were not morning people. However, the boys and girls in the shop classes were ecstatic to think that I wanted to get that dirty or greasy in any of those classes. For sure, it brought up interesting conversations both outside class as well as in my class. Having at least one student in each class who was also in "shop" or one of the other classes with me, helped to make learning fun in my classes. I loved these kids, and some told their parents about the shop classes and me.

Keep in mind that I had the cancer and implants, which brought on problems in the fall and winter. The most dreadful issue about the implants, especially after the fall weather blew in, was that they were continually cold on my body. It was like an ice-pack all the time. Therefore, I had a heating pad and a small electric heater to put under my desk. The heating pad stayed on, that I kept in my chair, which stayed under the desk. When students came into the classroom, I had special problems for them to be working on until time for the actual class time to start. There were also bonus problems on the overhead projector for them to begin as soon as they came into class.

During this time, I was trying to warm implants with the heating pad as well as getting my teaching aids out for use. The heating pad was slipped under my blouse so that no one would notice what I was doing, but warming those "ice-cube" implants. It helped, but it didn't last very long. I continually stayed cold. I didn't know if they knew of the cancer and they couldn't see what was happening with the heating pad. There was five minutes between classes and I stayed prepared for anyone to come in and observe.

I purchased an inexpensive computer and the computer classes offered by a company. I entered each student's scores in the computer and printed out a report for each of them each Monday. I had previously written a contract for each parent and student to sign. This in essence told them that I was there at 5:30 each morning to help with any problem that they may have in any of the math classes.

Along with the weekly report sent out each week, the parents knew how their child was doing. The students took advantage of this as well as their parents. Many calls went to the superintendent and principal about what I was doing and how much they appreciated this special act of concern.

I was grateful for this; I did it to have the smartest math students by raising their scores higher; more each year than ever. Then the "evening teachers" started helping students. The zero hour class was full of students who wanted to take the entire high school math courses offered at the high school. This made it possible for them to take summer classes and advanced calculus while others took computer classes. Wow! What a joy to have these students!

After my favorite principal retired, we received one from the school board office. This principal was even amazed when he found me in my classroom with a room full of students, before school. He was also surprised when he found his three boys in there also.

He didn't care for me at all, even though he praised me to others. He would never say a kind word to me until he observed for the one-hour review session. I used every method to make sure he understood as well as each student. He wrote a fine review and said that for the first time he understood something in math. He was a very poor administrator. He had been demoted from the school board as a supervisor for plagiarism. I couldn't believe that they even kept him in the school district. I didn't allow that bother me though because I knew that I was better at my job then he was at his.

CHAPTER 46

Cancer? Again?

"Oh my, I cannot believe this! Not again, Doctor why is this happening after three years?" I asked the doctor.

This dreadful news hit me like a boulder. I was quite frightened. I began asking the doctor so many questions, that he was speechless. He didn't know the answers. This had happened too often and he reminded me that I didn't take chemotherapy or radiation. He also remembered that we both knew that I couldn't miss school because I didn't have the days to miss.

Now the surgery must happen again, exactly as the last one. This will make one lumpectomy and a radical mastectomy and replacing the implants. If my dear friend had not been of utmost support, and God as my comforter, I don't think I could have made it. The wonderful students for the next three years were as much a dream as the previous three years. I loved those classes as well as the zero -hour classes and my two "off-hours" for the shop, auto mechanics and small engine repair.

Each year I had to go for my regular check-ups. Yet on another regular doctor three years later, I told the oncologist that there were strange little knots on each side under my arm. He immediately had some tests done. These showed that my cancer had come back and spread to other lymph nodes. At this time, teachers had an insurance policy (like an HMO), which paid everything. That was a blessing, but I still didn't want chemo or radiation as before. Teachers didn't get sick days. This will not work if you are on those treatments. You are sick a lot. I couldn't afford it. I had to trust God to take care of me. I could barely get by as it was, and certainly couldn't afford to pay a substitute teacher.

The surgery was done again, removing the implants and the nodules, and putting in another pair of implants of the same size. I was happy to have the my best friend again for her help at the end of school for each of these occurrences and then the summer to recuperate. The doctor thought that all was clean.

I was ready to go home again in four days. Just as before, I told them that I had a ride. I was glad that I had enough energy to drive home and in no time, I could mow my own yard again. I told my friends that, "one could do what they had to do." Now a new semester started. Most of the students were familiar with me, and knew what was expected as soon as they came in, so others followed. Just after all the books were given out, along with the contract for them and their parents, there was a knock on the door and a Special Education teacher with a student was there and I invited them in. She gave me his name and said that she would be his aid each day. I gave him a textbook with a contract.

I wanted him to be reading it as I asked the teacher to step outside the door. I told her that when he came into my classroom, that he was mine. He would not need any other help, she could do whatever she wanted but I would teach him. I also told her that if he needed help, that I would give it to him, because I was at school at 5:30 each morning to give help to any student in mathematics. She smiled and left with a copy of the contract. The young man, Sam Smith, was from Mississippi. He took a seat on the other side of the classroom about midway of the row. He had a "who-done-it" with him and he continued reading that, as he put his textbook and contract under his desk. He was a very tall and handsome young man with black curly hair and handsomely dressed.

After the lectures and problems still on the board and the overhead projector, I began going up and down the rows to see how the students were progressing. I had gone over each type of problem on the chalkboard. All were similar to each area of difficulty as those which had just been explained to them.

Then I arrived back at Sam's desk, from behind him and I put my arm around Sam and whispered in his ear, "I'll trade you for that beautiful Scottie plaid shirt you have on. I mean it."

He was pleased with that unusual attention. As I walked away without him noticing me, I looked back and was so pleased to see that he had put his book under his desk, and began working with the problems. Evidently, as he looked up again, he saw me smiling at him. That young man had been listening, and evidently watching, all the time, while I was lecturing. When he saw me smiling at him, he knew that I knew he had been listening to the explanations. This gave me the impression that he was smarter than all thought he was.

He never picked that book up again during the rest of the hour and worked diligently on those problems on the board before the bell rang. The students had their assignment for the next day. As Sam exited the classroom, he thanked me and I smiled and told him that I would see him in the morning if he needed me. Each morning before school, Sam was in my class to work or get help. He told me that when his parents were divorced and had sent him to live with his Grandmother. I thanked him for telling me, and I told him to invite her in any time if she needed to talk to me. He told his Grandmother and she was there the next morning.

She thanked me for helping and giving him the encouragement that he could do anything. She let me know that when he went home, he said that he had found the only teacher who made him think that he was as smart as the rest of the class. I didn't treat him like a special education student. This was the way he was treated each day.

He was thrilled and told the Special Education teacher that he wanted to be in all regular classes. She was pleased to make this arrangement and put it into action. He would still come into my classroom each morning to work even though he didn't have trouble in math.

He would work on history, English or any of the subjects. He just felt comfortable in there. This made me happy. Sam took geometry class with me the next year and he was great. Again, he came in each morning. His Grandmother was grateful to bring him to the early morning sessions, which I had every day. She was just as excited as he was. He was an "A" student in geometry, as he was with his Algebra 1 class with me. The next year the Counselor scheduled him in another class of algebra II. He came and asked if he could have it changed so that he could be in my class. I told him that he would have to ask them and see what would happen.

When I went to check to see if they had made the changes, they told me what he said. He told them he couldn't work with just any other teacher, and how much I had helped him. They made the necessary changes and he came in every day to work on any subject that he wanted to along with his math. He made another "A" in Algebra II. He took trigonometry from another teacher, which was a one-semester class, and then he took analytic geometry the next semester with that same teacher. He was as excited about learning as any student I had ever had. He kept the Special Education teachers informed of his progress. They were very proud of him also. He needed the acceptance from other teachers, and he got it.

That year he graduated and I didn't know whatever happened to him after that. Two years later, I was checking my mailbox near the office. It had a large legal size (yellow) envelope in it, and as I pulled it out my heart almost burst wide open. I just knew that the I.R.S. had found me and was ready to put me in jail. However, as I held it and noticed the return address the stiffness left me protecting something. I hurriedly opened it. It was from Sam. He had drawn a picture of one of the Space Shuttles that fell during the return of one of the missions and he had written the following:

There was a picture of the Space Shuttle with the American Flag at "Half Staff."

He continued on the side as it was directed to me.

He wrote, "Dear Mrs. Fromond, why is it always through tragedy that the nation recognizes heroes such as yourself? For people such as yourself, who commit a large part of their time and energy for little gain, I thank you. People like you make up the heart of America. What would we do without you? God bless you, Mrs. Fromond!" Love, Sam."

As I read this, I held it against my chest as tears started falling. I tried to hide this emotion as the principal came up to me and asked what was wrong. I gave him the picture, which Sam had drawn of the shuttle as well as the note at the side. He was very impressed.

He asked, "Where is Sam now?"

I replied, "According to the other note he sent with this, he was a sophomore at Texas A&M majoring in "Architectural Engineering."

I said to him, "Remember that he was the one who had been in Special Education, who was "mainstreamed into my class and wanted to try it. He was brilliant and no one tapped his abilities."

He could see tears in my eyes I know, because he gave me a pat on the back as he gave the picture back. It was all I could do, to walk back by the bathroom, wash my eyes, and get back to begin my first class. I had the picture and note framed. I have often wondered where and what all my students were doing after so many years had passed.

CHAPTER 47

Don't Tell Me!"

"Don't tell me Dr. Taylor that it is cancer again! Is it?" Am I going to live over this? Can all of it be gotten at one time? I just don't understand. Why is this happening every 3 years, Dr. Taylor?"

I kept popping the questions to the doctor. I was out of breath with one question after another, and now I had to stop for him to try to tell me something, if I would just shut up. He tried to make me feel better, but was quite puzzled himself. Exactly three years between each cancer surgery, the same problem was happening again. The cancer came back into more lymph nodes. He showed a picture of all the glands in the body, and that puzzled me for sure. I thought that if he had to remove all these lymph nodes in the body, I would die for sure. These were more in the backside under my arms. Now I was getting too concerned about my future. I didn't want the children to know or worry about any of this. God was giving me encouragement to keep my spirits up the best I could.

Therefore, the same procedures as were done before. I now had my third set of implants. Again, I was elated to have the summer to recuperate. Each time I was capable to take advantage of the computer classes offered the teachers at no expense. These courses helped me keep my spirits up.

Just before the next Christmas, there was news that was more distressing. Dr. Taylor sent me to a gastroenterologist for tests. This was extremely a scary experience. I had cancer of the transverse colon, which had to be done immediately. I had Christmas Break coming up the following week. There was no waiting around for this. I couldn't wait until school was out for the summer. The only time that I sobbed about all the cancers, was this time. I didn't believe that I would live long enough to enjoy my new dream and retire. I felt so alone, but had to get rid of those emotions straight away. I had been putting up with pain too long. Not all other cancer pained me, but this one did. I was beginning to get frightened that it was time for me to meet my "Maker."

The side of my abdomen hurt so badly, as if I had appendicitis. However, that had been taken out, many years back. It was tormenting, and I didn't want anyone noticing this. I had the "pre-op" done on Tuesday and surgery was done on Friday, taking one day off.

I was supposed to be out six weeks, but returned in two weeks (after the Christmas Holidays), trying to be very careful with staples holding a 19-inch incision. The doctor didn't know I had gone back to work after the holidays. The principal knew anything about it. My dear teacher friend kept my secrets, for me. I cherished her time and care with me. God had pulled me through so many tragedies, and He was keeping my spirits up.

By the Will of my Savior, I had recuperated well, and had taken even more computer classes the following summer. All teachers had to take at least one four to six week course in their field of teaching. I took two classes, which helped me in many ways. I used mine for the programming as well as the use of software offered by the company for teachers. The previous summer I had taken two other computer classes. As soon as School started back, I felt great and was anxious to get started with some new students and some I had taught before. These always set an example for the new students who were coming to me for their first time. I had the same messages on the overhead projector for the students as I had each semester. The parents of new students as well as the student needed this assurance that I was there to teach and help in any way that I could. Each student did exactly what he or she was asked. I allowed them to sit wherever they wanted until I saw that there was an issue, and made some adjustments without a comment opposing it. Then, I had asked them to begin reading the contract so that they could understand what was expected of them. This went on at the beginning of each class that day.

I had another comment on the "overhead projector" for them to begin reading the directions about the first page of problems. Next, I began teaching about everyday examples. These problems brought conversations I was having with them. I encouraged them to make up similar problems, and then the participation became a "fun" experience. This was what I liked. Choice involved them, and all got excited about making them up. I would do this until each understood the examples. I then went on with some other examples, which were a little more demanding (without letting them know that it was homework examples), and then some, which were more challenging. They had no idea what I had planned or was doing with all this "chit-chat" before an assignment was given.

Here, in essence, I gave them examples of the "A," "B" and "C" type problems dealing with each level of difficulty. This took most of the hour. At the bottom of the overhead projector, the assignment due for the next day was given. I always gave them the problems with answers in the back. I wanted them to see and feel success when they came back to my class the next day. What little effort, I thought to myself, for students to see that if you expect their best and nothing less, you will get their best. That will work every time with just a whisper.

I never had discipline problems. Students knew that when they crossed over the threshold into my classroom, all was in my control. This was true at 5:30 in the morning, when my first student came to class as well as other students who came at different times in the morning. It was not long until the room was filled with students who wanted to work. I turned down no one.

The principal saw students entering another morning when he drove up to the school and wondered what was going on again. With my classroom filled and other chairs brought in as needed, he came down and couldn't believe a room was full of students. There was no visiting just working. If a student or two finished and wanted to visit, they had to leave the classroom; I kept this type of discipline. It was a scene of ambitious students and the beauty. I had six tall windows in the back, with a huge fern hanging from each. He was in awe and gave me a pat on the back when he finished going up and down each row to see or ask the student a question. I could tell he was pleased. I never had a parent complain. His wife came often to visit, because she brought the boys by to work or for help. She was a special lady. I always had "thinking" bonus problems on the overhead projector, which could be used on any tests. Therefore, they were anxious to get in as soon as possible and get to work.

When the principal found out that I entered each student's grade in the computer and printed their average out every Monday to be signed by their parents He was somewhat impressed. He became more impressed when he found that I required the students and parents to sign a contract essentially saying that if a student needed help, they would get their child to me before school each day until the learning problem was solved. He got all the other teachers to help students before or after school. When these teachers found out who started it, some were quite upset with me.

On several occasions, different students would comment on how long it took a few teachers to get the students to calm down. One teacher (a close friend of mine) mentioned this to me and told about one of the students who initiated the chaos was also in my class. She said that he was the one who created chaos in her classes every day for science and another friend had him in biology, but he would first stop in her room and initiate a disturbance.

When I found out who it was, I just could not believe that he, of all students, would be guilty of doing this. Therefore, I didn't allow a day pass without telling the young man that I knew about it his behavior in my friend's class. I told him it hurt me to find that he was the "ringleader" of chaos in her class.

The student was quite embarrassed that I knew about this, was very apologetic and said that he would be a better student for my friend. He went to her that afternoon, apologized to her and told the rest of the class that they would start that day behaving as they did in their math class. He was the first student to be in for early tutoring each morning. His mother was so happy that he had a chance to catch up after he was transferred from out of state. He was so far behind that I was apprehensive as to whether he was willing to try hard enough to get the help he needed. But, he did and worked very hard every morning. His mother was one of many who wrote a letter to the superintendent, principal and a copy to me, telling about my early morning help. I did this each morning tutoring any student. I still have those and cherish each one. She was a special lady who worked sixteen hours a day, to get her son through school and saved for college. He also worked at the same hospital from 2 a. m. until time for my tutoring group.

My friend came to me to find out how I kept the discipline that the young man expressed to her class. I gave her some hints, which I used for having excellent discipline in my classes. I told her that they immediately came into the classroom and immediately looked to see what was on the overhead projector. I was ready for them to work when they came in. I also told her that there was no "recess" for the students, in my class. I was paid to teach and they were there to learn. When they crossed the threshold to come into my classroom, they were mine for the hour. I was in charge the entire hour and if any wanted out, to go right then to see a counselor for a change. None ever left.

However, I was, and just couldn't give up. I loved teaching and wanted to teach at least another year. I needed them, and they needed me.

CHAPTER 48

No!" Not Gene, Too!"

Gene finally told me what the dentist said was wrong was his gums, and not teeth. It made chills run up and down on me. I immediately thought of the HMO insurance that the teachers had. I could help and felt that God had taken care of me and filled me with a glow each day, that all was gonna be fine. I could help but wondered if God was testing me to see if I could care for someone else. As soon as Gene told me all about this, I had the answer right away. He needed help! It never occurred to me that this could get me fired from teaching anywhere or anytime. I had a friend who needed help and I felt that calling. This was strictly a platonic relationship and nothing more. I had no romantic relationship with him. He had no one who cared and I did. Was I trying to control my position with the superintendent who had called me in to show me all of the letters from parents about my teaching? These parents never had anyone to care for the students or give free tutoring so early in the morning.

Therefore, I said, "Ok, I'll marry you then, and you will have immediate coverage through the school system. However, he had to promise me that the next day he would go with me to the Oncologist to see my doctor."

He was thrilled and said, "I will, I do and everything you say, I promise that I will."

He was ecstatic. We hurried to the county court house; we got our marriage license and hurried back. I had papers to grade. He had work to do at home to prepare for a hospital visit, if that became necessary. I went to the school board the next day (Wednesday) and told them that I was getting married on Monday afternoon. I also told them that I wanted Gene on my insurance policy. Never was there an idea of the struggles and mystery of controlling one, which I cared for and the time involved in it.

The lady said, "Congratulations! All is in the computer now."

On Monday, at five in the afternoon, we got married at a Church where we had gone to services many times. The minister's wife was one of the witnesses, and they were the only ones there, except the lady who maintained the building, and the janitor. After the wedding, he kissed me for the first time, thank me for this opportunity, then he went to his home, and I went to mine. I took off a half day the next day on Tuesday to take Gene to my doctor. The doctor took a biopsy and did a "quick-freeze" to see if there was a problem, that either all was okay, or that more tests would be needed. He told us immediately that it was malignant and that he wanted Gene in the hospital on Wednesday afternoon to begin running test. The cancer was like an octopus with pinnacles which wrapped around anything within this area.

It "gutted" Gene's mastoid and deltoid muscles, carotid artery, vocal cords and some around the top of spinal cord. It took several doctors to complete the 12-hour surgery. They were exhausted!" I was also, from waiting for them to call me at school.

They were able peel the growth off one of the vocal cords, the spinal cord and carotid artery. One of the vocal cords was traumatized the other destroyed. The mastoid muscle was a mess. Gene's neck size went from a 17" to a 14 ½." He was in the hospital for one month. During this time, he was doing pretty well until Isabelle called and told the nurse that she needed to get in touch with me because Mama had died. The nurse immediately went to Gene's room and asked where I was. He motioned that I was in the hall.

The nurse told him, "Her Mother has died and I need to find her, quickly."

At this traumatic news, Gene's throat closed up from some sort of a spasm and he could not breathe. It was probably caused by the abruptness of the news from the nurse about my Mama's death and I would have to leave him. She called emergency and they had to do a tracheotomy immediately right there in his room. What a shock when I went in and all the commotion happening with doctors and nurses working on Gene.

When they did tell me about my Mama, I said to Gene, "I told you that I would stay with you and take care of you. Gene, Mama does not need me now. There are plenty of other siblings to take care of everything and I still have the best memories of Mama."

I was somewhat glad that God had planned this so that I could remember that sweet angel as I had always remembered her. Mama died just after turning 89 years of age. She had cancer of the reflux valve and the hiatal hernia.

Our God and Savior was the reason she didn't suffer. Had she not gone into a coma before she died, she probably would've been in great pain. I think of her so often because there were so many things that I wished I had told her or could've asked her. I know that she is in heaven and I will see her one day. I was unable to go to Mama's funeral. I was happy that I didn't go. I can remember her as we laughed, my cries, the walks, and talks while picking berries and helping me with a miscarriage. She was a precious lady beyond reproach.

During the month in the hospital, the doctors and nurses taught me how to care for Gene and all the machines, medication and feeding. This was rather traumatic for me because I had never done any of this before, but after a month, all of the machines were transferred to my living room. Five machines and my couch for a bed, just like a hospital room. I got up at about three a.m. and sterilized all of the equipment used during the night.

The bandage had to be replaced, surgical area cleaned and medicated. Then the feeding machine had to be cleaned, refilled and replaced the tube through his nose to his stomach, suctioned his lungs, cleaned the tracheotomy and the apparatus and checked his blood pressure, temperature and oxygen tank each a.m. and p.m. After all of this was done, I was off to school for my early morning tutoring as well as the "0" hour class. A nurse came once each day to check his vital signs and called the school for someone to let me know how he was doing. Two neighbors also checked on Gene until school was out for the day.

God gave me strength that I didn't know I was capable of doing. My days and part of the nights were totally used each minute. With the tracheotomy, Gene could only whisper a little. This condition was getting his emotions in a very depressed mood. I didn't know how to deal with that except to ask if there was anything else that I could do. He would always whisper an "OK."

I called his children and his former wife, who divorced him because of the drinking problem he had seventeen years before, at that time. This gave his "ex" a chance to humiliate him while he had to lie there and listen. I had left a key out so that they could see him whenever they wanted to and she chose to come while I was away at school.

I didn't realize that this was making him worse. His ex-wife made him think that all this was due to his drinking. I was not aware of this until it was too late. When he told me about it, I picked the key up, so that she could not come back without calling me. I left this same message on her answering machine. It took about half a year for him to get a little better, when he then began the deep depression, which I didn't know how to handle. In an effort to keep him engaged, I asked him to call out test scores so that I could record them, which he enjoyed, but that was about all the (whisper) talk he did. He enjoyed this and began to learn about each one. I had hoped that this would help his depression, but the excitement didn't last very long.

Through all of this, I continued to teach. The kids in my classes were helping me as much as the other way around. These wonderful students enjoyed learning. They were also encouraged especially by a handicapped blind student, "Dana" who made "A's" on everything. I am sure she was an inspiration to them as she was to me. Her reputation of abilities spread from one class to another. She was such a joy to know and to teach.

Dana would always say, "I see Mrs. Fromond."

Ahh! What a love this child was, with enthusiasm just as expressive as her eagerness to learn. Her textbook, was an inch thicker than the other student's textbook. To observe her as I demonstrated a problem on the board was most intriguing. She would be listening carefully, following the her text in Braille. Her comments astonished each student. She was a beautiful and charming student who asked me to write her a recommendation for a College in the northeast. I was happy to do it. She would have to be the best they had ever had. I have wished often that I could find out how all my students were doing.

Along with being accepted, I received a letter from the college thanking me for a very well written recommendation. It was succinct and to the point. He said that they didn't get many like that and was anxious to have and meet her. I knew they had to read hundreds of recommendations and if you wanted them to be read, it needed to be brief and to the point, otherwise they were "chunked." This letter of recommendation was similar to all the others. Dana was an extra special student like none I had ever had. Sam's letter was quite similar to Dana's, but different. I received several letters from the colleges about recommendations. However, none was like Dana's and Sam's.

The next year was great also, until a there was a dreadful happening on a band trip in the early spring. Someone took some brownies laced with LSD. Most chocolate lovers would say, "Who would turn down a brownie?" Some of the smartest students ate them and that was pretty much the end of their brilliant mind. After that incident, some were hooked on different drugs, from LSD, marijuana and crack. They were tricked into eating those treats on the bus. They had been taking seven classes each day as well as taking Junior College in the summer.

They were in my "0" hour class Had been in every kind of club, as well as being in all the AP classes. I never knew who was responsible . I would never get over this; it was too tragic. I just about cracked up. I loved them as if they were my own. They walked the tracks most of the time. This was so sad that I cried and prayed for these precious students every night. I knew I would retire if the Governor signed the "early out." I was diabetic, had cancer five times within ten years. I only told Gene, my children, the superintendent and my math teacher friend of my intentions.

CHAPTER 49

What's Depression?

I didn't know how to handle depression or despondency. I had never seen anyone like this, or in this mind-state and was quite bewildered. However, I had fought for Gene's disability all the way to the highest of judges. I would not give up. Those were the "sick" days I saved for "fighting for Gene" to win. He couldn't talk louder than a whisper or shake his head. We finally won the case for total disability and Gene would get the maximum for the salaries he had made over time.

I had volunteered for this job as well as encouraged him to have the surgery done. I married him so that he would have all expenses covered by my insurance. When vacuuming in his room, I moved his boots and saw all the money he had placed down in them. This was 14 months after his surgery. He probably had just gotten it and didn't know how to approach me about it. He might have put all in his bank account except that cash. I did not take it out or ask about it. If he wanted me to know, he would have to tell me.

Since he was under such stress by being unable to work, it was devastating to him. His speech was just above a whisper. He just could not take it. He read the newspaper while I graded class papers. He wouldn't talk or say anything. He wouldn't allow me to call the minister. I didn't know what to do. He had been taken care of, he had his own bedroom and I had mine. He did cook mostly for himself, and I had to have different kind of meals, so mine was microwaved dinners, because I didn't know how to cook and since I was diabetic, I couldn't have sweets. I had few funds, so I had to be frugal when buying groceries or Gene's ice cream, eggs and bacon after he was capable of eating regular food. His "energy" drinks for the feeding machines now were to be mixed with his ice cream for his evening meal.

I was glad that he had the money so now he could take care of himself. I should've asked the minister to come by without telling him. Maybe he could have helped him. I first saw the signs of depression beginning after his former wife blasted her way with him. I should never have allowed the visit unless I was home. Again, that was "20-20" hindsight.

The State Legislature met and one of the members had introduced a Bill for teachers who wanted to retire at the age of 55, they could do so. It was passed by the Legislature so all that was needed now was for the governor to sign it. I had planned to take advantage of it if he did sign the "early out." The surgeries for me and for Gene were more than enough for me. I had no idea that I would even live through another year of teaching. I had the joy of teaching and I decided to retire immediately after the last day of school.

CHAPTER 50

Answered Prayers

The Legislature had sent the Bill to the governor, and with overwhelming support for the Bill, they just knew that the governor would sign. He did sign it and I was overjoyed. Gene's condition hurt me and I felt so guilty that I couldn't take care of his mental condition. We could have enjoyed our walks each day for the summer if this depression had not hit him.

To retire, I had to buy up to a maximum of ten years of teaching experience from the money taken out when Jean didn't pay his taxes. It took $20,000 for the ten years. This was given to me out of the estate after my Mama died. I should've gotten much more than that. I was only offered $10,000 for the property and this was worth much more than that. Papa had more land than they claimed, but they had probably already acquired most of what he had before he died or before Mama died. My Papa didn't spend his money and was very well off with land, investments and savings. Just his financial worth which they claimed was so much more. They thought that Ted and I didn't know anything, but they forgot that we stayed on the farm when they took off for the service. Some of my siblings had died, and had the same misfortune before their death. I should've contested it, but they knew that neither Ted nor I would fight.

CHAPTER 51

Gene? Insured!"

One weekend, I called Jacques (my niece's husband) after I had slipped the house keys away from Gene, while he was mowing the yard with his mask and throat covering. When Jacques came up, Gene was very nice to him. One would think he was always like that and he used to be. I was somewhat shocked myself.

I said, "Gene, I had asked him to be here because married life was over for us. I can't cope with your depression, you refused to get help and you are well enough and could now afford to care for yourself. We will help you pack up and move."

Gene turned toward the house along with Jacques and began moving his belongings. He seemed to be glad that I asked, or was in complete shock. He moved and I got a non-contested divorce. That was in mid-spring and since the Governor of Louisiana signed the "early out" for retiring at 55; I took it the last day of school. I sold the house, and moved to Birmingham, and I never looked back.

The next year, Gene sent tax papers for me to sign, and mail back. Shortly afterwards he called and asked if he could come over. I told him he was welcome to come. He sounded like the person I use to know.

CHAPTER 52

My Last Move: Alabama!"

Gene's disability check was plenty for him to take care of himself and afford to live on his own. I was living with my daughter, Christine then in Alabama. Gene drove all the way to Birmingham to take care of the tax issues. I still had that feeling of guilt which I tried to conceal.

"This was going to be a special visit," he said.

He did not sound depressed or despondent. It was a delight to visit with him over the phone. He sounded like the guy I first met while working out after school. Christine was happy for him to come also. Neither of us knew how long it would take him to make the trip and neither did he.

However, he did say, "If it was all right, he would just park in the driveway if it was late during the night when he came. He said the he would sleep in the back of his pickup until we got up."

On Sunday, when we woke up, his truck was in the driveway. Both of us were excited to see him. He was a delight to have around, and we thoroughly enjoyed him. He wanted to visit since he was no longer depressed and had recovered from "not being capable of working" like a man should, and accepted things as they were. He was thankful to me, he said, for saving his life. I reminded him that all I did was marry him, and promised to care for him if what the dentist had thought was true, he would have insurance. The fourteen months at home, dealing with his illness, was quite a learning experience for me. God and no one else spared his life, that time.

After we visited awhile, Gene asked if we could listen to a tape that he had. I had a tape player in my small apartment on the downstairs portion of Christine's home.

He said, "I want you to sit down and hear this because it was something I want to say."

Christine told us to go downstairs and listen while she fixed breakfast. We went down and put the tape on to play. He had to play the song; because he said it was too emotional for him to tell me so the music would have to say it for him. It was a song about being thankful for the times that I had given him hope while he had cancer. The music did say that I made his life worth living, and he would like to spend each and every moment with me and that nothing should keep us apart again. As the song started, I jumped up to hug him. We kissed and just held each other and "swayed to the music." The song play over and over saying that I was a lady and that he loved me with each and every breath he took.

"Ahhh, thank you Gene; this was special." I said with tears forming.

"Will you marry me again," he asked, after the music stopped.

Yes, of course, and for love this time. I quickly answered.

He said that he had to go back and take care of some business and be back in two weeks, get married and then we would go hike the Appalachian Trail for our honeymoon. I was so happy and thought that I could not wait that long, but knew that he had to see the doctor for the last time, pack the truck for our trip, and wanted each of us to practice with our back packs. He packed mine with items we had and taught me how each pack should be loaded to distribute the weight.

The Appalachian Trail starts in Maine on Mount Katahdin and ends on Springer Mountain in Georgia. The trail passes through several states from Maine to Georgia. The trail is about 2,100 miles long and generally takes six to eight months to complete. This, of course, depended on whether we took "side-trips" or not.

I couldn't believe the drawings he had of plans for packers with different needs as the trip would carry us over different terrains. He had a list of each type of food as items needed for different areas of the trip as we would hike south. There would be items needed at the beginning of the trip that would not be needed for the rest of the trip.

He had done a professional's job and had never been on a hike longer than a week. He had done a lot of research for this hike. This was a wonderful time of visiting and having fun. We did some hiking out on the trails around Birmingham. He was a delight to have for this visit, and for the first time, he made my life worth living for me also.

We had always wanted to hike the Appalachian Trail. He planned the trip with the time to leave and return. He had the maps and the stops, which all hikers used for pickups and mailing addresses for the back-packers planned like a pro. We knew that it would take some practice with our backpack with him carrying 60 pounds and me with 40. He had the drawings of what the inside of a pack would look like, if the back was clear plastic. The visual made it easier to understand the reasoning behind his research.

He went back, took care of his business and practiced walking with his backpack. He had his complete body scan, and called after almost two weeks and said that all the scans were clear. We both were ecstatic!" He said the truck was packed and all ready for his return with a list of items needed for the each leg of the trip.

He was excited about the wedding on Saturday, and leaving on Monday for our trip. We would leave his truck at a safe park for hikers in N. Georgia. Christine would drive us to the airport for the flight to Maine, which he had previously purchased. We needed to be together and get away. After these visits, I think we were ready for each other. We could hardly wait for May 1 for us to go on the hike together. He said he would arrive on Wednesday, three days before the wedding and four before our trip

When he didn't show up, we assumed he must have had automobile trouble and was running late. He was not there on Thursday, or Friday. Something was definitely wrong. I called our friend to see if he knew what had happened. He said that Gene had gotten a clean bill of health; no cancer cells appeared anywhere. He was ecstatic, but added that Gene would not have been able to drive all the way in his condition. He said that early Tuesday morning, the doctor called and said that someone had given him an incorrect report. He was to get to the doctor, immediately, and was put in Hospice, for he was covered in all organs with cancer. I called the hospital.

He could hear the "sniffles" I'm sure, as I tried to hold back the crying. He didn't need that now.

"I love you, Gene and I am SO sorry, but I will be there as soon as possible.

I will drive or fly, which ever will get me there sooner," I said with a "quivering" voice.

"Don't come, sweetheart. I love you, too. You have done all that a human could do, and now I'm going to meet my Maker; probably before you could get here and I'll see you there", he said.

Oh my God, this tore me up because we had planned the rest of our lives together, getting re-married, going on the trail and having a great life. He was over his problem, and looking for his love, who he had always loved, but I would not give in. We did enjoy the church, hiking, working on machines and talking about students. But, I was afraid to be in love at that time. To me, he was a true friend whom I enjoyed talking, running, working and to learn about all that the heavy equipment which he used. He was very intelligent as well as knowing all about any machine.

Then God's plan was different. That was the last time that Gene was capable of talking to anyone rationally. I called our friend who said that the cancer had spread to his brain and he was not rational at all.

He said that all Gene would do was hike up and down the hospice hall. Getting married, and hiking the Appalachian Trail was all he was on his mind, as he hiked in the halls of the Hospice Center. And now, he was hiking to meet his Maker. The cancer spread to the brain rapidly. Our friend kept me informed to the end. He was a dream come true that never happened.

Why didn't some symptoms of feeling ill show while he was with us? In fact, he was happier than I had ever seen him. We hiked all around the area and we both had a grand time. How was he able to do all the hiking we did? Now this has happened in less than two weeks. I thought about what if this had happened on the trail. God knew best. God, in His infinite wisdom took Gene in less than three weeks. It was not meant for us to be together yet, but we will meet in a better place. A lesson all need to learn; just take one day at a time. It was not at all easy for me to accept. I had finally fallen in love, and lost him.

CHAPTER 53

A Changed Man

Two weeks before my Papa died at 89 years of age, he joined the church and was baptized. I was so thrilled when my Mama told me what had happened that morning at home, that I gasped for breath. My heart was throbbing for her.

My Mama's brother, Uncle Peter Cousteau, was a lay minister and preached every Sunday morning and night, as well as visited the nursing homes and held Wednesday night prayer service. He went to homes of the invalid, visited people who were ill at home or in the hospitals, nursing homes, as well as those who called for him like my Papa did.

On the farm, as you have read, it was quite laborious for each and every one. My Papa was a SLAVE DRIVER. You learned a lot about hard work, how it was done and when it was done, and learned that it went on for 52 weeks out of the year. Papa didn't get out and play with us; maybe he did when we were babies. I doubt that he ever played anything.

My Papa worked hard as a young boy until he ran away from home when he was twelve years old. Then he worked diligently for other people as he gained experience with the railroad company and worked them hard. Many couldn't do the hard work and quit. However, there were many people who needed work and many who "lay-in-wait" for someone to quit, so they were there to take the job. Some last longer than others did. My Papa was a slave driver and the company saw this young man, working like a slave and training others to do their job easier and safer. He knew so much about each area of logging, which the company knew little about, that they selected him to be the "Slave Driver," or "Manager" of the company. They recognized his drive, abilities and eagerness to do his best, and train others.

They paid him very well with the best horse, gun, whip, rifle and best of gloves; all he needed or wanted. He continued to work hard pushing all the workers as well as their leaders every single day of the year.

Then after ten years, he trained some men to take the place of many and trained others to take his place. The company admired his abilities as well as his ambition to succeed as he did his work and gave aid to others.

He made enough money to a buy a plantation, hired people to do the work and rode a horse with all his equipment, which included a pistol, rifle, rope and a whip. He was determined to succeed to get the land cleared; barns built as well as homes and got the job done quickly and correctly.

That was all a given in this novel. He wore gloves for at least ten years with the railroad. As a slave driver, they "punctuated" his attire for the remaining years as a plantation "Slave Driver." He was taught by the best: his Papa. His Papa had been his teacher and now he had taken his place.

Now, my Uncle Peter was a devout Christian man. He witnessed to everyone both sinners and Christians. Some were in the KKK and my Papa knew it. My Papa thought that Uncle Pete should not allow anyone connected to the KKK to enter his church. Papa thought that since the church had kicked his Papa (Grandpa Thibodeaux) out of the church for horse racing back home, that these people should be kicked out of the church also.

My Uncle was one of little "means," but made a mediocre living; nothing about him or his family was elaborate at all. His only mode of transportation was a mule, a school bus or one of the kid's bicycles. We, on the other hand, had mules, oxen, school bus, car and horses galore.

Uncle Peter probably didn't even own a pair of gloves, and probably never had nor used a whip or shot a gun. He was a minister, a bus driver and a gardener who fed his folks and others. He didn't curse, whip his girls or his son, and never had them working like a slave in the garden. They were allowed to visit and spend the night with the Grandparents and cousins. He didn't have a wife who any miscarriages that I knew of, and if she did, she certainly didn't have 22 of them as my Mama had, and maybe some that I never heard about. The girls helped their mother; learned to cook and sew and knew how to study the Bible. They went to church, school and brought books home to study or just read for fun. They were never allowed to come to our house, and our Papa never allowed us there.

How do you understand the different perspectives of two men.

Uncle Peter became a school bus driver just as my Papa did for the new school in the west end of the parish where my sister taught school. It was quite ironic that my Papa thought Uncle Peter was lazy. He was a bus driver, a kind and sweet man to his wife and children and all who met him. He also was one who preached for many people. He had a large garden, a mule and did his own plowing instead of requiring his daughters to plow.

He had only one son who was the youngest and was about the age of Andre (my brother), never did work as a field hand for his Papa. Uncle Peter did more physical labor; with the preaching, farming, gardening and driving the bus; that he actually worked harder than my Papa did. My Papa despised my uncle because he thought my uncle was lazy and only preached to get out of real work. All of Mama's other siblings worked hard, and two of them worked on the plantation like the rest of us. One of her brothers helped my Mama during this time of four miscarriages before she was 20 years old.

He also was most helpful with Isabelle when she had diphtheria. As far as I know, my Papa never spoke or visited with Uncle Chouteau and my uncle didn't visit or work for us. My Papa was good at controlling who went and who came to our farm. The day came when life took a different turn for Papa. He needed Uncle Peter immediately and didn't want anyone wasting time to get my uncle there. Papa called Mama to his bedroom door, in tears, trembling and wet with sweat. He was so frightened.

He began telling Mama why he was desperate for her brother to get there as soon as possible. He told Mama that Jesus Christ had just come to him and left. He said that Jesus was at the foot of his bed only a little while ago and told Papa he was going to die and go to hell and burn forever and ever.

Papa was so shaken when he called Mama and told what had just happened. He insisted that she call my uncle (the Preacher) right away. My Mama was so alarmed at this changed, old man she could hardly contain herself with a throbbing heart until the break of dawn.

It was at dawn that she called her brother and told him that Papa wanted to see him as soon as possible. They didn't ever come to blows that I ever heard about, but never visited. When my uncle passed on the road in his school bus, Papa was on the front porch, they waved and that was all.

Uncle Cousteau came down immediately after Mama called him and Papa told him what had happened that night and asked him if he could save him from going to hell. My uncle said that if he accepted Christ as his Personal Savior he could help him. Papa told him that after seeing Jesus, he certainly did believe in him and that he wanted to be baptized. The ceremony was performed right then and there, with just my Mama, Isabelle, (the oldest sister who was also called), to witness this glorious event. Papa said he was ready to give himself to Christ and that he swore that he believed in Him. My uncle, Papa, Mama and Isabelle were ecstatic over this change in my Papa's heart. It was ironic, that Richet (another brother) had visited with his minister about Papa the same morning that this event took place some 70 miles away. He lived in Baton Rouge and went to see his minister the same morning telling him about Papa.

He said that it weighed on his heart that Papa may not believe in Jesus Christ. He asked his minister if he would go with him to talk to Papa. His Preacher told Richet that he should go down himself to talk to his Papa. He did. Shortly after the trip getting there, Richet asked Papa to walk out in the pasture with him. He was unaware of all that had happened before his arrival back to the old place. They both went out into the pasture and Richet immediately asked Papa if he believed in Jesus Christ as his Personal Savior. Papa said that he did. However, Richet wanted to hear him say more than that because the Bible states that you must confess "out loud" to two or more that he believed in Jesus Christ to be saved.

Papa told Richet aloud, "that he believed in God the Father, Jesus Christ and the Holy Spirit and accepted Him as his Personal Savior."

He then said that he was sorry, but he just didn't know Him until the last night. He told Richet about Jesus coming to see him at the foot of the bed. He told Richet about having Uncle Pete come down, as well as the ceremony earlier that morning.

Richet told him that Sunday he would take both of them to church and walk him to the Alter. The following Sunday, Richet took Mama and Papa to the church where most of the family belonged.

At the end of the sermon, when the Alter Call was made, Richet took my Papa by the arm and walked up to the Preacher and said, "This is my Papa, Joseph Thibodeaux, and he has something that he wants to tell you."

Papa repeated all that he had said to Richet previously, to the minister. He wanted to be baptized immediately and the minister performed the Baptism right then. It happened just as he wanted it to happen.

The church was packed with standing room only. When members heard about who was going to join the church on Sunday, they couldn't believe it, yet very thankful for the change in his heart. He was known to be the meanest man to his family and would not allow them to go to church. That was the reason the place was packed inside and outside on a hot August Sunday morning.

This was a duty for both of them now to worship every day and night. I knew that he was going to be baptized and drove up from Baton Rouge to witness this myself. That day there was not a dry eye in the church as they watched all that was happening as well as being said.

I had just been there the weekend before. But, I didn't know about the whole story until after 36 years had passed. After the Baptism, I visited Papa and Mama along with my children who were with me to see and hug their Grandpa and Grandma Thibodeaux. After the visitations I returned .home.

CHAPTER 54

Letter

The Children's Thoughts: Written by: Marcel Fromond

Hi Mom,

I got your book in the mail today. I must tell you I was impressed by the size of your manuscript! I'm not sure what I was expecting, but I started reading it immediately and just finished an hour ago. It was obvious that you put your heart and soul into your writing, and I appreciate the opportunity to read it.

Your depiction of your childhood was painful to read. I knew, of course, that you had a tough childhood, but I guess I never understood the extent of it. You went through Hell! You and your siblings all did. Grandpa Thibodeaux was a proud man who raised his kids the only way he knew how; the way he was raised.

He didn't know any different, and I think that on some level he felt he was raising his kids the way he was supposed to. He was dead wrong, of course. I'm so grateful that you had Grandma to help buffer the situation at times, and it is easy to see that your upbringing went a long way towards making you the person that you are today. I've always been very proud of you Mom. You walked through Hell for 15 or 20 years and you overcame that diversity and rather than allow it to it to limit or restrict you, you channeled it so that it propelled and shaped your life.

There were several areas in your writing that expressed a hope that your kids would somehow forgive you for mistakes that you made in raising us. Mom, any mistakes that you made were forgiven when they occurred. You loved us, nurtured us, guided us and did your best to instill a sense of values, as well as provide us with the tools that we would need for our futures. There is no way I could even consider second guessing your decisions or your way of parenting, because I'm pretty happy with where my life is right now and a big part of that is thanks to the work you put in as a parent. I'm healthy, I have a wonderful woman that loves me, I have three incredible children and although I don't get to spend time with two of them right now, I know that in the future that will correct it.

I have a feasible plan for the future, I make goals, monitor my progress towards those goals, make adjustments where necessary, and I am looking forward to reaping the rewards of my efforts. Without your guidance and instruction, your love and nurturing, I have no doubt that I wouldn't be near, where I am today.

I know that Christine and Jean-Paul feel the same way, and we all three hope that we have caused you reason to be as proud of us as we are of you. As for the problems and issues that you had to go through with Dad and his family, I have known all along that those years were "no picnic" for you. I was too young during most of the goings on to understand what all of what was happening, but I knew that you were the one who was focused on the basics, providing for your family, supporting a strong education, and insisting on discipline.

Dad on the other hand was far less focused on these. I know that he loved all of us and wanted the best for us, but I don't think he fully understood what was important in providing for the future. He may have very well been a result of his upbringing and family much as you were. He obviously was brought up much differently and I'm sure if he had been subjected to more accountability for his actions growing up and as a young man, he would have made better decisions.

All in all, I know that I am a direct result of both of you, and I would not have it any other way. You showed all three of us how to behave, you taught us to believe in ourselves, you stressed the importance in education, and you have supported us in more ways than I can count.

I learned a lot from Dad also, although some of the lessons were how NOT to behave or live my life, a big part of who I am has been influenced by him. I miss him so much, and I have wished that he were still alive to see that I've been able to straighten myself out and get back on the right track.

I'm grateful that you are able to see the changes that I've gone through, and hope that you realize how important you have been in helping me make those changes. I have SO MANY wonderful memories of my childhood, Mom. Sure, there were some times where I wasn't so happy for one reason or another, there were probably times that I felt that you were being too hard or strict on us, or lacking in understanding, but everything happened for the best, and I would not change one thing.

Thank you so much Mom for everything you've done all along; for the sacrifices you made, the bull you had to go through, the heartache you put yourself through, and the confidence you had in us. Thank you for never giving up on me, and thank you for recognizing my progress. Thank you for writing this manuscript, and thank you for sharing it with me. I know it was not easy to do___it was not easy to read.

I love you Mom,

Marcel

www.ingramcontent.com/pod-product-compliance
Lightning Source LLC
Chambersburg PA
CBHW082010170626
46817CB00009B/3046